White Buffalo (New Beginnings) Series

DREAM DANCER & THE CELTIC WITCH

Lauretta Beaver

America Star Books

First printing

Softcover 9781611025033
PUBLISHED BY AMERICA STAR BOOKS, LLLP
www.americastarbooks.com

Printed in the United States of America

To: Don

SACRIFICES

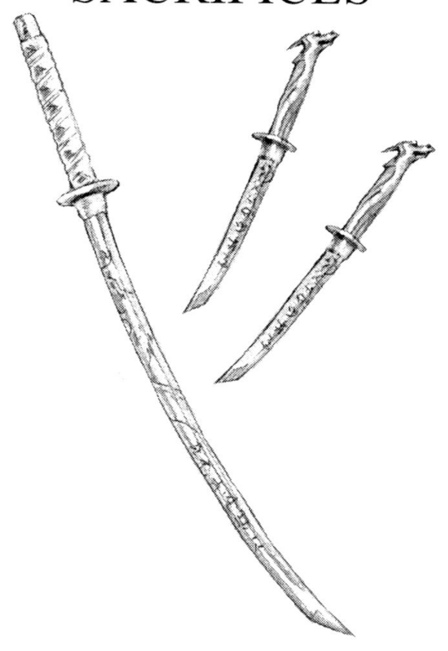

The Prophecy

"She will be called Cecille Luan Gweneal or White Buffalo to her people.
She will bring beauty to the earth as she keeps the evil at bay for another forty years.
In the new century evil will begin leaking out of its prison slowly, until the mists of
Snowdonia are no more than the six sentient stones will disappear.
The white buffalo will come back one final time as the rise of the Dragon begins!
There will be no turning back as judgement draws ever closer!"

Laurella Beaver

This book is dedicated to my father, Alexandre Charles Smith
Thanks dad for being there for me!
To my boss as well Marie Tunnell of the Girouxville Inn, your support and friendship have always been appreciated.

A special thank you goes to my fiancé Michel Pelletier for all his love, support, friendship, and help in editing this book.
Another special thank you goes to my best friend Patty Carson Jenkins for helping with the Prologue.
I also wish to send out a heartfelt thanks to everyone at the Eaglesham Golf and Country Club; in Eaglesham, Alberta, Canada:
Thank you for accepting me as one of your own; I have enjoyed golfing with all of you.

PROLOGUE

A young woman looked back over her shoulder fearfully as she shuddered in terror searching frantically for her pursuers. The white mare the girl was riding stumbled suddenly in exhaustion as she almost went down.

The woman gasped in shock as she quickly turned back to face the front. Desperately she grabbed onto the pommel to keep herself in the saddle as she felt herself slip slightly.

The only thing that saved her was her leg draped over the saddle. She was not use to riding sidesaddle at this speed, but straddling her mare right now was just too painful to contemplate. Riding sidesaddle was like being on a rocking horse it was smooth with no jarring or bouncing, unlike riding astride.

The young woman let out the breath she was holding in relief as her horse found her footing once more, before the mare continued her mad gallop through the nearly pitch-black night.

Only the extraordinary eyesight of her mare kept them going since the young woman could see nothing with the fog thickening all around them, blocking out the patchy moonlight that the girl had used earlier to guide her mare.

The woman was not sure how much longer her horse could maintain this speed; they were both fatigued to the point of dropping. However, panic drove the girl as she pushed her mare for more speed. The young woman knew that her pursuers were still behind her somewhere not willing to give her up so easily.

The young woman loosened her hold on the saddle in relief as her horse stabilized. She clutched her cape close to her almost naked body. She was freezing, getting colder by the minute as the wind howled fiercely. It made her shiver as goose bumps rose all over her body in reaction.

A drop of blood dribbled onto the sidesaddle; the bright red droplet slithered down before it finally dropped onto the silvery white sweat encrusted coat of her mare. If you looked closely at the mares sides, rivulets of blood were tainting the mares beautiful white coat. The bleeding had slowed considerably now though as the young girl's body worked to heal itself of the indignity she had suffered.

The woman sobbed in fearful disbelief as she pulled out her necklace before clutching the amulet in her left hand. She forgot for a moment that her palm was full of cuts, scratches as well as scrapes; they broke open once more, but she ignored the blood trickling down her wrists.

Usually the young woman had the medallion hidden under her chemise, but she needed its strength at this moment as she whispered softly in Celtic pleading desperately. "Please someone help me!"

A gusty wind blew up suddenly whisking her words away, which caused the fog to thicken even more, now she could barely see two feet in front of her. To make things worse, a steady rain began to fall as thunder sounded in the distance.

She huddled down further inside her cloak in despair, as she tucked the bloody amulet back into her chemise, but still, she continued whispering for help, almost chanting as her young mind flew back into the past…

*****

The woman remembered how her life was shattered suddenly when bandits killed both her parents. They were on their way back to Wales from Worchester, England. She had been sixteen at the time so had not understood how such an innocent outing could turn her life into a living nightmare.

The young woman's closest living relative was a third cousin who owned a neighbouring castle. He petitioned Queen Victoria so that the queen would grant to him guardianship of his sixteen year old cousin; at least until she was eighteen or decided to wed. Since his castle was not as important as the girl's was Queen Victoria decided that he would move in with his sixteen-year-old cousin immediately.

Everything went well for the first six months she thought; her cousin came and went whenever the whim took him so she did not see much of him at first. In those months, he only made small insignificant changes nothing to alarm anyone.

After the six months were up, he began hanging around more. He started mistreating the servants badly so her people turned sullen. Every day they withdrew even more, where once they laughed with her, now they ignored her. It was not just inside the castle either; he targeted everyone, even the guards.

A couple months later, she was forbidden to speak Celtic!

If that was not bad enough the guards that were loyal to her that should have been standing on the walls watching for intruders started disappearing, one at a time. Finally, her servants also vanished. By the end of his first year as guardian, he managed to run everyone off; then he too disappeared unexpectedly.

The young woman's home went from a happy thriving place to a deadly quiet rundown castle. The girl suffered quietly knowing that one-day things would change. She bit her tongue trying to do the best she could possibly do all by herself until she turned eighteen.

The next six months turned into a living nightmare as food became harder and harder to find. She outgrew all her clothes, so had to resort to wearing her mother's old clothes; they were way too big, but she managed.

Six months before her eighteenth birthday her cousin, which she had hardly seen, showed up with a wagon of food as well as gifts. He began hanging around the castle watching her with his ferret like, small beady black eyes, assessing her every move. At first all it did was cause her more work as she cooked plus cleaned after him.

Unexpectedly though, he started popping up around every corner trying to touch or kiss her as if he were her beau, teasing her about marriage. The more she tried to avoid him, the more persistent he became as he stalked her unmercifully.

The young woman did manage to find a hiding spot for a while, which finally made him leave the castle in a rage.

In relief, she started moving freely around her castle once more, but kept a wary eye out for him knowing instinctively that he would be back. He had given up way too easily; she could not help thinking.

The day before her birthday, dawned beautifully with barely any wind, which was unusual this close to the sea. She was in high spirits as she raced around the empty castle in joy knowing her life would soon be changing drastically, since her cousin's guardianship as of tomorrow would be null and void.

She had made herself a promise last night that she would forget about her troubles for one day at least. She was sure that her cousin would not show up until tomorrow, being as it was her birthday.

It was nearing the midnight hour when she finally left the balcony in her bedroom. She had spent over an hour basking in the rays of the bright full moon that shone down on her long coal-black hair.

She would have gladly stayed out longer, but the wind picked up blowing in the clouds that had been on the horizon to the south. A chilly shiver shook her as the moon disappeared hiding its glow behind the threatening clouds; they were in for a storm, she could feel it in the air.

Once inside, the young girl got ready for bed. She stripped off her dress then underskirt, followed by her bloomers and underwear; leaving them heaped on the floor. She decided to leave her chemise on for tonight since she was still chilled from the wind.

All of a sudden he was standing in front of her, where he had been hiding she did not know! She screamed in loathing as he threw her violently onto the bed; her cousin pushed her chemise up out of his way before dropping like a stone on top of her with such force that the air was driven from her lungs, she could not breath for a long moment.

With ragged breaths, she fought him desperately, but could not stop his dirty filthy hands from groping at her private parts, savagely raping her with no remorse for the blood pooling between her thighs.

The young woman begged and pleaded desperately as she pounded on his back until he managed to get a hold of her hands. Her feeble cries did her no good though as there was nobody around to hear her!

Once finished with her, he had stood over her gloating in glee as he rubbed his hands together in anticipation. "Nobody will want you now that I have broken your spirit, will they my haughty cousin? You should not have rejected me before when I tried so hard to woo you gently. So now, you have no choice but to marry me; like it or not since no man in his right mind will want your defiled body now. Your soul, as well as your body, belongs to me since I have stolen its innocence."

The young woman's cousin was completely wrong about the girl though, thanks to him, she had learned over time what real strength was. He might have defiled the young woman's body, but at that moment, she vowed silently to herself that never would she allow her spirit to be broken by the likes of him!

As soon as her cousin left her bedroom she grabbed her cloak as well as her amulet, but was too scared that he would come back before she could get away to worry about clothes. Besides, the young woman still had her chemise on; it would have to do! Most of her clothes were way too big for her anyway since they had been her mother's gowns. The chemise covered her decently enough draping below her thighs, so she rushed to the balcony not giving it anymore thought.

Lucky for her there was a little overhanging roof that was just slightly below her balcony, but a good three feet separated the two. Reaching it would be difficult because only a few inches stuck out enough for her to land on, which was not enough; she would also have to squeeze between a bedroom window overhang, as well as a statue.

If she stayed as far left as possible, the roof widened slightly in one spot giving her an extra three feet, so it would be big enough for her to land on. That would bring the girl into position to get to the balcony that led into the library below, which was her ultimate goal.

Climbing over the railing of her balcony, she carefully manoeuvred herself over to the left corner where she threw her cloak first, hoping to land on it instead of the rough roof. She eased herself down until she was hanging by her arms. She brought her legs up so that she could dig her bare toes into the side of the balcony in order to push herself far enough away, to give her a little more distance.

Pushing herself backwards like that would also arch her body perfectly to fit between the window overhang and the dragon. She had done this many times in the past to get away from her parents, but she had been younger more limber she could not help thinking.

Praying desperately, she hoped that she was right as she visualized where the roof below was. Now that the moon no longer gave off much light, she had to do this from memory as she shoved herself forcefully backwards away from the balcony hoping to miss the decorative dragon as well as the overhang that would snag her if she hit them, or maybe worse.

Good fortune was with her as she landed exactly where she had planned. It was all the luck she would receive though, as unfortunately only her head landed on the cloak. Landing hard, the air was knocked out of her for a precious fifteen minutes as she groaned painfully trying to catch her breath.

The rough roof against the girl's tender skin caused many scratches as well as bruising, since her chemise and cape had offered little protection. Her bare arms, the back of her legs, and buttocks got the worst of it.

Fortunately, her head was protected as it bounced off the cloak saving her from a nasty concussion. She could feel trickles of blood from the scratches, but she ignored them.

Finally, able to get up, she threw the cloak over her shoulders knowing that she would need both hands free for this next daring feat. She crouched before carefully negotiating the steep incline of the roof as she made her way to the very far edge.

The young woman paused for a good fifteen minutes as she pulled out her medallion to pray asking for the Lords help. When she was done, she tucked the medallion away before taking a deep breath of courage as she prepared herself. A miscalculation here could cost her dearly, even her life.

Turning herself backwards, she carefully lowered herself so that she hung suspended in mid air from the roof knowing it was a forty-foot drop to the courtyard below. Her arm muscles screaming as they strained to hold her weight, but she had to make sure that she was exactly in the center of the little overhanging roof because the balcony to the library was not very big.

In addition, there was a six-foot gap with a slight drop from the edge of the roof to the balcony below. Satisfied with her position, she swung her legs back and forth several times gaining momentum before praying she let go.

She miscalculated slightly causing her to hit the corner of the balcony railing. Once again, the air was knocked out of her lungs as pain exploded in her chest. Desperately she made a grab for the top of the railing, but missed!

Good fortune was with her as she managed to hook her left hand into one of the trellises as she fell; preventing her from falling the thirty-five feet to the courtyard below. Hanging from one arm, she gave a small squeal of alarm.

Fighting to regain her breath, she shook her head trying to stop herself from passing out from the excruciating pain. Finally, she managed to pull in a much-needed breath of air so the spots floating in front of her eyes disappeared.

Quickly remembering the layout of the balcony, she felt around with her left barefoot trying to find another piece of mortar that jutted further past the balcony. It was the match to the one above, also in the form of a baby dragon; both were decorations that her mother had requested her father add.

Finding it at last, she lifted her leg before carefully manoeuvring so that her leg was draped over it. That way she would be sitting behind the dragon giving her some stability when she let go of the balcony.

Once in position she was able to release her precarious hold on the balcony trellis, but it took her a few precious minutes to regain the rest of her breath before she was able to grab the top railing as she pulled herself up.

Now standing on the dragon, she quickly climbed over the railing then dropped thankfully, into a sitting position. She held her left hand painfully against her chest for a moment as she rocked back and forth, tears of pain streaked her face. She wiggled her fingers before rotating her wrist checking to see if she had broken any bones.

It hurt something awful, but thankfully, it was not broken. She could feel several cuts as well as scrapes on her palm where her hand had dug into the carvings on the balcony trellis, but it would have to wait!

The girl wiped the blood on her cloak as she sent a silent thank you prayer to her mother for adding that little dragon since it had just saved her life. She inhaled deeply a couple times, thankful she had not broken any ribs either.

Reassured that she had not damaged anything, she quickly got up not wanting to stay there any longer. She hurriedly raced through the library to a set of stairs leading to a landing before turning right. She ran down more stairs as she made a beeline for the door, praying that her cousin would not see her.

Once outside the castle, she paused at the entranceway door. Two door-height statues of dragon's one male and one female flanked it. Quite a few times the girl had squeezed behind one of the dragons to hide in a little niche behind them. It had hid her from her cousin many times in the past.

Just past the dragons was a set of stairs, which would bring you into the courtyard. The girl raced down the six steps, turning left she quickly ran to the stables. She saddled her mare with her mother's sidesaddle, since it was the easiest one to get too.

Once saddled, she led her mare out the back way. She snuck through the garden to the gate in the very back corner quickly she disappeared!

*****

The young black haired girl sobbed loudly, which brought her back to the present as she hunkered further into her cloak for protection. She should have known what he was up too. However, she was young as well as innocent with no guile or duplicity in her nature at all.

The young woman had been completely sheltered by her adoring parents when they were alive, which put her at a big disadvantage when dealing with people like her cousin.

The woman bent forward suddenly in terror as she whispered urgently to her mare at the sound of the baying hounds behind them. "Run Mist, you must go faster we are almost there! Please hurry!"

The mare's ears flickered back at her mistress's urgent command as its stride lengthened obediently. Mist could not maintain that speed for long though as she tried hard to obey, but she was too weary to go any faster, so the mare's stride slowed once more.

Thankfully, the girl saw a hill ahead rising up out of a denser fog that surrounding it. She could not see much, but it was enough as they raced on trying to reach the safety of the thicker mist ahead.

She wanted to get there desperately, but dreaded reaching it at the same time. If she reached it her pursuers would never find her, but legend also warned that once you entered the fog there was no way out.

The hill was called Snowdonia, it was rumoured to be haunted by the locals. According to legend, twenty-five years ago, several teenagers dared each other to push up against the mist; so spacing themselves out around the fog, they all tried to enter together. Three of them suddenly disappeared, and were never seen again!

The deep pearly grey wall of mist surrounding the hill never dissipated even on the sunniest days. It was said to be impenetrable by most; only a chosen few were permitted entry.

The black haired girl fearfully searched behind her, her dark silvery-grey, crystal eyes filled with terror as she saw the hounds closing on them. She turned back frantically urging her exhausted horse for more speed as she grabbed her amulet through her chemise. Clutching it desperately, she prayed for all she was worth in Celtic to be allowed entrance into the thick impenetrable fog.

Legend also spoke of many would be adventurers trying to enter only to come up against a thick grey wall that stopped them. Try as they might they could not step foot into the mist.

The young woman was on the very edge of the fog. Almost, but not quite into its safe reaches when her mare Mist had to stop short as several massive hunting dogs surrounded them.

Mist, neighing in fear, backed away before rearing slightly in alarm, trying to keep the snarling dogs away from her; the mare struck out at them with her front hooves.

The huge hounds, bred for bringing down large game, circled the horse looking for an opening as they growled viciously. Lunging, a Karelian Bear dog snapped its great jaws at Mist as it looked for an opportunity to bring the mare down by reaching the horse's throat.

The woman held on for dear life as Mist almost unseated her; in desperation, the woman did something that she had never done too her mare before. Although the girl had always carried a whip, never once in all these years that she had her horse did she ever need to use it on Mist, but the girl was frantic.

Screaming in Celtic at her mare in encouragement, the young woman reached behind her with the whip before slapping Mist as hard as she could on the rump. She made sure to hold onto the saddle horn for dear life, knowing that her mare was going to bolt ahead. "RUN MIST! RUNNN!"

The mare screamed in shock before instinctively leaping forward when her mistress hit her. As Mist surged ahead, one of mastiffs in front of her lunged for the horse's throat, but the dog was too late as the terrified mare slammed into it knocking the huge English Mastiff to the ground.

The young woman winced slightly in remorse as she heard the mastiff scream painfully as her mare trampled it into the ground. It was not the dog's fault the girl could not help thinking, but its master!

Tendrils of fog reached out engulfing Mist and her rider as they rushed ahead; quickly the pair was swallowed up into a world filled with heavy misty vapour. No longer were they able to hear, or see, as dead silence surrounded them.

Mist stopped short in uncertainty not sure what to do next. She only paused for a moment though as her ears perked forward; she relaxed, calmed by something that only she could hear.

The black haired woman shuddered in relief as she threw herself forward hugging her mare in apology as the girl whispered softly in Celtic. “I am so sorry Mist; I promise I will never hit you like that again. Please forgive me!”

Mist nickered softly as she bobbed her head accepting her mistress’s apology before the mare began slowly walking forward.

The young woman sat back up before urging her horse on gently; all the while, the woman continued whispering to her mare in excitement. “We made it Mist! I am so grateful that the fog accepted us. Thanks to our God he who watches out for us!”

The black haired woman let her mare find her own way; the woman was unsure where to go, but knew that she could trust her horse’s instincts. The girl relaxed back in the saddle letting Mist roam where she would.

They wandered aimlessly, becoming lethargic as time moved on, seemingly endless.

*****

It was hours later, but felt more like days as they slowly continued on their way. Mist was not sure where they were going, but the mare knew that she must keep going. Something was compelling the horse to do so; the impulse was so strong that Mist could not refuse it.

The young woman finally roused herself from her lethargy as she frowned in surprise at a dark unmoving grey shape ahead. She sat up in the saddle in fearful anticipation before an uneasy feeling surfaced causing her to brace herself, unsure if they should go any further.

The woman tried to pull her mare to a stop. “Whoa there girl. Mist, please stop!”

Mist showing no hesitation at all, ignored her mistress’s repeated attempts to stop her.

Abruptly, a huge grey stone archway was directly in front of them; now, it was too late to stop.

The young woman’s mouth dropped open in awe as they walked through. She could see ancient symbols written all over the stones, which spoke of peace; as well as tranquillity, to all who came under its protection. Her horse shuddered under her as they entered its sacred walls.

Mist came to an uncertain halt in the center of the six huge towering rocks that surrounded them. The compulsion the horse felt to continue on ended, quelling the inner urging as suddenly as it had appeared.

The young woman stared around in apprehensive wonder, still unsure if they should be here. There were six towering grey stone rocks spread out in a circular pattern, all were about fifteen feet high. If you included the stone archway though, that would make seven stones. For some reason the woman did not think the archway was included though, why, she could not say for sure!

They all had different carved patterns going up about half way, which was about seven feet; then a deep engraved line separated the next section.

Directly above the line was a single elemental symbol a foot high before another line separated the next section; each stone had a different element. Stone one had an air symbol. Stone two, had the fire element. Stone three, had a water symbol. On the fourth stone, there was the earth element.

Surprisingly stone five had an aether or quintessence symbol, which was a spirit element; because there was no physical attribute to the spirit element, five circles entwined were used; this element was often forgotten as one of the elements. The sixth and final stone had the sun/ moon symbol, which brought to mind light and darkness.

Past the elemental symbols just above the line, a picture formed for the last six feet of each pillar. It was an engraved picture of Jesus or God encircled by the angels as they helped fight an immense black dragon or serpent of some kind. Why each pillar had the same picture at the top was a bit confusing to the girl because below everything was different.

The girl lowered her gaze to the last seven feet of each stone; there were so many symbols that almost every available space on each pillar was covered. Most, the girl did not even recognize, it could take a lifetime to be able to understand them.

There were markings associated with healing, and some regarding sacrifices, plus many more. It confused the girl greatly as to why they would have protection, as well as warning symbols on the same pillar. It was same with the healing and sacrifice stone, both were opposite to each other on the same pillar.

The woman shook her head irritably to clear it because each time she tried to focus; the symbols began to run together. Finally, she looked away trying to distract herself. It was not until that moment she noticed the shorter stone that was in the center. It only stood about ten feet and was pure ebony black; not grey, as the others were. It also had markings carved on it, but they were indistinguishable since the stone was too dark to see from where she was sitting.

The grey stones surrounding it seemed to be keeping watch over the ebony stone, as if trying to keep it contained inside the circle of stones. The young woman dismounted then stood gazing about her in wonder.

The girl frowned in anxious puzzlement all of a sudden as a niggling thought pushed itself into her conscious thought clearing her head slightly, there was something not right here! She knew that nobody outside the fog could see what was hiding in the mist, but inside the stone formation there was no fog at all; it was clear as day with even a little sun shinning off the stones, but yet it was not an enclosed circle there was a five-foot gap between each pillar. She could see mist swirling between the stones, but it almost looked like the fog was not allowed to enter here.

Did that mean the girl was now stuck in this formation of pillars forever? That thought disturbed the young woman even more making her stiffen in fear, but quickly it disappeared from the girl's mind as the mist swirled around the formation calming her, putting her back into a dreamy, lethargic state.

Now distracted from her thoughts and fears the dark grey-eyed woman took a hesitant step forward then a second; she was surprised that her legs held her up with only a slight wobble. She was just thankful that the pain of her ravishment, as well as all the scrapes and bruises that she had gotten when trying to escape, had almost completely disappeared.

The young woman gazed at the towering black rock in front of her in fascination before approaching it, curious. She touched it hesitantly with her left hand, forgetting that it was still very tender and bloody, wanting to feel the patterns engraved into the rock with her hand.

Instantly the black haired woman snatched her hand away in revulsion before backing away uneasily. She was not sure if she should have touched it as she shook her hand before wiggling her fingers painfully, not realizing that she left a bloody handprint on the ebony stone.

Standing by her mare once more, she put a hand over her mouth stifling a huge yawn, suddenly feeling very tired. The young woman forgot everything else as the thick lush emerald green grass tickled her bare feet enticingly.

Wiggling her toes in delighted surprise at the feel, she gave into her need for sleep. She lay down as she gave another huge yawn, nestling into the thick grass she instantly fell asleep.

The young woman cried out once in her sleep as she mumbled desperately for help in Celtic. "Please someone help me!"

A soft wind blew over the woman in order to calm her as it whisked her words away into the eerie stillness.

A drop of blood trickled its way down the inside of the young girl's thigh before falling onto the emerald green grass. Suddenly the grass turned a blood red as the six sentient stones standing guard, blackened almost instantly.

The thick fog that was once a pearl grey, darkened to a deeper steal grey. An evil chuckle made the hill shudder painfully in reaction, but it was incapable of stopping what was taking place.

The once innocent maiden thrashed as her body arched in excruciating pain as she slept an unnatural sleep, but still she tried desperately to fight off the dark mist that was entering her through every open wound she had. Although she tried desperately, she was unable to stop what was happening to her.

The evil that was hidden here since the dawn of time overcame her resistance as it took over her ravished body.

Nothing could stop it now!

CHAPTER ONE

WALES October 6, 1860

The Earl of Summerset stood with his back to the ballroom looking out the window in brooding discontent. He could hear the music behind him as well as the laughter from a distance, but was not really paying any attention. The earl hated these functions with a passion!

Edward still could not figure out why she had followed him here! Even though she had said that she would come, the earl had not really believed her. Especially since everyone considered his estates in Conwy, only a couple of days from the border of Snowdonia to be haunted.

It seemed like only yesterday, but it was actually a month ago today that Edward was standing exactly the same way staring out a different window longingly.

Edward was at his estate in Summerset entertaining Queen Victoria at his castle in North West Summerset not far from Clevedon when a burning urge took the earl away suddenly to visit his castle in Wales.

Edward could not help sighing in aggravation as the earl thought back to that night…

*****

Edward remembered turning from the window as another shiver of need shook him. The earl looked around hurriedly for the brown haired, blue eyed,

Queen Victoria. She was not difficult to find as Edward waded through the crowd surrounding Victoria before bending to whisper a plea for privacy.

Queen Victoria looked up at Edward's upset expression before nodding as she waved her hand in dismissal to clear the antechamber where she was holding court. Once everyone was gone, Victoria looked up inquisitively. "What seems to be the problem Earl Summerset?"

Edward sighed in relief when they were left alone. The earl had thought that it would be more of a fight to get Queen Victoria by herself, but thankfully, it was not.

Edward dropping to one knee in front of Queen Victoria, he knew how much she hated looking up at anyone. Especially because Victoria was only five feet tall, which she did not like at all. "Your Majesty I ask your leave to go to my estates in Wales tomorrow there is something bad happening or going to happen, so I need to be there. I just can't explain this weird feeling of need I am experiencing!"

Queen Victoria frowned in surprised disapproval as she instantly opened her mouth to deny his request, but shut it quickly as Victoria smiled suddenly with a wicked chuckle instead.

Queen Victoria knew that her husband hated Wales with a passion, so it would be the perfect place to take Albert next. They had been ignoring each other for a week now, ever since they had argued over him paying too much attention to one of Victoria's ladies-in-waiting.

Queen Victoria had sent the poor unfortunate girl home, even though deep down she knew that there was nothing going on between the two. Victoria just could not help the unusual feelings of jealousy she was feeling.

Afterwards, Queen Victoria took everyone to Earl Summerset's since she knew that her husband would not like that at all. It was petty of her of course as Victoria chuckled silently to herself, but oh so satisfying to punish Albert so subtly that the prince consort did not even realize that he was being chastised.

Queen Victoria grinned like a naughty girl making her look years younger, Wales would be perfect to finish off the prince consorts punishment. She finally nodded in permission at Edward as Victoria's grin widened in anticipation. "Oh Wales, I haven't been there in quite a few years. I think I will join you there in a week or so!"

*****

Edward returned to the present with an angry frown; he had thought Queen Victoria was joking of course, but he should know her well enough by now to know that Victoria always did what she said. Still the earl could not help but feel a little annoyed by the queen's presence since now he felt trapped here!

Edward tensed slightly in suspicion instantly as the hairs on the nape of his neck bristled in warning at a whisper of sound behind him; immediately his guard rose as he waited for whoever was approaching to make the first move.

Edward's nose twitched as he inhaled slightly, he smelt Queen Victoria's perfume before she touched him to get his attention, so he relaxed as he turned around quickly. The earl made absolute sure that his expression was void of all emotions as he bowed deeply to Victoria in greeting. "Your Highness?"

Queen Victoria snapped her fan closed in irritation as she eyed the slightly dusky skinned Earl of Summerset. It was hard to believe sometimes that he was three quarters Cheyenne with his dark blond auburn streaked hair, as well as the distinct Summerset deep green eyes.

Queen Victoria's father had banished his grandfather to the new world; there, the late Earl Summerset met a Cheyenne maiden that he later married. He died not knowing that his banishment had ended when she had taken over the throne.

When Queen Victoria found out that the late Earl Summerset's grandson was coming instead to attend school, she had been dead set against him. There was just no way, she was going to allow a savage into her kingdom to stay or allow him to become an earl of the realm. Not while Victoria was the queen, she had insisted to her husband Prince Albert.

What happened next, Queen Victoria had no explanation for it at all! As soon as she saw the boy, with his unmistakable Summerset eyes, a weird feeling had came over Victoria. Instantly she knew that Edward was meant to be at her side.

Where the feeling came from, Queen Victoria had no idea. Why she felt that way was even a mystery. It had turned out to be the best decision the queen had ever made though, since Edward had saved Victoria's life many times already.

Still Queen Victoria did not like this feeling of being indebted to anyone, especially a savage from across the sea even though Victoria felt drawn to Edward unwillingly.

Queen Victoria's husband Prince Albert had been furious with her when Victoria had allowed the savage to stay in England against his wishes.

Queen Victoria's friendship with Edward had grown over the years though, so Victoria had pushed her qualms aside tucking them further and further away into her subconscious mind. Until, they were all but forgotten now.

Occasionally though, Queen Victoria would get a nagging thought that would surface, how did she allow this to happen, but instantly it would disappear again. The queen had never told Edward any of this though since most of the time Victoria did not remember it herself.

Queen Victoria tapped Earl Summerset smartly on the arm in angry demand as Victoria waved in aggravation. "What is troubling you tonight you have been restless all day? It is not like you at all to be this edgy. So for goodness sakes what is troubling you, Edward?"

Edward regarded Queen Victoria reflectively not sure himself what the problem was as the earl shrugged self-consciously before lowering his voice so that no one else could hear their conversation.

Edward was glad that he had encouraged the English nobles to fear him over the years, now everyone stayed clear of the dangerous earl. "I am sorry Victoria, but remember that urgency I felt in Summerset. Tonight it is even worse! I feel as if I should be out there somewhere, not in here entertaining a bunch of pompous fools. I keep thinking someone or something is in trouble and will need my help!"

Queen Victoria looked at Edward sharply in surprised disapproval. In the nine years that she had known him, never had the earl called Victoria by her first name or referred to his abilities in public, only in private.

Queen Victoria's frown eased as she smiled inwardly in pleasure, well that was perfect timing now she had an excuse to stay longer. Her husband had insisted that they leave tomorrow, but Victoria was not done punishing him yet!

Queen Victoria motioned irritably, she ignored Edward's use of her name only because he kept giving her the opportunity to punish the prince consort more, without Albert becoming suspicious. Victoria was enjoying her husband's discomfort, maybe a little too much she couldn't help thinking.

Queen Victoria finally nodded her blessings. "If you must go you have my permission; I am sure you will come to my room immediately once you return to give me all the details. If you need me for any reason just send someone, I will come to you!"

Edward bowed deeply as he kissed Queen Victoria's hand in gratitude that she extended to him for the expected kiss. As the earl stood up, he could not help but wink down devilishly at Victoria. "Thank you your Majesty, I will tell you everything when I get back, I promise!"

Queen Victoria reached up teasingly before patting Edward's cheek with a knowing smile. "Of course you will my boy, I expect nothing less."

Edward turned away from Queen Victoria as soon as she removed her hand from his cheek with a wicked chuckle at her dramatic statement. He did not dare move away until Victoria allowed him to.

Once Queen Victoria removed her hand Edward raced out of the ballroom as the earl hurried up to his room before Victoria could change her mind.

Edward was stripping out of his hated finery even before he entered his room, but once inside the clothes came off faster almost in unseemly haste. He dropped them on the floor as the earl headed for his closet in order to get his old buckskins that he had brought with him from Montana.

Inside the closet, Edward grabbed a shirt that had once been fringed as well as beaded. However, the earl had removed the beadwork and the fringes after an embarrassing confrontation with some of the lords who did not know him. He did have one more set though, but they were ceremonial so they stayed hidden away.

Edward grabbed a saddlebag that the earl always kept inside; it was filled on one side with extra clothes. There was also a couple of hunting knives, some dry kindling plus a little bit of wood since Wales was so wet most of the time dry wood was almost impossible to find.

On the other side of the saddlebag was a hatchet, as well as other survival necessities, that Edward always kept nearby. Old habits died hard even this far away from his old home. The earl changed inside the closet before stepping out with saddlebags in hand.

Edward heard a faint noise of to his left, instantly he dropped the saddlebag as he crouched. Spinning to the right the earl instinctively lifted his arm up over his head. He just managed to save his skull from a hard thwack.

Edward made sure to keep a hold of the stick so that his attacker would not be tempted to try another crack at him. The earl had made the mistake of releasing the stick too quickly only once since he had begun his training.

Edward had ended up with another whack for his inattention, but it had been a good lesson to learn. He stood up to his full six feet four inches before letting go of the stick as the earl bowed deeply to the five foot grey haired man standing in front of him.

Everyone mistook Edward's teacher for Chinese, but if you looked closer you could tell Dao's Oriental mixed blood by his looks. His face was round with eyes angled downward typical of the Chinese people, but his eyes were larger as well as wider with a pronounced nose bridge that spoke of his Japanese descent.

A dark complexion, as well as Dao's short slight frame, pointed to his Vietnamese heritage. Surprisingly his pronounced nose bridge flared out before broadening. Edward's teacher also had single eyelids with black pouches under his eyes, which showed off his Korean descent.

Edward's teacher did not seem to know why Zevak was part of his name since it was Hebrew, as far as Dao knew there was no Hebrew in him.

Dao smiled in approval as he returned the bow slightly. He stood up eyeing Edward's old clothes in surprise before gesturing casually. "You are going somewhere I take it Dream Dancer?"

Edward nodded instantly never having kept anything from his faithful companion. "Yes, someone is calling me for help I think. Can you keep the servants in line please? Plus keep Queen Victoria entertained until I return, teacher?"

Dao nodded slightly used to his student's unexpected departures; he never needed to ask, knowing that Edward would tell him the details later.

Even after all these years, Dao still thought of Edward as his student even though his training had long been completed. "As you wish Dream Dancer!"

Instantly Dao turned away as he scurried out.

Edward smiled after the little Oriental that he called Dao in public, but teacher in private. Dao always insisted on calling him Dream Dancer in private. He was adamant that Edward's Indian name suited him much better.

For the past ten years now, Dao had been Edward's teacher as well as his companion. Even though the earl's training in the Oriental arts had long since finished, his teacher still occasionally tried to catch Dream Dancer off guard.

Several times over the years, Edward had a hard lump on his head to prove that Dream Dancer was still a little slow.

Edward shrugged off his reflective mood as he grabbed his cloak before putting it around his shoulders. Dream Dancer picked up his bedroll and grabbed the saddlebag that he had dropped to protect his head.

Edward raced out of his room before going down the backstairs that would take Dream Dancer outside into the back courtyard of his castle where the stables were located.

Edward barrelled through the back door before jumping over the four stairs. He landed soundlessly cat like in a crouch. Immediately Dream Dancer put his free hand down pressing it flat on the firm ground feeling for any vibrations that would tell the earl others were coming or nearby.

Quickly Edward looked around, but not seeing anyone and with the Mother Earth being silent, Dream Dancer put two fingers in his mouth before giving a shrill whistle of command.

Edward stood to his full height listening intently, waiting. He finally heard the expected answering whinny from the back of the paddock where he kept his special horse in satisfaction. Dream Dancer listened to the thunder of hooves as his horse obediently jumped the fence before racing towards him.

Edward strolled purposely toward his horse to meet him halfway. He reached up to pat the sleek pitch-black coat of his stallion in praise as Dream Dancer switched his language too his native tongue. "Good boy, Cheyenne, come I need to get some stuff in the barn."

Obediently the black stud turned before following his master without hesitation making sure his nose did not quite touch his master's right shoulder so that Cheyenne would not be crowding him.

Edward quickly saddled Cheyenne before going to the back tack room in order to grab his rifle. If Dream Dancer did not think, he would need the bedroll; saddlebags, or the rifle he would have just jumped on his stallion bareback.

However, Edward had a sense that he would be gone for at least two or three days, so it was better that Dream Dancer was prepared for the unexpected.

Edward went into his private back room where he had jerky hanging as well as hardtack stored. They made excellent travelling food plus kept for a long time without spoiling, so Dream Dancer always had some handy for emergencies.

Once finished, Edward led Cheyenne out of the barn before mounting him. He sat quietly for a moment closing his eyes; Earl Summerset let his mind drift remembering who he really was.

Edward tucked the gentler Earl of Summerset away as he released Dream Dancer the stronger half of himself, the Cheyenne half!

When Dream Dancer opened his eyes, they were so dark a green they were almost black. Now having a sense of where he was going Edward turned his horse towards the open gates of his castle before kicking Cheyenne into a gallop.

As they thundered out the gate, Dream Dancer turned his horse south towards the border of Conwy and Snowdonia.

Knowing it was going to be a long ride Dream Dancer let his mind drift as he remembered back to that long ago day ten years ago when Edward left his homeland for good. Although it seemed like only yesterday sometimes, it had been over a decade already.

Dream Dancer missed Montana fiercely, but Edward had never once regretted coming to England in order to become the next Earl of Summerset…

*****

Dream Dancer remembered fondly the last hug he had given his sister. Edward squeezed Raven fiercely in farewell. "I love you! I will miss you terribly while I am gone. You take good care of that new husband of yours. Try to keep him out of trouble too, okay. Remember if you need me I will know and will come to you!"

Raven stepped back as she wiped tears from her eyes before motioning plaintively. "I love you too! Are you sure you do not want us to come to Boston with you I do not like the fact that you are going alone."

Dream Dancer smiled reassuringly at his sister as Edward reached out to squeeze her hand in promise. "I will be fine Raven; I must do this alone it is my destiny, not yours. The Great Spirit has commanded me to go. Besides, you still need to help grandfather. I will write you when I get to Boston before I leave for England, I promise!"

Golden Eagle standing behind Raven put his arm around his wife as he pulled her back against his side in rebuke. Devon looked at her chidingly as she looked up at him. "Let your brother be Raven he will make out alright. He must do what he thinks is best! Besides, he will be riding with White Buffalo as well as Grey Wolf to North Dakota before catching a train to Boston. They will not let Dream Dancer get into any trouble I am sure!"

Golden Eagle let go of Raven as he turned to his young brother-in-law Dream Dancer. Devon bowed deeply in farewell. "You take care of yourself Earl Edward William Charles Summerset! Always remember the lessons I have given you, they will help you to fit in with the nobility. I have no doubt that you will do just fine in England."

Dream Dancer smiled in gratitude at Lord Devon Rochester who was now known to the Cheyenne as Golden Eagle.

As Devon stood up, Edward stepped forward to clasp Golden Eagle's arm in the traditional Cheyenne way as he grinned at his new brother-in-law. "Goodbye blood brother, I will remember your teachings. You take care of my sister for me, please! Try to make sure that Raven does not get into anymore mischief while I am gone."

Both men chuckled knowingly at an indignant huff behind them before Dream Dancer turned away without another word. Edward walked to his horses with a smile of pleasure; there were three of them in total.

The gelding Dream Dancer had trained himself, which he had ridden since he was eleven years old. A mare that was being used as a packhorse, but eventually he would breed. Plus, his gift from Raven a coal black two-year-old stallion Edward would use in England as a stud.

Dream Dance had named his horse Cheyenne to remind him of his home roots, as well as the other half of himself, so that Edward would never forget.

*****

Edward's mind returned to the present suddenly as Dream Dancer reached down to pat his black horse in appreciation. "Well Cheyenne you were the best present ever, plus you remind me of home every time I ride you."

Cheyenne snorted as if in agreement.

Edward laughed at his horse before sighing plaintively, Dream Dancer missed his family fiercely at times especially Raven, her husband Devon, as well as his Cheyenne grandparents.

Edward grinned suddenly in anticipation as he remembered Raven's last letter, Dream Dancer had received it only two weeks ago. Devon's brother here in England was dying; since Earl Rochester had no heirs to replace him, Golden Eagle would have to come here to claim the earldom for his ten-year-old son.

Raven had said that she would be coming as well for a visit.

Edward chuckled in delight before sighing slightly in anxiety as he pictured his wild rugged sister in England. As soon as he had read the letter, Dream Dancer had warned Queen Victoria immediately.

Queen Victoria of course had waved away his concern with a laugh as the queen joked that her court needed livening up anyway, but Victoria had no idea what was in store for her.

Raven was not like the delicate nobility here in England, not even a little. She wore pants, a man's vest, a Stetson, with moccasins or riding boots on her feet. She even had a lethal colt revolver on her hip that she was a crack shot with.

Not only that, but Raven was a full-fledged Cheyenne warrior. The Cheyenne referred to her as their 'Protector' since she was the buffer between her Cheyenne Tribe and the whites.

Raven was not a delicate rose like the women here, but more like the thorn that pricks you when you least expect it. She always laughed heartily, joked with the best of them, who could out drink almost anyone, as well as hold her own in a fight.

In Montana, Raven was unbeatable with a bow in her Cheyenne village!

Edward could not help chuckling to himself in anticipation. Now Raven would have real competition though since Dream Dancer was sure that he had surpassed her in the last few years because of his training with Dao. They would have to put on a demonstration for Queen Victoria to see who the best was now.

Edward laughed in delight just thinking about Raven. Dream Dancer could not wait to see his sister it was going to be an interesting visit, to say the least!

One of the reasons Edward had fit in so well with the English nobility was because of Raven; his sister had known before he was born that he would be coming to England so had made sure that Dream Dancer was prepared.

Edward did not spend much time with their Cheyenne family, but he had been brought up at their ranch. Dream Dancer had also gone to a white school, unlike Raven who had quit school as soon as their parents died.

Raven had taken her responsibilities of raising her brother Edward very seriously, as well as managing the huge sprawling ranch that their parents had built up.

Lucky for Edward, Raven's new husband Golden Eagle who happened to be an English lord had spent as much time as possible with him before he left Montana. Lord Devon Rochester had taught Dream Dancer English etiquette as well as about the nobility hierarchy.

Thankfully, it had helped Edward's transition go smoothly as Dream Dancer settled into his earldom with hardly any problems.

Edward shook off thoughts of Raven as he looked around it was getting late, time to stop for some much needed sleep. It would be another full day tomorrow before he got to the border, Dream Dancer was almost positive that Snowdonia was where he was going to end up.

Normally Edward would have just kept going, but since he had been entertaining Queen Victoria's court half the night, Dream Dancer needed some sleep.

Remembering an Inn that Edward had stayed in not too long ago, the earl turned southeast heading to a little town in the distance. It was not very far out of Dream Dancer's way, so hopefully he could sleep there for a couple hours at least.

Suddenly Edward doubled up in pain before falling out of his saddle to the hard ground. Hitting his head on a rock, Dream Dancer's eyes rolled back in his head as he lost consciousness.

Cheyenne stopped instantly; the black stallion turned back around before going to check on his master. He nudged Edward with his nose curiously in concern as he snorted gently. When he got no response, he lay down against Dream Dancer keeping him warm as well as protected as he waited patiently.

*****

Edward groaned as he came too suddenly. He had not been out very long, maybe half an hour at the most he figured. His head really hurt, Dream Dancer put his hand up so that he could feel the small lump before bringing his hand in front of his face.

Edward could not see anything, but he could feel a wet sticky substance. Dream Dancer must have broken the skin slightly, which would account for the blood.

Edward opened and closed his hands a few times in surprise his palms were burning; the back of his arms also, most of his back as well as his buttocks too. It almost felt as if Dream Dancer had slid on his back down a hill scrapping every inch of his skin on the way down.

Of course, Edward had not; Dream Dancer still lay exactly where he had fallen.

Edward was not exactly sure what had happened! He did have a hunch though that it had something to do with whoever was in trouble. If that were the case, it would mean that they were somehow connected. That would not be good at all especially if Dream Dancer was going to be falling of off his horse without warning.

Edward knew that he had not passed out before falling off his horse though. He did not even think that he would have passed out at all if Dream Dancer had not hit his head on a rock.

It was the sudden feeling of falling through space, as well as the unexpected pain in Edward's back that had Dream Dancer tumbling out of the saddle so abruptly.

Edward sighed grimly as he sat up slowly. He turned to smile at his horse in thanks. Glad now for the long hours he had spent sleeping with Cheyenne when he was a colt; this was not the first time he had curled up beside Dream Dancer to keep him warm. "I am okay now Cheyenne, up you go we need to get going!"

Cheyenne obediently got to his feet; he stood steady, as his master got ready to mount again.

Edward squealed in surprise before he could even put his foot in the stirrup. Dream Dancer stumbled backwards away from his horse in shock instead.

Again, Edward felt that feeling of flying through the air. He grunted as Dream Dancer doubled up in half before grabbing a hold of his chest, as the wind seemed to be knocked out of him.

Edward sat down hard on the ground panting in exertion trying to catch his breath. He grabbed his left hand as it stung and burned for a moment; thankfully, it only lasted a few minutes.

Cheyenne turned when his master stumbled backwards before going over to him. He nudged the sitting Edward in demand trying to help him rise. This was not the first time this had happened as the stallion snorted in rebuke trying to help Dream Dancer to his feet.

Edward pushed his horse's nose away as the gentle nudge almost toppled the unfortunate Dream Dancer backwards. He chuckled grimly; this reminded him of his last drinking episode. He had been so drunk Cheyenne had to resort to lying down to help him mount.

Twice Edward had gotten on his horse only to fall off again as soon as Cheyenne stood up. His stud had been very patient with him that night, Dream Dancer could not help laughing again out loud remembering.

Edward wondered if Cheyenne remembered that too! The next morning bruised as well as very hung-over, Dream Dancer had vowed never to drink that much again. "I am okay Cheyenne just give me a minute!"

Edward slowly got up testing his stability as he moved around. He sighed thankfully when no other incident occurred so going over to his horse Dream Dancer finally mounted.

Edward sat for a bit waiting, but nothing else happened. Dream Dancer sighing relieved before turning his horse southwest once more.

Now that Edward had a little siesta, unwillingly he could not help thinking with a little unamused chuckle, Dream Dancer decided to keep going.

Whoever was in trouble obviously could not wait for Edward much longer so sleep would have to wait a little while. Dream Dancer would have to sleep sometime though, but he would go as far as he possibly could tonight.

Edward looked up before chuckling or today he should say since daybreak was just starting. Dream Dancer frowned grimly as he kicked his horse into a ground-eating cantor as he continued on.

CHAPTER TWO

Dusk was just beginning as Edward leaning precariously in his saddle to the right jerked himself awake once again as his chin dropped to his chest. This was the third time Dream Dancer had almost fallen out of his saddle.

Edward was finding it more difficult to stay awake as each hour passed, but he could see storm clouds in the distance so he did not want to stop just yet. They were not that far from the border as he watched lightning flare in the distance with a grim frown, Dream Dancer hoped to reach Snowdonia before stopping to sleep.

That storm was getting closer though as daylight waned, it would not be long before it overtook them. Edward had managed to keep himself awake for most of the day with only one stop to rest his horse. Dream Dancer had caught a second wind while eating a light meal, so they had continued on.

To take his mind off his need to sleep, Edward allowed his mind to wander back into time once again as Dream Dancer remembered his first view of Boston…

*****

Edward could still remember that long ago day as if it were yesterday; Dream Dancer jerked awake at the loud call of the conductor as the man yelled out so that everyone could hear him above the noise of the train. "One hour to Boston folks!"

Edward smiled in anticipation before sighing thankfully, as he sat up with a giant yawn; finally, he was here. He had ridden across Montana into North Dakota with Melissa as well as her husband Jed. Dream Dancer had stayed with them for two days, but Mell was too busy getting her towns back in shape after being gone for almost two full months.

Edward had laughed in delight when he had heard Mell mumbling under her breath about how incompetent her deputy marshals were. It would have been rude of him not to stay at least two days since they had asked Dream Dancer to while travelling.

Edward roused himself; pushing his thoughts away, he looked out the window in anticipation not wanting to miss anything. Dream Dancer's first sight caused him to sigh in disappointment though.

Boston looked exactly like the towns close to the ranch except it was much bigger. It was also disgustingly dirty compared to their towns; even his grandfather Chief Giant Bear's Cheyenne village was better kept.

The Great Spirit had promised Edward that he would get help here; how, he was supposed to find anyone in this vast city was beyond him. Why he needed help from someone not of his own people baffled him, but Dream Dancer knew that it would be revealed to him when the time came.

The train slowed, so Edward shook off his reflective mood as he grabbed his gear that he had put on the seat beside him so that nobody else could sit with him. He got up before heading towards the rear compartments where Dream Dancer's horses were being kept.

Edward arrived just in time as he heard his stallion screaming in anger as he reared up. Dream Dancer ran towards the idiot trying to lead his stud out of his stall. "Stop, get away from that horse before you get yourself killed!"

The tall burly brown haired man backed off quickly with a grunt of exasperation as the young fellow grabbed the lead rope away from him.

Edward's voice lowered soothingly as Dream Dancer talked calmly in Cheyenne to quiet the agitated stallion.

The stocky black stud stood there quivering in anger as he blew hard threw his nostrils in distress, but his ears perked forward listening attentively to his master's quiet reassurances as he finally calmed down once more.

Edward heard the other man mumbled irritably under his breath as he shook his head in disgust. "Damn half-breeds and their horses!"

Edward frowned angrily at the man's prejudice comment, but did not criticize him; it would not help anyway he could not help thinking. Dream Dancer had learnt that lesson many years ago when staying with his grandfather's people.

As the train came to a complete halt, the large door dropped to the ground. Edward led his stallion out before tying him securely to the hitching rail. Even though Dream Dancer knew the stud would not stray unless spooked, there was way too much noise as well as people to take that chance.

Edward raced back up the platform as he went to get his mare next. Dream Dancer tightened the mare's packs before leading her out to stand beside the stallion.

The man, who had tried to take his stallion out of the stall, led his more passive gelding out.

Edward nodded his thanks as he took the rope from the man before tossing him a penny for his help. Dream Dancer tied his gelding up as well before heading into the train station.

Once Edward had directions, he went back out then tied his stallion's lead rope to the back of his gelding's saddle. Next, he tied his mare on the opposite side of his saddle close to the left stirrup. Dream Dancer finally mounted heading north.

Edward's sister Raven with the help of their lawyer in town had made all the arrangements for him. He would stay in Boston for three days before catching a ship to England; the Summerset lawyer would meet Dream Dancer there.

The lawyer would take Edward to one of his townhouses, once there he would be outfitted in the proper clothing so that Dream Dancer could be taken to Queen Victoria to be properly introduced.

All the arrangements were already made for Edward's schooling; he was to start at Oxford in the fall. Dream Dancer's English grandfather, the late Earl Summerset, had attended the same school.

Hopefully, in a few years Edward would be a full doctor. At first, he had wanted to be a lawyer, but his blood brother Devon had advised Dream Dancer to become a doctor instead. Golden Eagle had insisted that being a doctor would help to hide what he really was from England's corrupt nobility.

Edward looked around curiously as the buildings got smaller; they were mostly lean-tos now with a lot more garbage lying around. He noticed a group of men standing together, so he slowed curiously. Dream Dancer had never seen people like them before.

Jed had warned Edward that he probably would see them here; he had called them Orientals. They had coal black hair done in a long thin braid down their backs some almost to their hips. Others had theirs up in a bun on top of their heads with a braid hanging down as well; Dream Dancer could see various styles in the dozen men standing around.

They were dark skinned like Edward's people, but their skin had a bit of a yellowish tinge. Their eyes were anywhere between a deep brown to black with a slight tilt some upward others were downward, depending on where they lived.

Most of them wore funny looking clothes some almost looked like dresses or skirts to Dream Dancer. Several styles did remind him of buckskins with the long shirt and leggings underneath. They had no fringes though or beadwork, he could see what looked like paint on some of them though.

Jed had also told him that they were treated worse than the Indian tribes were. Most of them laboured in mines or on the railroad, he said that they were treated like slaves. A lot of them died from starvation or diseases.

Edward rode on as he shook his head sadly, most of the time he was terribly ashamed of his white blood. He turned onto his street before continuing on, as Dream Dancer rode along the houses changed becoming better kept as well as expensive.

Edward finally saw the hotel so turned into the stables; Dream Dancer dismounted leading his horses in.

A large bulky dark haired bear of a man in an apron bustled up to Edward as he knuckled his forehead in respect. "What can I do for ya young sir?"

Edward nodded cordially back. "I am booked into the hotel for three days; can you look after my horses for me? Be careful of the stallion though he gets a bit ornery with strangers."

The man inclined his head in agreement; he turned before bellowing loudly to someone in the back. "Hey Chink, comes out den take dose hoses en feed em!"

A five-foot tall Chinaman came out of the back room immediately, he glided towards them it seemed to the impressionable young earl. He had a bun on top of his head with two braids hanging down one on each side of the bun. He wore a plain black flowing long shirt with pants.

The Chinaman put his two hands together as if in prayer before bowing slightly, but not once did he look at the big stableman. "As you wish!"

The little man walked over to the black stallion first unhooking his lead rope.

Cheyenne rolled his eyes angrily as the stud backed away with a warning snort ready to rear up.

The Chinaman reached out calmly as he touched the stallion's nose in reassurance before talking soothingly to him in his own language.

Cheyenne's ears perked up as the stud calmed almost immediately before following the little man docilely.

Edward shook his head in disbelief that was the first time Cheyenne had allowed anyone near him without hardly any fuss. Satisfied that his horses were in good hands, Dream Dancer pulled off his main saddlebag before turning to the stableman. He tossed him a half dime. "Please have the rest of my packs brought to my room."

Edward turned back to unhook the lead rope from the mare so that he could personally hand the rope to the Chinaman. He turned to the Oriental as he came to take the mare before handing him the lead rope with two bits hidden in his palm as Dream Dancer smiled in thanks.

Edward did this to make sure that the money was hidden from the stableman not wanting him to take it from the Oriental.

The little man backed away bowing with his hands pressed together, but a little deeper compared to the one he had given to the stableman. "Thank you young lord."

When the Chinaman stood back up he looked up at the young man staring into his eyes intently for a long moment assessingly. A slight curl to his lips in approval was all the emotion he showed before he turned away leading the mare to a stall without further comment.

Edward frowned in puzzlement, when the little man had looked into his eyes he had felt a slight tingle of something. Almost of recognition or anticipation, but he had never seen him before that he knew of. Dream Dancer shrugged uneasily, somewhat disconcerted as he left quickly.

Edward went to the front door of the hotel before entering the lobby. He looked around curiously. The counter was on his left with a stairway on the right leading up to the rooms, just past that was a door Dream Dancer assumed led into the dining room.

Edward walked up to the counter, but nobody was there so seeing a little bell on top Dream Dancer rang for service.

A huge barrel of a man came out of the back rooms nodding in acknowledgement. "Yes sir, may I help you?"

Edward smiled in surprise; the man was enormous at least three hundred pounds if not more, but he was short compared to the young earl. He resembled the stableman slightly, so Dream Dancer guessed that they were probably related somehow.

The hotel clerk was assessing Edward just as intently. Curiously, he eyed the light brown almost blond auburn streaked haired stranger with the deepest green-eyes he had ever seen. He wondered if this was the young earl that he had been instructed to watch for. If it were, he was tall for sixteen at six foot already. The clerk liked the honest straightforward expression of the young man.

Edward reached across the counter so that he could shake the hotel clerks hand in greeting.

The clerk approved of the firm, but not crushing handshake the young man gave him as he grinned knowingly. "Names, Edwin."

Edward inclined his head as he released Edwin's hand. "I am Earl Summerset, but everyone calls me Edward."

Edwin nodded in delight his suspicion confirmed. "I have been expecting you."

Edwin reached under the counter pulling out his special key that only a few were ever privileged to use before walking around the counter. He beckoned the young earl to follow him.

Edward obediently trailed the clerk. He was led towards the door of the dining room, but the clerk unexpectedly turned right as he walked under the main stairway that led up to the rooms. Dream Dancer had not noticed the hallway on his first inspection, there was one door down the hallway on the right almost in the center.

The clerk unlocked the door before opening it with a flourish as he waved for the young man to precede him. He handed the key to Edward as he walked past.

Edward walked in before his eyes widened in surprise. The room was made up in royal blue colours it was enormous. It even had its own bathtub off to the right partially hidden by a screen. The bed was round it would hold three people comfortably without crowding each other; Dream Dancer was sure.

Edward turned to the fireplace before smiling in satisfaction; they had clearly expected him today since a fire was already crackling cheerily inside. He turned with a grin of pleasure to the innkeeper. Dream Dancer dug out a half silver dollar for a tip in thanks. "It is beautiful!"

Edwin waved off the tip with a smile of pleasure at the young earl's obviously delight in his room. "No need for that it has already been taken care of, so under no circumstances are you to tip anyone here. Your lawyer already made sure that everyone was looked after. Now Susan will be here soon she will take care of all your needs while you are here. The rest of your saddlebags will be delivered directly, enjoy your stay here Earl Summerset.

Edward nodded pleased he was very confident that he would enjoy it. He waited for the stout innkeeper to close the door before the Dream Dancer dropped down on the bed with a satisfied sigh as he fell asleep almost instantly; trains were just so uncomfortable.

*****

It was getting late when Edward left the hotel to go to the saloon Edwin had recommended. He had turned seventeen yesterday, but had been unable to celebrate that fact on the train. Dream Dancer decided to do so tonight.

Edward was about halfway there when he felt a prickle of warning on the back of his neck. His hand dropped to his gun quickly as Dream Dancer spun around looking for whoever was watching him so intently, but nobody was there.

Edward frowned perplexed as he looked everywhere, but to no avail. That feeling of being watched did not go away, however. Dream Dancer shrugged dismissively as he turned back around before continuing on. He released his gun with a chuckle at his foolishness.

The gun was a new addition to Edward's wardrobe, a gift from Mell. She had insisted on teaching him how to use it, but he knew deep down that he would not be able to kill anyone unless given no other choice. It just was not in him Dream Dancer was a healer not a killer.

Edward was close to the saloon when he heard a woman scream in terror off to his left. The dreadful sound echoed eerily from an alley in-between two buildings. Instantly without thought for his own safety Dream Dancer raced in that direction so that he could help whoever was in trouble. He was halfway down the alleyway when he heard a grunt of effort with a fainter call for help.

Edward's pace quickened when he saw two men struggling with a young woman, she was on the ground sobbing hysterically. One man was holding her down while the other one was in the process of raping her.

Edward did not even hesitate for a second as he grabbed the man lying on the woman. Dream Dancer heaved him bodily across the alleyway off her.

The man holding the woman down jumped up in surprise going for his gun instantly.

Edward was faster though as Dream Dancer's left foot rose rapidly connecting under the man's jaw.

Instantly the man dropped stunned to the ground.

The man Edward had thrown across the alley raced back towards Dream Dancer.

Edward crouched readying himself as both arms came up in a fighting stance that Dream Dancer had learnt from his Uncle Black Hawk and his sister Raven.

The rapist wanted nothing to do with the towering stranger though. He got to his friend to help him up before both men turned tail as they fled.

Edward waited for a few moments in order to make sure that they were not coming back. Once sure they were gone, Dream Dancer relaxed his stance as he dropped down beside the sobbing girl.

Edward looked around making sure nobody was nearby before eyeing the girl in reflection, obviously he had been too late she had been raped at least once. Dream Dancer frowned angrily; maybe he should go after those men after all.

Someone should make them pay for what they had done as Edward looked at the girl a little more closely, she could not be more than fifteen. Judging by the coal black hair, dusky yellowish skin, she was Chinese like the man in the stables.

Edward moved closer to the girl as Dream Dancer rubbed his hands together chanting softly in Cheyenne.

The girl stopped sobbing suddenly as she listened to the big man above her chanting; she could not understand what he was saying, but it calmed her to listen to him. She watched curiously, as he continued to rub his hands together before reaching out to her. She automatically flinched away thinking he wanted to hurt her too.

Edward never once wavered or stopped his chanting as he brought Dream Dancer to the surface. He reached out with his hot hands towards the girl, not letting her fear stop him. He laid one hand on her forehead as well as one hand on her stomach still chanting in Cheyenne.

This was only the third time in his life that Dream Dancer had done this. The first time was by accident with Edward's brother-in-law Devon. The second time had been with Jake's son after he had been shot.

Dream Dancer was not even sure that he could do it out here so far away from his people and homeland, but he did not let that stop him as Edward tried to help the girl's body heal itself.

When Dream Dancer's hands touched her, he was surprised to feel a painful, burning jolt race up his arms. It took all of his concentration to continue as the pain intensified, but finally Edward felt his healing powers reluctantly come to life once more.

The shock was something new; Dream Dancer had not felt that with the other two. He felt the power in his hands wane, so he released the girl abruptly. Edward came back to himself as his eyes went back to their customary dark green. He sat back on his haunches rubbing his hands together painfully.

Edward dropped his head in his hands for a moment hoping the slightly woozy feeling in his head would not last long. Dream Dancer sighed in relief as the feeling subsided after only a few minutes she had not been hurt that badly.

The girl smiled gratefully at the strange young man sitting in front of her. She was not sure what he had done, but she felt warm as well as tingly all over.

Suddenly her eyes widened in stunned disbelief at something behind Edward. Instantly she got to her knees before kneeling with head bowed as her two small hands came together in a prayer like position as she started babbling in her own language fearfully.

Edward spun around quickly as he instantly went into a fighter's crouch readying him self, unsure what the girl was so upset about. He looked up in surprise at the little man from the stables that had looked after his horses. Dream Dancer had not heard the man coming at all. The earl hoped that the man had not seen what he had done to the girl!

The man stared down at the girl in disapproval as she continued to babble incoherently. Finally, his hand came down in a sharp silencing motion as he spoke harshly to her in his own language.

Instantly the girl quieted as she bowed down deeper. Now her forehead was almost pressed against the little man's feet as she listened to him respectfully. She jumped up suddenly without warning as she bowed to the Oriental man first before turning to her rescuer with another deep bow. Without looking at either of them, she turned scurrying away as fast as she could go.

Dao watched his granddaughter disappear reflectively. She had disobeyed him again this time with disastrous consequences, but he would deal with her later.

Dao turned slightly before regarding Edward intently as the young man crouched in front of him. He stared down into the dark green eyes relentlessly; waiting for the earl to turn away as every white man had done since he had arrived in Boston searching for his destiny.

To Dao's surprise though, the young man's gaze never once wavered. He watched in fascination as Edward's eyes darkened from a deep green to such a dark green that his eyes were now almost black. He had watched the earl kick his opponent before crouching in a fighting stance it had pleased him to see that.

Even though Edward had a gun, he had never made one move towards it as he had done earlier while Dao had watched him so intently from the shadows of the buildings. It was good that the boy showed such well-developed warrior instincts; the young earl was obviously a fighter not a killer, which he had just demonstrated while rescuing Dao's granddaughter.

Now that Edward's eyes were black, Dao could feel the chaotic power radiating from him. He had felt it slightly earlier in the stables, which was why he had looked at the young earl so intently.

Dream Dancer forced to the surface by the Orientals intense gaze stared up just as fixedly refusing to relent. He felt his power surge in his body as his eyes changed, but this was different they were so black Edward wondered if they were actually coming right out of his head it was that intense of a feeling.

The power rushing through Dream Dancer's body was so determined to be released that it was becoming excruciatingly painful as he fought desperately to hold it back. He was sure that there must be sparks or lights flaring around him as Edward fought not only his unmanageable power, but also the fear mounted within him.

This had never happened to Dream Dancer before the man was doing something to him. Edward refused to look away though knowing deep down that if he did; it would be disastrous for him.

Dream Dancer knew that he had to figure out how to bury his power somehow; it was almost beyond his control now. So chanting softly, he slowed his heartbeat down a little at a time. As he did so, he could feel the blood in his veins slowing as Edward relaxed every part of his body one muscle at a time.

Black Hawk, Dream Dancer's uncle from his grandfather's village, had taught him to do this when using the bow. Edward had to be careful though too much could stop his heart altogether.

As Dream Dancer's heart slowed down more, so too did his body relax, as it calmed the power finally dissipated now under his control once more. Edward could feel his eyes changing back to their usual deep green; still he refused to look away from the little man.

Unexpectedly the Oriental released Edward's gaze. As Dao stepped back, he clapped twice in admiration before bowing deeply with both hands pressed together.

Dao's bow this time was much deeper, with a great deal of respect now showing compared to this afternoon. "You have saved my granddaughter, I owe you a debt. To repay this obligation, I will accompany you on your travels so that I can teach you how to control your powers, your mind, as well as your body. This is my destiny I have been waiting a long time for you!"

Edward frowned slightly confused as he stood up to his full height. Dream Dancer looked down at the little man who still stood bent over. "You cannot come with me I am going to England in a couple of days!"

Dao stood back up before inclining his head at Edward knowingly. "I have knowledge of this already, even if I have to pursue you from a distance I will still follow. Your powers are getting stronger; as you age, they will also grow within you. Without my help, you will not be able to use them to their full potential. Without my help, they will also become unmanageable for you one day soon. Already I can feel it rebelling!"

Edward grimaced in anxiety very much aware of that now; he had just felt what that would be like while healing the girl. Dream Dancer definitely did not want to have that feeling of unpredictability ever again.

Edward smiled suddenly as he nodded pleased; the Great Spirit had not steered him wrong after all, as he remembered his thoughts from the train. Dream Dancer had just found the help that he knew deep down he needed.

Edward's sister Raven had been worried because it had been so long since they had a shaman with Dream Dancer's ability. There had been no one to teach him how to manage the power that had just begun to grow stronger.

Edward felt intense relief as the two walked out of the alleyway together. Dream Dancer looked sideways at the little man. "What should I call you?"

Dao looked up in amusement. "Dao Ba Zevak Hajime. The meaning of my name is complex; Dao means sword in Chinese. Ba is Vietnamese; it means third. Zevak is Hebrew; it means sacrifice. Hajime is Japanese; it means beginning. To make it easier for you just call me Dao, or you can call me teacher if you prefer since that will now be what I am to you."

Edward smiled curiously, as he tried to figure out why the Oriental would have a name that means so many different things. If Dao's people were anything like his, a meaning or warning would be hidden in his name. However, sword, third, sacrifice, as well as beginning just did not make much sense to Dream Dancer. "I take it you are not full Chinese? Is there a particular reason for your name?"

Dao shrugged as he looked up at Edward. "You are correct I am not full Chinese, but a mixture of cultures. Why this is so, has not been revealed to me as of yet. Our names always have great meaning, but why is not always revealed to use until the end of our lives."

Edward nodded thoughtfully. "I will call you Dao when we are in public, but I think teacher will be a lot better when we are alone together. You can call me Edward or Dream Dancer that is my Cheyenne name."

Dao grinned teasingly before chuckling in amusement. "I will call you Earl Summerset in public, but Dream Dancer in private since it suits you best."

When Edward took his teacher back to the hotel, he arranged to purchase Dao's bondage papers in order to free him. In the morning, Dream Dancer would seek out all the papers for Dao's family as well so that they too would be released from slavery.

Edward had a bed put in his room for the mixed Oriental.

As predicted Dao refused to leave his new students side; he always stayed one-step behind respectfully in public. In private though, he became Dream Dancer's shadow teacher.

*****

Edward shook himself from his contemplation as he looked around dejectedly. The wind had picked up with a thick fog blowing in suddenly as Dream Dancer finally rode into the storm that had been on the horizon all day.

There was very little shelter out here though being a little too open.

Edward could see trees a few miles to the west, but he did not want to veer off course again. When Dream Dancer had tried that early this morning, he had fallen out of his saddle.

Edward did not think the fall had any bearing on his direction change, but he did not want to take any more chances. He stopped his stallion figuring he was on the border of Snowdonia at last. Dream Dancer dismounted before stripping off his horse's saddle so that he could rub him down.

Cheyenne was soaking wet from the long hard ride, but not blowing hard so he would be okay for the night.

After Edward finished with his horse, he set up a camp for himself as lightning flared all around bringing rain. As the wind gusted harder, the rain turned into a torrent as it fell steadily. He did not bother with a fire he was not that hungry anyway, but he did chew on some jerky. Afterwards, Dream Dancer wrapped himself in his bedroll to sleep.

Cheyenne wandered around eating grass for a bit before going over to his master; he dropped down beside him for some much needed warmth

Edward's dreams were wrestles as the urgency he had felt continued to plague him. Dream Dancer mumbled suddenly in fear at the sound of dogs baying loudly. "Please hurry you must get away, do not let them catch you!"

Edward quieted suddenly in relief as his sleep deepened. In the morning, Dream Dancer would not remember his dream.

CHAPTER THREE

Edward was jolted awake just before dawn by his own voice as Dream Dancer screamed aloud. "I'm coming; hold on, I am coming!"

Edward sat up trembling in reaction, but could not remember who he had been talking too. All that Dream Dancer could remember was him self, screaming out his final words of reassurance.

It was unsettling to say the least, especially since Edward always remembered his dreams since Dream Dancer had shaman powers. That is what shamans do they interpret dreams their own as well as others.

Disconcerted Edward got up before going over to his pack to pull out some dry kindling, as well as some wood for a small fire so that he could have a cup of tea. Dream Dancer chewed on dried jerky while he waited.

Once finished, Edward doused the fire as Dream Dancer repacked everything.

Edward finally saddling his stallion getting ready to leave, when he was done he looked around to make sure that all traces of him were gone. Satisfied Dream Dancer mounted before nudging Cheyenne forward to resume his journey; he continued going southwest.

There was still some lingering fog, but thankfully, the rain, wind, as well as the lightning had quit. It was deadly quiet now with not even a puff of wind, which was highly unusual for Wales especially here in Snowdonia. In all the time, that Edward had lived here it was either windy, raining, and foggy or sunny with wind. Not very often was the wind completely silent.

All that Edward could hear at this moment was the steady cadence of his horse's hooves, as well as an occasional squawk of a bird.

To take his mind off the eerie stillness, Edward remembered his first sight of England that long ago day. Dream Dancer had to admit that he was not very impressed when he had first seen it, but the British Isle had grown on him as time passed…

*****

Edward remembered how depressed he was at his first sight of England it seemed like only yesterday that he had docked in London. It was foggy, cold, and drizzling steadily when Dream Dancer came up on deck to look around curiously. It reminded him a lot of Boston dirty, dreary looking, but even bigger.

People were rushing around frantically it seemed to Edward if they bumped into someone they just kept going without a sorry or an excuse me. Nothing, no politeness in these people at all that Dream Dancer could see from the ship.

Edward sighed dejectedly feeling very lonely suddenly as he grimaced missing his home already. Dream Dancer went down below decks to help Dao with his horses.

Once all of the horses were safely off the ship Edward helped Dao with saddle packs as well as their luggage before going to stand on the docks. Dream Dancer put the mare's packs back on while they waited since it gave him something to do.

Edward was unsure where to go next, so figured that it was best to stay where they were. Dream Dancer's lawyer was supposed to meet them here by the ship. Finished with the mare, he tied his stallion as well as the mare to his gelding's saddle. He walked back around his horse as he stood by his teacher waiting impatiently.

It was so crowded on the docks that it was hard for Edward to distinguish exactly what happened next. Unexpectedly a red haired boy stumbled, or maybe he was pushed up against the earl. It did not really matter to Dream Dancer one way or the other though how it happened, only that it did.

Edward reacting instantly reached out before the boy could make a clean getaway, or even realized what was happening; Dream Dancer grabbed him by the shirtfront. He lifted the youngster bodily off the ground so that they were nose to nose.

Edward stared intently at the dirty scrawny golden-brown eyed boy; he could not be more than thirteen. Dream Dancer's eyes narrowed dangerously as he held up his free hand; the earl opened it so that his palm was facing upwards. "I would not do that if I were you, now give it all back!"

The youngster squealed in fear as he looked into the icy deep green eyes before reluctantly putting Edward's watch as well as his purse in the open palm.

Edward dropped the boy unceremoniously without any warning.

The young boy yelped in protest as he sprawled on the dock in a heap. The air was instantly knocked out of him so that he could not rise as he watched the Bobbies walking towards them in a panic.

Edward dug in his purse before pulling out a silver dollar. Dream Dancer flipped it to the boy with unusual bright carrot red hair; the hair colour really made his golden-brown eyes stand out. "Here go buy yourself something to eat, make sure to let your friends know that Earl Summerset will not tolerate thieves!"

The boy finally caught his breath as he nodded mutely before jumping up as he raced away in relief, extremely glad that the earl did not call down the Bobbies on him. The three policemen that had began walking towards them had stopped only because Earl Summerset had thrown him a coin, so they had figured he was doing an errand for the earl. The dockside police were notoriously cruel to thieves, especially if they were in a guild as he was.

*****

Dao just chuckled beside him. "That will not help you know!"

Edward grinned in humour as Dream Dancer inclined his head. "I know, but it was worth a try."

A sandy brown haired man dressed in fancy clothes walked up, he stopped knowingly in front of the green-eyed earl. "Earl Summerset I am Sir James Bertin, my family has been the Summerset lawyer since we came from France a hundred years ago."

Edward nodded before reaching out to shake his lawyers hand in greeting. "Yes, I am Edward Summerset how do you do."

James looked at the offered hand in surprise not having expected that from an earl even one from the new world. Reluctantly James Bertin shook the hand before turning away as he beckoned Edward to follow him. "This way please your carriage is waiting at the end of the dock."

Edward frowned disgruntled after the retreating lawyer; well obviously shaking hands in this country was frowned on. Dream Dancer grabbed his gelding's reins before helping Dao by grabbing one of his bags as they followed dutifully.

The lawyer reached the carriage first so waited impatiently for the earl. Once the two men joined him, James gestured in apology as he looked up at the much taller earl. "Unfortunately you are not going to be able to have clothes made up for your first visit with Queen Victoria. You are around the same size as your grandfather was though so we will stop quickly so that you can change into one of his outfits. The queen wants to see you right away!"

Edward inclined his head a little surprised by the haste before helping Dao up into the carriage. Dream Dancer turned away to mount his gelding, he did not want to ride in that stuffy looking thing.

James frowned up at the young earl in disapproval sitting up on his horse before finally turning away with a dismissive shrug. He climbed into the carriage with the funny looking little man wondering if he were a servant or a family friend.

*****

Edward could not help but chuckle, which returned him to the present as he remembered the many battles between him and his lawyer over the years. Sadly, James Bertin died a few years ago; Dream Dancer still missed their fights sometimes. His son Charles Bertin had taken over as the Summerset lawyer, but he was more laid back hardly ever arguing with him.

Edward's thoughts turned back to his first day in England…

*****

Edward grinned as he remembered how frightened he was to meet a real live queen. Dream Dancer decked out in his grandfather's outdated court clothes walked into the Palace.

Edward was trembling inside in fear, but none of the whispering men or women watching him would have guessed as the impassive Dream Dancer refused to show these people one speck of emotion.

Edward heard the whispers of savage Indians, he frowned angrily someone had already leaked out the fact that he was three quarters Cheyenne. It would be almost a year before Dream Dancer found out that he already had an enemy at court, Queen Victoria's husband Prince Albert, unfortunately.

Edward refused to look right or left as he walked ahead. Remembering his brother-in-law Devon's instructions, Dream Dancer made sure to keep his right hand on his sword hilt as well as his eyes on the back of the man leading him.

The man stopped suddenly before bowing, he backed away leaving Edward alone.

Edward quickly dropped to one knee gracefully, he bowed his head waiting for permission to rise; Dream Dancer did not dare look up either.

"Stand young man so I can have a look at you!"

Immediately Edward stood up before looking at Queen Victoria for the first time. She had brown hair with light blue eyes, she was slightly chubby not fat though. She had a bit of a homely appearance until she smiled; it lit up her face giving Victoria a glowing mischievous look.

Queen Victoria frowned disgruntled, as she looked him over assessingly. She had not expected a savage to look so much like an English lord, even though his grandfather had been one.

The fact that the young man looked exactly like the late Earl Summerset in a painting that Queen Victoria had was uncanny; she had not expected that at all. She was intrigued slightly by the fact that he already seemed versed in court manners since Victoria had watched him closely, but he had done all the right things so far.

Queen Victoria smiled enticingly; she wanted to know more about this young savage in their midst, afterwards Victoria would send him away. "Yes, you look just like the portrait I have of your grandfather. Of course, I never met him since my father had banished him before I was born. My Uncle King George the fourth had talked about sending for him a few times, but we got the sad news that he had passed away just a few days before my uncle died as well."

Edward unaware of Queen Victoria's intention of sending him back to Montana sighed sadly, as he motioned in regret. "Yes I never met him either; maybe sometime you can show me the portraits you have. I have all the papers you need here with me if you would like to see them now your Majesty?"

Queen Victoria waved her hand dismissively. "Later my boy, now come over here I want you to sit beside me so that you can tell me all about yourself."

Edward sat down before doing what he was told.

Later Queen Victoria had introduced all the waiting nobles, but it took Edward almost a year to get them all straight.

*****

Edward chuckled quietly to himself, as he shook off the memory; Devon would have been proud of his first meeting with Queen Victoria. It was only because of Golden Eagle's teaching that everything had gone so smoothly, especially when Victoria called Dream Dancer in to see her as soon as he landed in England.

Edward's brother-in-law Devon had figured that Queen Victoria would let Dream Dancer sit for at least a week or two, but Raven's husband Golden Eagle had been wrong.

Edward having been lost in thought for quite some time had not noticed the fog thickening, or the wind gaining strength as the day wore on. He had a sudden need to turn west, which had Dream Dancer reining his horse in that direction.

It was not long before Edward saw a darker steal grey almost black thicker fog ahead. When he looked up higher, Dream Dancer could see that a hill or mountain was within the mist.

Edward was about a quarter of a mile away from the wall of fog when Dream Dancer's horse unexpectedly stopped dead. Cheyenne reared slightly before backing up several steps in alarm refusing to go forward another step.

Edward taken completely by surprise was almost unseated; he let his stallion back up until he came to a halt on his own. Feeling his horses fear Dream Dancer tried to calm him as he put a hand down on the side of his stud's neck patting him soothingly in concern. "Whoa there Cheyenne what is the matter, big boy?"

Cheyenne snorted uneasily as he stood quivering in fear pawing at the ground anxiously. The big black threw his head around before backing up several more steps as he snorted blowing hard.

Edward jumped off Cheyenne before stroking his sweating neck soothingly, something was not right. Dream Dancer looked towards the darker mist ahead grimly; obviously, it was the fog upsetting his stallion.

Having grown up in Montana with his sister Raven, she had taught Edward from an early age to trust his horse's instincts. If Dream Dancer's stallion refused to budge, there had to be a very good reason for it.

An urge to go south had Edward turning in that direction. The change in direction meant that they would stay at a safe distance from the mist. Dream Dancer's horse was still very upset, but obediently walked ahead when they changed directions.

Edward decided it was best to continue leading Cheyenne for a while until his horse calmed down. Dream Dancer had a feeling that they would not be going much further anyway.

They circled the dark fog going around slowly, but now they stayed at a safer distance. There was something here Edward could feel it, so not wanting to miss whatever it was Dream Dancer continued walking even though Cheyenne was calm once more.

Cheyenne's head jerked up suddenly, his nostrils flared when the wind shifted as he caught an enticing scent. He neighed loudly as he arched his neck before prancing in excitement.

An answering dainty neigh just ahead of them echoed in the deadly silence.

Edward put his hand up to his stallion in caution. "Shush now!"

The big black quieted instantly as his master walked up to him.

Edward went around his horse in order to get to his rifle; he cocked it so that it was ready for instant use just in case this was a trap. Cautiously they advanced with Dream Dancer still leading Cheyenne.

Something white flickered in the distance, but disappeared again just as quickly as the mist shifted hiding it from view once more. Edward stopped instantly waiting for whatever was ahead to advance. The minutes ticked by, but nothing happened; cautiously he took two more steps, still nothing moved in the fog. All of a sudden, Dream Dancer quickened his step as he caught sight of a silvery white riderless mare.

When Edward got closer, he saw a bundle lying on the ground still as death. Dream Dancer turned to his horse in command. "Stand Cheyenne!"

Edward let the hammer down on his rifle before putting it on the ground. Not wanting to spook the horse, Dream Dancer chanted reassurances to her as he cautiously advanced towards the mare soothingly talking in Cheyenne.

Mist nickered uneasily before moving to protect her mistress unsure about the strange man walking towards her. She half reared in warning as she used her front right leg to try driving him away as she struck out at him.

Edward stopped instantly as the mare became much more agitated the closer he got. Dream Dancer did not want her to back up at all; it could cause the horse to step accidentally on the bundle behind her.

Edward squatted where he was showing her that he was no threat, but continued chanting almost hypnotically. The mare settled down finally, so Dream Dancer waited for a good ten minutes to pass.

Edward stood up again slowly; he tried to walk forward, but stopped instantly as he dropped back to his knee once more as the mare squealed angrily. Again, she tried to strike at Dream Dancer.

Edward stopped chanting; he frowned grimly this was not working for him at all. The mare was protecting whatever was in the bundle, so refused to let Dream Dancer come any closer.

Edward turned as he looked at his stallion thoughtfully; Dream Dancer had grain in his saddlebag to try enticing her

Edward stopped in mid thought as he smiled suddenly at an idea before whistling to his horse so that he would come over to him. As soon as Cheyenne trotted up Dream Dancer got up to strip off the saddlebag, bedroll, saddle, as well as the bridle off his stallion.

Edward spread out his bedroll in preparation so that Dream Dancer could put whatever the mare was protecting inside it.

Evening was fast approaching, so the wind was getting even stronger.

Edward patted his stallion before waving at the mare. "Okay, Cheyenne, I want you to get her out of there for me!"

Cheyenne nickered in understanding this was not the first time that he had to move a reluctant unbroke horse for his master. He pranced towards the mare before dropping his head down so that he could push her out of the way.

Mist absolutely refused to move at first as she squealed angrily trying to strike at the stallion. She did not want to leave her mistress; the mare had tried since early this morning to wake the woman by nudging her insistently, but it had not roused her.

Cheyenne was not intimidated at the mare's show of defiance as he moved in using his head, as well as his muscled shoulder; he pushed the mare sideways away from the bundle.

The further they got from the bundle, the more Mist neighed in fear as she tried to get past the stallion. Snorting she bit at the stud before trying to go around him, but it did not help her; the mare could not get past him.

Cheyenne continued shoving her until his master was able to rush forward to pick up the limp bundle. Once his master was gone, the stud stopped shoving the mare before draping his head over her neck consoling her as he gave her comfort.

Edward carried the cloak to his bedroll it weighed next to nothing, so he wondered in apprehension if it were a child he was rescuing. Dream Dancer put the bundle down before he removed the upper part, so that he could see what was inside the cloak.

Edward's breath caught in shock as he stared down at the beautiful young woman Dream Dancer uncovered.

Her hair was white, a pure white. Her face still had a slight girlish look to it she was not very old; it was delicate as well as deathly pale. Edward checked her pulse in dread wondering if he were too late! Dream Dancer let out his breath in relief at the faint heartbeat he felt.

Quickly Edward covered her with her cloak as well as his bedroll to keep her warm before turning away to gather the rest of his kindling. He took out the last of his dry wood as well to start a fire. Dream Dancer looked around, but there were no trees close for more wood.

Edward could see trees a few miles away, but it would be too wet anyway with all the rain Snowdonia seemed to be getting; even the ground was saturated so dry wood would be impossible to find.

Edward eyed the spot where the mare had been standing in relief as he smiled. She must have been there all day guarding her mistress. He jumped up as he went to the piles of dung before grimacing in distaste Dream Dancer carried several loads over to where he wanted the fire to be.

Edward built his fire before putting some dung in, the rest Dream Dancer piled up for later. It gave off an awful smell, but dung burned a lot longer in comparison to wood; it would also give them more heat since horse dung also burnt hotter.

Edward went to his saddlebag again, after digging around inside he found a pouch that he always kept full of oats. The mare would have eaten grass, but Dream Dancer wanted to check her out more closely so this would hopefully keep her still long enough for him to examine her.

Edward walked over to the now quiet mare, as she ate the oats he examined her meticulously. He frowned uneasily at the sight of the dried blood speckling her silvery white coat.

Dream Dancer checked her carefully, but thankfully, the blood was not from her.

Edward quickly gave his horse some oats before turning away instantly in anxiety; Dream Dancer was not worried that either horse would budge.

Edward rushed to the woman before stripping off the bedroll as well as the cloak looking for a wound. As the cloak fell away, Dream Dancer frowned grimly. She was almost naked with only a chemise covering her, her legs were bare.

There was dried blood everywhere, but what had caused the amount of blood on the mare was the question ringing in Edward's mind.

Edward scowled grimly already guessing what had happened to her, but wanted to make sure. He checked both arms first as well as her head. Next, Dream Dancer turned her on her stomach before checking her back.

Just with a glance, Edward could see that the girl did have a lot of cuts with quite a few scrapes as well around her buttocks, legs, and feet. She also had several long scratches with many deep cuts on her hands as well as on the back of her arms. She was black and blue everywhere from multiple bruises. If Edward had to guess, it was probably from a fall or maybe from trying to escape that would be more like it.

Edward frowned as he remembered yesterday falling off his horse at the feeling of falling through space as well as the burning he had felt in his hands, back, arms, and buttocks. Now Dream Dancer knew for sure that he had been right they were connected somehow.

There was quite a bit of dry crusty blood from a possible fall, but it would not have been enough to cause the blood splatters on her mare. There was also, where the blood was situated on her horse; since she was riding sidesaddle, Edward was sure it came from her lower body. He had checked the upper part though just in case Dream Dancer was wrong.

Edward went lower to check both her legs thankfully neither were broken. Again, the amount of blood on the back of her legs still would not have produced enough blood. He turned her back over, he sighed grimly as he saw blood on the inside of her thighs as he pushed her chemise up. He sat back on his haunches as Dream Dancer nodded angrily now that his guess was confirmed; she had been raped! By the amount of blood, it must have been a brutal attack.

It could not have happened here there was too much blood on her mare, so she must have escaped trying to find help. The blood on her thighs was dry and crusty, so Edward figured one maybe two nights ago at the most.

Edward grabbed his canteen so that he could put some water in a bowl to heat in order to clean her up a little. Dream Dancer would have to wait until he got her back to his castle for anything more.

Edward took out some herbs from his medicine bag to boil for some hot tea for her to drink. The biggest problem was hypothermia; she was freezing right now so if Dream Dancer did not warm her up quickly, she would die soon.

Once the tea was hot enough, Edward brought it over to her; he put a little in his own mouth before bending over her. Dream Dancer put his lips to hers as he carefully dribbled a little bit at a time into her mouth, all the while stroking her throat to encourage her to swallow.

Once Edward had enough in her to satisfy him, Dream Dancer set the cup down.

Chanting in Cheyenne, Edward brought Dream Dancer out so his healing powers would be at the surface ready for use. He laid one hand on her forehead, as well as one on her abdomen; letting his Cheyenne blood take over his eyes darkened to black almost instantly.

Without any warning, Dream Dancer screamed in agonizing pain. He fell backwards in a shocked stupor laying there unable to move. He could see a dark fog coming from the woman it was entering Edward through his palms the pain was excruciating as it invaded him slowly.

Suddenly Dream Dancer could feel the presence creeping through his bloodstream taking over his body slowly as it infested his limbs. First, his hands before going up into his arms slowly agonizingly it reached his shoulders; it began working its way downwards next. If it reached Edward's major organs he was in big trouble, there would be nothing to stop it.

Calling on the training his teacher had given Dream Dancer over the years, he put himself in a trance. He had done this once before when he first met Dao; Edward had also done something similar when Queen Victoria had been poisoned.

This was different though, at those times Dream Dancer had just slowed everything down to gain control of his body. This time Edward would almost have to die in order to get rid of the evil that was invading him.

Dream Dancer began by slowing down his heart first, as it beat slower his pulse becoming fainter with each passing minute. Soon his blood also slowed until it was barely moving through Edward's body.

Dream Dancer could feel the evils desperation as it pushed against his veins trying to get past the diminishing blood flow, but Edward persisted not giving in as he slowed his heartbeat one more time.

Now Dream Dancer was so close to death that if he did not hurry his organs would starve without fresh blood causing him to die within the hour. Quickly shoving at the evil, Edward pushed for all he was worth, but the evil defied him trying to resist.

Heaving in panic Dream Dancer managed to force it back up into his shoulders, down into his arms before forcefully pushing it back into Edward's hands.

Dream Dancer quarantining it in his hands for a moment, so that he could gather all the strength Edward had left for one more violent assault.

Feeling his organs screaming for blood Dream Dancer was out of time so in desperation he gave one more tremendous surge. His body arched as he screamed in agony, urgently Edward bore down on the mist pushing it towards his palms before finally expelling it from his body.

The mist flew out of Dream Dancer's hands back into the woman with a squeal of rage. The woman sat up for a second screaming before dropping back onto the bedroll still unconscious.

CHAPTER FOUR

Now taking control of his body once more Dream Dancer accelerated his heart slightly just enough to give Edward's organs some much-needed blood.

Now that his organs were no longer stressed, Dream Dancer slowly searched his system for any traces of evil that might have slipped past his quarantine. Feeling none, he sped up his heart a little more. Again, Edward did another check. Feeling nothing, he allowed his heart to resume its normal beat.

Dream Dancer sat up slowly still chanting making sure that he was fully clean, once satisfied he sighed in relief before opening his deep green eyes as Edward returned to himself once again.

Edward frowned grimly; well healing her with his power was out of the question for now anyway. He knew eventually that Dream Dancer would have to try again, but now he knew what he was up against so would be more cautious.

The woman's ravishment was not the problem there was something evil in her. How Edward was to cure her of that, he had no idea. He would have to ask the Great Spirit what to do later when he returned home since Dream Dancer had everything he needed there for the rituals.

Dao might have an idea as well since he was his teacher of the Oriental arts.

Edward looked up eyeing the darker mist just a quarter of a mile away. He grimaced thoughtfully. Between his horse refusing to go anywhere near that fog, as well as the dark mist that had come out of the woman's body as it tried to invade him; plus the dream that he could not remember from last night. Dream Dancer was almost totally convinced that the dark fog in the distance was the cause of all these sinister occurrences.

To test out his theory Edward got up to walk toward it in suspicion wanting to make sure that he was right. When he was close enough, he reached out his hand. Instantly he snatched his hand back without actually touching the mist before backing away grimly; Dream Dancer's hunch was now confirmed. He could feel the same evil presence inside that the girl had in her.

Edward walked back; he knelt down to check the water he had heating. It was hot enough, so he took a cloth from his saddlebag before gently washing her thighs. When he finished, Dream Dancer threw the water as well as the cloth away in disgust.

Edward would love to get a hold of the man who had done this to her though. He would teach him a thing or two about respecting women, but it would not be gently done that he could promise. Dream Dancer hated rapist with a passion to him they were the lowest form of humanity on earth!

Edward stood up as he stared down at the girl contemplatively before stripping, but left his loincloth on. He had touched her quite a bit; he had even put his lips on hers with no problems. It was not until he brought his power to bear that the evil inside the woman had tried to gain control of Dream Dancer.

Therefore, Edward would have to do this the old-fashioned way, with body heat.

Edward crawled in the bedroll with her; he put his arms under her head before pulling her against his body. Instantly he hardened in desire as he gazed down at her; she was such a beautiful little thing. Dream Dancer pushed his need away, angry with himself for even thinking such things.

To take his mind off the woman in his arms Edward let his mind wander back to the day he had graduated, as well as how Dream Dancer had become not only Queen Victoria's friend, but also her personal physician…

*****

Edward could still remember the feelings of fearful dread he had experienced that long ago day when Queen Victoria had finally found out about Dream Dancer's secret which he had carefully guarded.

Edward was sitting on Queen Victoria's right eating the feast that was prepared for him in celebration of his success in finishing his schooling; Dream Dancer was now a practicing doctor.

Edward had set up an office in the poorer section of London down by the docks in the hopes of helping people who could ill afford the outrageous fees most doctors charged here in England. Queen Victoria had not approved of that at all, but Dream Dancer had ignored her objections.

Edward turned as Queen Victoria touched his arm to get his attention. He smiled curiously before frowning in concern as Dream Dancer noticed her face turning purple suddenly as Victoria grabbed at her throat gasping, unable to get a breath.

Edward jumped up instantly in fear as Dream Dancer quickly swept Queen Victoria into his arms before turning to the prince consort. "Hurry, take me to the queen's bedchamber she is sick!"

Queen Victoria's personal doctor rushed up instantly; he beckoned to Edward so that Dream Dancer would follow him since Prince Albert just stood there staring in bewildered shock.

As they rushed to the royal bedchamber, they were followed by the bloodthirsty royal court. Edward could hear them as they whispered in fearful excitement of poison and treason.

Edward turned at the door with a growl of rage as Dream Dancer's eyes narrowed dangerously. "I better not see even one of you enter this bedchamber until I give you permission!"

The throng stopped instantly cowering back from the dangerous Earl of Summerset.

Edward turned back around as he walked into the royal bedchamber; Dream Dancer made sure to reach his foot back to push the door closed hard so that it would slam shut on the curious faces trying to see in.

Edward carried Queen Victoria to her bed, Dream Dancer gently laid her down before kneeling beside Victoria watching the doctor closely.

Queen Victoria's doctor rushed up to loosen the collar on Victoria's dress. "The queen has been poisoned again I think!"

Edward nodded in agreement, but Dream Dancer did not say anything just continued watching the blond, brown eyed, skinny five foot eight doctor closely as Doctor Andrews grabbed a bottle from his bag.

The doctor put some drops in a glass then added some water. He mixed it before lifting Queen Victoria's head in order to force her to drink it. He laid her back watching her closely; the medicine would take about five to eight minutes to work.

Ten minutes later Doctor Andrews checked Queen Victoria's pulse, but it was weak very feeble the medicine had not worked! Victoria's physician looked at Edward sadly, as he shook his head in deep regret. "It is not working; I do not know what kind of poison they gave her this time, but it is not the usual stuff. My potion is not affecting it at all; I am afraid she is going to die this time!"

Edward growled furiously at the inept doctor as Dream Dancer pointed at the bedchamber door in anger. "Out, get out! I will tend to her myself!"

Doctor Andrews drew himself up infuriated; he was the senior physician here not this savage who had just graduated, even if it were with honours! He finally shrugged in relief letting Edward have his way, at least when Queen Victoria died the doctor would not be held accountable for a monarchies death.

Besides, it really was not wise to argue with Earl Summerset several men had already died in duels with the Indian over the years. There was no way that Doctor Andrews wanted to be one of those casualties. "I will inform the prince consort before sending him in."

Edward jumped up impatiently; he needed to get rid of Doctor Andrews immediately in order to save Queen Victoria's life. Dream Dancer had to make absolute sure though that they would not be disturbed.

Edward deadly serious glared into the doctor's eyes grimly, making sure that the threat was clearly evident in Dream Dancer's voice. "You will do no such thing! I do not want to see even one person showing their faces in this bedchamber until I call them, or you Doctor Andrews will be held personally responsible, is that understood!"

Doctor Andrews squeaked in fear before nodding as he turned racing out of the room without another word spoken.

In relief, Edward heard the door slam shut behind Doctor Andrews, so he dropped back down beside Queen Victoria. Not even hesitation knowing that it was extremely dangerous for Dream Dancer to show Victoria his abilities, but not having the time to hide what he was doing the earl started chanting in Cheyenne.

Edward reached out quickly placing both hands on Queen Victoria's stomach, he allowed Dream Dancer to come out as his healing powers surfaced.

Heat filled Dream Dancer's hands instantly before entering Queen Victoria's body in a rush; the queen's back arched as she shuddered in shock as the poison was slowly drained out of her stomach.

Dream Dancer let go of Queen Victoria all of a sudden, he fell to the floor writhing painfully as the poison entered his body. Still chanting he held onto his stomach as he slowed his heart and blood to keep the poison contained before slowly using his training Edward pushed the poison upwards.

Dream Dancer needed to get it past the lower esophageal sphincter; it was a bunch of muscles that kept food in the stomach from going backwards, which would bring it back into ones esophagus. Unfortunately, that muscle was not under voluntary control so it would be very difficult to open it.

It took Dream Dancer several long agonizing minutes to force it open before Edward could push the poison up into his esophagus, but finally it was travelling upward; it had about eight inches that it needed to travel along the esophagus before it stalled once more.

Dream Dancer had one more bunch of muscles to get past called the upper esophageal sphincter this muscle kept food from going down your windpipe. It was also the muscles that controlled burping, breathing, eating, and vomiting.

It was no trouble for Dream Dancer though since those muscles were under conscious control, so it was easy to pry open. Suddenly a white substance dribbled out of Edward's mouth.

Queen Victoria sat up so that she could watch Edward; Victoria frowned in fear as she saw a white liquid dribbling out the corner of Earl Summerset's mouth, but he continued to chant in a strange language.

Suddenly it was over, Dream Dancer stayed on the floor waiting for the dizziness to disappear. It took him a good fifteen minutes before he could bring Edward back to the surface, but finally he was able to sit up weakly.

Queen Victoria had been so close to death that Edward could have died while healing her. He had known that of course, but had not let it stop him. Dream Dancer looked up at Victoria grimly wondering what she would do with that information.

Edward's brother-in-law Devon had warned Dream Dancer not to let anyone here in England, know about his gift. Golden Eagle had told him that the English nobility were notorious for exploiting others if it was in their best interest or if they had something to gain from it.

Queen Victoria eyed Earl Edward Summerset thoughtfully. She had known he was three quarters Cheyenne of course, but she had not known Indians could heal. Were the whites murdering a race of healers that could be useful to them? Maybe Victoria should have several shipped to London to have them examined by her scientists to figure out how they did it!

Queen Victoria pointed at Edward in command. "You will be my personal physician from now on; I want you to tell me what you did! How it is even possible that you healed me, can all Indians heal as well or just you? What else can you do, I want to know everything?"

If Edward could have read Queen Victoria's thoughts at that moment, he would have been afraid for his people. He sighed before nodding in resignation as Dream Dancer obediently told Victoria about his shaman powers.

Edward reassured Queen Victoria that other Indians could not do what he does; Dream Dancer also explained that it had been over a hundred years since a shaman had the power to heal.

For some reason the Indians had lost the ability to heal by touch, as well as several other unique abilities like shape shifting, and walking through the dream world. Until Dream Dancer was born that is.

Shape shifting had actually died out way before the others as far as Edward knew anyway; it had been well over five hundred years since the last shape shifter had been born. Dream walking had also been gone for about four hundred years or so, why he had two of the abilities was still a mystery to him.

Queen Victoria nodded in disappointment that there were not others out there like him. Victoria had kept his secret all these years, as they became friends.

*****

Edward chuckled in delight as his thoughts returned to the present. He could not help thinking about Bailey now though, the black and white royal beagle. Dream Dancer had brought Queen Victoria a dog a year later that he had personally trained himself. She was trained especially for sniffing out poisons in food.

Now Queen Victoria would eat nothing without her dog trying it first if Bailey refused to eat something Victoria would not eat it either. She took the dog everywhere with her, so the poisoning had stopped, but not the attempts on her life, unfortunately.

Edward looked down at the woman he was holding. Dream Dancer touched her cheek, as well as her arm before nodding in satisfaction; she was beginning to warm up already.

Edward yawned, suddenly very tired from his struggle with the evil fog, almost instantly Dream Dancer fell into a deep unnatural sleep.

*****

The dark mist feeling the shaman finally falling asleep advanced quickly as it chuckled evilly. Swiftly it encompassed the two sleeping entwined together in the bedroll, keeping them trapped!

Time in the fog flowed faster since it had no boundaries; what seemed like minutes were actually days, and days were years. If one were in the mist for ten days, their body would age one year. If they managed to leave the fog their bodies would still be a year older in the human world, but they would not even realize it.

In the human world, once they stepped out of the mist it was as if they had not left at all so time had seemed to halt for them. In fact though it had just slowed to a crawl, five minutes in the real world would be five years in the fog.

*****

Edward was walking through a deep mist searching desperately for something that seemed just beyond his reach. Suddenly in front of him was a huge grey stone archway that Dream Dancer walked through in awe.

Edward hardly could believe his eyes, there were beautiful carvings all over the stones, but Dream Dancer did not understand their meaning.

It was not until Edward stepped through the archway that he saw the woman on the ground. He walked to her cautiously not sure at first who it was, but it did not take Dream Dancer long to realize that it was the same woman that he had found earlier not far from the mist.

The woman looked different here though; she had long midnight black hair spread out like a cloud against the bed of emerald green grass that she was laid out on.

Edward knelt beside her in concern; Dream Dancer wondered why she was here, she looked so peaceful laying there. She opened her eyes all of a sudden staring up at him intently.

Edward gasped in amazement as he stared down in surprise at the lightest grey eyes Dream Dancer had ever seen. It was almost as if he were staring into glass they were crystal clear with a dark black ring on the outside of her iris as well as a tiny spot of black in the center for a pupil.

She smiled sweetly as she reached up before pulling his head down for a kiss as she tenderly started making love to him. At first Edward tried to pull back knowing instinctively that this was wrong, but she was persistent refusing to let him go. His treacherous body refused to listen to him as well, as it hardened instantly in desire against Dream Dancer's wishes.

She was such a beautiful woman especially now that she had black hair and grey eyes, one could forget for a moment the white hair of earlier. Edward found it almost impossible to stop his body from reacting!

As they made love, the grass beneath them turned black. So too did the six sentient stones, but Edward never noticed. Dream Dancer unable to help himself entered her swiftly groaning in deep pleasure.

Edward's head jerked up suddenly as he heard someone screaming his name in warning. He cocked his head listening intently, it had sounded like his sister Raven's voice. He tried to get away from the woman again as Dream Dancer strained to hear his sister's desperate calls.

Edward's lover would have none of that though as she reached up pulling his head back down for a deep demanding kiss, refusing to let him go. She wrapped herself around him tightly holding Dream Dancer against her as she whispered a spell in Celtic hypnotizing him.

Edward forgot everything as if nothing else existed for him as she forced him to finish making love to her. As he surged against her Dream Dancer came to the surface turning his eyes black, blacker than they had ever been before.

Dream Dancer screamed out in gratification as he lost control of his emotions as his seed filled her. Edward dropped his head down on her shoulder for a moment as his eyes turned back to their customary deep green before rolling away, but the earl took her with him so that they could lay entwined; content to just hold her he finally fell back into an unnatural asleep.

*****

The mist shuddered in satisfaction as the shaman slept; he was too powerful for the dark fog, but the woman was easily gotten too. It must keep the woman in the mist now until it was born or all could be lost! The offspring would be able to release his master, but it must be done quickly before the Great Spirit realized that one of the serpent's minions was awake.

The dark evil mist must also find a way to keep the shaman from realizing that he too was trapped inside. All the fog needed was to keep the woman here in the mist for seven days, which would only be a second in the shaman's world; failure was not an option it was a sentence of eternal pain.

*****

Edward woke instantly knowing that something was not right; what had woke Dream Dancer was the hairs on the back of his neck prickling against his skin telling him that he was in some kind of danger.

How long Edward had slept he did not know; too long he could not help but think, three maybe four days! Why he even thought that, he had no clue. Dream Dancer looked around wondering how he had gotten there.

Edward was confused and disoriented as again he felt a prickling of warning course down his spin. He heard someone whispering or chanting it was coming from the woman. How Dream Dancer had managed to get past the spell being chanted was a mystery.

Edward sat up; he looked down at the woman curiously wondering what she was saying or who she was talking too. Instantly Dream Dancer gasped in fear, the woman's hair was now completely white. She also had eyes that were a milky white with no hint of a pupil evident. It almost looked as if she were blind.

The woman had a gloating look on her face as she smiled in evil satisfaction as she continued whispering a spell trying to put Edward back to sleep.

*****

Dream Dancer cried out in denial; it wrenched him out of the dream world, which caused his black eyes to pop open now instantly awake. He frowned perturbed wondering why his heart was racing in fear, he calmed it down slowly very confused. Once relaxed, Edward felt his eyes changing back to a deep green.

Edward scowled even more surprised, what was that all about. Dream Dancer could feel sweat covering his whole body as the cool wind caused goose bumps to rise all over him.

Edward frowned even more perplexed the woman was still sleeping on his shoulder, but they were not in the bedroll anymore. They were now closer to the fire, so he must have been thrashing around; which was the only explanation Dream Dancer had for them moving out of the bedroll.

Edward looked to the left the mist was only an arms length away, he frowned in surprise as he disentangled himself from the woman before sitting up. Dream Dancer looked down to check on his patient.

Well at least Edward had not disturbed the woman; her colour was better too with a blush of rose now on her cheekbones. It would not last out in this cold though Dream Dancer could not help thinking.

Edward looked to the left again searching for the fog, but it was gone now; Dream Dancer shook his head in confusion his eyes must be playing tricks on him he could not help thinking.

Edward got up before carefully lifting the woman so that he could put her back in his bedroll. Dream Dancer stood back up getting ready to crawl in too, but paused in mortification as he looked down at a slap of cloth against his skin.

Edward noticed his tie on the left side of Dream Dancer's loincloth was loose.

Edward tied it tight before crawling in mumbling irritably to himself all the while that this would not have happened if Dream Dancer had not been thrashing around in his sleep; obviously, he had a nightmare of some kind. The earl had never been prone to them in the past though, he could not help thinking.

Edward frowned troubled trying to remember what he had been dreaming about that would cause him to move around like that; all that he could recall was hearing his sister screaming at him insistently. What Raven had said Dream Dancer could not remember now at all!

Edward shrugged mentally to himself, he yawned deeply exhausted. Why he was so tired was beyond him, it almost seemed that he had not slept at all. Dream Dancer looked up in surprise as his horse Cheyenne trotted over to him before laying down against his side staring to the left intently.

Edward chuckled in pleasure as he reached over giving Cheyenne a pat. He frowned in surprise as he heard another horse coming. Dream Dancer looked to the right to see the white mare walk over; she dropped down beside her mistress.

Edward frowned in confusion as the mare also stared off to his left. Too tired to figure out what was up with the two horses Dream Dancer fell into a dreamless uneventful sleep.

*****

Raven's scream of warning echoed eerily of the cabin walls; it even drowned out the noise of the storm raging all around them. Terrified she jumped off the bunk in despair as her arms lifted in supplication trying to reach out to her brother as she stood there, not even realizing what she was doing since she was still sound asleep.

At the same moment, the ship bucked as it dropped into a deep trough as huge waves tossed the ship around unmercifully. Raven did not hear the wind howling, or the storm outside raging as she fell to the floor unable to keep her feet under her as the ship did a nosedive almost straight down. She curled herself into a protective ball unknowingly in self-preservation.

Raven cried out Edward's name again in forewarning. "DREAM DANCER!"

Devon rolled off the bed after his wife as he sat on the floor with his back to the bunk; he picked Raven up before putting her in his lap cradling her tenderly. Golden Eagle held her in fear not sure what was going on as he crooned soothingly. "Shhh it will be okay love, shhh!"

Raven shook her head in horror as she clutched at Devon desperately; still she did not wake up as she called out to her brother Edward again in despair. Letting go of her husband Golden Eagle she reached out with her right hand trying to grab onto something that only she could see as she wailed forlornly. "She is evil, it is not a dream! Dream Dancer, it is not a dreamm! Please do not; get away from her! Too late! It is too late!"

Raven slumped against her husband Devon suddenly as the dream let her go unexpectedly; she woke trembling in terror. She looked up at Golden Eagle in desperation. "We have to hurry or Dream Dancer will be lost to us, the witch has him now!"

Devon scowled grimly as Golden Eagle shook his head hopelessly. "We have only been on the ship for two days Raven; we are still thirteen days away from England. We can't make the ship go any faster, love!"

Raven shuddered uneasily what kind of place is this England to have such evil present. Somebody must have known about it why was it not stopped!

Dream Dancer had made love to the witch even though he had thought it was a dream; Raven knew that it was not. If she did not get there in time, the witch would gain complete control of Edward with no one to stop her.

Raven shivered in dread if the witch became pregnant the baby would be dangerous. With evil witch powers, as well as shaman powers combined what would the baby become!

Devon lifted his wife off the floor before putting Raven back in the bunk. Golden Eagle crawled in with her a few minutes later making sure he was on the outside so that she could not jump out of the bunk again without him knowing.

Devon pulled Raven up against him as Golden Eagle kissed her forehead lovingly. "Go to sleep love, there is nothing we can do to help him tonight. All that we can do right now is pray to the Great Spirit to keep your brother safe until we get there."

Raven nodded reluctantly as she curled up against her husband Devon for reassurance before falling into a dreamless sleep almost immediately, too exhausted to think anymore.

Devon held Raven close making sure she was sleeping before joining her a few minutes later. Golden Eagle's dreams were filled with unease as well as fear for his wife. He cried out in his sleep beseechingly. "No, God, please! Not my wife!"

*****

Pastor Daniel Brown sat up in his bunk shivering in fear. He was not sure what he had been dreaming about; the need to pray overcame him though, so he crawled out of his bunk. Daniel knelt as he clutched his cross desperately still he was unsure what to pray about, so he just knelt there remembering how he had come to be on this ship.

The pastor remembered how lost he had felt until Raven and Devon had shown up at his mother Melissa's. It was at a time in his life that he had felt his most vulnerable. Daniel's wife Pamela had died three months before that in childbirth finally having the girl she had always wanted.

The pastor's faith in his God survived his wife Pamela's death! Although at one point in Daniel's life, it might not have…

*****

The pastor remembered back fifteen years ago, but even now it seemed like only yesterday. Daniel shuddered dejectedly at the memory of almost losing his faith in God as they travelled across Montana on their way to his father-in-laws Chief Giant Bear's village.

The pastor's Cheyenne wife Pamela or Morning Star to her people was swept away in a raging storm as they tried to cross a river. Unfortunately, the Blackfoot found her before they did so they had taken her captive to their village.

Instead of trusting God to help his wife Pamela, the pastor had strapped on the guns that he had sworn never to wear again. Fortunately for him he never had to use them as they got his wife Morning Star back peacefully, but just the fact that Daniel had put them on made him think that he had lost his faith in his saviour.

The second day the pastor had worn his guns again much to his family's dismay. On the third day, Daniel was praying over his wife Pamela as the fever inside her raged; Morning Star had been hurt very badly in the river, so none of them thought that she would even survive.

Unexpectedly the pastor felt another presence beside him touching his shoulder in reassurance. He had known instinctively that Jesus was beside him at that moment. Just because he had made a mistake did not mean that he was lost; Daniel knew that God had forgiven him.

The pastor remembered a passage in his bible that Daniel had forgotten; it was in Romans five verse three and four. ***'We can rejoice, too, when we run into problems and trials, for we know that they help us develop endurance. And endurance develops strength of character, and character strengthens our confident hope of salvation.'***

The pastor had put his guns away after that for good, not once in all these years had he touched them again. Daniel's faith in God, as well as in himself, was now stronger than it had ever been.

*****

The pastor smiled serenely as he remembered sitting at his mother's table eating supper six days ago with Raven, on the other side of her was Devon. They were both talking excitedly about going to England to see Dream Dancer after an eleven-year separation. Suddenly an urge to go to his church took Daniel by surprise, after supper he had followed that urge.

The pastor walked the two miles slowly enjoying the beautiful evening, it seemed to him that the stars were brighter tonight and so too was the full moon as it shone down on him. Daniel lifted his face to bask in the healing light of the moon's brightness as his heart, which was filled with sorrow, began to heal slowly.

After entering his church, the pastor knelt in front of his pulpit praying for direction when suddenly his bible slipped out of his hands. He reached down to pick it up as Daniel lifted it his eyes caught on a passage; Acts sixteen eleven ***'We boarded a boat at Troas and sailed straight across to the island of Samothrace, and the next day we landed at Neapolis.'***

The pastor read the passage again as he thought of England. He had jumped up in excitement before racing to his mother Melissa's place to see Raven and Devon. Daniel had informed them immediately that he was being called by God to accompany them to England for some reason.

The pastor left his children with his mother Melissa until Daniel returned.

*****

The pastor shook of his thoughts as he returned to the present with a grim sigh of frustration, now here he sat praying again for guidance still confused about why he needed to go to England, but Daniel trusted that God would reveal all to him when it was time.

The pastor got up feeling much better all of a sudden before crawling back into his bunk; it did not take Daniel long to fall into a dreamless sleep.

CHAPTER FIVE

Edward woke disoriented; he wondered why he felt so funny this morning something was nagging at him. Dream Dancer tried to remember what he had dreamt about last night, but again he could not remember his dream.

Edward looked in surprise at the two horses still lying on either side of them; Dream Dancer frowned completely confused as he nudged Cheyenne. "Okay up you go now, I am awake!"

Cheyenne instantly stood up satisfied that his master now awake would not disappear on him again as he had last night. The stallion wondered off with the mare following him to eat.

Edward disentangled himself from the woman before getting up to dress. He turned looking towards the thick dark fog in the distance as he frowned grimly. It had to be that mist causing the disruption in his dreams, as well as the funny behaviour of the horses; Dream Dancer needed desperately to get away from Snowdonia.

Edward turned away to stir up his fire. Once it was hot enough, he grabbed some jerky, hardtack, as well as some tea from his saddlebag. He broke several jerky up before throwing it in a skillet; Dream Dancer added water next for broth. When he was finished, he set it on the fire to cook.

While it was cooking, Edward made himself some tea before leaving it to steep. He grabbed his canteen to put a little water in his mouth so that when he bent over the woman Dream Dancer could give her some, that way he would keep her hydrated. Between the water, tea, and broth she should get enough moisture to keep her cells as well as her major organs from becoming over stressed.

By the time, Edward was satisfied that she had enough water the tea was ready. He drank half of it saving the rest so that he could give her some. Dream Dancer ate the jerky out of the pan with his hardtack before feeding the broth to the woman, as well as the now lukewarm tea.

Once finished, Edward saddled his stallion then the mare before tying her to the back of Cheyenne's saddle. Dream Dancer figured the mare would follow the woman anyway, but just to be on the safe side he tied her anyway.

Edward went back so that he could douse the fire before bundling the woman tight in his bedroll. Lifting her Dream Dancer took her over to his horse; luckily, she weighed next to nothing.

Edward's voice brooked no disobedience as it deepened in commanded. "Okay Cheyenne, kneel down for me now. Down you go, boy!"

Cheyenne obeyed quickly as he buckled his front legs so that he was kneeling, this way his master could mount without difficulty.

Edward straddled his horse before clicking in demand. "Up now boy, slowly!"

Cheyenne lifted himself carefully as he snorted in exertion. Once standing he shook his head irritated at the blanket draped awkwardly on his right side.

Edward chuckled not worried that his horse would refuse to carry the extra weight. "Sorry about that old boy! Home now Cheyenne, let's go home!"

Cheyenne obediently turned northeast for two hours before turning north heading straight towards Conwy at a steady ground-eating cantor.

Edward held tightly to the woman letting Cheyenne find his own way, as well as set his own pace. Now that they did not have to follow directions or contend with the fog, it should be a shorter trip.

Especially with both horse and rider fully rested, so Edward hoped to be back at the castle by midnight. Dream Dancer did not plan to stop unless the woman woke up before they got there or the horses needed a rest.

*****

Edward sighed in relief as the gates of his castle came into view; they had made it before midnight thankfully. He was exhausted as well as starving, since they had only stopped once. Dream Dancer had fed the horses plus chewed on some jerky and hardtack as well as gave the woman more water. Within an hour though, he was back in the saddle.

The woman still had not woken up now Edward was getting really concerned.

Edward stopped to wave up in reassurance at his sentry, once he was sure that the guard saw him Dream Dancer continued on.

Edward guided his horse towards the stable, which would also take him to the back entry of his castle. Dream Dancer stopped Cheyenne as they got to the stairs that the earl had jumped over only three days ago. "Down you go, Cheyenne!"

Cheyenne obediently knelt before standing up once his master was safely off.

Edward hefted his bundle in a better position as Dream Dancer walked up to his horses head. "Of you go Cheyenne; James will look after you both."

Cheyenne nickered in farewell as he went to the barn obediently still leading the white mare knowing that oats would be waiting for him there.

Edward turned to the back entry into his castle; he took the stairs two at a time. He stopped short in surprise before smiling in greeting as Dao opened the door for him. Dream Dancer shook his head in amazement as he grinned in relief at seeing his teacher.

Even after all this time Edward still could not figure out how Dao always knew when Dream Dancer needed him. It did not seem to matter what time of day or night, always his teacher was there! "Is Queen Victoria still here teacher?"

Dao nodded decisively. "Of course she is did you really expect anything else from her Dream Dancer? There was no budging Queen Victoria until she found out exactly what was going on."

Edward chuckled knowingly. "I can just imagine what Victoria would have said to you if you tried to get rid of her! I need the rose room made up immediately, please. You can send someone to get Queen Victoria to come see me there also!"

Dao snorted in exasperation as he shook his head at Dream Dancer. He should know better by now; he was always one-step ahead of Edward at all times. "It is already made up for you. Queen Victoria is there waiting right now, impatiently I might add. As for your unasked question, yes there is food in the room waiting for you as well!"

Edward laughed in amazement. "Someday teacher you are going to have to tell me how you do that. I need you with me too!"

Dao pressed his hands together as if in prayer before bowing deeply with a little smirk. "Maybe someday Dream Dancer I will tell you, maybe someday!"

Dao was actually very glad to see Dream Dancer; he had been extremely worried there for a while. For almost two days he had not sensed Edward at all, which only happens at a students death usually.

Dao had been meditating this morning trying to find out what was going on when suddenly he had felt Edward's heartbeat once more in relief. He shook off his grim thoughts knowing Dream Dancer would tell him everything later. The earl took the lead, so he obediently followed.

Edward snickered knowingly already aware that his teacher would never divulge his secret. He went up the back stairs without further comment. Dream Dancer walked down the hallway passed his rooms on the right to the adjoining room.

Edward had been told when he first came here that it was for the mistress of the castle. Dream Dancer had snorted in disdain when he heard that, no wife of his would sleep in a separate room whether she liked it or not.

Edward brought the woman in before gently putting her on the bed.

Edward turned to Queen Victoria as soon as he backed away from the bed. Dream Dancer bowed low in greeting. "Your Highness!"

Queen Victoria chuckled as she walked over before waving the bow away. "None of that now since we are alone."

Queen Victoria walked to the other side of the bed; curiously, she pushed the bedroll as well as the cloak aside so that she could see what was inside. Victoria frowned thoughtfully down at the young girl with white hair.

Dao hissed in fear as soon as he saw the girl, Edward's teacher rushed over putting himself between Queen Victoria and the girl. He bowed low both hands pressed together in deep apology. "You must not go near the girl your Highness; she has a devil inside her!"

Queen Victoria stepped back in shocked surprise never in all these years had Dao ever came this close to Victoria.

Dao spun around quickly as he eyed Edward in concern. "Have you tried to heal her Dream Dancer?"

Edward nodded before frowning grimly as he told them what had happened to him when Dream Dancer had tried.

Dao scowled uneasily, now he knew why he had not sensed Edward for almost two days. "After you eat Dream Dancer I want you to come to your room, I need to make sure that you are completely purged. I will have Edith come tend to the girl since you are sure touching her has no ill effect."

Edward nodded before going over to the sitting area so that Dream Dancer could eat hungrily as Dao left to prepare.

Queen Victoria continued to stare down contemplatively at the girl there was something very familiar about her; suddenly Victoria turned to Edward thoughtfully. "Where did you say you found her?"

Edward poured Queen Victoria some tea as she came over to sit beside Dream Dancer. "I found her in Snowdonia halfway around the dark fog!"

Queen Victoria took a sip of her tea as she tried to remember what was on the other side of the mist that never dissipated even on the sunniest days. Everyone said it was haunted, but Victoria had never believed that until now that is!

After a few minutes of thought, Queen Victoria frowned as she asked Edward curiously. "Was she riding a white mare?"

Edward looked up from his meal in surprise. "Yes she is at the stables right now, how did you know that?"

Queen Victoria grimaced as her guess was confirmed; Victoria told Edward everything she knew about the girl. "I gave her that mare ten years ago when I was doing an inspection at her parent's castle. About two years ago, bandits killed both of Crystin's parents. I granted her third cousin Lord Ernest of Pwllheli Castle custody of my ward until she turned eighteen. If I remember correctly her eighteenth birthday was three or four days ago, but her hair should be black not white. Her name is Lady Mary Crystin Alexandrina of Llannor Castle. Mary is after her great-great grandmother, who happened to be Queen Mary of Scotland at one time. Crystin is after her father's Welsh mother, the meaning of her name in Welsh is, 'a follower of Christ'. Her third name, Alexandrina, is after her godmother, which happens to be me. Mary of Scotland's son brought the game you love so much from Scotland into England, when he became King of England. It had actually been outlawed in Scotland for a long time before that. Queen Mary of Scotland was also the one who first named the caddie. Do not tell anyone that I told you any of this; England has always claimed golf as their own. Crystin is not only my goddaughter, but we are also related. I would have to look up her lineage; I think we are fourth or fifth cousins or some such thing. It was rumoured that her father's mother, who was pure Welsh, was a witch. A white witch, hence the name Crystin since they converted to Christianity. All that really means is that she was a good witch, one that dealt mostly in the healing arts. I only know this because when I was a child my mother Victoria Louise the Duchess of Kent took me with her to see the late Lady Crystin. My mother was dying and the doctors could not seem to help her. Lady Crystin healed my mother, so I have always had a special relationship with her family. Crystin is a splitting image of her Welsh grandmother, or she was when she had black hair."

Edward frowned thoughtfully something was tickling the back of his memory; he finally shrugged dismissively he just could not grasp it. After he was finished with his teacher, Dream Dancer would have to go out to his sweat lodge tucked away in the back courtyard where no one else is allowed to enter.

It was in the form of a tepee of course, Edward's sister Raven had shipped him the hides he needed to cover it; Dream Dancer could have gotten some here, but he did not have time for hunting or tanning hides at first too busy with school.

Edward needed to go talk to the Great Spirit in private so that Dream Dancer could find some answers!

Edward finished eating quickly; he got up before walking over to the bed as he gazed down at the girl. Queen Victoria had called her Crystin; Dream Dancer tried out the name silently to himself.

Edward reached down to brush back a white strand of hair gently; he tried to picture her with black hair, but for some reason Dream Dancer could not.

Queen Victoria walked over as well; she watched Edward's intense expression with interest before grinning knowingly. This would solve a problem Victoria had pondered only last month.

Llannor was in the middle of a little jut of land called Llyn Peninsula. It was in between Caernarfon Bay and Cardigan Bay both bays went out to the St George's Channel, which led into the Irish Sea. There are six small castles right on the cliffs that keep watch for invaders, but Llannor is the main defence of the inlet.

Queen Victoria had been hearing recently that she had made a big mistake giving Crystin's cousin guardianship. He had totally run the place down with no guards standing on the walls since he had taken over.

Queen Victoria's husband Prince Albert had been hounding her lately about finding the girl a husband that was loyal to the throne. With war always being a threat, having Wales protected was very important. They did not want an invading army to try sneaking into England through their back door again.

Queen Victoria cleared her throat noisily in order to get Edward's attention. "Do you want her?"

Edward's head jerked up instantly as Dream Dancer frowned in surprise. "What do you mean, do I want her?"

Queen Victoria grinned mischievously. "I am going to betroth her to you. I will have my priest read the bans right away so that he can marry the two of you as soon as she wakes up."

Edward turned away from Queen Victoria so that she could not see Dream Dancer's anger. "She is a woman, not a horse to be sold! How do you think Crystin is going to feel when she wakes up after being raped by a man then told that she has no choice but to marry me, she will hate me?"

Queen Victoria sighed in aggravation; she could hear the anger in Edward's voice, but she did not let that deter her. Victoria needed someone that she could trust at Llannor Castle; the queen knew without a doubt that she could trust Earl Summerset with her life.

Queen Victoria shrugged dismissively, how her goddaughter Crystin would feel had no bearing on Victoria's decision at all. She wanted Edward at Llannor Castle; the queen's ruling was final!

Queen Victoria knew that Edward would be difficult though, but suddenly she remembered the earl's aversion to one of her lords. Maybe Victoria could convince him after all! "I had thought of giving her to Lord Palmerston until I caught him sneaking into one of my ladies-in-waiting bedchamber, besides he is too old for her. I can hear the disapproval in your voice, but this is how things are done in England. Almost every noble except a few that snuck off to get married without my royal permission has arranged political motivated marriages. My goddaughter will be no different, either you take her or I will find another one that won't care if she has a maiden head!"

Edward grimaced in defeat knowing that Queen Victoria had finally won, the fact that he had managed to keep the queen from forcing him into a loveless marriage so far was only because she owed him her life. Dream Dancer knew though that he could not stop Victoria from forcing Crystin into marriage.

Edward remembered a conversation he had with Raven about this same subject when she was being forced to marry Devon by their grandfather. He turned once more to look down at the pale white haired girl. For some reason he felt the need to protect her, why he was not sure; there was also his feeling that somehow they were connected. Until he found out how or why Dream Dancer had to keep her close to him.

Edward sighed in frustration as he looked over at Queen Victoria before Dream Dancer nodded unwillingly. "Yes, I will marry her if you insist!"

Queen Victoria clapped her hands in glee, glad that her reference to Palmerston had worked. Victoria had tried many times to arrange a marriage for Edward, but he had resisted every time. "Excellent Earl Summerset, I will go inform the priest immediately so that the banner of your betrothal will officially be raised in the morning."

Edward frowned disgruntled as Queen Victoria hurriedly turned rushing out quickly before Dream Dancer could change his mind.

Edith came in a few minutes later; the maid curtsied deeply in hope. "My lord wished to see me?"

Edward nodded curtly. "You will look after my betrothed she is unconscious, but bath her anyway. There is an ointment on the bedside table make sure you put it generously on all her scrapes and cuts, make sure you get the ones on her back, as well please. You will also need to find her proper nightclothes, go ask Queen Victoria's maid I am sure she has extras. Try to get her to drink more water as well as some lukewarm tea. If Crystin awakes call me immediately!"

The maid sighed in disappointment as the good-looking earl hurried out, oh well she had hoped for something else. She turned her attention to the white haired young woman; Edith scowled grimly as she uncovered the nearly naked girl.

The maid frowned in surprise; she had never heard of the earl forcing himself on a woman before, but obviously this one had been raped so Edith would have to ask the old cook since she had been with Earl Summerset the longest.

The maid shook off her thoughts as Edith got down to work seeing to her new mistress.

*****

As Edward walked into his room, he could not help smiling in delight. In every nook and cranny candles flickered, Dream Dancer sniffed appreciatively; incense was also burning. It smelt so good that the scent calmed him immediately.

Edward stripped before crawling into the tub of hot water that was waiting for him. He looked over at his bed knowingly; on top was his silky Oriental clothing that he wore for training with Dao. They were white with a flowing loose top, as well as pants; Dream Dancer loved to wear them they were so light it almost seemed he was naked.

Edward scrubbed himself with the special soap that Dao made just for him. Dream Dancer finished washing just as his teacher came in with a bucket of warm water, as well as towels.

Dao waved at his student to get up. "Kneel Dream Dancer, I will rinse you off."

Edward obeyed before getting out of the tub to dry himself. Dream Dancer dressed in his white garments while Dao went to the left corner of his room.

Dao rolled up the Chinese carpet that he had put there long ago, underneath were symbols that he had painted when they had started coming here regularly so that Dream Dancer could meditate whenever the need struck him. They sat in the center of the symbols facing each other cross-legged.

Taking deep breaths Edward placed his arms lightly on his knees before touching his middle finger to his thumb, which helped to put him in a trance as he chanted in Cheyenne releasing Dream Dancer.

Dao watched him intently, when he felt that Dream Dancer's meditation was deep enough, he started chanting in his own language. He reached out his hands, but did not touch the earl. He just moved both of them in front of his charge feeling his aura. If even a hint of evil remained in Edward, his teacher would feel it.

Dao stopped suddenly before sitting back frowning as he stared at his student Edward in bewilderment. He could feel no evil present, but there was a disruption in Dream Dancer's aura so something else had happened.

Dao was not exactly sure what the cause was yet; to Edward's teacher it almost seemed that Dream Dancer had aged unnaturally. On the other hand, even more confusing to him was that those two days seemed to be missing completely from his student's aura.

Dao was totally baffled how could days be missing from Dream Dancer's life, but yet still Edward seemed older. Not by much mind you four or five months he would guess; it just made no sense at all, whatever had caused this was not a good thing.

Dream Dancer opened his black eyes; he blinked as he tucked the Cheyenne half of himself away once more so that now Edward's eyes were back to their original deep green. "Well teacher, am I clean?"

Dao nodded disgruntled totally frustrated. Edward's teacher gestured in demand needing answers. "Yes, there is no evil present, but something else is not right. Tell me everything right from the time you left here until you rode in do not leave anything out Dream Dancer, even if it seems insignificant to you."

Edward told his teacher everything about the disruption in his dreams, as well as how he seemed connected to the woman. He also told him about his suspicion that the dark mist surrounding the hill of Snowdonia was evil. Dream Dancer was still sure that it was the cause of all this.

Finally, Edward also told his teacher Dao about both the strange occurrences with his stallion. He went into way more detail though about the second event when Cheyenne and Crystin's mare laid down keeping him as well as the woman guarded. It seemed to him just before he had fallen asleep that both of them were staring towards the fog. Their behaviour had Dream Dancer extremely baffled.

Dao listened intently before leaning forward urgently. "It is your dream that is missing, that is what I felt. Something important happened in one or maybe both of your dreams. You must find a way to remember them Dream Dancer the key is in the dreams somewhere."

Edward nodded thoughtfully. "I am heading to my sweat lodge as soon as I am finished here to talk to the Great Spirit."

Dao got up immediately. "Go Dream Dancer, I will clean up before meditating as well hopefully one of us will find the answers."

Edward nodded as he got up to strip out of his Oriental clothes. He went into his closet next to pull out a large package hidden in the back. Dream Dancer put the buckskins on that he had taken off for his bath.

Finally, Edward grabbed the packet on his way out before racing down the back stairs to a side door; Dream Dancer slipped outside into the garden.

*****

Dao stood there for a few minutes contemplating Dream Dancer's theory that the mist was evil; he frowned troubled by Edward's description of his stallion's odd behaviour. He turned suddenly for the adjoining door to the rose room before walking over; he knocked waiting impatiently.

Dao smiled as the maid Edith opened the door. "Can I come in; I need a few minutes with the woman please."

Edith backed away letting Earl Summerset's manservant in; she had always been slightly scared of the funny looking little man even though he had never done anything to her. The maid always got a weird shiver every time she was near him so tried to avoid him at all costs.

Dao walked over to the bed before turning to the maid Edith. "Go have something to eat since you will likely be here the rest of the night. I will watch her for a bit, come back in half an hour."

Edith nodded in relief; she needed to get tea as well as some water anyway for her new mistress, so she left without asking questions.

Dao turned to the woman as he frowned thoughtfully; he did not want to touch her just in case the evil in her tried to gain control of him, so he just put his hands out feeling her aura. Dream Dancer's teacher was hoping that his suspicions were not right. He started from her head working downwards slowly; the evil inside her was very strong as it tried to hide its identity from him.

Dao groaned it was taking all his considerable power to continue as the evil battered against him trying to resist, he persisted as he chanted calling on his master to help him to see!

Suddenly Dao stopped in shock halfway down the woman's body before jerking his hands away unable to continue. Edward's teacher sat down hard in the chair that Edith had put beside the bed in order to stay close to the woman.

Dao sat there stunned as he shook his head in denial; it could not be he was not ready yet! There was one other way he could be sure that he was right though, so he jumped out of the chair heading to the door.

He opened it before walking into the hallway of the castle, he saw Edith coming but he never said anything to her not wanting to be distracted now. He hurried quickly down the hallway.

Dao went immediately to the stables; he walked over to Cheyenne as he chanted putting his hand out so that Edward's stallion would walk over so that he could touch him. As Dream Dancer's teacher touched the stud's nose, he changed his chanting. Seeing what he feared he sighed grimly as he stepped back.

Turning Dao rushed out of the stables up to his room where he knelt on his carpet meditating looking for answers. Unfortunately the answer he received left Edward's teacher flabbergasted as he groaned. He would have to wait for his student's vision as well to be sure of course.

Dao dropped his head in his hands in fear, he was just not ready yet; Dream Dancer was not ready yet either, but above all the world was not ready for it!

CHAPTER SIX

Edward followed a path going through the center of his garden until it took him close to the thick rose bushes that ran along the edge. It did not take Dream Dancer long to reach a gate that was kept locked.

Edward pulled out a key that he always carried around his neck in order to unlock it. Dream Dancer entered before closing and locking the gate behind him.

Edward followed another short pathway into the deep thick woods behind his castle until he came to a clearing with his tepee in it. He had set it up nine years ago to use as a sweat lodge for when he needed to meditate in order to talk to the Great Spirit or when Dream Dancer wanted to dream walk in privacy.

Edward went to gather wood first from behind the tepee; next, he went inside to build his fire. He came back out to strip out of his buckskins before hanging them on a branch; now Dream Dancer only had his loincloth on as he sat on the ground.

Edward decided against starting the little fire pit in front of him, the big one in the sweat lodge would do for tonight. He began chanting as he opened the large package Dream Dancer had taken from his room.

Edward pulled out a bear fur; it was the last animal he had hunted while still in Montana. It held a special link to his birthplace that Dream Dancer had needed at first when the Cheyenne half of him was released.

Edward did not really need the hide anymore though since his training with Dao was complete so now he could bring out the stronger Cheyenne half of himself anytime or anywhere he needed him. It did not matter where Dream Dancer was on this earth he had become that powerful.

Still Edward liked to use it though as well as painting his face because to him it just seemed the right thing to do there were rituals for a reason, so Dream Dancer preferred to use them whenever he possibly could.

Edward continued using his sister Raven or Devon at first in Montana when learning to dream walk greater distances since he did not have trouble finding them. Both of them were used to him walking in their dreams so they were more receptive to his invasion. Anyone else Dream Dancer would have had trouble with because not everyone would allow him in.

Edward was now at the point though that he could enter almost anyone's dreams without difficulty, but he tried not to intrude unless he had permission first. There was one exception though for some reason Dream Dancer could not get into his teacher Dao's dreams at all.

Dao must have his dreams protected some how, Edward had never asked him why not wanting his teacher to know that Dream Dancer had tried sneaking into them once or twice to see what he was dreaming.

Edward shook off his thoughts before putting the bear fur aside. He opened three pouches of paste one was yellow; one was black, with the last one being red. He pulled out three small bowls that had obviously been used to make his paint for many years. Dream Dancer put a little paste in each container making sure the proper colour was in the right bowl.

Edward grabbed a canteen that he always kept full of water; it was sitting at the entrance of the tepee. He added a little water to the three bowls before looking around to find a twig so that he could stir the contents. Finding what he needed Dream Dancer stirred the contents reflectively. It was a little too thick, so he added some water until it was the right consistency.

Not once throughout Dream Dancer's routine did the most powerful shaman in a hundred years stop chanting. When the paint was ready, he dipped his fingers in the bowl as Edward proceeded to paint his chest as well as his face with various symbols of the Cheyenne Indians.

Afterwards Dream Dancer added several Oriental symbols that Dao had taught him. They represented what he was now because of the ceremonial differences he practiced since his shadow teacher Dao had taught him his Oriental traditions also. Edward had blended the two cultures within himself, which gave him an edge.

Dream Dancer had found over the years that it had given him much more power, especially for long distance dream walking. Edward could now go anywhere on this earth and be able to read someone's dream.

Dao had put Dream Dancer to the test a few times by having him find someone in his homeland that was dreaming about his teacher. Never having been there in his life the earl had learned to find that person by just concentrating on an image of Dao as Edward walked the spirit world.

As Dream Dancer walked around looking for certain dreams; pockets of dreams from every person sleeping would materialize for a few minutes before disappearing. If he wanted to see that dream, he would have to touch that person's dream receptor in their mind bringing the subconscious fully awake so that Edward could follow the dream.

In the spirit world what seems like hours were only seconds in the real world. Luckily, it gave Dream Dancer plenty of time to find the one with Dao prominent in his dream. Once he found the image he was looking for Edward would enter that man's dream to find out his name.

It had amazed Dream Dancer how Dao arranged to have these people in his homeland dream about him on those specific nights. His teacher had to of arranged it somehow because once Edward found that person's dream, he would only be allowed in for a moment. As soon as he was given a name of the person having the dream, he was pushed out again almost immediately.

The first time Dream Dancer had went into one of their dreams; he had tried to go back in once he was pushed out. Like Dao though they could block him from re-entering the dream, how they did it Edward could never figure out.

Of course, walking in others dreams was not what Dream Dancer was doing since even though he called it a world it was not. There was no real substance to it, so Edward was not actually walking physically anywhere.

It was actually Dream Dancer's spirit that would travel around weaving in and out of the spiritual world. He always did like to give himself substance though. He could be anything he wanted in the spirit world, but Edward chose to be himself.

Dream Dancer liked to use the word, 'world', even though it was not a separate place or a substantial one because it was just easier to explain to someone who did not know what it was like.

Everyone had a part of their brains that were susceptible to dreams. Dream Dancer's was just more advanced allowing him to see other dreams or even participate, he could also change someone's dream if he wished. How it was possible or even how Edward did it most of the time was a mystery even to him.

Dream Dancer getting annoyed at him self for becoming distracted shook off his thoughts, which is what happens when you are overtired, Edward turned back to what he was doing.

Dream Dancer grabbed a small packet tied with a special yellow died rawhide. He opened it adding two pinches of leaves to another bowl before adding some water. It would be heated slightly in the fire so that Edward could drink it.

Last, Dream Dancer grabbed another packet with the rawhide dyed black; picking up his peace pipe Edward filled the bowl with the special leaves harvested only for this purpose.

There were some people who would use these leaves for their pipe all the time liking the other worldly feeling they got preferring to live in that world, but Dream Dancer was not one of them as far as Edward was concerned they were for rituals only.

Dream Dancer was getting low, but his sister had promised to bring him more as well as some seeds to see if he could grow his special ceremonial leaves here. She was also supposed to bring Edward seeds for his special drink; hopefully, they would grow here as well.

The special leaves for a shaman's drink were not widely known since shaman and medicine men refused to allow others to use it fearing it would be abused. It was a powerful hallucinating drug if not used properly it could cause brain damage or even death so Dream Dancer guarded the secret closely.

Dream Dancer really did not need these drugs to dream walk now, but again it was a traditional ritual that Edward was determined to keep using.

Dream Dancer shook off his thoughts once more before throwing the bear hide around his shoulders; he picked up his peace pipe as well as the bowl with the darkening liquid inside. Edward went in the sweat lodge still chanting in his native language.

The heat hit Dream Dancer as he entered; it almost took his breath away, but his chanting never faltered. Edward set the bowl of liquid on the hot rocks to heat up a little before adding more wood, as well as more rocks to the fire.

When Dream Dancer figured the fire was strong enough, Edward poured his special scented water on the hot rocks. The hiss of the water hitting the hot rocks caused a billow of steam to fill the tepee.

Dream Dancer inhaled blissfully at the scent of home, satisfied with the amount of steam he sat down as he picked up his pipe. Edward lit it before inhaling deeply; he blew smoke up towards the Great Spirit as well as down at Mother Earth.

Next, Dream Dancer blew smoke to the west as well as to the east because that is where the sun rises and sets; it gives precious light as well as life in an otherwise dark world.

Dream Dancer picked up the bowl of black liquid; he downed the foul tasting stuff in a single gulp, it made Edward shudder slightly at the bitter taste before setting the bowl down.

Dream Dancer continued smoking the pipe until he felt the tepee starting to spin. He put the pipe down; Edward rocked back and forth rhythmically, as the world began to spin as well. Still the Cheyenne shaman continued to chant.

Dream Dancer asked the Great Spirit to help him remember not only his dream, but how to get rid of the evil mist in the girl also. Immediately his spirit left his body; Edward flew to a ship before going down into a cabin.

Dream Dancer saw his sister laying on the floor screaming at him in warning, he saw Devon climbing out of the bunk pulling her into his arms. Edward heard her cry out his name again as she continued screaming out desperately. "She is evil, it is not a dream! Dream Dancer, it is not a dreamm! Please do not; get away from her! Too late! It is too late!"

Suddenly Dream Dancer was whisked away to another cabin. He saw Daniel kneeling praying to his white God. Daniel was Melissa and Jed Brown's oldest son; he was also a Baptist Pastor. Edward had gotten to know Daniel on their travels to North Dakota when he was sixteen before catching a train to Boston.

Dream Dancer frowned perplexed wondering why Daniel was on the ship or what he had to do with all of this. It confused him greatly why would Edward be shown the pastor!

Dream Dancer was taken out of the ship before he was brought back to his sweat lodge once more. Inside were Crystin, Raven, Devon, Dao, Daniel, and himself it would take all of them to heal the girl. Edward sighed in relief, well now he knew why the pastor was on the ship.

Suddenly Dream Dancer was lifted out of the tepee again as he raced through time. It seemed to be a long journey so had to be quite some time in the future, how long Edward could not say for sure.

Unexpectedly Dream Dancer stopped abruptly as he was taken to a castle; Edward did not recognize the castle at all so it could not be one of his. A severe storm was raging outside as waves swamped the inlet.

Dream Dancer was drawn into a bedchamber where a woman was screaming in pain, as well as fear. He saw himself helping this woman in childbirth, a squalling blond haired baby boy landed in Edward's hands. Quickly he tied the umbilical cord before handing the baby to a woman waiting; it looked like Queen Victoria to him.

The woman lying on the bed shrieked in denial as she wailed forlornly in despair before lifting herself slightly in agony.

Dream Dancer's spirit looked at the woman closely causing Edward to hiss in shocked disbelief. It was Crystin, but she had black hair instead of white.

Dream Dancer looked back at himself; Edward watched in amazement as his other self caught another baby, a girl with a full head of white hair.

Crystin took one look at the baby girl in fear before her eyes rolled back in her head as she fell back onto the bed now unconscious or possibly dead!

Dream Dancer wailed in denial as his spiritual body was quickly pulled back to the sweat lodge to be reunited with his body. His eyes turned back to a deep green as Edward came to surface as his Cheyenne half faded to the background.

Edward dropped his head in his hands in despair there was something wrong with the girl child, Dream Dancer had felt it, what it was he did not know.

Edward remembered his sister Raven screaming her warning; he shivered uneasily as a memory tickled Dream Dancer's mind before it was gone again. What dream was she talking about being real?

Edward shook his head in confusion; Dream Dancer was not sure what Raven was talking about at all. Dao too had insisted that an important dream was missing for some unknown reason.

Being whom Edward was he knew how dangerous dreams could actually be; take a sleepwalker for instance, they could walk outside in the dead of winter and freeze to death unknowingly or even kill someone else in their sleep. They could walk into a kitchen looking for food or something to drink, but grab poison by mistake killing them.

Some dreams were so powerful that a person falling can actually stop their own heart if they believed that they died when they hit the ground. Dreams were nothing to kid around about; most people did not even realize how dangerous they could be, especially the ones as soon as you fall asleep most did not remember those dreams. It was the ones just before a person woke up that they were more likely to remember since your subconscious was beginning to wake itself.

Edward shook off his thoughts as he remembered his vision about Crystin, at least now Dream Dancer knew how to heal his wife-to-be.

Edward's mind drifted back to the twin's, the boy had been perfect as well as healthy; Dream Dancer had felt nothing sinister about him at all.

The girl, on the other hand, was a mystery. Edward had not heard her cry or seen her move at all. Was she born dead or did the girl child have another meaning? There might not be a girl child even born; the Great Spirit could be trying to reassure Dream Dancer that the evil died with the birth of a son.

Edward was not sure about his wife either; it could also be a warning to Dream Dancer that she would die in childbirth.

Edward slowly got up before dousing the fire as he left the tepee; he was just too tired to think anymore. He cleaned all four bowls out as he repacked everything, once done Dream Dancer tied the packet back up.

Edward dressed quickly; exhausted he stumbled back to the castle then thankfully into his room. Dream Dancer quickly stripped before washing himself clean of all symbols, so that he could put on his dressing gown.

Edward was just about to crawl into bed when an urgent knock had Dream Dancer turning instead towards the adjoining door to the rose room. "Yes!"

Edith poked her head in the door. "Sorry Earl Summerset, but the woman is awake. She says she is leaving immediately!"

Edward rushed towards the door. "Go get Queen Victoria, tell her that her goddaughter is awake so will need her!"

Edith nodded before scurrying away as Edward rushed into the room in concern.

The young woman spun around in fear; she screamed at the sight of the strange man coming towards her before running into a corner as she cowered there in terror. She held up her left hand trying to stop him from advancing.

Edward kept his distance, but Dream Dancer made sure to block Crystin's escape until Queen Victoria arrived.

A few minutes later a concerned Queen Victoria rushed in, taking in the scene at a glance Victoria waved Edward back before kneeling in front of her godchild. "Crystin, it is okay now you are with friends!"

Crystin shook her head in confusion. "Where am I?"

The young girl dropped her head in her hands in despair as she wailed in fear. "Who are you? Who am I?"

Victoria sat back in surprise. "I am Queen Victoria your godmother. You are Lady Mary Crystin Alexandrina, we are at Earl Summerset's castle in Conwy; he is a doctor that I have looking after you. Can you remember anything at all?"

Crystin looked at Queen Victoria in bafflement before shaking her head in fear. "No, I do not remember anything!"

Queen Victoria reached over to help her goddaughter Crystin to her feet. "That is okay dear you just woke up; you have been unconscious for at least two days maybe more! I am sure you will remember tomorrow; come I will help you back to bed."

Queen Victoria put her goddaughter Crystin into bed before beckoning Edward out. "Could she have amnesia or is it the evil inside her?"

Edward shrugged unknowingly. "I do not know for sure, but tomorrow I will examine her more fully. It could be amnesia or maybe it is the trauma of being raped! Go back to bed your Highness, I will have Edith stay with her for the rest of the night to keep an eye on her."

Queen Victoria nodded as she turned away. "Goodnight."

Edward bowed in farewell before entering the rose room once more. Edith was tucking the girl in, so Dream Dancer motioned the maid over. "See if you can get her to eat or drink anything, I want you to stay with her just in case she tries to slip away. If she does, wake me immediately!"

Edith nodded as she turned away.

Edward went back to his room before finally climbing into bed, Dream Dancer fell asleep almost instantly too exhausted even to think anymore.

*****

Dream Dancer's spiritual body was walking through a thick dark grey mist searching for something. Since this was his own dream he did not need to visualize a body, Edward already had real substance here!

Edward knew it was Dream Dancer, not the earl because he could feel that his eyes were black not green. He saw a flicker of movement ahead; he strained to see before taking a couple cautious steps.

Dream Dancer was just in time to see him self, standing in front of a grey towering stone archway. He was only wearing a loincloth, so it must have been last night when Edward was trying to keep the woman warm. He watched himself slip under the arch disappearing inside.

Dream Dancer hurried forward wanting to follow to see what his other self was doing. He rushed to the archway quickly; unexpectedly he slammed into a solid object stopping him instantly. He pushed against it, but was unable to go any further! It was as if Edward was pushing against a solid wall, it was that impenetrable.

Dream Dancer ran around the archway and saw a gap in the pillars, so he raced to it before smashing into another grey wall unable to go between. Edward could not even see inside since the wall of fog between the stones was so thick.

Suddenly, the emerald green grass under Dream Dancer's feet withered dying before his very eyes as the ground turned a blood red! He watched in horror, as the grey stones in front of Edward ever so slowly turn pitch-black.

Dream Dancer heard his sister Raven screaming all around him, it echoed eerily in the deathly stillness as she desperately tried to warn him. Again, Edward tried to get inside shoving urgently at the invisible wall needing to see what was happening, but he was denied access.

Dream Dancer jumped back in fear as he heard an evil sinister laugh. The hill Edward was standing on shuddered so hard in pain that it felt like a small earthquake. He fell suddenly to his hands and knees unable to stay on his feet.

With both palms pressed to Mother Earth, Dream Dancer felt her agony as his own causing tears to stream down his face as Edward shivered in despair. All of a sudden, it was mercifully over as the hill became silent once more!

Dream Dancer dropped onto the ground before curling himself up into a fetal position as he tried to gain control of his emotions. What had he done in there? Edward had done something unthinkable, but what it was he still could not remember.

Dream Dancer's sister Raven was right though this seemed to be a dream, but it was clearly not; it was very real!

The mist disappeared suddenly as Dream Dancer once again played out the vision of him helping with the birth of the twin's. Again, Edward got the sense that there was something wrong with the baby girl.

Although, Dream Dancer was still not totally convinced of that yet. Since, it still could be some kind of warning. She could even be a message, but Edward just could not see what the vision was trying to tell him.

Dream Dancer was wrenched from the birthing unexpectedly before he was whisked away, now Edward was standing on the wall above the gates into his castle.

Dream Dancer frowned in puzzlement as he heard the baying of hounds as well as the unmistakable sounds of horses. A few minutes later Edward saw foot soldiers marching purposely towards his open castle gates.

Dream Dancer could see the sun just starting to rise as Edward screamed at one of the guards in warning. "Close the gates!"

Of course, it was only a dream, so the guard never heard Dream Dancer.

*****

Edward sat up in bed instantly wide-awake. He jumped out of his bed quickly before getting dressed in a rush. He ran out of the bedroom so that Dream Dancer could give warning hoping it was not too late.

CHAPTER SEVEN

Edward ran frantically down the stairs across his main hall before going through the kitchen into the armoury where Queen Victoria's guards were sleeping. Dream Dancer cupped his mouth with his hands before hollering out as loud as he positively could manage. "Intruders are coming; all of you up man the gates quickly! Protect your queen!"

Instantly pandemonium erupted as the hundred soldiers crowded in the armoury jumped out of bed as they rushed into their clothes.

Edward hurried into the next room where all the squires, pages, and musicians of Queen Victoria's were sleeping. Dream Dancer roused them in a similar manner before turning to the youngest. "You boy run up to the tower, I want you to ring the bell, hurry now! We need to ready the castle for an attack."

The brown haired page nodded fearfully as he ran out.

Edward followed the boy out before going back the way he had come. Dream Dancer just reaching the top of the stairs when Dao came hurrying out of his room.

The bell had not even sounded yet, but already his teacher seemed to know. How Edward did not know, sometimes he wondered if Dao could see into the future as Dream Dancer could.

Dao frowned grimly. "Are we under attack yet Dream Dancer?"

Edward shook his head in reassurance as Dream Dancer pointed down the hallway. "Not yet, but they are coming. Can you wake Queen Victoria for me I need to go put on my chain mail; I will meet you at the gates."

Dao turned away instantly as he rushed down to Queen Victoria's apartments.

Edward went to his bedchamber; he pulled out his chain mail shirt. It did not take him long to slip into it; Dao would do up the buckles once they were up on the gate. Dream Dancer buckled on his sword next.

Edward ran out of his room down the side stairs that lead directly to the stables where Dream Dancer grabbed his bow and arrows, as well as his rifle.

The English did not have repeater rifles thankfully since they preferred the single shot Enfield muzzle-loading rifles with bayonets on the end to stab their enemy. Edward knew that eventually they would get them though!

Edward grabbed his six-shooter, as well as two boxes of shells for each gun. He ran out of the stables to the outer bailey before climbing the stairs two at a time so that Dream Dancer could see who was coming.

Thankfully, the gates were closed already; usually Edward left them open day or night in invitation never having had a problem with guests coming or going.

Edward propped his rifle against the wall before shoving his pistol in his pants to free up his hands so that he could pull his bow over his head. Dream Dancer grabbed ten arrows out of his carrier; he propped them against the wall in easy reach.

Edward prayed that he did not have to use anything he had with him, but he had to protect Queen Victoria at all costs, so Dream Dancer would use them if given no other choice.

Dao materialized beside him silently; his teacher was dressed in the same type of flowing outfit that Edward had on yesterday, but black.

Edward knew though that his teacher would have underneath his shirt a kusari gusoku, which was a Japanese chain mail shirt; Dao had brought it from his homeland. The mail shirt was made for a Samari warrior Dream Dancer had been told.

Edward's teacher Dao had told Dream Dancer that in his homeland it was a mark of distinction as well as wealth to wear your kusari gusoku for all to see. Here in England though it would be seen as an act of aggression being as he was a foreigner.

These days only castle guards or Queen Victoria's soldiers wore armour all the time. It was not like the old days where everyone had to wear armour; they were more civilized now since Victoria had become queen.

The shirt was made with links that were lacquered black to prevent them from rusting; it was always stitched onto the backing of a cloth or leather jacket. The kusari was sometimes concealed entirely between layers of cloth or it could be worn in pride as a jacket.

Dao had told Edward that in the last few years; ever since the invention of bullets, most of the time the links were doubled up. Sometimes they were even tripled in an attempt to make the kusari bullet resistant. Of course, it had not worked; his teacher had told Dream Dancer.

If Dao were still in his homeland, he would have worn it outside his clothes with several accessories like hoods, gloves, vests, shin, shoulder, thigh guards, even kusari tabi socks. Now that Edward's teacher was in England though he did not wear most of his armour only what he felt necessary.

Dao also carried a Japanese sword he called Masamune's secret, if it had another name Edward did not know it. According to Dream Dancer's teacher, it had been made secretly in a ritual performed by the Tianming Monks. These monks were a secret as well, but he had promised to tell Dream Dancer about them someday.

Dao had told Edward how the sword was made though, but he had not understood any of it. A Japanese sword, nihonto his teacher had called it, could cut through armour it was that sharp. They used double quenching as well as up to three different metals, Dream Dancer's teacher had explained.

They also used a folding method that Masamune had perfected to get the blade into three different thicknesses; it gave the blade a thin razor sharp edge, with a slightly wider center that had a soft core to give it flexibility so that it would not shatter, as well as the thicker back to give it strength.

Masamune had also perfected Nie, which produces crystal brilliance on the blade; the nie on Masamune's swords was a grey line running smoothly on the front of the blade. Dao explained that an undulating notare hamon was harder steel that gave it a leading edge with a softer pearlite steel of the cutting edge. Kinsuji lines were like streaks of lightning throughout the blade.

Edward had not understood any of this, but had nodded trying to be polite as he listened attentively. Dream Dancer had seen a blue streak coming from the blade while it was in use though, as it reflected the light, it helped him to grasp some of Dao's explanation.

A dragon graced the first part of the sword going about a third of the way up the blade, with Japanese symbols running the rest of the length almost to the tip of the blade. What they meant Edward had no idea, but Dao had said that someday he would explain it to Dream Dancer.

The pummel was wrapped in a red cord that gave it a sure grip. The tasuba a disc shaped guard between the blade and the handle was intricacy designed with crosses as well as doves entwined.

Dao had held the sword up with two fingers, just below the tasuba showing Edward how perfectly balanced it was. It had a slight curve in the blade, which made it perfect for drawing before striking your opponent in one swift motion. That is why Dao always wore it blade up, Dream Dancer was told.

Edward had examined it in awe; the blade was spectacular it was the most beautiful sword he had ever seen. His grandfather had collected swords Dream Dancer had found out when he had first walked into his ancestral home, but none of them even came close to Dao's Masamune sword.

While Edward was contemplating the sword, Dao was busy doing up the buckles on his student's chain mail. As soon as his teacher finished Dream Dancer walked to the wall to get a better view.

The sun was just coming up when Edward heard the hounds as well as about fifty horses, with another fifty-foot soldiers at least approaching. They stopped a quarter of a mile away.

Only two men came forward one was carrying a banner, they stopped just before the moat. The men on the wall could clearly hear the horses as they pranced impatiently in place, neighing eagerly wanting to rush ahead as they chomped at the bit.

Edward took a quick tally of the waiting men, he was right there were about a hundred of them. He frowned; the banner they carried was unknown to Dream Dancer. It had a castle with crossed swords beneath it with a quarter moon over the top of the castle.

Edward looked back at the two waiting men below before Dream Dancer called out loudly. "State your business?"

*****

Ernest counted the soldiers standing on the wall, he frowned there were a couple hundred, but he did not let that stop him. "I am Lord Ernest of Pwllheli Castle you have my betrothed Lady Mary Crystin Alexandrina of Llannor Castle in your midst, I want her returned to me!"

*****

Edward turned in surprise at a commotion behind him; he saw Queen Victoria walking purposely towards him. Dream Dancer frowned in disgruntlement how was he to protect Victoria if she were up on the wall. He grinned in delight as he eyed the attire she was wearing.

Queen Victoria had on a hauberk, which was called a king's maille shirt because they used double riveting as well as welding the metal links making them solid thicker pieces, it was solid enough that even arrows or spears could hardly pierce it.

Queen Victoria had modified it slightly since it would normally be too heavy for her to wear if made out of iron or metal. It fell to about mid-thigh, the links were made mostly out of silver and gold mixtures that Victoria had her blacksmith make for her.

The blacksmith had suggested adding just a hint of metal to give it a harder texture so that it would still be lighter, but give Queen Victoria more protection. To go with that he had made her matching chausses to protect her legs. He had also made her a coif for her head, which was a chain mail cap.

Queen Victoria had been so impressed with his work that she had also had him make her a sword that was now strapped to Victoria's waist.

Queen Victoria stopped beside Edward with a regal nod.

Edward chuckled as he bowed deeply in appreciation. His voice held no humour in it though as Dream Dancer chided Queen Victoria in grievance. "Your Highness you should not be up here!"

Queen Victoria's personal guard surrounded her protectively; they looked around apprehensively none of them looked pleased that the queen had insisted on coming up here either.

Queen Victoria waved away their concerns before turning she walked up to the wall as she regarded Lord Ernest in anger. Victoria had heard Ernest's demand, as well as his outrageous statement that he was betrothed to Lady Crystin.

*****

Ernest stared up at the queen in fearful anger. He looked up at the flags again in surprise; he had not noticed her banner since the sun was directly behind the castle. It had distorted her flag, which proclaimed to all that Queen Victoria was in residence here.

Now Ernest knew why there were so many guards; most keeps only had fifty-to-a-hundred. If Queen Victoria found out what he was up too, he was a dead man! He put his right hand to the left side of his chest over his heart quickly as he dropped his head in trepidation.

Queen Victoria watched Ernest bow from his saddle, but she was unimpressed. Victoria let the silence deepen for effect before calling out loudly so that all could hear her. "You lie Lord Ernest; I did not betroth you to Lady Crystin. Nor did I receive or approve any petition from you requesting her hand in marriage. I have betrothed her to Earl Summerset; they are to be married immediately. You had better hope that Lady Crystin's amnesia continues, because if I find out that you were the cause of my goddaughter's dishevelled condition you will rot in Negate for the rest of your life! Now be gone or I might change my mind and have you arrested anyway for threatening your queen!"

Ernest looked up at Queen Victoria's speech in surprise as he dropped his hand; he trembled in relief at the news that Crystin had amnesia; he prayed that she never recovered her memory. "My apologies your Majesty, I did not realize that you were here. Crystin had just turned eighteen, so I have not had the chance to make my request for her hand in marriage. I only said that she was my betrothed hopefully to secure her release faster. I came to rescue my ward because I thought that she had been taken against her will. She disappeared several days ago so I have no idea what condition you found her in, but I vow it was not by my hand!"

Ernest clasped his hand to his chest once more as he bowed his head hoping Queen Victoria would accept his lie. He backed his horse away quickly before racing back to his men in a rage.

Now what was he going to do, Ernest needed Llannor Castle desperately. He had made promises to certain unsavoury characters; with them you could not back out, the only way to be released was through death!

They were several miles away when an idea formed; he beckoned his captain of the guard forward. "Go recruit as many mercenaries as you can in London, afterwards send them to me at my castle."

Ernest's captain nodded; he broke away from the main body of men as he turned towards London without questioning his lord.

The first part of his plan started Ernest headed to Llannor Castle to set in motion the second part of his plan.

*****

Edward sighed in relief as Ernest left with no casualties; he had heard the fear in the man's voice though, so had not believed his lie. However, without proof what could Dream Dancer do about it?

Edward turned to Queen Victoria before bowing in respect. "That was very nicely done your Majesty."

Queen Victoria frowned as she looked back out to where Ernest had disappeared; Victoria had not believed him either.

Queen Victoria turned to Edward fretfully. "I think we better marry the two of you tonight just to be on the safe side. We need to leave tomorrow anyway; your tournament is in less than two weeks, so you need to be out on the course for a few days at least. I will go talk to Crystin immediately."

Edward nodded before frowning in warning as Dream Dancer motioned grimly. "She will not like it you know!"

Queen Victoria shrugged dismissively. "That may be, but Crystin will marry you none the less!"

Edward sighed uneasily at Queen Victoria's determined expression as she turned away. Dream Dancer scowled grimly he knew that he did not like being forced into marriage, so he was sure that Crystin would hate it even more.

Edward turned to the captain of his guard. "Keep the gates closed for a few days, as well as several men up here to keep watch, just in case Lord Ernest decides to double back; I do not trust him at all!"

Captain Davies nodded as he left to assign extra men on guard duty.

Edward turned to Dao thoughtfully as Dream Dancer gestured towards the dust from the retreating soldiers. "I do not think we have heard the last of that man!"

Dao inclined his head in agreement before shrugging dismissively. There were more important things that they needed to worry about right now. "Come Dream Dancer we need to discuss your vision from your Great Spirit last night."

Edward nodded grimly as Dream Dancer followed Dao to his room, they did not want to be disturbed so his teacher's room would be the perfect place for them to hide for some much needed privacy.

Dao led Edward to the special carpet that he had on this floor, it was exactly like the painting in Dream Dancer's room that he had put on his students floor ten years ago. Unlike the carpet in the earl's room though, this one would not be removed they would kneel on it.

Edward unbuckled his sword before putting it aside since Dream Dancer would not be able to sit down or even kneel comfortably with it on; afterwards, Dao help Edward out of his chain mail shirt.

Dao went behind a Chinese screen that he had imported long ago, once hidden Edward's teacher strip out of his clothes to remove his armour before putting his shirt back on. Never in the ten years that they had known each other, had Dao allowed Dream Dancer to see him without a shirt; it was not time yet!

Dao walked back over as they both sat down on the carpet facing each other cross-legged. The carpet had a power unknown to anyone; even Edward was unaware of it. Dream Dancer's teacher leaned forward intently. "Well, what did you see?"

Edward told his teacher everything he had seen in his dream before Dream Dancer banged a closed fist on his knee in frustration. "I do not understand what I could have done that would even cause the Mother Earth so much pain! And why can't I remember it?"

Dao frowned thoughtfully as he sat back before gesturing inquisitively. "You said the grey stones had symbols on them can you remember any of them?"

Edward shook his head regretfully. "I do not think so!"

Dao leaned forward earnestly. "Will you let me see what you saw Dream Dancer?"

Edward frowned in surprise; he had not known there were others who could do what he did. In all these years, Dao had never once mention that he could also dream walk. Dream Dancer wondered why his teacher had not told him, they could have gone together.

Edward had begun to be suspicious though the last few years, ever since Dao had challenged Dream Dancer to dream walk with some of his teacher's friends that he had in his homeland. They always seemed to know that he was coming, as well as when. "You can do that?"

Dao nodded decisively. "Of course, I can't dream walk like you do but I can see what you see; all you need to do is go into your usual meditation. I will put two fingers on your temples so that I will be able to see whatever you wish to show me. It is similar to when we open our minds to each other; we can both see the same thing at the same time. Remember you have the control until we get to where we need to go, I can only ride along. Make sure when you are going into the trance that you concentrate only on your visions so that I will see exactly what you do."

Edward sighed in relief, Dao could not really dream walk so Dream Dancer felt better knowing that his teacher had not kept anything from him.

After thinking about it for a few minutes, Edward frowned before nodding grimly; he was willing to try anything that might give Dream Dancer some answers. "Okay teacher, let's try it."

Edward put his arms on his knees touching his thumb to his middle finger before chanting he let Dream Dancer out; as he did, he concentrated on his visions of last night.

Dao got up once he was sure that Dream Dancer was deep enough in meditation that outside influences would not bother Edward before walking behind him, but made sure that he was still standing on the carpet.

Dao put his first two fingers on Dream Dancer's temples as he began chanting in his own language bringing the power of his carpet to life. He was taken to the ship first, where he saw Raven trying to warn her brother.

A moment later Dao saw the pastor praying before he was taken into Dream Dancer's tepee. He saw himself, as well as all the others needed for the healing, which he was already aware of.

Suddenly they were in the dark grey fog; Dao saw the other Dream Dancer in a loincloth disappear inside the archway. He left his student to play out his dream as he hurried forward.

Dao did not have much time; he had to be back before the dream ended, or he would be lost here. He eyed the archway speculatively reading quickly before running around until he reached the second stone pillar; he read it as fast as he possibly could without missing anything.

As quick as possible Dao raced to the next one, there were six besides the stone archway, so he tried to hurry. He was on the second last stone when the grass became red under his feet.

The hill trembling, almost knocking Dao down. He dashed as fast as he could go to the last stone, but it was turning black already so he could not read it. He raced back around looking for Dream Dancer, he saw him just getting up of the ground.

Desperately Dao lunged forward, he just managing to grab a hold of Dream Dancer's arm before they were flying through time until they were inside Crystin's birthing room in an unknown castle.

As soon as Queen Victoria took the squalling baby boy, Dao reached out touching his forehead. The boy had no powers that Dream Dancer's teacher could distinguish; Edward's son would grow up to be a great earl someday.

Dao turned quickly as the baby girl fell into her father's hands. He reached out to put his hand on her forehead, immediately Dream Dancer's teacher began chanting in his own language.

Quickly Dao drew as much of the evil dark mist into himself as he possibly could before putting a protective spell on the tiny baby girl. Dream Dancer's teacher also added a charm so that the powers he could feel raging in Edward's daughter would be kept under control until she was eighteen.

Dao could not suppress her powers completely because Dream Dancer's daughter needed to be taught how to control them at an early age before she became too powerful to handle.

Suddenly the baby girl gave a deafening high-pitched screech of rage and denial.

Dao turned desperately as he grabbed onto Dream Dancer, cringing in pain.

As Dao came back to himself once more inside his bedroom, Dream Dancer's teacher fell withering on the floor holding his head in agony.

CHAPTER EIGHT

Dream Dancer pulled himself out of his meditation quickly; his eyes turned back to a deep green as Edward returned to himself before hurriedly he turned to his teacher in concern. "Are you okay, what happened?"

Dao groaned as he slowly sat up still holding his head; Edward's teacher looked at Dream Dancer's earnest expression sadly. "My time on this earth is short now; I need you to promise me that you will give my sword, as well as this carpet to my son. He will be taking over soon; he will be your daughter's teacher as well as her guardian as I have been yours."

Edward sat back in shock; the dream had been exactly the way he had seen it last night Dream Dancer had not even felt his teacher Dao with him at all. "I do not understand what happened! Did you see something that I did not?"

Dao sighed in relief as some of the pain in his head eased slightly; it would never go away though. He had one more thing left to do before his destiny, as well as his purpose on this earth was fulfilled; afterwards Dream Dancer's teacher would die.

Dao moved back over to his side of the Japanese carpet staring down at the intricate designs thoughtfully. It was because of the carpet that Dream Dancer's teacher had been able to go into Edward's dream in the physical sense in order to do what needed to be done.

This carpet was the only one of its kind in existence. It was made not long after Jesus had risen from the dead. A decade later, the Tianming

Monastery was built on a hidden island away from prying eyes. Within a year, recruiting across the land had begun bringing in many students eager to join.

The first head master of the newly formed Tianming Monks was said to be the one, with the help of an unknown source, to weave the carpet into existence even before the monastery was built. Dao had often speculated that it was Jesus or an envoy of the Great Spirit's that had helped in the weaving, but Dream Dancer's teacher had no proof of that.

If it was true though, the carpet might be some kind of a portal or a manipulator of time and space to different dimensions. To where or for what purpose Dao was not entirely sure. If he had to guess, it would be a portal to heaven because the spirit symbols of the chosen ones were trapped in it.

Dao figured that is how he was able to contact his master so far away in his homeland. It was also why, he was able to talk to or get instructions from the Great Spirit when needed.

Dao had also figured out that he might be a descendant of the first head monk, but again there was no real proof to back up his theory so he had kept it to himself. Why else would his family be the only ones able to use the carpet.

The one that had control of the carpet was the only one who could use the sword made by Masamune as well; according to legend, the carpet had been used to make the sword. That meant Dao's descendants were the only ones who could use the sword as well. Because of this, they both needed to be returned to his family nobody else could use them.

Dao looked up at Edward intently trying to convey how serious he was. "Dream Dancer I am not just your teacher, I am a master of a special sect of Samari Monks that call themselves Tianming Monks. Tianming has many meanings, mandate of heaven, divine mandate, the Great Spirit's or God's will. It can also mean fate, destiny, or ones lifespan. They are Samari, but not just limited to that. They also study Ninja, Subak, Vovinam, Buddhism, as well as various other fighting styles; it is all part of our training. It is very secret not even the emperor knows about us. That is why I can speak such good English. Right from birth, I was taught many languages. It is our destiny to find people with special abilities like you so that we can help them. When our purpose is fulfilled, we die. I have a son that was born five years before I met you. He came very late in my life since I already had grandchildren, but none with the unique gifts needed to become a Tianming Monk until he was born. Before I left with you, I sent him back to my homeland to be taught by the head monks. We have the ability to take away evil or put charms and enchantments when we feel evil brewing. Once we take any type of evil into ourselves, our time is limited, so we must die! Even take our own lives if necessary, so that the evil cannot gain full control of us. I could not read all the symbols on those stone pillars, but enough of them to know that they are guardians of an evil that was hidden at the dawn of time. Your wife-to-be now has part of this evil in her. Since the evil could not get a hold of you directly, it had to find another way to get to your powers. The evil trapped you in the mist while you were sleeping. Afterwards, it enticed you to made love to that woman; unfortunately, the evil was already inside her. It did this so that you would impregnate her. Your sister tried to warn you that it was not a dream even though you thought it was. The reason the evil fog kept you trapped is that time flows faster in the mist so it needed to keep Crystin trapped inside until she had the baby. I do not know how you managed to get away from the fog the first time, but it saved both your babies lives as well as Crystin's. Your stallion coming to lay with you saved the both of you from becoming trapped a second time. That means Crystin is pregnant already; because the two of you were in the mist for quite a while, she is actually five months pregnant! Your son will be a fine earl someday there are no powers in him at all. Your daughter was a different matter! I could feel your shaman powers as well as the evil fog in her fighting each other for dominance, which is why she did not cry at first. If one could not claim dominance by the end of the night, she would have died by dawn. If the evil won, I do not know what she could have become! To help her I drew some of that evil out, I also put a charm as well as enchantments on her. You, as well as her guardian, will have until she is eighteen to teach her without fear. I could not draw all the evil out, but enough that now she has a choice on what she becomes in the future.

The mist is small enough in her now that unless she wishes to become evil, it cannot overtake her."

Edward sat back stunned with his mouth hanging open unable to say anything for a long moment; never in his wildest dreams would Dream Dancer have thought any of this was even remotely possible.

Edward finally managed to snap his mouth closed with an audible crack! Dream Dancer shook his head in amazement. "I do not understand any of this! Five months pregnant you say with my twin's; how is that even possible? Why, and why me?"

Dao sighed grimly as the Tianming Monk shrugged. "None of us really understand why things happen as they do. All I can tell you is that to have balance, evil must exist as well as good, one cannot be without the other. There is always a constant battle between the two. We had to study not only our own religion, but also all other religions past as well as present. In all religions throughout history, good and evil at all times exist together. Take the Baptist Pastor we saw on the ship, he believes in God as well as his son Jesus. That religion seems to be taking over all other religions since Christ was born. The Tianming Monks believe in this God, which we call Shen it means spirit. Like your people though, most of the time the Tianming Monks just refer to Shen as the Great Spirit. We believe in Shen because the Great Spirit preaches of love, as well as peace. The Tianming Monks believe that they are doing the Great Spirit or Shen's will. Satan, or Mara, which is what we call the devil, balances even the Great Spirit. It is the same in pagan religions; religion itself is a form of evil, there has been more killing in the name of religion since time began. Humans make it evil, not Shen. The Great Spirit wants us to love one another not kill or prosecute in his name. All anyone can do is seek council from Shen and pray that we will be led down the right path that we need to take. The Great Spirit would not give us abilities that we could not handle. We are all born, but we must all die as well it is part of the life cycle! How we live is up to us except for a chosen few, like you that must follow certain paths. That is what happened when we were given free will. People like me are born to help keep the balance between good and evil, so that neither can take full control at this time. We do this in secret, so that nobody realizes that there is an unseen war being waged even now."

Edward frowned thoughtfully; Devon had told him almost the same thing when he was sixteen, that the Great Spirit would not have given him powers if Dream Dancer could not handle them. He would just have to try keeping that in mind in the future. He turned back to his teacher Dao knowing that he was not done yet so waited patiently for him to continue.

Dao paused as he frowned thoughtfully for a moment trying to figure out how to explain the working of the mist to Dream Dancer. Sighing in frustration Edward's teacher finally decided to try using age as an example. "Now the dark fog that you got caught in was guarding a minion of Mara's, a very nasty creature that if release would find a way to release his master that is its ultimate goal. The mist is there to hide the portal that contains this creature, there are several portals scattered throughout the world most cannot be gotten too or even seen. Unfortunately, this portal as you now know can be accessed; why that is so I have no idea! Your wife unknowingly opened that portal slightly not enough for it to be released fully, but enough for it to try finding a way out. The fog is timeless it flows faster then a blink of the eye because it is trapped between worlds. The longer you stay in the mist the faster you will age. When you come back into this world your age will slow back down, but you will still be older. For instance if you stepped in the fog at forty-five and aged five years in the mist when you step out of the fog you will be fifty even though time here had only advanced five minutes."

Edward turned the conversation back to Dream Dancer's vision, seeking reassurances from the Tianming Monk. "You saw all of us in the tepee to heal Crystin; do you really think that will stop the evil mist?"

Dao shrugged unknowingly; the Tianming Monks had several different abilities, but seeing into the future was not one of them. Unless the Great Spirit wanted them to see it, at that time it would be shown to him. "I do not know, but it is worth a try. I had to make a decision on which one I was going to help, so I chose your daughter. As soon as I helped her all my powers disappeared since we are only capable of taking in evil once in our lifetime. The reason for that is so we can continue battling on for however long we are needed. As long as the evil we take in is not enough to turn us evil we can prevail; then and only then can our destiny be fulfilled! We are just going to have to trust in the Great Spirit for the rest."

Edward nodded as he stood up to leave now that he understood a little more Dream Dancer felt slightly better, but still confused. "I will go change, brunch should be ready soon; I will meet you in the great hall, I need some time to think about all of this! I am just not sure how to take having a wife that is already five months pregnant even though I only just impregnated her two days ago. I need to talk to the Great Spirit also to be positive that the babies are mine!"

Dao stood up as he said goodbye to Dream Dancer, he had no worries that Edward would accept the twin's; the Tianming Monk knew the earl too well to have any doubts about that.

Once Dream Dancer left, Dao sighed dispiritedly as the Tianming Monk dropped onto his knees in the center of his carpet. He held his head in his hands in regret for a moment; he had left a few things out of course.

Like whom Dao really was, as well as what the grey stone symbols had revealed! Although, with the last stone not read the Tianming Monk had no idea what the outcome would turn out to be in the end.

Dao had also omitted the fact that to save Edward's wife-to-be, as well as the twin's; three willing sacrifice must be made. The Tianming Monk could not tell Dream Dancer because if he knew, he would not allow it.

The evil mist would now begin to grow; they needed to stop it so that it could not reach the border of Snowdonia. As the evil grew, it would affect others causing strife to increase across England before leaking into the rest of the world. That is why Dream Dancer had felt the earth weeping.

Dao heard a rustling at his window, so the Tianming Monk looked up in despair. "Great Spirit, I do not know if I can do this!"

A dove cooed at Dao from his windowsill, quickly he closed his eyes in awe as a beam of sunlight warmed his face. The Tianming Monk felt the Holy Spirit enter him before he felt something touch his shoulder, but he kept his eyes tightly closed not wanting to see what touched him.

"**You are troubled, chosen one**?"

Dao bowed down to the floor quickly so that the Tianming Monk's forehead touched the carpet not wanting to be tempted to look. "I do not know if I can do what must be done; I am afraid!"

"**You are one of the Great Spirit's chosen warriors; do not be afraid the Holy Spirit will be with you guiding you every step of the way. You will also have the aid of one of my special envoys; he will be with you when it is time. You must be strong and believe that 'I AM' will be with you, it is not time yet. The serpent, Mara, is getting desperate trying to free itself. It must be kept contained until the appointed day**!"

Dao heard the wind whistle through his bedroom window, as well as a final coo of the dove. The comforting hand on his shoulder disappeared suddenly as the Tianming Monk heard the flapping of wings getting fainter.

As soon as Dao felt the warmth from the sunbeam shining through his window disappear, the Tianming Monk knew that he was now alone.

Dao sat up with a frown this was not the first time Shen had used the term, 'I AM'. Several places in the bible it was also used when the Great Spirit referred to itself, it made the Tianming Monk wonder why.

Finally, Dao shrugged dismissively; Shen had many names it did not really matter what name you used as long as you believed.

Dao smiled calmed once more his faith in himself and the Great Spirit was stronger than ever. He could not falter now; he had to stay strong to complete his destiny if he wished to have his reward. The Tianming Monk got up to change, what would be must be, there was no way to stop it now!

*****

Queen Victoria entered her goddaughter's chamber before smiling at the picture she made. Victoria had sent over a royal purple gown; it showed off Crystin's white hair dramatically. "Do you like the dress my dear?"

Crystin reached down to stroke the silky material in appreciation as she nodded before smiling in pleasure as she looked up at Queen Victoria. "It is beautiful!"

Queen Victoria sucked in a shocked gasp as Victoria caught sight of Crystin's white eyes; no hint of an iris was present at all! They should have been a steel grey; it had been too dark last night for the queen to notice the colour change in her goddaughter's eyes.

Queen Victoria walked over before lifting her goddaughter's chin as Victoria examined Crystin's eyes closely. "Can you see?"

Crystin nodded in confusion. "Of course I can see, why what is the matter?"

Queen Victoria waved the question away not wanting to scare her goddaughter. "Do you remember anything yet?"

Crystin shook her head uneasily. "Nothing!"

Queen Victoria sighed in disappointment before sitting down as Victoria took her goddaughter Crystin's hand in hers. "That is okay dear someday you will remember I am sure, but I have something very important to talk to you about. Did you hear the alarm going off this morning?"

Crystin nodded in confusion. "Yes, but I did not know what it was about."

Queen Victoria sighed in aggravation as she thought of Crystin's third cousin with his small beady black eyes; she did not like or trust him one little bit. Why Victoria had given him custody of her ward she could not remember. "It was your third cousin on your mother's side; he came here with about a hundred men to attack this castle not realizing that I was here. This man is very bad; he insisted that we give you to him. I refused of course, because when Earl Summerset found you; you had been raped. I am sure that your cousin Ernest did it, but without you being able to remember anything, I have no real proof. So I have decided that tonight you will marry Doctor Summerset to keep you safe from your cousin."

Crystin wrenched her hand away from Queen Victoria's as she jumped up in fear shaking her head in denial. "I will not, I do not even know the man!"

Queen Victoria nodded as she got up as well to face Crystin with a look of grim determination. "I know you do not dear, but that is beside the point. Doctor Summerset is willing to marry you even though you might be carrying another man's child. You must think about your future, besides as your queen as well as your godmother I insist that you do so tonight!"

Crystin stared stubbornly at Queen Victoria's resolute expression as she asked angrily. "What if I refuse?"

Queen Victoria shrugged dismissively as Victoria growled in warning. "If you do not I will find an old crippled man three times your age who would not care whether you are a virgin or not!"

Crystin sighed dejectedly as her shoulders slumped in defeat. "How do you know I do not already have a husband out there somewhere? What about my parents what would they say?"

Queen Victoria walked over before taking Crystin's hand into hers consolingly. "Your parents died when you were just about sixteen you have been my ward since, so you could not have married without my consent. I guarantee you that there is no other man out there!"

Crystin frowned in forewarning as she pulled her hand away from Queen Victoria angrily in a fit of temper. "If you make me do this I will hate you, you know!"

Queen Victoria shrugged flippantly as Victoria waved negligently. "Right now maybe, but someday you will understand that I do have your best interest at heart. Besides I am a queen everybody hates me, so one more will not make much difference!"

Crystin scowled surprised by the acceptance plain in Queen Victoria's face, her expression softened for a moment before hardening in anger once more.

Crystin folded her arms under her breasts in grim resignation as she vowed childishly. "I will marry him if you force me too since it seems that I have no choice in the matter, but I will not love him!"

Queen Victoria smirked knowingly as she thought of the gorgeous hunk of a doctor, if she were not married as well as older; the queen would have kept Edward for herself. Victoria had little doubt that Crystin would be able to stay immune to the good-looking Earl Summerset for long.

Especially once Crystin got to know Edward better even being a queen, Victoria was not immune. There was just something about Doctor Summerset that drew a person to him Queen Victoria could not explain it.

Even though Queen Victoria had vowed to send Edward back to his home in the new world, Victoria herself could not help but succumbed to the earl's charms letting him stay in England. She even went against her husband Albert's wishes, who she loved above all others.

Not only that, but Queen Victoria had let him take over his grandfather's estates. It still baffled her on why she had let a savage from the new world have an earl's title. Victoria's frown of thought disappeared as the feeling of unease vanished once again, as if it had never been.

Queen Victoria winked suggestively as she beckoned to her goddaughter so that she would follow her to the dinning room, but paused for a moment as Victoria teased before leading Crystin out the door. "You will learn as you get older that love has nothing to do with marriage my dear. What you make of the marriage is totally up to the two of you, it is not my business at all! If I were you though I would not take too long deciding, there are a lot of women standing in line hoping for the dangerous good-looking doctor to crook his little finger towards them. Come it is time for brunch."

Crystin walked behind Queen Victoria wondering what her godmother meant by dangerous doctor crooking his finger. She had not really seen the earl last night; she had been too afraid as she cowered in the corner. She would have to look at him more closely at brunch as she followed Victoria reluctantly.

*****

Edward rose instantly as Queen Victoria, her ladies-in-waiting, the queen's faithful hound Bailey, as well as his future wife Crystin entered. Dream Dancer bowed deeply as did the other five nobles sitting around the table.

Thankfully, the other two hundred had left before Edward had gotten back; Dream Dancer hated dealing with the buffoons that followed Queen Victoria everywhere. Lucky for him Victoria had sent them away before he had returned.

Edward walked around to hold out the chair for Crystin, while Queen Victoria's husband did the same for Victoria. The five nobles scrambled to help the other ladies-in-waiting into chairs too.

Queen Victoria waited until everyone was seated then cleared her throat to get everyone's attention. "Tonight we will be celebrating Earl Edward William Charles Summerset and Lady Mary Crystin Alexandrina's wedding. Tomorrow we will be heading to Scotland for the first Open Championship. The queen's champion must have a few days to practise before the tournament. There are only eleven days left until the big day so we must try to leave here first thing in the morning."

There were excited whispers from the nobles sitting around the table. Earl Summerset had won every tournament around England as well as Scotland for the last two years much to Queen Victoria's delight, but her husband Albert's anger.

Prince Albert had placed second every time; last year he had tried to sabotage the earl's equipment, but it had not helped him. As Queen Victoria's husband Albert should have been Victoria's champion for the first open, which only enraged the prince further. It also helped to fuel the prince consort's hatred towards Edward.

Crystin peeked over at her future husband Edward in surprise as an image of an older man holding a funny looking stick materialized in her mind. He was smiling down lovingly at something; the image disappeared suddenly as the servants started dishing out brunch.

Crystin tried putting a name to the face, but could not.

Edward watched Crystin frown wondering if Queen Victoria's announcement about their marriage tonight was upsetting her. Dream

Dancer could not help that, he had to marry her in order to save her from a beast like Palmerston.

However, if Dao were right Crystin would already be five months pregnant with Edward's children. There was no way that he would allow another man, especially Lord Palmerston who Dream Dancer loathed with a passion, to raise his children.

Edward knew that Queen Victoria had used his aversion to Palmerston as a weapon. That is why she had mentioned him as a prospective husband knowing that Dream Dancer would not allow that to happen. Victoria had no idea why he hated Palmerston since the earl refused to tell her why.

One day Edward would get Palmerston alone, when he did there would be a reckoning. Dream Dancer shook of thoughts of Lord Palmerston since it was giving him indigestion!

Absolute quiet descended while everyone ate silently. As usual, Edward's cook had out done her self again; she had cooked his favourite chicken soup with dumplings for an appetizer. There was also big juicy beefsteak with Yorkshire pudding mashed potatoes, and fresh vegetables for the main course. For those who did not like beef, she had included lamb chops with homemade applesauce. For desert, she had made Dream Dancer an apple cobbler knowing how much he loved it.

Since this was their last day here and Edward's cook would not be needed again for a while, she had cooked up a feast. Later on, she would lay out a cold meal so that everyone could help them selves.

Queen Victoria had tried several times to steal Edward's cook, lucky for Dream Dancer his cook was loyal refusing to leave him.

Edward looked around with a smirk of satisfaction, not a soul looked up from their food. Forks scrapping plates was all that could be heard as they eagerly devoured almost every morsel on the table, as they ate a meal fit for a queen!

CHAPTER NINE

Raven walked down from the captain's deck luckily it put her back to the severe wind; she stumbled to the stern of the boat where the pastor was standing.

Raven had to scream so that she could be heard above the wind as she bent forward getting close to Daniel's ear. "Come for lunch in my cabin!"

The pastor looked at her in confusion wondering why she wanted to see him. Finally, Daniel nodded before taking Raven's arm as they fought the wind to the door that lead down to the cabins.

Two sailors were just leaving Raven's room having set up a table with chairs for their afternoon lunch, which was highly unusual. Most of the time, they ate with the captain in his cabin. They both nodded in greeting as they went past them, but did not say anything.

Devon as well as Trevor was already at the table waiting impatiently for them.

The new arrivals just sat down when two of the captain's own servants came in with a large fish caught yesterday. Potatoes, carrots, as well as cabbage, were arranged artfully around the plate.

The other servant had bread, tea, plus dessert; they put everything on the table before leaving without a word.

The pastor looked around at all the food as his mouth watered in appreciation at the enticing scent emanating from it before Daniel grinned in delight. "Are we celebrating something?"

Raven grinned teasingly before waving upwards towards the top deck. "Captain Roberts wanted to say thank you for all of your help."

The pastor frowned puzzled as Raven dished them up a good helping; Daniel put a hand on his chest in surprise. "Thank you to me, but I have not done anything? What could I have done that would be a cause for celebration?"

Raven shrugged dismissively. "Captain Roberts thinks you have as do all the crew; I will explain it to you after we finish eating."

The pastor nodded still perplexed before Daniel smiled hopefully as he gestured around at the bountiful food. "Do you mind if I say grace?"

Raven gestured encouragingly. "By all means Pastor Daniel, please do."

The pastor bowed his head giving thanks for the captain's generosity. Daniel also asked for God's blessing on all who sat at the table, as well as for the sailors risking their lives so that they would make it safely to England.

Everyone said amen before absolute quiet descended as they all ate. All that was heard in the small cabin was the scraping of forks on their plates, with an occasional outburst from the crew on duty up on deck, as well as the whistling of the gusty wind making the ship creak and groan eerily.

Trevor was the first one finished, the light blond almost white haired greenish-grey eyed ten year old jumped up imploringly. "Mom, can I go up on deck to help the captain?"

Raven frowned in disapproval at her oldest son's impatience. She looked over at her husband Devon for his approval.

Devon nodded slightly in agreement.

Raven turned to her son Trevor before shaking a finger at him in warning. "Okay Little Cub, but do not get in the way. Make sure you mind the wind as well, it is blowing something fierce up there!"

Trevor raced for the door hoping to escape, but stopped short in disappointment as his mother called out knowingly. Little Cub turned back towards Raven listening respectfully as she gave prohibitions.

Raven's voice brooked no disobedience as she warned her son Little Cub grimly knowing that is the first place he would be heading. "Trevor, stay out of the rigging today it is too windy up there for you!"

Trevor knew that there was no use arguing when Raven used his white name; she could not be budged. Little Cub could not help trying anyway, as he pleaded with his mother in anger. "But, ni-go-i!"

Raven held up her hand to forestall Little Cub's objections. "I mean it Trevor, if the wind dies down by tomorrow we will discuss it at that time!"

Trevor sighed forlornly as he nodded in disgruntlement. He turned to the door, after opening it Little Cub gave a dejected answer before closing the door behind him. "Alright mom, I can wait."

The adults finished eating so Raven poured tea for the three of them. She handed the pastor a cup last before grinning at Daniel in delight. "Captain Roberts said for me to say thank you to you, as well as your God for the wind today. I am also to tell you he hopes that the wind will continue for the rest of the trip. He said if it does we should be in England in ten days instead of twelve, we will also beat the current record of thirteen days twenty hours."

The pastor shook his head decisively completely flabbergasted at first that Captain Roberts thought that Daniel was responsible for this wind. "This is not my doing I did not pray for it!"

Raven shrugged as she motioned flippantly. "You were standing on deck when it started this morning. The captain and his crew are highly religious, as well as superstitious you know. He told me that in the thirty years he has made this run never had he felt a wind this strong without a storm cloud to be seen. His sails are so full of wind that they might not hold all the way to England if it keeps up."

The pastor chuckled in delight. "Well if he is that happy about it, I will pray that it keeps blowing for him."

Raven sobered in worry as she thought of her brother Dream Dancer still at least ten days away if not more, but all she could do was pray hoping to make it to England on time. "I would appreciate it if you did pray Pastor so that the wind will continue as well, I know I am!"

The pastor eyed Raven curiously. "Do you believe in God, Raven?"

Raven nodded decisively. "Of course, don't we all?"

The pastor frowned perplexed. "But you pray to the Great Spirit, do you not?"

Raven sighed in disappointment as she eyed Daniel the Baptist Pastor. He looked a lot like his father Jed Brown, but with his mother Melissa's blond curly hair.

Was the pastor's religion as rigid as the others, she hoped not. Raven leaned forward earnestly! "Do you think because we call God the Great Spirit or Heammawihio, which is what we call him; that it is not the same God as in the bible? I have read that the bible from cover to cover. The Old Testament is very good reading it gives good examples of why we should not act as God's chosen people the Jews do. However, the New Testament is the gentiles' bible; is it not. When Jesus, God's son talked to his disciples, he told them that he would die before rising again. He also said that after he had risen he would proclaim to all nations across the earth his, as well as his father's glory. In the New Testament, God also speaks of working through other nations, not just the Jews. We did not have written words as you did when we were new, but our stories tell of our journey to God the Great Spirit. When we were young, a man led us out of the darkness into the light. He had a glow around him; he taught us how to plant food so we would not go hungry. He taught us how to hunt; he taught us to pray, as well as how to give thanks to Heammawihio the Great Spirit, how to give praise for the food that was provided. He told us never to take advantage of or loose respect for the earth or animals that he had provided for us. He did not give us tablets with the Ten Commandments on it, but he did give us guidelines to live by. It is very similar to the Ten Commandments. I have listened to all the old stories of the elders; almost every tribe of Indians has a similar story. I believe that it was Jesus who came to my people in order to lead us into the light."

The pastor stared at Raven incredulously for a long moment he opened his mouth to refute her, but snapped it shut again very flabbergasted not quite sure what to say at first. Could she be right only God would know that for sure of course? Daniel was going to have to pray to see if Jesus would answer that question for him.

The pastor chuckled as he shook his head resignedly. "Well I must say that you have given me something to think about. I am not sure if you are right or not. As long as you keep praying to the Great Spirit, but continue to believe that he is God I suppose that is better than what some people think."

Raven laughed at the flustered Baptist Pastor. "Well I am not sure if I am right or not, most of my people would not necessarily agree with me either. Every time I read the New Testament though, I just get a feeling that I cannot explain. Take revelations, for example, it talks about Armageddon, which also means new beginnings. It is a written prophecy, unlike ours that is passed down orally from generation to generation. The prophecy we have is that once the white eyes have begun destroying the earth no white buffalo will come again for many generations. Not until just before the world ends, at that time the white buffalo will return once more. When they do, we must be ready because soon afterwards we will resume our place as caretakers of Mother Earth as a new beginning is ushered in. Can you see the similarities in the two; of course the bible gives way more details on how that will happen."

Devon having heard these views many times in the past could not help feeling sorry for the pastor as Daniel sat there with a bewildered look on his face.

Devon shook off his thoughts with a grin of delight as he turned back to the conversation; Golden Eagle had to admit though that Raven had a way of putting it that made perfect sense.

Raven unaware of her husband Devon's amusement continued the discussion. "Your mother was named White Buffalo by my grandfather; nobody could understand why a white woman would be called as such, but to us a white buffalo also means new beginnings. Your mother was instrumental in helping to bring my grandfather's people into a new beginning, which is why the white buffalo spirit claimed her. I have a feeling though that there was another reason, I just have not been able to figure out what it is yet."

The pastor frowned curiously remembering the confusion he had felt when his mother Melissa had unexpectedly handed him her buffalo robe. Daniel rubbed his chin thoughtfully wondering if Raven would know what that was all about. "My mother gave me her white buffalo robe, as well as her medicine bag to give to Edward. She said that she had a dream that the robe was to be returned to the Cheyenne people. I am to give it to Dream Dancer he will know what to do with it; do you know why my mother would do that?"

Raven shared a concerned look with Devon before she turned back to the pastor. She shook her head perplexed. "No, I do not know why she would do that either, but like I said with the dwindling of our sacred buffalo it might be the last white buffalo hide in existence. Why Melissa was told to give it to my brother instead of to our medicine man is very confusing."

Devon frowned thoughtfully if Melissa had instructions to give the hide back; he could only surmise that her time was nearing its end. Why else would she be told to give the hide back to the Cheyenne? Golden Eagle kept his opinion to himself not wanting to upset the pastor when Daniel was so far away from home.

Devon sat back with a quiet chuckle as the two went back to debating whether Raven's theory about the Great Spirit being the one true God was right; the discussion ran late into the night.

*****

Edward was showing Crystin around the castle, which would now be one of her new homes. He had managed to evade most of her questions so far; thankfully, this was their last stop so Dream Dancer could take her back to her room.

Crystin had taken several quick sideways glances at her husband-to-be; she had to admit that her godmother Queen Victoria was right Doctor Summerset was sinfully handsome. He moved with a silent grace that reminded her of a lion; where she had seen a lion before she was not sure.

Edward made Crystin extremely nervous though, every time he touched her arm or back to steer her in a different direction she wanted to scream or run away in fear. Why she was afraid of the earl, she did not know.

Unless Crystin's godmother Queen Victoria was right, maybe her cousin had raped her. That made no sense either though, why would she be afraid of Edward he was not her cousin.

The last stop was at the library; Crystin looked around in disapproval there were no drapes in the windows, or carpets on the floor. There were hardly any books on the shelves with sheets covering all the furniture. No fire or candles were lit; the only decoration visible was a portrait of an older looking man that resembled the man standing beside her.

Crystin looked up at Edward inquisitively. "You do not live here do you, or even visit very often?"

Edward inclined his head solemnly. "You are right my ancestral castle is not far from Clevedon in North West Summerset. I have three townhouses one in London, Oxford, as well as one in Windsor. I also had a ranch in Montana, but I gave that to my sister Raven. I do come here sometimes, but I do not stay here for long."

Crystin frowned perplexed as they got to her room. "What is a ranch? Where is this Montana?"

Edward shrugged dismissively before Dream Dancer bowed in farewell. "I will explain it someday or maybe I will even take you there. I will leave you now to get ready for our wedding."

Edward turned away quickly leaving without another word not giving her anymore chances to ask questions, it would just have to wait until after the wedding. Crystin was too skittish as it was.

Edward had felt Crystin jump every time he touched her. Dream Dancer did not need her refusing to marry him now. Once they were married, it would be too late for her to back out.

Crystin watched him go in irritation, why would Edward not answer any of her questions. She had asked him quite a few since they had begun the tour of his castle, but he refused to answer almost all of them. She wanted to know more about the earl; finally, she sighed in frustrated disappointment as she went into her room.

Edith was waiting with Crystin's bath water.

Crystin stripped before crawling in with a sigh of pleasure. Her maid wet her long hair before scrubbing it briskly much to Crystin's delight, she groaned ecstatically.

Crystin peeked up at Edith inquisitively maybe she could get some answers from her instead; servants were always gossiping. “Do you travel around with the earl or do you stay here?”

Edith shook her head with a horrified look at that thought. “No, my lady, I would not leave my home.”

Crystin nodded in understanding. “How often does the earl come here?”

Edith shrugged negligently. “Several times a month it depends on how often my lord wants to hide in the deep woods behind his garden where we are forbidden to go. It is kept locked at all times, me as well as the keeper of the keys figures he has a pet hidden from his homeland inside. Even the keeper of the keys does not have a key for that gate; the earl keeps the key around his neck at all times.”

Crystin frowned in surprise. “Edward is not from England?”

Edith shook her head emphatically. “No, me lady, the earl’s grandfather was banished to the new world that is where he died. It caused quite a scandal when the old King found out Earl Summerset married an Indian maiden. Our lord is a barbarian from the new world, a heathen, an Indian, a savage!”

Crystin shuddered in revulsion. “Why would my godmother Queen Victoria want me to marry a heathen?”

Edith shrugged grimly. “Because, Queen Victoria loves him of course!”

Crystin looked up in shock. “But my godmother is married; do you think they are having an affair?”

Edith shook her head in horror at that thought. “Oh my lady I did not mean to give you that impression. No, no only one man has ever dared say anything about a relationship between them. The earl immediately demanded a duel; he killed the unfortunate Count. No, Queen Victoria loves him because he has saved her life many times, now he is her personal doctor.”

Crystin frowned thoughtfully. “My godmother had mentioned that he was a doctor. I suppose he only doctors Queen Victoria’s court?”

Edith chuckled at the disapproval she heard in her new mistress’s voice before the maid shook her head negatively. “No, my lord refuses to doctor anyone but Queen Victoria or her direct family. She was very angry when she found out that he had opened an office down by the docks, so was administering to the poor with only a minimal charge, but he will not doctor any of the queen's court!"

Crystin nodded pleased to hear that before getting out of the tub. She dried herself off, but continued the conversation to find out more about this so-called savage. If Edward were a savage, why would he be administering to the poor?

In addition, how did Edith know so much when according to the maid, she did not travel around with the earl? "I thought you said you never leave Wales, so how do you know all of this stuff?"

Edith snickered as she helped dry her mistress's hair. "The cook my lady goes everywhere with the earl. She has been with him since he arrived in England, anything you want to know she can tell you. All you have to do is put a little brandy in her tea; afterwards she will talk your ear off."

Crystin chuckled in delight. "That is very good to know."

Once dry Crystin walked over to the vanity, she sat lost in thought as her maid brushed out her long white hair. She frowned thoughtfully wondering what an Indian was; heathen, barbarian, even savage she understood, but Indian was an unfamiliar word.

Crystin's contemplation was interrupted as Edith finished with her hair; her new maid beckoned her over so that she could help her into her new bloomers, a camisole before finally into the corset.

Crystin would have to remember to thank her godmother Queen Victoria later for the new clothes. She groaned in pain as her maid tightened the torturous contraption, Edith had to give an extra yank on the ribbons because Crystin's belly was a little too big; she could barely breathe by the time the maid was done.

Edith clucked in sympathy before walking over to the closet, the maid pulled out the dress Queen Victoria's maid had brought over earlier while her new mistress was busy with the earl.

Crystin gasped in admiration as she caught her first look at the beautiful exotic white wedding dress. The bodice came down in a deep

V, which made it very low in front; it would show off her small perky breasts nicely.

It was gorgeous in its simplicity the only decoration was around the waist. It had a cream coloured cloth belt that would be tied in the back; the front of the sash had black symbols as well as several different flowers painted all around it giving it a mysterious foreign look.

Crystin frowned uneasily for a moment as a memory teased her tried to come alive. She had seen some of those symbols before, but she was not sure where or when she had seen them.

Edith unaware of her mistress's confused grim thoughts brought the dress over.

Crystin stepped back afraid refusing to let her maid Edith put it on her.

Edith stopped uncertainly at her mistress's look of fear. "My lady is there something wrong?"

Crystin blinked in surprise as the feelings of unease, as well as the momentary terror that she was experiencing disappeared suddenly as if they had never been. She shrugged in confusion not having any idea what her maid Edith was talking about at all. "No, why do you ask?"

Edith shook her head in disapproval; her mistress was definitely a strange one the maid could not help thinking, but so too was the earl.

The maid brought the dress over before helping Crystin into it.

CHAPTER TEN

Crystin put a shaky hand on the Prince Consort Albert's arm. Since her father according to Queen Victoria was dead, he had agreed to give her away.

Crystin looked around wildly in panic; she really did not want to do this! What choice did she really have though? She was trapped in this castle with no memories, clothes, or money with a cousin who she did not remember at all somewhere out there hunting her for some reason; according to her godmother Queen Victoria anyway. What was so important about her that is what she did not understand!

Crystin felt totally helpless with only Queen Victoria's assurances to go by; a woman that said she was her ward as well as her godmother, but that Crystin did not remember at all. She was also quite confused by how her cousin had gotten guardianship of her if she was the queen's ward.

Everything was happening so fast! Nobody had explained anything to Crystin not how she had gotten here or where she was from. She was frustratingly confused as well, by why the earl would want her even though Edward knew that she was no longer a maiden.

This just did not make any sense to the terrified Crystin at all, what was all the rush for anyway! Why oh why could she not remember anything? As she got closer to the priest as well as her husband-to-be tears of fearful uncertainty sprang to her eyes. She did not want to do this it was wrong; there was something very wrong about all of this.

Crystin had no way to stop this madness though; she could not run away, where would she go? Did she have any friends out there or even a home? All these questions and fears kept running through her mind. She was so disorientated all she really wanted to do was sit in a corner screaming out her uncertainties!

Unexpectedly Crystin's godmother Queen Victoria elbowed her sharply in the ribs. Crystin jumped in shocked surprise having been so engrossed in her thoughts that she did not hear Victoria coming.

Queen Victoria scowled grimly as she chided Crystin in exasperation. "Put a smile on your face for goodness sake, the tears are not going to help you now!"

Crystin nodded jerkily as she wiped her eyes on the hankie the prince consort handed her. Handing it back, she pasted on a wobbly smile; it was the best that she could manage under the circumstances.

As Crystin got closer she stared at Edward in panicky fascination he was one of the handsomest men she had ever seen, he even put Prince Albert to shame. Queen Victoria had said that there was a lot of woman standing in line willing to go to him, so why did he want her?

Crystin shivered in foreboding, as she got closer before cringing in fear as a memory trickled to the surface making her halt instantly in surprise. She saw a man, with a concerned expression bent over her, Crystin was sure it was Edward. She saw herself reach up drawing his head down for a kiss.

Not realizing what she was doing Crystin dug her long nails deep into the prince consort's arm; it was not until she heard him gasp in painful surprise that she realized she was hurting him.

Prince Albert quickly grasped Crystin's fingers trying to pry her nails out of his arm.

Quickly Crystin let go as the memories faded unsure where it came from or even why her future husband Edward who she had never seen before that she knew of was part of a memory, one where obviously they were intimate. Unless it was just her mind playing tricks on her, or maybe it was a dream she was remembering.

Queen Victoria took her goddaughter's hand before squeezing it tightly until Crystin winced in pain. Satisfied that she had her goddaughter's full attention, Victoria let go of the hand irritably. "Get a hold of your self Crystin, now is not the time for having daydreams!"

Crystin stifled another pained grimace as she wiggled her fingers; reluctantly she put her right hand back on the prince consort's arm following mutely.

Crystin tried hard to quiet her thoughts they were not doing her any good anyway, but it was almost impossible! Reverberating through her skull was a voice screaming at her to run, as far and as fast as she could manage!

*****

Edward frowned in concern as Crystin halted suddenly staring at him in recognition. He did not really want her to remember just yet; Dream Dancer had a feeling that if she did she would refuse to marry him, that he could not allow.

Edward's daughter would need special handling if he were to keep her evil side dormant Dao had told him. Dream Dancer sighed in relief as Queen Victoria grasped Crystin's hand thankfully distracting her as he saw the recognition disappear from her eyes.

It still took several long agonizing minutes before the procession started once more, as they got ever closer it seemed to Edward that time seemed to slow down as the wait became excruciating for Dream Dancer. Finally, Crystin was in front of him; thankfully time once again speeded up to its normal speed.

Edward smiled at Crystin in sympathetic encouragement before reaching out he tenderly pried the hand she had clutching the prince consort's arm loose. Dream Dancer pulled a reluctant Crystin up beside him.

Edward turned to face the minister eagerly just wanting to get this all over with before anything else happened to stop the proceedings. Dream Dancer nodded impatiently for Queen Victoria's priest to begin.

*****

Most of the ceremony was a blur for Edward with only one problem surfacing with Crystin, but Queen Victoria quickly stepped forward before whispering something in her ear. What Victoria said to her goddaughter Dream Dancer had no clue, but whatever it was, it worked!

Jerkily Crystin nodded as she whispered almost too low for anyone to hear. "I do!"

The priest quickly finished as Queen Victoria impatiently waved him to hurry this up suddenly it was mercifully over.

Edward bent slightly, lightly he brushed his lips against Crystin's cheek as she turned her lips away, but Dream Dancer did not protest.

Edward tucked Crystin's left hand into the crook of his arm as he led his new wife out of his small chapel; Dream Dancer bent slightly in order to whisper so that nobody else could hear. "I gave you my grandmother's ring, but if you do not like it you can choose another one?"

Crystin looked at the delicate diamond clustered ring; the center stone was the size of her pinkie nail with six just slightly smaller diamonds encircled it. The new countess was quite happy with the one Edward had chosen. "It is beautiful I will keep this one if you do not mind, thank you very much."

Edward nodded pleased that Crystin liked his choice there had been several bigger rings in his grandmother's jewellery box, but Dream Dancer had liked the smaller one better.

Edward led his new wife towards the ballroom in relief, Dream Dancer was certainly glad to have gotten the ceremony over with at last. Queen Victoria's own musicians would be playing for a while before a light supper would be layed out buffet style, followed by more dancing if they wished afterwards.

Edward squeezed Crystin's hand gently as Dream Dancer bent slightly once more trying to put his countess more at ease. "You look lovely my dear!"

Crystin blushed in pleasure before peeking up at her new husband shyly; she only came up to Edward's shoulder, so the countess felt very delicate next to him. "Thank you."

Quiet descended as Edward led Crystin into the ballroom.

Crystin frowned perturbed, but tried hard to hide it from her new husband. She was even more confused now, as soon as she had said

'I do' the voice that was screaming in the countess's head had silenced almost immediately.

It seemed to the bewildered Crystin now that the voice in her head must have come from another source, so was not her at all! The new countess grimaced in uncertainty, but finally she shrugged it off wanting to forget everything for the moment especially the fear!

*****

Raven looked around her tiny cabin uneasily as a shiver rippled down her spine. Suddenly the hairs on the back of her neck bristled unexpectedly standing straight up in warning. She looked around again in confusion; it was almost as if she could feel someone watching her.

All of a sudden, the feeling was gone before Raven felt a surprising sense of great loss; it was so overwhelming that tears sprang to her eyes, even though she had no clue what it meant.

The door burst open behind Raven making her jump slightly in surprised fright not having expected that. She spun around as she stared at her husband Devon forlornly with tears streaking her face.

Devon groaned in exaggeration as he playfully stumbled inside; turning instantly, he pushed against the door pretending it was taking all his strength to shut it. With a chuckle, Golden Eagle turned around putting his back to the door as he huffed and puffed playfully teasing his wife. "That wind is trying to carry me away! I swear it is getting stronger it followed me all the way down…"

Instantly the teasing smile disappeared as Devon's face sobered in concern when he saw the tears. Quickly pushing away from the door Golden Eagle rushed to his wife Raven in apprehension. "What is the matter?"

Raven looked up at her husband Devon in dismay as she shrugged in confusion. "I do not know! I had this weird feeling that someone was watching me for a brief moment before a sense of deep loss caught me by surprise, it was as if someone important were gone!"

Devon gathered his wife Raven in his arms anxiously dreading to ask, but knew that Golden Eagle needed to know. “Your brother Dream Dancer maybe?”

Raven shook her head emphatically. “No, I do not think so if it was my brother Edward I would have known instantly!”

Devon sighed grimly in relief. “Well come to bed I tucked Trevor in already, now it is your turn my love.”

Raven nodded mutely as she crawled into their bunk without arguing on who was tucking who in.

Devon frowned grimly; usually his wife Raven would not have let him off with that last statement, so it worried Golden Eagle considerably. Any other time they would have ended up tussling together in laughter, trying to be the first one to get the other undressed quickly in order to tuck them in first.

Devon undressed before crawling in; he gathered his wife Raven close protectively as he sighed apprehensively this trip was getting more bizarre every day. If Golden Eagle had his way, they would be turning this ship around right now to head back to Boston so that they could go home.

Unfortunately, it was not up to Devon as Golden Eagle silently wished that they had never left home!

*****

“Dream Dancer!”

Edward sat up with a shocked jerk, as he looked around the room uncomprehending for a moment; it took him a few minutes to realize where he was. Dream Dancer shivered forlornly as he called out plaintively. “Nam-shimi’!”

Edward turned quickly looking down at his new wife Crystin to make sure that Dream Dancer had not disturbed her sleep.

Fortunately, Crystin was still curled up in a fetal position on her side of the bed as far from Edward as she could get. It had been quite a fight when he had insisted that the countess sleep in his bed with him even Queen Victoria had gotten involved much to Dream Dancer's displeasure.

In the end, Edward had gotten his way by promising Crystin that he would not demand his husbandly rights for the time being. As soon as the countess was assured of that, she had agreed.

"Dream Dancer!"

Again, Edward heard the pleading far off whisper as he shook off thoughts of his wife Crystin. Frowning grimly he crawled out of bed, he tiptoed to his closet so that Dream Dancer could grab his Indian articles before leaving his room as quietly as he possible could.

Edward raced down the back stairs as he ran out into the garden. Hurriedly Dream Dancer pulled the key out from under his nightshirt to let himself into the deep forest behind his garden.

In too much of a hurry Edward decided not to bother locking the gate it was late enough nobody else in their right mind would be up anyway. Even if they were, Dream Dancer had forewarned everyone years ago about staying away from this place, so he never gave it another thought as he rushed up the pathway!

Edward dropped his saddlebags by the entrance of his tepee as he rushed behind to gather a large armload of wood. Quickly beginning his chanting already, Dream Dancer went inside to start his fire in the center fire pit.

Edward waited until it was high enough so that when he put the rocks in the fire it would not be extinguished by mistake. He watched for a bit to make sure the rocks Dream Dancer put inside were getting red-hot before leaving.

Once outside, Edward started his little fire not far from the tepee.

While Edward waited for it to get stronger, he unpacked his package taking everything out except the hide. Quickly he released Dream Dancer as he mixed his special tea; he put the last of his special leaves in his pipe before mixing his paint.

As fast as Dream Dancer could go without making any mistakes, he painted his face meticulously. When finished Edward stood up as he stripped out of his nightclothes before painting his chest next.

Now only in his loincloth Dream Dancer grabbed his bear fur out of the package before draping it around Edward's shoulders still chanting rhythmically.

Dream Dancer squatted as Edward drew deeply on his pipe, blowing the smoke in the air towards the heavens at the ground towards Mother Earth as well as to the west, and finally to the east.

Still chanting Dream Dancer lifted the bowl with his special ceremonial liquid up high before downing the bitter concoction that he had made; He shuddered, as the foul taste seemed to linger on Edward's tongue this time.

Twice more Dream Dancer drew on his pipe before finally ready he put the pipe down as he stood up once again. Looking up at the full moon Edward sighed resignedly. He did not want to go in there, but had no choice HE was waiting.

Dream Dancer turned ducking into the tepee before grabbing a canteen that was only half-full of water. He had forgotten to refill it after last night; it still had some of the sweet scent that reminded him of home though. Edward dumped the rest of the water onto the red-hot rocks.

All that could be heard was the hiss of the water hitting the rocks, as well as the rhythmic chanting of one of the most powerful shaman's in the Cheyenne history. Steam billowed out encompassing every inch of the tepee.

It was because of Dao's training that Dream Dancer would be able to find his sister on the ship even though now Raven would no longer be where Edward had found her last night.

When Raven got here, she would find a lot of it very familiar since when spirit walking Dream Dancer would bring her as well as her husband Devon to his home in Wales while they were dreaming. Sometimes Edward even manipulating their dreams taking them places that they had never been before.

Dream Dancer sat cross-legged rocking back and forth, as he let his spirit fly across the Ocean. Edward found the ship instantly, remembering where Raven was he flew down to the cabin.

Dream Dancer stared down at his sleeping sister hating to disturb her as he paused for a moment, but not for long knowing that he must hurry time was of the essence. Finally, Edward reached out touching the part of Raven's subconscious that was receptive to dreams bringing her into his vision.

They flew across the sea; Dream Dancer could not help the impulse to stop for a moment at the ranch. He missed the place dreadfully sometimes, of course it had not changed much just gotten bigger. Edward only stopped for a moment, since they did not have time to linger long.

On their way once more, they went up into the familiar mountains before going into his grandfather Giant Bear's thriving village. Well it was not his grandfather's anymore, but his cousin's. Running Wolf had taken over as chief a year after Dream Dancer had left for England.

Dream Dancer stopped in front of his grandfather Giant Bear's tepee; he really did not want to go in, but knew that he had no choice. Finally, they were inside, immediately Edward heard his sister Raven's cry of pain.

Dream Dancer tried to comfort Raven as best he could; inside, their grandmother Golden Dove was laid out peacefully already being readied for burial. Their grandfather Giant Bear was lying beside his wife waiting for them not wanting to go until he could at least feel his grandchildren's presence, one last time.

Giant Bear turned his head as he looked directly up at Dream Dancer smiling serenely as he felt both of them here. "It is our time Dream Dancer and Raven, please do not weep long for us. We have fulfilled our purpose on this earth; someday we will meet again in the happy hunting grounds of the Great Spirit. Take care of each other, may your lives be long with as much happiness as ours has been!"

Dream Dancer smiled down sadly as Edward reached out to touch his grandfather's dream receptor so that Giant Bear could hear the whisper of his far off voice. "Goodbye nam-shimi' we both love you, we will miss you!"

Giant Bear smiled peacefully before drawing in one final breath content now that he knew both his grandchildren were beside him one last time. A moment later, he was gone to be with his Golden Dove not able to live even a moment without his beautiful golden haired wife.

Instantly Dream Dancer could hear the wailing of grief throughout the village at the death of their former chief. Giant Bear would be forever remembered as one of the greatest chief's that had fought to protect his people by bringing his tribe into a new era with the whites, with as little bloodshed as he possibly could!

Songs would be composed of Giant Bear's love for his white wife Golden Dove, as well as his life; they would be sung by the Cheyenne for as long as there were Cheyenne.

Dream Dancer shuddered in sympathy as he felt his sister Raven's pain. Looking down one last time at his grandparents lying peacefully beside each other, Edward saw that their hands were entwined even in death; he could only hope to have such a loving marriage someday.

Dream Dancer caught a sob back before turning he took his sister back to the ship, they went down to the cabin to where her husband Devon who was frantically trying to wake Raven up. With a last comforting word to his grief stricken sister, Edward left her as he flew back to his waiting body.

With tears of grief streaming down his face, Dream Dancer grabbed a hunting knife that he always kept by his fire. Wailing he cut a furrow on the back of his bicep, making sure that he did not go too deep. Edward pulled the knife out of his arm as he cut two furrows one in each leg.

Reaching up Dream Dancer grabbed handfuls of shoulder length hair as he chopped it off short before dropping several fistfuls into the smouldering fire. The foul stink of burning hair brought him to his feet quickly, so Edward grabbed a bucket of water dousing his fire.

Still cutting small furrows in his chest, Dream Dancer stumbled outside bleeding clutching his knife not finished yet.

Dream Dancer stopped in shock as Edward instantly spun around at a frightened cry off to his right! He watched in disbelief as his new wife Crystin crumbled in a heap at the earl's feet.

CHAPTER ELEVEN

Crystin heard Edward cry out in his sleep, but she remained motionless pretending that she was still asleep. The countess was still very upset with the earl so did not want to talk to him at all.

When Edward had insisted that she sleep in his bed now that she was his wife, Crystin had tried throwing a tantrum. Weeping the countess had pleaded trying to convince him that decent woman did not sleep in the same bed as their husbands, but to no avail; he would not listen to reason at all.

Edward had stood there with his arms folded resolutely, refusing to budge even when Queen Victoria had told him the exact same thing the earl would not give in to Crystin's wishes.

Crystin had not really trusted Edward when he had promised not to demand his husbandly rights, but he had been true to his word. The countess had lain the whole night in this same spot petrified, unable to sleep this close to the earl.

It had annoyed Crystin to no end when she heard Edward snore softly; obviously, he had no trouble sleeping. She turned before staring at him speculatively this was the first time the countess actually had time to look at him closely. He was shamefully handsome with his dusky sun kissed skin, dark blond-auburn streaked hair, which set off his deep green emerald eyes. His cheekbones were set very high giving him a more aristocrat air, with a hawkish nose that fit his face perfectly; he had a chin that jutted just a little giving him a stubborn look at times as well.

Crystin shuddered there was something about the earl that still made her afraid, but she was not sure what the cause of it was. It almost seemed to her at that moment that it had a lot to do with the countess not wanting to remember something that she had done.

Crystin frowned angrily at herself that could not be it at all what could she have possibly done that would make her reluctant to remember; she did not even know the man. Sighing in frustration the countess turned back around to try to get some much-needed sleep.

Crystin just started dozing off when Edward sat up with a jerk. He cried out a word that she did not understand it was in a language she had never heard before. The countess peeked as he jumped out of bed; since the earl's back was to her, she continued watching him as he rummaged inside the closet.

Crystin frowned perturbed as Edward left without even looking once towards her. She got up quickly as she slipped into her dressing robe, automatically she slipped on her Celtic medallion feeling naked without it; at the same time the countess was also putting on her slippers.

Crystin rushed out following Edward down the back stairs, but paused on the landing as she waited until she heard the door close. As soon as she heard it shut, the countess ran down the stairs before cautiously opening the back door; it was all clear, so hurriedly she followed the earl.

Crystin waited several minutes at the back gate before cracking it open cautiously to see what Edward was doing. There were way too many trees though, so the countess slipped through the opening running behind one of the trees before rushing to another tree.

Crystin followed Edward carefully staying far enough back that hopefully if she stepped on a branch the earl would not hear her. She stayed close to the pathway that had been used often by the looks of it, not wanting to get lost. The countess was not sure how far this forest went, but it was really thick so would be easy to get lost in she figured.

Crystin was just in time to see Edward duck into a funny looking cone shaped cloth like building. Finding a tree closer that the countess judged was big enough to hide her completely, she rushed to it before she knelt down waiting patiently. Carefully she peeked around the tree to watch curiously.

Edward came out a few minutes later; Crystin watched in fascination as he built a fire before making up three bowls of something. Once done, the earl started to put whatever was in the bowls on his face. It must be paint; the countess could not see what designs they were though.

Edward stood up as he striped out of his nightshirt. He stood there bold and proud in nothing but a funny looking piece of cloth that covered the earl's genital area, another flap of cloth covered part of the earl's buttocks, but not all of him.

Crystin was close enough that she could see that it was tied at the hip. She could not help but wonder if she pulled on the string if the whole thing would fall to the ground. The countess shivered as a tingly feeling ran all over her body; she pulled her dressing gown closer blaming the cold for the shivering.

Crystin cocked her head trying to hear what Edward was saying, but it was no use she could not discern any real words. Only some kind of chanting; the countess wondered if the earl was a warlock, a male witch that would explain some of his actions.

Crystin watched in fascination as Edward proceeded to paint his chest next, now she could see colour, so the countess knew that it had to be paint of some kind. The earl put several different pictures on his deeply muscled chest.

Crystin could not help but stare at Edward's large biceps as they flexed moving with the earl's hand movements. A tingly feeling raced throughout the countess' body giving her goose bumps as another shiver shook her, this time she could not blame it on the wind.

Crystin was thankful when Edward finally reached down pulling out a pitch-black hide of some kind, the earl draping it around his naked shoulders so that he was now covered somewhat.

It only took Crystin a moment to realize that it was a bear hide. He knelt before grabbing what looked like a pipe, but longer more intricately designed compared to any that the countess had ever seen.

Edward blew smoke in four different directions, now Crystin was even more convinced that he was a warlock. He picked up another bowl, still chanting he lifted it up above his head. The earl mumbled unintelligible words that the countess still could not understand since it was in that strange language.

Crystin watched Edward drink the liquid with a visible shudder. He drew on his pipe a few more times before getting up; he paused for a moment looking up at the full moon, but finally the earl headed inside his funny looking building.

Crystin waited a good ten minutes, when Edward did not come out she cautiously went over to the earl's fire. The countess picked up the pipe to smell what was in it, whatever was inside smelt awful it made her slightly dizzy.

Crystin put it down before bending to dip her finger in the leftover liquid in the bowl; she touched it to her tongue. The countess shuddered as she spit out the awful tasting stuff; her tongue tingled where the liquid touched.

Crystin turned staring at the cone shaped building with interest; the countess looked up to the very top and saw tree branches sticking up out of a hole, a lot of smoke was pouring out of it.

Curiously, Crystin walked around the building stroking the velvety feeling cloth, hides. Some kind of animal hide was sewn together; she did not recognize the animals so it must be from his homeland. On the hides it looked like there were animals, as well as other things painted on them. They reminded the countess of the images painted on Edward's face.

Crystin pulled out her necklace; she looked down at it in speculation. She knew what it was, how the countess knew she was not sure. Her maid had said that she was wearing it when she had first come here.

It was a Celtic witches medallion, where Crystin had gotten it she did not know. Did that mean she was a witch? Is that why the earl really wanted to marry her? That would mean Edward had known who Crystin was before they were married, could he be lying to Queen Victoria!

At their wedding Crystin was sure that she had seen him before somewhere; had the earl manipulated the countess' godmother Queen Victoria in order to have a witch for a wife.

Determined to find the real reason behind it all, Crystin marched around the animal hide building when she heard Edward come out. The countess stopped short in shocked terror with a squeal of fear as she stared at the bleeding, sobbing, knife wielding Earl of Summerset.

Crystin did what every woman in her particular situation would do. The countess crumbled to the ground in a dead faint.

*****

Dream Dancer halted instantly in stunned surprise; he watched as his new wife Crystin fell to the ground out cold. Edward grumbled irritably under his breath. "Fool women anyway, where did she come from?"

Dream Dancer's eyes went back to green instantly as he brought Edward back to the surface before dropping his knife by the fire pit. He kicked dirt on his fire to extinguish the still smouldering coals. He bent lifting Crystin up as he marched determinedly out of his sanctuary.

Edward set Crystin down outside the gate; that would teach him not to leave his gate unlocked in the future. Dream Dancer turned the key with a resounding click that echoed loudly in the silence.

Edward scooped Crystin up once more before marching purposely down the pathway. Dream Dancer shouldered open the back door as he took the stairs two at a time rushing to Dao's room.

Edward pulled his foot back to kick at the door, but it never reached its target as the door opened unexpectedly before it could connect.

Dao beckoned Dream Dancer inside as he stepped back holding the door open wider, without questions. "Put Crystin on my bed!"

Dao frowned in concern at all the blood the Tianming Monk saw on his new mistress' nightclothes. "Is she hurt?"

Edward shook his head negatively as Dream Dancer stood back.

Dao looked at Dream Dancer more closely before shaking his head as he tisked knowingly. Now the Tianming Monk knew why he had woken half an hour ago with a stabbing pain in his bicep. He had just gotten dressed to go see what that was all about knowing immediately it had something to do with his student Edward.

Dao sighed grimly as he eyed all the blood on Edward. "I see it is not the countess' blood, you must have given Crystin quite a fright did you? Who died that you felt the need to cut yourself up so badly Dream Dancer?"

Dao of course was aware of all Cheyenne customs; he knew just by looking at all the shallow cuts, as well as the partly scalped short hair on Dream Dancer's head, that someone important must have died, the Tianming Monk hoped it was not Raven he needed her for the healing.

Edward sighed forlornly. "My grandparents!"

Dao frowned in surprise. "Both of them?"

Edward grimaced sadly, as he nodded. "My grandmother Golden Dove died first. I took Raven to see grandfather we arrived just in time for Giant Bear to say goodbye. My nam-shimi' could not live without my grandmother!"

Dao inclined his head in understanding, the Tianming Monk was well aware of who Giant Bear was; he was also aware that the old chief's white wife Golden Dove was not Edward's real grandmother even though he thought of her as such. "Go finish your grieving Dream Dancer; I will look after the countess for you."

Edward sighed in relief before turning he left Dao's room. Dream Dancer went back to his private garden making sure to lock the gate this time. With a loud clank, the rusty old lock echoed in the deep silence.

*****

Dao was kneeling on his carpet waiting, trying to ignore the slight sting of Dream Dancer's knife every time Edward cut himself. He was praying quietly when he heard a moan. The Tianming Monk got up before walking over to the bed.

Crystin looked up at Edward's servant in panic; the fear was plain to see on the countess' face. "Is the earl going to kill me?"

Dao burst out laughing; he just could not help himself. Dream Dancer was one of the gentlest men he had ever met. The Tianming Monk shook his head as he sobered before smiling placatingly. He could not resist teasing Crystin just a little bit though. "No my dear Edward will not kill you, not today anyway! Your husband is way too soft hearted for that Countess. You should not have trespassed where you were not wanted though!"

Not pacified by Dao's obvious humour nor did the countess appreciate his joking attitude. Crystin scowled angrily as she turned her head away grimly. "Edward is a warlock is he not, I have a witch's medallion around my neck so the earl thinks that I am a witch doesn't he?"

Dao frowned irritably at Crystin's assumptions. "No, Edward does not know who you are; I do though, believe me you are not a practicing witch. Your grandmother on your father's side was though that is her medallion you are wearing, but you do have her blood in you. This makes your marriage to the earl very dangerous!"

Crystin's head swung around in shock as she stared at Dao hopefully, but was very confused by his last statement. "You know who I am; did you know my family as well? I do not understand why would my marriage to Edward be dangerous?"

Dao shook his head negatively. "No, I did not know your parents personally I just know of them. Your marriage to Edward is dangerous because of what you have now become!"

Crystin frowned perplexed, what did Dao mean by that statement? Unfortunately, not remembering anything the countess had no idea what she was like before. "I still do not understand any of this!"

Dao nodded, well aware of that wondering if it were a good idea to let Crystin see the truth. He was not sure if touching the countess was such a good idea either; what if the Tianming Monk drew more evil in unwillingly!

If Dao did draw in more even by accident he would become evil, so would have to die before the proper time. Which would endanger Crystin, as well as the twins that the countess was carrying; it was too risky the Tianming Monk could not help thinking.

Dao scowled grimly before shrugging resignedly the Tianming Monk was just not willing to take that kind of chance. "I know you do not countess, but someday you will. I put an Oriental robe at the foot of the bed you can have it; go behind the screen that is in the corner so you can change out of your blood soaked nightclothes, just leave them on the floor I will look after them. When you are done, go back to bed Edward will be closeted in his garden until sometime tomorrow stay away from the earl until he is finished!"

Crystin sat up before looking down at her bloody dressing robe as she grimaced in disgust as the countess looked at Dao angrily. "Why was the earl cutting himself is it some kind of warlock ritual?"

Dao shook his head negatively before sighing in aggravation at Crystin's insistence that Dream Dancer was a warlock. "Edward is not a warlock that is the Cheyenne way of grieving, the earl's Cheyenne grandparents both died so leave him be!"

Crystin scowled in surprise not having expected that at all; she opened her mouth to demand how Edward would know that when he was here in England not in the new world, but snapped it shut angrily when Dao put up a restraining hand to forestall the countess' questions.

Dao shook his head resignedly as the Tianming Monk stopped Crystin from uttering anything further already knowing what the countess was going to say. "No more tonight, it is not up to me to tell you anything; if the earl thinks you need to know he will explain it to you himself, when he is ready."

Crystin nodded irritably as she got off the bed; she grabbed the garment lying at the bottom not even paying attention to the soft silky gown she held. In aggravation, the countess marched behind the screen Dao had indicated.

Hurriedly Crystin stripped as she shook out the long flowing gown; finally, the countess noticed the beautiful flowers as well as the many different symbols intricately patterned on the exotic material.

Crystin put it on with a sigh of bliss as the silky material caressed her naked body in ways that she would never have thought was possible. The countess shivered in pleasure as she tightened the sash before stepping out.

*****

Dao chuckled low at Crystin's show of temper, she was no wall flower that one; the Tianming Monk frowned in thought when he saw the Celtic medallion that had slipped out from under the countess' nightdress swinging back and forth with her angry movements as she marched to the screen.

An idea began to form suddenly; Dao nodded to himself it just might work, with Shen's help of course, the Tianming Monk couldn't help thinking.

Quickly Dao went around lighting all his special candles, as well as his incense before walking over to his carpet; he knelt in the center. The Tianming Monk put his two hands together in prayer as he looked up hopefully. "If it is your will Shen show the new countess who she really is. Great Spirit, please help Crystin to remember; she needs your assistance only you Lord can help her!"

Dao's prayer now done he sat back on his haunches as he waited patiently for Crystin to come out. The Tianming Monk closed his eyes as he hummed softly, preparing himself hoping this would work.

*****

When Crystin stepped out she looked around in surprise candles of every design and shape flickered eerily around the whole room casting strange shadows everywhere. She sniffed appreciatively at the heavenly scent emitting from them it calmed the countess' anger relaxing her instantly.

Crystin looked over, but saw Dao kneeling humming softly to him self. Not wanting to disturb him the countess tiptoed towards the door before stopping short in surprise as Edward's servant spoke.

"Countess come kneel across from me, I will explain what the flowers symbolize on your robe if you like?"

Crystin looked at the door tempted to leave. The countess looked back at the waiting Dao thoughtfully. He had not once looked in her direction how he had known that she was leaving baffled her.

Crystin had asked her maid about the strange looking little man that Edward had for a servant. Edith had not known very much about him except that Dao was an Oriental, but she did not know where exactly his hometown was since he never talked about himself at all. The countess' maid also did not seem to know how Dao even became Edward's servant only that the Oriental was with the earl when he first came to England.

Crystin looked down at the beautiful flowers on her robe as she sighed resignedly, curious to know about them the countess walked over before kneeling down waiting for Dao to speak impatiently.

Five minutes went by, but Dao continued to hum softly eyes closed not saying a word. Crystin grimaced irritably as she looked down noticing the beautiful carpet for the first time. It had the same flowers as well as other strange symbols on it, just like the robe the countess was wearing.

Crystin studied them in interest remembering that her wedding sash on her dress had some of these flowers on it with a few of these strange symbols too. The countess jumped in surprise as the quiet was shattered suddenly as Dao once again began to speak.

"Take out your medallion Crystin; I want you to hold it in both of your hands. I want you to close your eyes let yourself feel every curve as well as the intricate Celtic knots on your necklace. Concentrate on the medallion countess let your mind wander where it will."

Crystin frowned taken completely by surprise wondering what that had to do with the countess' new robe, but did as she was told anyway. There was something so intense about Dao at this moment that it made one listen to him without knowing why they were doing it.

Besides Crystin was curious to find out what this strange little man was up too. Edward seemed to trust him, so the countess decided to go along with Dao's unusual request what could it hurt.

Crystin pulled out her medallion; she obediently clasped it in both her hands before closing her white eyes. The countess listened to Dao as he slowly hypnotized her without her being aware of it. He continued to give her instructions in a soft soothing whisper as the Tianming Monk pulled Edward's wife deeper into meditation.

"Feel the energy from your medallion, feel your grandmother pulling at you through your necklace. She is calling for you to remember who you were, as well as what you have turned into now. Let your Celtic blood flow to the surface Crystin, as you do think of your father with your mother…remember!"

Dao droned on hoping that she would remember on her own if the countess did not the Tianming Monk would not be able to help her any other way. He could not risk touching her at all.

CHAPTER TWELVE

Crystin heard a far off giggle of a child in her mind; the countess saw a black haired man holding a long wooden stick showing a small five or six year old black haired girl how to hold it properly.

"Here Crystin feel the weight of the club swing it back and forth that's it now step forward so that you can hit the ball that is on the ground. We want to surprise your godmother Queen Victoria next time she comes for a visit on how well you are learning to play golf."

The little girl obediently hit the ball.

The tall black haired grey-eyed man clapped in approval when the ball flew through the air disappearing out of sight.

The little girl looked up at her father in pleased delight. "I did it Papa!"

The man beamed down in loving approval. "Yes you certainly did love."

*****

The scene dissipated; Crystin whimpered in denial aching to continue the vision. As her life went from one moment to the next, but did not stop as time moved on quickly. It did not let the countess linger even though she desperately wanted too until suddenly it slowed once more…

*****

Crystin saw an older teenage girl standing at the steps of a carriage with tears streaming down her face.

The young black haired teenage girl stood with her arms folded in anger as Crystin pleaded desperately. She dropped her arms in exasperation trying one more time to convince him. "But Papa, I want to go watch you win the tournament for Queen Victoria. It will be so exciting to see you become godmother's champion; please I beg you let me come too!"

The same man, older now as well as almost bald smiled down at his angry daughter. "Not this time love, your amateur tournament is coming up in two weeks we will be gone until the day before so it would not give you enough time to practise. You stay with Marie she will help you, no tantrums now we will see you before your tournament Crystin I promise!"

Crystin frowned crossly, but finally nodded in reluctant agreement as she leaned forward for a farewell kiss. She waved forlornly as her parents disappeared from her life never to return.

When Crystin's cousin had brought her the news she had screamed in disbelief running to her room she had hid in there as the promise that had been made by her father was never fulfilled.

It took Crystin's nurse Marie two days to get her out of her room. It was hunger that finally drew her out though since her nurse absolutely refused to bring her food in her room.

*****

Crystin's life again flickered from one moment to the next in quick succession never stopping though; the countess watched in horror as her life become a living hell once her cousin took over as her guardian.

Crystin's golf clubs were the first thing that disappeared, the guards on her walls next before her nanny too vanished. It was not long until all the servants vanished one by one, until the countess was alone in the huge castle left to fend for her self.

Crystin whimpered in pain then fear as tears streamed down her face as the countess watched her cousin with loathing as he tore her undergarments off forcing himself on her; raping her savagely with no remorse what so ever!

Crystin saw her daring desperate escape next. Before finally, the countess saw her other self now racing across the pitch-black night praying for help.

As Crystin saw, her lips move; five shimmering green sparkles came out of them. She watched as they fluttered in the wind being carried away. Curious the countess followed it back in time, how long in the past she was not entirely sure.

Suddenly Crystin was in front of this castle before being pulled inside, the countess saw her new husband Edward talking to her godmother Queen Victoria. What they were saying she could not hear.

The fluttering stopped in front of Edward; they burst suddenly disappearing into thin air, Crystin heard her soft call for help. The desperate plea rippled in the quiet of the dream world that the countess seemed to be in, eerily.

Instantly Crystin was outside the castle watching Edward mount his black horse, racing towards Snowdonia. The countess saw him turn away going in a different direction, so she screamed for him to stop, but suddenly for no reason that she could see the earl fell of his horse knocking himself out.

When Edward came to he tried to mount again, but he fell down once more. It almost seemed to the countess that he was drunk, but he had not looked drunk to her at the castle. Finally the earl was able to mount, the countess sighed in relief as he turned back towards Snowdonia.

Crystin continued following Edward watching as he used his stallion to move her mare so that he could get to her. The countess blushed shamefully as she watched him clean her thighs of blood.

Crystin frowned puzzled as Edward started chanting in that strange language before falling to the ground. She was not sure why, but when he laid his hands on her the earl screamed in shock and pain. The countess watched him withering on the ground beside her not sure what that was about at all!

*****

Crystin was pulled back to her mare as they galloped madly through the fog trying to get away from her pursuers. Mercifully, she was unexpectedly enveloped by the dark grey mist before the dogs could bring Mist down. The countess watched as her horse carefully walked forward time seemed to stop as they wandered.

*****

It was not long though before the white haired Crystin saw herself disappear between two pillars. The countess followed curiously watching as her other self reached out to touch the pitch-black pillar in the center of the grey stones.

As the black haired Crystin reached out her hand to touch the pillar, the white haired countess that was watching her cried out in warning, but it was no use as she felt the shock travel throughout her body as she left a bloody handprint on the stone.

The white haired Crystin saw herself lay down; the countess watched horrified, as the ground beneath the black haired Crystin turned a blood red before the six grey stones began to turn black slowly inch by inch the colour ran up the pillar. It almost seemed that the pillars were absorbed her hair colour. As they drew in the colour, her black hair bit by bit turned snow white! The mist darkened to a dark steel grey, which reminded her of the colour of her eyes! What had she done?

*****

Time quickened once more for a short period before leisurely it played out in slow motion once again as Crystin watched Edward rush to her to help as she lay in the grass that had mysteriously turned green once more.

Where the earl came from she had did not know or why they were both in the mist now baffled her. Her hair too was back to its normal black; the countess frowned in puzzlement, when did that happen? She was sure she had seen it turn white not that long ago!

The white haired countess observed her other self in disbelief as the black haired Crystin reached up to force Edward's head down so that he would begin to make love to her. Horrified by what was happening the white haired countess watching was incapable of stopping it.

The white haired Crystin unexpectedly heard an unknown female voice screaming all around the countess it echoed eerily off the stones. The woman that was screaming was trying to warn Edward that the black haired Crystin was evil.

It dropped the white haired Crystin to her knees in the grass as the countess wailed forlornly in denial.

Unfortunately try as the white haired Crystin might she could not get the vision to release her. The countess rocked back and forth keening in disbelief as she knelt there helplessly watching as she saw Edward once again try to get away from the black haired Crystin.

Hardly believing what was happening, the white haired countess heard herself weave a spell that she had no previous knowledge of at all. Before forcing Edward's head back down as the black haired Crystin wrapped her legs and her arms around the earl in demand refusing to let him up.

As the other Crystin forced Edward to make love to her, the grass again turned a blood red beneath her. A few minutes later, the countess' hair began turning snow white as the pillars turned black once more.

*****

Finally, it was mercifully over as Crystin shuddering in horror dropped to the carpet in Dao's room. The countess curled herself into a protective ball as the tears streamed down her face in despair.

What had Crystin turned into, she had went from being a victim to being just as much of a rapist as her cousin was. The countess had felt Edward's reluctance, but the evil surrounding her had forced the earl to relent against his will.

The female voice that Crystin had heard screaming out the warning had been right it had not been a dream, but all too real!

Dao watched Crystin as she cried out her remorse; the Tianming Monk let her be, until the tears quit on there own. Finally, he beckoned the countess to get up. "Come now what is done cannot be undone so dry your eyes. I want you to sit up so that we can talk!"

Crystin nodded unhappily, but did as she was told; the countess wiped her eyes before blowing her nose delicately in the handkerchief Dao handed her.

Dao waited patiently until Crystin finished as the Tianming Monk leaned forward earnestly. "Crystin, you must make sure that Edward does not make love to you again. If he does, he might not be able to withstand the evil that is inside you a second time. If the evil gains control of the earl, we are all doomed! There are things about Edward you do not know; right now, it is best that you do not. Once you are free of the evil the two of you can become a married couple in every sense. It is too late for your children though, one will be born with the evil inside her. I have given her a special charm so that the earl will have until she is eighteen to teach her without fear. Put this necklace around your neck, when your daughter is born put it around her neck. Make sure that you teach her never to take it off, even when she bathes or sleeps."

Crystin dutifully took the necklace putting it around her neck, the flower nestled perfectly in the hollow of her throat. The countess frowned earnestly as she looked at Dao in hope. "You can cure me?"

Dao gave a small nod. "Yes, we are waiting for several more people who are on their way here as we speak; when they arrive we will give it a try. I am not going to guarantee it of course only the Great Spirit knows what is to come, but if I were you I would pray every night for help."

Crystin frowned suddenly as the countess remembered what else Dao had said. "You mentioned children?"

Dao nodded grimly as he gestured down at Crystin's belly. "Yes you are already carrying Edward's babies, twin's, a boy as well as a girl. Because the two of you were in the mist for so long you are actually five months pregnant already!"

Crystin's hand dropped instantly to her stomach in fearful denial as she shook her had not believing that for a moment. "That is impossible, there is no way I can be that far along! How do you know they are Edward's anyway; my cousin raped me first remember!"

Dao smiled gently in reassurance as Crystin grimaced in anger. "I know he did, but unknown to him is that he was a pawn. That evil black pillar used him so that your body would be open as well as receptive to the evils invasion. If you had still been innocent, the evil could not have used you to get at Edward. It is actually the earl that the evil was after, or a child of Edward's would suffice."

Crystin frowned in confusion before the countess grimaced uneasily. "Why, what is so unique about Edward or me, I do not understand?"

Dao sighed knowing his explanation really would not help Crystin because he could not tell her the whole truth, but the Tianming Monk did tell her almost everything he had told Edward earlier.

Dao even went so far as to tell the countess about the mist keeping them both trapped so that her pregnancy would advance quicker. The Tianming Monk did not tell her why the evil wanted to keep her there though knowing she would not believe him anyway. He could see from her expression that she still did not understand, but it was the best that he could do for now.

Dao stood up before beckoning Crystin to stand. "Off to bed with you now the necklace will protect your sleep, so the evil cannot control you while you wear it. Edward will be in his sanctuary for the night. Sleep well, Countess, goodnight."

Crystin nodded as she left without any further questions even though she had many that she wanted answers too. Exhausted beyond thought, the countess went to her room before slipping into her bed. Instantly she fell into a deep asleep; she dreamt of her parents as well as happier times.

*****

Devon kept himself braced against the wind watching his wife closely as she cut herself. She had changed into one of her buckskin dresses as she knelt on the ships deck mourning for her grandparents. He understood Raven's customs of course; Golden Eagle had lived with the Cheyenne long enough that even he had cut himself several times as well as cut his long hair to above his shoulders.

Trevor being as young as he was had only been allowed a few shallow cuts. They had also let Little Cub cut off his hair; shorter than his father had, but not as short as Raven would do Devon was sure.

The pastor was staying with Trevor making sure that Little Cub did not cut himself anymore while his parents were occupied.

Devon stayed at a respectful distance as he watched Raven making sure that his wife did not over do it. Golden Eagle had seen a few Cheyenne die because their grief was so bad that they had cut themselves too deeply, bleeding to death.

Raven was kneeling at the bow of the boat keening; she was not paying any attention to the wind or the crew standing at a distance watching her fearfully.

A very concerned ship's captain had cornered Devon earlier when the wailing had first begun wanting to know what was going on.

Devon had explained the Cheyenne grieving ritual to Captain Roberts. Of course, Golden Eagle had not told the captain how they had found out.

Captain Roberts had shaken an angry finger at Devon in warning. "I do not know or care how Raven found out about her grandparents death, but if she throws herself overboard or dies from loss of blood it is not my responsibility! Do I make myself absolutely clear on that?"

*****

Devon winced as Golden Eagle watched Raven lift each braid cutting them off almost at her scalp before tossing her beautiful hair that was once past her buttocks over the ship's railing into the sea.

Finally, Devon had enough as he rushed up to Raven taking the knife away from her. Golden Eagle tucked it into his pants as he lifted his limp sobbing wife before carrying her to their cabin.

Devon laid Raven on the bunk, he grimaced at all the blood; enough was enough if he let her continue she would kill herself. Golden Eagle poured water into the basin before turning he strip her lovingly, he cleaned the blood away as his wife continued to sob softly.

Devon rummaged under the bunk pulling out his medicine pouch; he put a few herbs in a glass of water before washing Raven some more. He did not have any hot water, so Golden Eagle mixed a few herbs in the cold water forcing her to drink it. He had put a painkiller with a mild sedative, as well as a healing herb in the glass. He smiled down sympathetically at his wife's grimace of distaste, but made her drink it all.

When the glass was empty, Devon nodded in satisfaction before putting the cup away as he stripped himself. Golden Eagle crawled into the bunk with Raven as he gathered his wife close lovingly. "Shhh love, sleep now you have grieved enough for tonight. Your grandparents would not be happy if you over do it."

Devon crooned to Raven softly gently stroking her short hair until Golden Eagle felt his wife's sobs subside as the sedative began working helping her to sleep so that she could heal.

Devon kept a silent vigilance all night, making sure that Raven did not slip away on him. Tomorrow his wife would be back to normal, until that time Golden Eagle never let his guard down once.

*****

Edward looked down at himself in trepidation as he sighed, some of his cuts were a little deep; he had not intended to go that far. His hair was shorn short right up to his scalp; he could also feel a slight sting there. Clearly, Dream Dancer had gotten too close to his head trying to scalp himself.

Edward stood up to leave, but dropped to his knees almost instantly as a wave of dizziness hit Dream Dancer.

Suddenly Edward felt another presence; he looked up at Dao in apology. Dream Dancer was not sure how his teacher had gotten in here without a key, but he was too woozy to ask questions. "I think I over did it a little?"

Dao shook his head in disapproval as Dream Dancer fell sideways out cold from loss of blood. Having come prepared, the Tianming Monk put one blanket to the side with his medicine pouch before spreading the other blanket that he had brought with him out on the ground.

Dao rolled Edward onto the blanket first; turning away, the Tianming Monk filled one of Dream Dancer's bowls with water adding the herbs afterwards. He cleaned the earl's wounds stitching the deeper ones, when he was finished he put the other blanket over his student to keep him warm.

Dao stood back as he stared down reflectively at his student, charge, and friend. The Tianming Monk sighed sadly, soon he would be leaving Dream Dancer; he would have to make sure that Crystin was prepared to help her husband Edward through that process.

Dao knew that Dream Dancer would take the Tianming Monk's death hard, maybe even harder than Edward had taken his grandparents death. In all these years Dream Dancer had never figured out that they were connected, but soon Edward would.

That is why Dao always knew when Dream Dancer needed him, the Tianming Monk could feel his students need. When Edward was hurt, his teacher could feel his pain as his own.

Of course, Dream Dancer did not feel it as much as Dao did. The Tianming Monk grimaced as he rubbed his arm where one of Edward's wounds had been too deep that one had definitely hurt.

That is why Dao was here now, he had known Dream Dancer would die without his help; that the Tianming Monk could not allow to happen!

Dao silently disappeared leaving Dream Dancer to sleep so that Edward could heal. Maybe they would be leaving tomorrow, but maybe not by the looks of the Tianming Monk's student.

Dao sighed in exasperation he understood Dream Dancer's need to grieve, but cutting oneself was a useless effort as far as the Tianming Monk was concerned. Of course, he would never tell Edward that.

Once inside the castle Dao paused at Dream Dancer's bedchamber. He stood at the door for a moment with his eyes closed feeling for any disruption in or around the castle. Feeling nothing the Tianming Monk glided silently to his rooms, it almost looked as if he never once touched the floor especially with his robes hanging down to his feet.

Dao entered his room; quickly the Tianming Monk went to his special carpet before sitting in the center. Instantly he was in a trance as he felt his Tianming Master touch his mind, so he gave his report.

It did not matter where in the world Dao was; as long as he had this carpet, the Tianming Monk could contact his master in his homeland.

When Dao opened his eyes, the Tianming Monk felt relief, as well as a slight lifting of his burden. Help was on its way; more time was all that was needed, but could he hold the evil at bay long enough.

Dao just hoped that he would get to see his son once more, but it was such a long perilous journey from the Tianming Monk's homeland.

Dao crawled into his bed humming his protection song before finally falling asleep as the Tianming Monk felt the castle come to life. He would know the instant anything entered or moved that was not supposed to be there.

CHAPTER THIRTEEN

Edward groaned painfully as he rolled over. He could hear the birds cheerily singing outside; Dream Dancer frowned at the blanket covering him, suddenly it all came back to him.

Edward pushed the blankets aside before looking down at his red scabbing wounds; he shook his head in anger at himself. If it had not been for Dao, Dream Dancer probably would have bled to death last night.

Edward sighed regretfully as he got painfully to his feet. Gathering the blankets, he left his tepee. Dream Dancer let himself out of the gate making sure to lock it tight before heading to the back entrance of his castle.

Edward opened the door, but stopped short when Dream Dancer saw Dao standing there waiting for him with a disapproving frown.

Without a word, Dao beckoned demandingly.

Edward obediently followed Dao upstairs feeling like a chastised kid as he went into his teacher's bedchamber. Dream Dancer sniffed appreciatively at the smell of the incense; every candle was lit of course.

A tub full of hot steaming water was waiting for Edward; he could see an oily film floating on top of the water. Dream Dancer knew that the water was laced with healing oil that Dao always put in his tub when he was hurt.

Edward knew words would not be tolerated right now, so he stripped silently as he crawled thankfully into the tub of hot water. He soaked for a good ten minutes before washing himself. Once finished, Dream

Dancer knelt as his teacher came over with a bucket of warm water to rinse off the excess soap as well as oil before handing the earl a towel.

Dao gestured silently at the foot of his bed where Edward's training outfit was laying waiting for him. The Tianming Monk walked over picking up the shirt he turned silently holding it out for this charge to put on before handing the earl his trousers; finally his teacher beckoning Dream Dancer to come kneel on his carpet.

The two knelt humming softly as they both went into a deep meditation.

Edward felt himself relax at the approval of his grandparents as they left this earth now able to rest in peace before Dream Dancer smiled serenely letting them go to the great hunting grounds of the Great Spirit.

Dao feeling Dream Dancer's changing mood from grief to acceptance stopped humming as the Tianming Monk opened his eyes. "Are we still leaving today or do you need a day to rest?"

Edward opened his green eyes before shaking his head at his teacher. "Nope we will be leaving today time is running short! Crystin, how is she doing?"

Dao smiled in reassurance as the Tianming Monk gestured placatingly. "Fine I helped her remember last night, so her memories have now returned. She also knows that she is pregnant with your twin's!"

Edward frowned troubled. "She does, how did Crystin take that news?"

Dao grinned as the Tianming Monk gestured cautiously. "Better than I thought she would do, actually; your countess has strength of character that is unknown in the nobility. I am sure she will make you a good wife someday. I think you should let Crystin sleep in her own room for now though, until the healing at least. You must resist any efforts the evil will take for you to make love to her again!"

Edward shook his head adamant. "No, Crystin will sleep with me that way I can keep an eye on her!"

Dao inclined his head giving in. He was not sure why it was so important for Crystin to sleep in the same bed, but the Tianming Monk could tell by Dream Dancer's tone that Edward would not budge on that issue.

Dao rose gracefully before waving Edward out. "Go, I will rouse the servants to pack up. Go see your countess, make sure you have something to eat as well Dream Dancer you need your strength."

Edward nodded as he rose before turning he walked out. He frowned angrily at himself thinking of his insistence that Crystin sleep with him. Dream Dancer was not sure why it was so important to him, but it was. A wife's place was beside her husband, not in another room!

Edward had never approved of that custom of the English nobility. He had been quite vocal on that subject many times over the years, so Dream Dancer could not back down now.

Without thinking Edward walked into his bedchamber still lost in thought; instantly Dream Dancer spun around with a grin at his new wife Crystin's angry outraged squeal of shock.

Crystin grabbed her bed robe that she had just removed; quickly the countess put it back on indignantly as she sputtered angrily. "You can at least knock before you walk in, Edward!"

Edward coughed into his hand trying to hide the laughter. "Sorry my dear, I will make sure to bang on the door next time."

Edward heard a giggle off to his right from Edith before Crystin's maid went over to the bed depositing the garments she held.

Crystin harrumphed not pacified by her husband's promise.

Crystin frowned in annoyance at her giggling maid before waving Edith out. "Be gone, come back in half an hour!"

Once Edith disappeared, Crystin sighed plaintively. "You can turn around now."

Edward turned slowly; Dream Dancer was careful to keep his expression of amusement hidden. "We will be leaving today; I will have a wardrobe made up for you when we arrive in Scotland."

Crystin opened her mouth to snap at Edward angrily that she had her own clothes, but closed it quickly with an audible snap as she remembered her pitiful wardrobe. Most of it was made up of her mother's old outdated clothing at her castle, the countess reluctantly nodded. "As you wish!"

Crystin eyed her new husband critically. Edward had several scabbing cuts on the back of his hands. The long shirt with the pants underneath hid the rest of him from view, but she knew that he would have more cuts on his legs and torso. The countess frowned in disapproval at his short hair. The earl definitely looked better with long hair. "Do you have scissors, Edward; I will fix your hair for you? You made quite a mess of it I must say!"

Edward shrugged. "No, but I have a razor you can just shave it all off for me it grows fast. If you would not mind I could use a shave as well."

Crystin nodded hesitantly never having shaved anyone before the countess was unsure where to begin.

Edward grinned at Crystin's hesitation, but did not change his mind. Dream Dancer walked to his vanity so that he could pour water in the basin as he wet his hair, as well as his face. Afterwards, he grabbed a towel that he used to shave with before draping it around his shoulders.

Edward proceeded to put soap on his face then wet hair before sitting down in a chair. Dream Dancer picked up the straight razor holding it out to Crystin in invitation. "Here you go my dear."

Edward watched Crystin approaching him hesitantly in the mirror; Dream Dancer wondered if this were such a good idea. He had decided that scissors were too impersonal if his wife had to shave him she would have to touch him, which would bring the countess into closer contact.

Edward hoped that it would help Crystin get use to him faster, oh well if he got a few nicks in the process so be it. Especially, if his plan worked by getting the countess to relax a little more around him. Dream Dancer snorted in sarcasm to himself quietly, it could not be any worse then what he had done to himself anyway last night, he was sure of that!

Crystin took the razor before taking the last step behind Edward. She hesitated at first, but suddenly an image of her parents surfaced. The countess had often watched as her mother shaved her father when she was little.

Crystin's father had lost most of his hair in his later years before the bandits killed them both. The countess' mother use to shave the few scraggly hairs on top of her father's head. She had always teased her husband that he looked hilarious with a dozen scraggly hairs on top of his bald pallet. When he went to court, he always wore a wig anyway.

Crystin shook off thoughts of her parents as the countess got down to business.

Crystin ran her fingers through her husbands hair pulling it all back so that the countess could get start shaving Edward from front to back. The earl had an awful lot of hair, so it was slow going at first.

Edward watched Crystin's intense face through the mirror on the vanity in pleasure; he was enjoying every changing expression on his wife's face. Dream Dancer could not help grinning slightly; the countess had the cute habit of biting her lower lip when concentrating.

Crystin finished the top before pushing Edward's head down so that she could get at the back. The countess noticed quite a few red angry scabs from her husband's attempt at scalping himself last night. She was careful to go around them not wanting them to start bleeding again.

Finally finished, Crystin took the towel from Edward's shoulders as she wiped all the excess soap off to make sure that she had gotten all the hair. Satisfied the countess walked around her husband before eyeing the dry soap on the earl's face.

Crystin tisked irritably as she bent over to reach the basin of water. It was on the right side of Edward, so she had to reach around her husband to dip the end of the towel into it so that the countess could wet his face again.

Edward held perfectly still not wanting to scare Crystin away as her breasts brushed against his arm, all that moved on Dream Dancer was his nose as he inhaled the rose scent his wife's maid had put in her bath water. The countess smelt heavenly, instantly he hardened in desire.

Crystin unaware of her affect on her new husband Edward stood back up as the countess went to work on getting the soap on the earl's face to soften so that it would lather back up.

Edward closed his eyes so that Crystin could not see the fire blazing in them not wanting Dream Dancer's throat slit by accident.

Crystin bent closer; she could not help inhaling the musky scent of Edward's soap it smelt so very good. The countess tried to place the scent, but could not. She had never smelt anything like it before.

A slight tingle distracted Crystin for a moment as she felt herself blushing in reaction. She had felt the exact same shiver in the woods last night while she had watched Edward paint his chest. The countess peaked at her husband, but the earl's eyes were thankfully closed.

Crystin exhaled in relief that Edward had not noticed her flushed face. By the time, she finished shaving her husband the countess' entire body was tingling, so quickly she began wiping the earl's face with the towel.

Before Crystin could move away, Edward opened his deep green inflamed eyes.

Crystin's breath caught in wonder at the passion flaring in her husband Edward's eyes.

They stared at each other intently as slowly their lips drew closer, ever closer, together. Unfortunately, their lips never got the chance to touch as the door behind them swung open unexpectedly.

Crystin jumped back guiltily as if caught with her hand in the cookie jar. The countess' hip hit the vanity hard; she would have fallen if Edward had not reached out to steady her.

Edith unaware of how close the two had come to kissing bustled in. "The castle is in an uproar my lady almost everyone is ready to go except you, let's get you dressed now!"

Edward got up out of the chair once he was sure that his wife Crystin would not fall; keeping his back to the two women so that they could not see his obvious desire. Dream Dancer went to the wardrobe before grabbing a change of clothes. "I will go change in Dao's room!"

Once the clothes were in front of Edward, Dream Dancer felt relief since he was finally able to turn. "I will send Dao down in half an hour to pack up our room."

A shaken Crystin still standing propped against the vanity could not help the grin that spread across her face at Edward's unseemly haste. She chuckled well that was definitely interesting; having never seen a man's obvious desire for her before she found that she actually liked the warm tingly feeling that she had experienced. The countess wondered if that feeling would come back again next time they were that close to one another.

Crystin only had one other incidence to go by; that was the perverted one of her cousin Ernest's, which caused her to shudder in angry distaste. Quickly the countess pushed that thought away not wanting to wreck the pleasurable feelings Edward had unwillingly unleashed in his new wife as she turned to Edith to get ready for their trip to Scotland.

*****

Edward leaned against the door of his room in relief; well that was definitely a narrow escape. Obviously having Crystin shave him again was out of the question for now anyway. Once his wife was healed, Dream Dancer would definitely ask her again to shave him though.

Edward grinned in delight his idea had been a complete success. The budding passion Dream Dancer had seen in Crystin's eyes made him hopeful for the future of their marriage.

With an obvious spring in Edward's step, Dream Dancer pushed away from his door before hurrying to Dao's room to change.

*****

Raven groaned as she carefully rolled to the edge of her bunk as she sat up; she put her head in her hands before running her fingers through her short-cropped hair. She could not help thinking how light her head felt now.

A cup of tea materialized in front of Raven as if by magic, so she looked up with a shaky smile at her husband Devon. "Thank you!"

Devon smiled sympathetically before sitting down on the bunk beside Raven. "Are you okay love?"

Raven nodded, but did not answer as she sipped her tea in appreciation.

Devon gave Raven a few minutes to relax before looking over at his wife enticingly. "I talked the crew into heating some sea water for you if you would like a bath. We set a place up on the deck with a barrier around it so that you could have some privacy. The captain wants you to come up on deck anyway so that the crew can see that you are okay, you gave them quite a fright last night. The wind is still howling pretty good out there, so you better leave your hat here."

Raven nodded as she got up to dress in her dirty clothes; she grabbed clean pants, shirt, and socks before finally underclothes. She slipped her boots on eagerly; a bath right now was just what she needed.

Raven turned to her husband Devon as she wrinkled her nose. "You as well as Trevor can both bath after me, you stink!"

Devon chuckled in delight as Golden Eagle bowed in humour. "As you wish, madam; I serve and obey!"

Raven snickered as she turned away. "Lead on my handsome servant."

Devon stooped his shoulders as he tucked his head down pretending to have a bad leg as he shuffled to the cabin door. Opening it with a flourish Golden Eagle bowed again as his left arm came out before sweeping it towards the door. "After you my beautiful lady!"

Raven laughed making sure to give Devon a slap as she passed by.

Devon chuckled as he followed Raven out before taking the lead, once up on the deck Golden Eagle took his wife's arm to help her over to the bathing area that the crew had set up for her. They had to fight the wind the whole way.

Devon pulled one of the barriers away so that Raven could slip inside. Golden Eagle closed it again as he went to go find his son.

Raven quickly stripped before crawling into the tub cautiously. As the salt water hit her scabbing sores, she hissed slightly in pain. Once she was fully submerged though the sting faded so she sat back with a sigh of pleasure as she soaked away her aches and pains.

*****

Complete chaos filled the courtyard as horses stamped, neighing impatiently eager to be off. Pages, stableman, as well as soldiers ran around yelling trying to make sure nothing as well as no one was forgotten.

Instant silence fell as the men bowed suddenly; quickly the women curtsied deeply as Queen Victoria followed closely by the Prince Consort Albert stepped out of the castle, they both paused on the landing.

Earl Summerset with his new bride was next as they walked behind the royal pair.

Prince Albert led Queen Victoria to her dun coloured dainty thoroughbred mare before helping his wife Victoria mount, afterwards Albert went to his carriage. He hated riding, so always preferred using the carriage unless it was for a hunt or his favourite sport polo.

Queen Victoria loved horses so always wanted to ride; she used a sidesaddle unless they were riding with the hounds, at that time Victoria would ride with a split skirt since she used a regular saddle.

Crystin had requested a split skirt as well as a regular saddle; when she saw mist standing there waiting for her, the countess gave a cry of pleasure as she rushed over for a hug of relief. "Oh my Mist, I am so glad that you are here with me. I have missed you so and was very worried!"

Mist nickered in greeting before nudging her mistress for a scratch when Crystin stepped back.

Edward waited patiently as Crystin greeted her horse, knowing how close they were Dream Dancer allowed his wife a moment; he had forgotten to mention to his wife that her mare was here safe. Finally, he helped the countess mount before vaulting up on his own horse.

It took a few more minutes as everyone else mounted or found carriages.

Edward rode to the front; he lifted his arm before dropping it so that the procession to Scotland would begin.

Crystin rode up beside Edward after a few minutes. "You are my godmother Queen Victoria's champion for the first Open Championship?"

Edward looked over at Crystin with a smile as he inclined his head with a little chuckle of amusement as Dream Dancer remembered last years near mishap. "Yes, believe me the prince was not happy about that! Albert tried to sabotage my clubs last year; luckily, I had an extra set. Do you like golfing?"

Crystin frowned sadly as the countess nodded wistfully. "I use to golf all the time. I was supposed to golf in the girl's amateur tournament the same year that my parents were killed, but it never happened. It was not long after my parents died that my guardian Ernest took my clubs away from me; he said that girls were not allowed to play golf anymore!"

Edward grimaced in sympathy as he gestured curiously. "How did your parents die? Queen Victoria had mentioned it when I first brought you here, but I can't remember now what Victoria had said."

Crystin sighed unhappily as the countess fidgeted with her reins. "Bandits killed them! Nobody seems to know why; they were on their way back from a golf tournament just on the other side of the border of Wales and England. They had no money or jewellery nothing was taken anyway, but all were killed even the driver as well as the two servants!"

Edward frowned thoughtfully; it was unusual for bandits to kill because once their victims died they had no chance of holding them up again. Most bandits in England and Wales kept to the same area so would end up hitting the same person two to three times in a single year. For the most part the thieves did not do it for the wealth; most did it to feed their starving families.

Of course, there were always exceptions to any rule; some did do it just for the pleasure. Others did it to get rich, since stealing money from the rich did not require them to put out as much effort as working for a living.

The fact that nothing was taken, made Edward very suspicious. Maybe, it was not a robbery that had went bad; who would want Crystin's parents killed though. Dream Dancer would have to talk to Queen Victoria about it later.

Edward looked over at Crystin before smiling enticingly wanting to get rid of the painful frown on his wife's face. "Well, I will get another set of golf clubs made for you so that you can play again if you want."

Crystin's face lit up in pleasure. "Really Edward, you would not mind if I played again? I would love that!"

The two lapsed into silence as a glimmer of hope for their marriage began to grow between them, now content they rode side by side.

*****

Raven walked into her room, she had gone to the galley earlier for a cup of coffee. She smiled over at Devon in approval. "Well, you look way better!"

Devon grinned in delight as he slicked back his wet hair with his fingers. He backed away from the door as he sat back down on the bunk once more. Golden Eagle was just about to leave their room to go find his wife when Raven had came in saving him a trip. "I feel better too."

Devon paused at a knock on the door before Golden Eagle got back up curiously. "Come on in!"

The pastor pushed the door open with his shoulder; Daniel walked in holding something white. "I brought you mom's white buffalo hide it needs to be given to Dream Dancer."

Raven frowned perplexed as she rushed over to hold open the door for the pastor; she had forgotten that he had mentioned it the other night. "Did your mother say why it was to go to my brother instead of our shaman? Or how Melissa knew that the hide was to come here instead of Montana?"

The pastor shrugged as he nodded his head, but Daniel was still confused by it. "Only that she had a dream of a white buffalo standing beside me on a ship; when it got to where it was going Dream Dancer was waiting to lead it away. Mom said that in the dream, she was standing on the docks with the hide draped around her at first, suddenly she was waving goodbye to the white buffalo. The hide was gone from around mom's shoulders, so that is why she did not come as well, she knew that only the hide was to go, not her."

Raven nodded puzzled it was very unusual for a spirit to leave its host until death, but Mell was still alive when they left. Very strange indeed, confused as well as still somewhat mystified by the fact that it was to go to Edward; Raven took the hide from the pastor. She turned putting it down at the end of her bed, she was sure Dream Dancer would have the answer for her when they got to England.

Raven turned back to the pastor. "We are just going for lunch would you like to join us, Captain Roberts sent out an invite for you as well."

The pastor nodded as they left for Captain Roberts' cabin.

*****

Queen Victoria rode up to Edward; Victoria pointed towards the ocean. "I want to go along the coast maybe we can find a ship to take us, it will be faster. We should have left a week ago if we had we could have rode instead. A ship will mean abandoning the carriages, but if we can be at the golf course tomorrow I would prefer that!"

Edward nodded already having thought of that, but grinned in praise giving Queen Victoria all the credit. "Good thinking your Majesty; if we cannot find a ship though we will have to find a train as soon as possible. At least it will get us there in four days instead of six by horse."

Queen Victoria frowned in distaste as Victoria waved in aggravation. "I know Edward, but I still prefer travelling by horse the loud stinky locomotive just does not appeal to me at all!"

Edward grinned in agreement. "My sentiments exactly your Highness; I would rather take a few extra days with the horses, but we do not have the time right now we dawdled way to long as it is."

Queen Victoria grimaced as she nodded reluctantly. "If we have to take the train we might arrive only a couple days before the tournament if we are lucky, not much time for you to practise."

Edward shrugged not worried in the least. "That's okay a couple days to practise will be enough."

Edward pointed northwest. "There should be a ship at Victoria Pier by now I would think. They will have to be unloaded then loaded again with cargo, so hopefully they will be just about ready to sail when we get there."

Edward looked behind him searching for his page; seeing Craig holding his banner Dream Dancer waved for him to come over to him. "Craig we need a ship, so I want you to go to Victoria Pier along the north coast just past Bae Colwyn to see if there is one there yet. If they are ready to sail make sure to stop them, but if they are still loading just keep an eye on them. Make sure you get Queen Victoria's page on your way so that you have both banners with you, but do not show them unless you have too. Some captains hate having women on their ship's even a queen!"

Craig nodded as he turned his horse away looking for Queen Victoria's page.

A few minutes later, Edward nodded satisfied as the two boys raced away with both banners tied down inconspicuously. Dream Dancer turned back to Queen Victoria. "We should make it to Victoria Pier just after lunch if we do not stop; high tide is around three o'clock."

Queen Victoria nodded in satisfaction as Victoria fell back to her husband Albert's carriage to let the prince know.

*****

Raven stood at the stern with her husband, Captain Roberts, as well as her son Trevor talking to the captain about his beautiful ship. She was listening with half her attention on her son Little Cub, not interested in spars or mainmasts, but tried to be polite. It was just nice to be outside without the wind howling constantly. Much to everyones surprise, it had almost quit completely about an hour ago.

Raven watched Trevor fidget hopping from one foot to the other impatient to be off to see his friends. She made Little Cub wait though trying to teach her son patience.

Captain Roberts paused for breath so Raven smiled at him before lifting her hand to halt him in apology. "One moment captain, please!"

Raven turned to Trevor in irritation. "Okay Little Cub you can go. I want you to stay out of the way though; be careful as well the wind has calmed down a lot, but it is still pretty gusty at times."

Trevor nodded elated as he took off before his mother Raven could change her mind, Little Cub headed to the stern looking for his new friend.

Raven turned back to Captain Roberts. "Sorry about that please continue."

Captain Roberts smiled before rubbing his hands together in anticipation. "Well my ship the Princess was only built two years ago, so I am hoping to beat Lightning's record of thirteen and three quarter days from Boston to England. If this wind keeps up, we should make it in twelve days."

Again, Raven listened with half an ear to Captain Roberts. She just could not concentrate today something was distracting her; all of a sudden, it got worse. She just could not figure out what it was.

Raven sighed irritably at herself as an annoying irritation itch suddenly started on the back of her neck niggling at her insistently. It almost felt like the short hairs on the back of her neck were standing straight up, but there was no reason for that. It had to be the shorter hair that was bothering her, Raven could not help thinking; she was just not use to it yet!

*****

Edward sighed in relief as Dream Dancer saw the majestic spires of a ship docked at Victoria Pier; they had made it in time.

The two boys waiting came galloping up to Edward.

Craig grinned in relief to see them here at last. "The Scottish Maid she is called they are almost done loading though."

Edward nodded pleased. "Okay, unfurl your banners before we go talk to the ship's captain."

Edward turned to Queen Victoria's captain of the guard. "Abandon the carriages while I am gone; I want you to get the horses ready to be load also please."

The captain of the guard nodded before turning away.

Edward with the two boys following went to talk to the captain of the ship. It took about two hours to get everyone, as well as all the horses on board the ship. They built a makeshift corral on deck for the horses instead of stowing them below decks since it was only a four-hour journey.

Finally, underway Edward sighed in relief as he went to stand with the captain. The Prince Consort Albert was there already with Queen Victoria, as well as his wife Crystin, so Dream Dancer joined them at the wheelhouse.

Dao stayed with the trunks since the Tianming Monk did not trust anyone near his precious carpet or sword.

*****

Raven grimaced in aggravation as she rubbed the back of her neck once again. They had followed Captain Roberts from stern to bow listening as he explained the workings of his ship.

It had taken them just over an hour to get the inspection done, the whole time Raven had fought this sense of unease. She was beginning to wonder what her brother Edward was doing, maybe it had something to do with Dream Dancer!

All of a sudden, Raven stopped dead in her tracks not moving a muscle; she paused only for a second before turning she sprinted towards the mainmast without a word to anyone, not even her husband Devon.

Devon frowned perplexed as Raven took off without a peep being spoken. Golden Eagle watched his wife run wondering what that was all about; suddenly he heard a scream of fear.

"NI-GO-I!"

Devon looked up in dread for a split second when he heard his son Trevor screaming out for his mother in Cheyenne. Instantly Golden Eagle was sprinting towards the mainmast as well as Trevor dangled upside down hooked by his right foot in the rigging way up there.

CHAPTER FOURTEEN

Raven reached the mainmast, not even hesitating she jumped for the ratlines. She scurried up the rope ladder as fast as she could possibly go, praying for all she was worth.

Of course, Trevor could not have stayed closer to the deck. No, Little Cub had to be up on the tallest mast the second sail from the top, which Raven had just learned was called the main upper topgallant sail.

The sail above that was the main royal with the one below being the main lower topgallant sail. It took Raven no time to pass the main course bottom sail, the main lower topsail before finally the main upper topsail.

Now that Raven was at the main lower topgallant sail, she started looking frantically for a way to get to her son Trevor. She eyed the yard speculatively if she negotiated here she could get below Little Cub, which would put her in a position to reach his hands.

Instantly Raven discarded that thought, she would not be able to untangle Trevor that way. Plus, realistically she would still be too far away to reach his hands. If his foot slipped out, Little Cub would take both of them to the decks below.

Raven eyed the sail next, speculatively; she could jump up grabbing a hold of the rope on the main upper topgallant sail above her. Captain Roberts had described the lines running down the sails as buntlines. The ones at the very end of the sail were called clewlines.

Raven could climb up the buntline, which would bring her next to her son Trevor. The problem with that is she would only have one hand to do anything with so she would not be able to cut Little Cub's foot free from there!

Suddenly the wind gusted, so the sail billowed out. As the wind filled the sail to capacity, it hid Trevor from Raven's view. She frowned grimly, nope that definitely would not work.

Trevor had used the shallow footrope that the sailors used to cross the yard of the main upper topgallant before trying to step down to the Flemish horse. It was a smaller deeper rope almost at the end of the yard that the sailors used so that they were low enough to work on the lines at each end of the yard.

The problem was Trevor with his slightly shorter legs, being young as well as always in too much of a hurry, had not been paying attention to what he was doing. As Little Cub tried to step down, he had miscalculated so his foot had tangled in both lines right where the two lines crossed each other.

When Trevor tried to untangle himself, he had fallen so now Little Cub was hanging upside down between the main upper and lower topgallant close to the very end of the yard.

Unfortunately, Raven would not be able to use the footrope that ran from one end of the yard to the other or Trevor's foot could come loose before she got to him; or it would tighten the ropes wrapped around Little Cub's foot cutting off all circulation. If that happened he could loose his foot or worse his whole leg, depending on how long it took Raven to free him.

Getting an idea, Raven scurried up to the main upper topgallant yard, which set her above Trevor. She pulled off both boots as well as her socks, hoping that her bare feet would give her a stable purchase.

Raven glanced down seeing nobody she threw her boots slightly so that they would land on the captain's main deck, which they called the quarterdeck.

Even though it seemed to Raven as if it was taking her forever to come to any conclusion on how to get to Trevor, it had only taken her precious seconds to make a final decision.

Devon was still only half way up the ratlines as Golden Eagle tried to reach them, as were two other sailors. Raven sighed in relief she would have time before the men got to where she wanted them.

Raven waited until the wind died down then holding the yard with two hands she pulled herself onto it. She squatted there for a moment to make sure that she was balanced properly before standing up.

Precariously Raven made her way across the yard slowly one foot in front of the other with both arms out for balance. She had to negotiate around the mast pole, which gave her some support for a few minutes as the wind gusted before settling down once more. The yard luckily was bigger compared to a tightrope that the people in the circus used, but they had years of training; she did not!

Carefully now past the mast pole Raven made her way across, all the while praying that the wind would not gust again till she got to where she was going, which was on the other side of the dangling Trevor. If it did, the yard that was not actually stationary could move throwing her off balance causing her to fall to the decks below.

Luck was with Raven, she thanked the Lord for all the years of training to be a warrior that her Uncle Black Hawk had put her through in her lifetime.

Carefully Raven knelt; she turned herself around so that she was facing the ratlines that she had just left. She sat straddling the yard for a moment making sure that she could lock her ankles together underneath the yard to keep her in place even when the wind gusted before letting go with her hands.

Finally, Raven pulled out her hunting knife from her belt pouch in preparation.

Raven looked over at the ratlines; she saw her husband Devon where she wanted him so she called out to stop him. “Golden Eagle, do not go any further! Get as close to this end of the ladder as you can, when I get a hold of Trevor I will swing Little Cub over to you!”

Two sailors spaced themselves out below Devon so that if he missed at least one of them would be in a position to try catching Trevor.

Devon nodded as he went as close to the edge as he could go before putting his right foot through the loop in the ladder to hook his foot in place. Now Golden Eagle was straddling the ladder, this way he would be able to lean out past the ratlines in order to reach out further for Trevor, it also freed up both hands. "Okay, but for God's sakes Raven, be careful!"

Raven waited until Devon was looking at her so that Golden Eagle would see her nod of reassurance before looking down at Trevor.

Raven smiled calmly down, even though she was anything but, trying to keep Trevor from seeing just how scared she really was. "Little Cub, I am going to flip myself so that I am hanging upside down; I want you to reach up to take my left hand. Pull yourself up as soon as you have a good grip that way you can grab my sleeve with your other hand. Afterwards, I want you to hold on as tight as you can. Once I cut your foot loose, your legs are going to drop down so that you will be hanging by your hands. Once I get a good grip, I am going to swing you to your father; he will grab you and help you down. Can you do that for me sweetheart?"

Trevor looked up at his mother Raven trustingly as Little Cub nodded in agreement. "Okay!"

Raven's smile widened proudly at her calm son glad Trevor was not the type to panic before putting her knife in her mouth. Carefully she flipped herself over so that she was hanging down towards the deck below.

Raven did not release her hold on the yard with her hands until she did one final check to make sure that her ankles were locked together tightly enough so that they would not let go. She hoped anyway, once satisfied she let go of the yard so that she was hanging upside down.

Raven's head was now just below her son's foot just passed Trevor's ankle; she extended her left hand down as far as she could reach so that Little Cub did not have too far to grasp it.

Trevor latched onto Raven's hand; he pulled himself up slightly so that he could grasp her shirtsleeve in a tight fist with his other hand. Little Cub held on as tight as he possibly could manage as his mother had instructed him to do.

Raven took her knife out of her mouth with her free hand. "Are you ready?"

Trevor nodded vigorously. "Yes!"

As fast as Raven could manage, she sliced at the ropes; luckily, neither was that thick so it only took her a minute to free Trevor. She grunted slightly in effort as her son's legs dropped down jerking her slightly as her arm muscles strained against Little Cub's weight keeping him in position.

Hoping nobody was directly below them; Raven quickly dropped the knife so that she could take the hand Trevor had clenched in her shirt before her arm came completely out of its socket.

Once Raven took Trevor's other hand his weight became more evenly distributed giving her arm some relief. "Okay Little Cub, hold on tightly now; swing your legs so that you can help me get enough momentum to throw you over to your father!"

After several tries, Trevor was finally swinging at a good speed. Raven yelled out in warning. "I am going to drop your right hand this time. I want you to reach out for your father; he will catch you when I let your left hand go!"

Trevor obediently let go of Raven's right hand, but before she let go of his left one Little Cub looked up mouthing anxiously. "I love you!"

Raven smiled in reassurance as she swung Trevor as hard as she could manage, praying she released her son Little Cub.

*****

Edward could not help but chuckled at Crystin question; the earl opened his mouth to tease his wife, but all that came out of Dream Dancer was an eerie screech of fear in his native language.

"NI-GO-I!"

Immediately with no hesitation or explanation at all Edward turned jumping over the five stairs leading from the quarterdeck, where the captain was steering them through the channel, to the main deck below.

Edward landed in a crouch before jumping up he raced as fast as he could to the mainmast, Dream Dancer dropped to his knees in front of it lifting his hands up skywards pleadingly.

Instantly Dream Dancer came to the surface as Edward's eyes turned black, blacker than they had ever been before totally drowning out the green.

Chanted in Cheyenne, Dream Dancer watched the scene across the ocean happening in horrified dread at the same instant it was happening.

*****

Dao pushed through the crowd gathering around Edward angrily. The Tianming Monk turned to face the curious group before pointing imperiously in command brooking no disobedience. "GO NOW!"

Everyone stepped back from the furious Oriental; never had anyone seen Dao take such command before now! They backed away even further because of his daunting presents as the Tianming Monk drew himself up further overshadow them.

It even seemed to everyone watching that Dao grew in stature becoming so large that the Tianming Monk completely blocked the wailing Earl Summerset from their curious view.

*****

Dream Dancer still with his arms up imploringly tried to help his sister as he chanted to the Great Spirit beseechingly. Edward watched fearfully as Raven negotiated the yard; finally, she was hanging upside down so that she could grab his nephew Trevor.

Dream Dancer knew that Raven's legs were not going to hold for another desperate rotation. Especially, since Edward's nephew Trevor had dislodged his mother slightly when Little Cub's legs had dropped down.

Quickly Dream Dancer sent Edward's spirit flying out giving Raven the added strength she needed to throw Trevor at her husband Devon.

Suddenly they were both falling!

*****

Devon grunted in shocked surprise as Trevor slammed into him harder than Golden Eagle figured was possible as they both almost toppled backwards. The only thing that saved them was his leg hooked in the ratlines.

There was just no way, that Devon's wife would have enough power to throw his son that hard; as strong as Golden Eagle knew Raven was from her many years of training to be a Cheyenne warrior.

Devon righted them both, before looking over frantically at a squeal of stunned disbelief, but Raven was gone. Golden Eagle screamed his wife's name in horrified dread. "RAVEN!"

*****

Dream Dancer still chanting grabbed his left arm as he doubled up in pained shock as he felt himself falling with his sister, Raven. Never had Edward ever had such a powerful vision before or been present as the event was happening.

Usually Dream Dancer dreamt about something happening before or after, but never in all these years had Edward actually participated in an event.

Although, Dream Dancer did have a brief spell when he was looking for Crystin that said they were connected somehow. Edward had not actually gone to where his wife was at to help her get away from her evil cousin.

Dream Dancer had just felt a little of what Crystin was feeling, as his wife tried to escape her cousin, so this was very different.

Not only could Dream Dancer feel everything his sister Raven was feeling, but he was also participating as it happened. Edward could not seem to stop this phenomenon as they both fell towards the deck below, headfirst!

Dream Dancer could not help thinking frantically that if Raven hit the deck below killing herself, would Edward also die with her!

*****

Raven felt her brother, Dream Dancer with her as she gave one more tremendous heave before letting Trevor go. As she released her son Little Cub, her ankles unlocked; causing her to fall head first down the main upper topgallant sail.

Raven saw the yard of the lower topgallant sail getting closer, but she was too far away to grab it as she dropped unexpectedly to the main lower topgallant sail with a slight scream of surprise.

Suddenly the wind gusted, so the sail billowed out further keeping her from free falling. Raven was now sliding down the sail still head first with her belly scraping against the sail.

Raven made a grab for one of the buntlines that were spaced so many feet apart. She managed to get a hold of it, which turned out not to be a good thing after all.

Unexpectedly Raven's left arm was wrenched out of the socket causing her to scream out in excruciating pain. Since Trevor had already strained her arm when Little Cub's feet had dropped, it did not take much to pop it out of the joint completely making it even worse.

The pain was so agonizingly painful that Raven could not keep a hold of the rope. Involuntarily her hand, which she could not feel anymore, released the buntline as she shrieked again. Before she let go though, her weight pulled on the line hard enough that it flattened the sail pulling her in as it slowed her momentum down.

The only good thing to come out of grabbing that buntline was that it flipped Raven around completely. She was still falling, but feet first now as her belly continued scraping on the sail.

Raven was now closer to the yard of the upper topsail, but was starting to gain more speed as she rushed towards it. She knew that she was going to hit it, so she extended her right arm hoping to catch it. She did managed to get a hold of it, but the air was knocked out of her lungs as she hit way too hard.

The wind gusted again so that the sails filled; it almost caused Raven to lose the precarious hold she had on the yard. Desperately she tried to hold on, but the pain of hitting the yard at that speed almost made her black out.

With Raven's left arm hanging limply by her side, she was not sure how long she could hold on as she struggled for breath knowing that she had at least cracked a rib or two. Already she could feel herself slipping.

Raven knew the footrope was close, so she tried to find it with her barefoot as the wind died down. She strained knowing it was there, but suddenly she was falling once again.

The sail billowed out suddenly as Raven continued her downward momentum feet first. She tried to find something to grab onto, but it was useless. She tried to dig her fingers on her right hand into the fabric of the main upper topsail, but the sail was stretched too tight.

Raven was now too far away from any of the buntlines for them to be of any help to her. She slid down the sail gaining more speed, as the main lower topsail yard got ever closer.

*****

Dream Dancer was getting desperate as he felt Raven fall again; Edward had slumped down onto his knees in relief when she had gotten a hold of that yard. Suddenly he jumped back to his feet again imploring the Great Spirit to keep the sails full of wind, as his sister's precarious hold on the yard was lost.

As long as Raven was sliding down the sail, it was keeping her downward momentum slowed. Even though it did not seem like it, if his sister was free falling there was no way that she would have a chance of surviving a fall from that height.

Dream Dancer was also very aware of the fact that if Raven lost the sail now she would hit the lower topsail yard. Edward knew that if she did hit it, just by the way that she was positioned, she would not be so lucky this time.

Dream Dancer watched in dread as Raven got closer to the end of the upper topsail. Thankfully, she dropped to the lower topsail just missing the yard, which caused Edward to sigh in relief even though his sister was not out of danger yet!

Dream Dancer could see a rope on Raven's right, when she had dropped to the next sail it had moved her over enough that now she should be able to reach it. Edward extended his right arm; he wiggled his fingers willing his sister to reach out for the buntline.

*****

Raven screeched in fright as she dropped form the main upper topsail to the lower one just managing to miss the yard, but the drop caused her to gain some momentum again.

Desperately Raven tried to slow herself down, but she could not find anything to hold onto. She tried curling her legs slightly to dig her toes into the sail, but all that did was burn her feet; she was falling way too fast for that to help her any.

Suddenly Raven heard a voice screaming in her head as Dream Dancer tried to tell her something important. Nodding that she understood she reached her right arm over trying to find the buntline that her brother Edward was referring to, but that she could not see.

Finally finding it, Raven managed to get a hold of it just as she reached the end of the lower topsail. As she grasped it her momentum stopped suddenly it flipped her so that now her back was against the sail, so she was facing outward with her left arm still hanging limply.

Raven hanging by her right hand grimaced in pain as she slowly slipped down the line. The moisture on her palm was making it almost impossible to keep a hold of it; the rope was leaving deep burns in her palm as she slipped down another inch.

Raven was now hanging between the main lower topsail as well as the main course sail. She could see the yard below her, facing this way if she hit that yard she would be in real trouble.

Raven could also see the deck below; thankfully, it was getting closer, but it was still not close enough. She quickly calculated the risks of dropping to the next sail wondering if it were possible for her to get a hold of the buntline on the main course sail.

Unexpectedly the wind died causing the sail to go completely limp abruptly.

Immediately it yanked Raven backwards, she screamed in painful shock as she felt her other shoulder wrench from the socket as her hand let go of the buntline involuntarily.

Raven knew no more as her head hit the yard on the way down knocking her out cold!

Now Raven was free falling to the deck below!

*****

Dream Dancer screeched in excruciating alarm as he tried to grab his right shoulder, but his left arm was useless. Edward's hand was burning as well and he was having a hard time drawing in a breath.

Dream Dancer with both arms hanging limply staggered in bewilderment; suddenly he felt an explosion in his head before Edward unexpectedly dropped like a rock to the deck of the ship, unmoving!

CHAPTER FIFTEEN

Devon quickly passed Trevor down to the sailor below before untangling himself as he scurried down the ratline as fast as he could go. Golden Eagle jumped down the last few feet as he searched the sky desperately for his wife Raven, but could not see her anywhere.

The wind died suddenly giving Devon a glimpse of her hanging by one arm from the yard of the main upper topsail.

Captain Roberts rushed up behind Devon looking, so Golden Eagle pointed up at Raven as he turned frantically to the captain. "She is not going to be able to hold out for long!"

Captain Roberts nodded in agreement; the captain turned to his second in command, he gestured at the deck. "James, I want you to go below to get that old sail we kept. I want you to gather the crew too, HURRY now!"

James raced away immediately already knowing what the captain had planned.

Captain Roberts turned back quickly as he heard Devon inhale in horror. They both watched helplessly as Raven fell again.

Suddenly the wind gusted filling the sails to full capacity so that they lost sight of Raven once again. Twice more they caught quick glimpses of her as the sail deflated slightly almost seeming to be teasing them before filling once again hiding her from their view.

Occasionally Devon would cringe in fear as a squeal or scream sounded from above; helplessly Golden Eagle stood there unable to do anything to help Raven. Never in all their years together did the Englishman ever feel this powerless.

The pastor rushed up to Devon in concern. "Is there anything I can do to help?"

Devon turned to the Baptist Pastor with an anguished expression. He was just about to shake his head no when Golden Eagle saw Trevor standing by the ratlines with tears of fear streaming down his son's face.

Devon frowned grimly, Trevor did not need to see Raven fall to her death after saving Little Cub's life, so Golden Eagle needed to get his son away from here.

Devon looked at the pastor earnestly as Golden Eagle pointed at Trevor before nodding. "Please take my son to your cabin Pastor; I do not want him present if the worst should happen. I would also appreciate it Daniel if you would pray for my wife Raven to be spared!"

The pastor nodded in agreement before Daniel turned away taking a reluctant Trevor with him.

James finally rushed up with twenty crewmembers; they unfurled the sail spreading out. He turned to Captain Roberts in apprehension. "I cannot see her, where should we stand?"

Captain Roberts calculated as quickly as he could manage before pointing. "If Raven follows the sail it should be right about there."

The twenty crewmembers spaced themselves out further as they pulled the sail tighter between them. Everyone looked up waiting, but the minutes ticked by with nothing happening.

Devon frantically searching raced towards the mast, he stared upwards grimly. Finally, Golden Eagle could see feet dangling between the main lower topsail as well as the main course sail.

Captain Roberts joined Devon a minute later looking up as well. Again, the captain judged the distance; he raised his arm to send the men out a little further, but suddenly he was frantically waving for his men to come towards him as the wind died unexpectedly.

Devon heard Raven let out a blood-curdling scream of pain as the sails flattened abruptly as the wind completely disappeared without warning. Golden Eagle watched horrified as his wife was pulled backwards away from the sail that the crewmembers were holding out to catch her.

Everything was happening in slow motion suddenly it seemed to Devon as the crew members tried to get underneath Raven in time.

They were not going to make it!

*****

Dao turned to Dream Dancer in apprehension as he heard his student collapse behind him with a loud thump as Edward dropped to the deck out cold. The Tianming Monk rushed over to kneel beside the earl.

Queen Victoria grabbed Crystin's hand as she pushed through the crowd pulling her goddaughter with her.

The crowd opened instantly to let Queen Victoria through.

Queen Victoria turned them around before putting herself, as well as Crystin between Edward and the crowd of people as she pointed imperiously. "GO!"

Immediately the men bowed as the women curtsied before dispersing.

Queen Victoria satisfied turned pulling Crystin over to Edward as they both knelt down on the earl's left side.

Dao looked over at Queen Victoria as the Tianming Monk shrugged in confusion. "Edward is out cold; I am not sure what that was all about!"

Edward groaned as he sat up painfully before putting his head in his hands; Dream Dancer had an excruciating headache, both his arms felt as if they had been ripped right out of their sockets as well. The right one was the worse off if that were possible.

Dao moved in front of Dream Dancer so that nobody else could see him talking. "Raven?"

Edward nodded painfully.

Dao looked over at Crystin, the Tianming Monk pointed towards the quarterdeck where the captain was standing. "Can you go ask the captain where you can get some hot tea please?"

Crystin jumped up immediately as the countess hurried away.

Dao frowned grimly as the Tianming Monk looked back at Dream Dancer hopefully. "Do you know if Raven is okay?"

Edward groaned in agony as Dream Dancer shrugged grimly. "I don't know all I can feel is this blasted headache!"

Dao nodded in sympathy as the Tianming Monk got up. “Be right back!”

Dao trotted over to his trunk; he unlocked it before rummaging inside until he found his herb pouch. The Tianming Monk pulled it out then re-locked the trunk. He turned to go back to Dream Dancer.

Crystin was just coming back as the countess held out a glass to Dao. “There is no tea only water.”

Dao nodded it would have to do; the Tianming Monk knelt as he added some herbs to the water before giving it to Dream Dancer. “Drink it all!”

Edward took the cup; he wrinkled his nose at the foul smell before downing it as quickly as he possibly could. Dream Dancer shuddered at the awful taste as he closed his eyes waiting.

Edward went back to rocking himself humming low and easy willing the headache to disappear so that he could find out if Raven was okay. Dream Dancer was sure his sister was not dead because he knew that he would have died with her.

How badly Raven was hurt was another matter though, just because Edward’s sister was not dead now did not mean that she could not die later.

*****

Raven screamed painfully as she tried to sit up as the ship’s surgeon popped her left arm back into its socket, but Devon held her down tight. Mercifully, she passed out once more.

Devon looked down at Raven in sympathy knowing that they still had one more shoulder to put in place and it was the worst one.

Devon still could not believe that the sailors had gotten to Raven in time, but it had been a close call. She had fallen on the very edge of the sail before sliding down to the center, a few inches over she would have hit the deck instead. From that height, his wife probably would not have died. She would have broken almost every bone in her body though Golden Eagle was sure.

As it was until Raven woke, they would not know the full extent of her injuries. The fact that both her arms were right out of the sockets was obvious, as was the rope burns on her hands, so they both could be treated immediately.

Raven also had a large lump on the back of her head that was a bit of a concern.

To find out if there were any other injuries though they would have to wait until Raven was awake.

Devon watched the doctor closely as he rotated Raven's arm feeling around the top of her shoulder before moving his hand underneath. Satisfied that he had set it properly, he laid her arm back on the bed.

The two men turned Raven the other way making sure that both her arms were supported before Devon laid on her once again holding his wife down.

Devon watched the doctor closely as he inspected her shoulder, looking for the best angle in order to pop it back into place. The doctor did not look at all sure of himself, which worried Golden Eagle immensely.

The doctor frowned grimly as he looked at Devon in deep concern. "This arm is in bad shape not only did Raven pop this one out of joint, but I think every muscle and tendon was ripped or stretched. It is swollen pretty badly already, so it is going to take a lot of manipulating to get it right. I cannot guarantee either that Raven will have full use of it again, but I will do my best. Make sure she does not move I need her to be as still as possible!"

Devon scowled in apprehension, but he really had no choice. He had to rely on the doctor there was no one else who could help Raven. Finally, Golden Eagle nodded for the doctor to begin; they could not leave it as it was. If they did, his wife would never be able to use it again.

The doctor re-probed the arm for a bit until satisfied with what he found he took a hold of Raven's hand before grabbing a hold of her upper arm. He braced himself against the bunk with both feet as he carefully pulled rotating her arm trying to get it to settle back into her socket.

Raven let out a blood-curdling scream of agony as she tried to get away from the pain.

Devon knowing how strong Raven was covered her entire body with his; still it took his full strength, as well as Golden Eagle's big body, to keep his wife in place.

The doctor sweat pouring down his face could not get the arm back into the socket. He was getting desperate if he could not get it in soon he would have to give up causing Raven to lose total use of her right arm as well as her hand.

*****

Edward his headache almost gone looked up as he smiled at Dao in reassurance, Dream Dancer could now feel that his sister was alive at least.

Unexpectedly Edward screamed as Dream Dancer grabbed his right shoulder, doubling up in painful shock. Quickly he got to his knees as he began chanting rocking back and forth.

Edward hurriedly released Dream Dancer once again as he flew to the ship Raven was on before going down to his sister's familiar bunk.

Taking in the scene with a quick glance, Dream Dancer did something he had never done or even attempted to do before as his spirit flew into the doctor! There was only a brief struggle as Edward blocked the doctor's conscious mind.

*****

Devon was strained against the thrashing Raven trying desperately to keep her still. Golden Eagle could tell by the doctor's grim sweat encrusted face that he was not making any headway at all.

Devon opened his mouth to scream at the doctor to stop unable to handle any more, but Golden Eagle snapped it shut in stunned amazement as all of a sudden the doctor started chanting in Cheyenne.

Devon watched in astonishment as the doctor's eyes turned black before Golden Eagle felt Dream Dancer's presence.

*****

With one tremendous pull, Dream Dancer felt as well as heard a satisfying pop as Raven's arm settled back into its socket. Quickly knowing he did not have much time, Edward released his healing energy into his sister repairing as much of the damage as he could.

Dream Dancer was not quite finished what he was doing though, when suddenly Edward was ripped away from the doctor.

*****

The doctor released Raven's arm as he fell backwards, stunned. He was not exactly sure what had happened to him. He shook his head to clear it before scooting back over to check his patient's arm.

The doctor checked out Raven's shoulder in relief as he looked over at Devon with a huge smile of satisfaction. "Well I am not sure exactly what I did, but whatever it was it worked. The swelling is already almost all gone so now we just need to wait to see what happens. That lump on the back of her head concerns me though it might take some time until she comes around."

Devon nodded as he got off his wife thanking God for Dream Dancer's help. Golden Eagle knew that it was Edward; it was not the first time he had felt his brother-in-law's healing presence, so was not concerned about the lump at all.

*****

Dream Dancer once again collapsed on the ship's deck out cold.

Dao frowned in unease whatever was going on did not sound good at all as the Tianming Monk began to fret. Something was obviously very wrong with Raven.

Dao looked over at Crystin before handing the countess the empty glass. "You better get me some more water as well as a wet cloth, please!"

Crystin jumped up immediately very glad to have something to do as she left, it did not take her as long since she now knew where to go. She did not understand any of this, her new husband Edward was beginning to scare her badly. The countess rushed back before handing Dao the cloth as well as the water.

Dao accepted them both before putting the cloth on Dream Dancer's forehead hoping it would wake him up, but it did not. He wiped the sweat off Edward's face; the Tianming Monk was starting to get apprehensive now.

Dao sat back wondering if he should unpack his carpet, but if he did, he would have to get the sailors to move Dream Dancer to a room. There was no way that the Tianming Monk would be able to use his carpet out here with everyone still standing around gawking.

Dao was just turning away to get a couple of sailors when thankfully the Tianming Monk turned back at a groan from Dream Dancer.

Edward sat up slowly; he rotated both arms experimentally, but felt no pain. Next, Dream Dancer moved his head back and forth as well as up and down, but his headache was gone. So too was the pressure in his chest.

Edward sighed in relief as he gratefully accepted the water that Dao handed him. He sipped at it appreciatively; Dream Dancer's throat was sore from chanting for well over two hours.

It took Edward the rest of the trip to Scotland to explain what had happened to Dream Dancer to his three very concerned friends; mercifully, the rest of the journey was without incident.

*****

Devon sat diligently by Raven's bed with his hand in his wife's right one. His head dropped to his chest for the third time; Golden Eagle was finding it almost impossible to stay awake now that everyone was okay. It had taken quite a while before the initial furrow had died down.

Devon had to deal with a steady stream of visitors until about an hour ago, now Golden Eagle was exhausted both physically as well as mentally.

Trevor had been the hardest one to deal with wanting to stay with his mother Raven.

Devon had finally taken Trevor to bed earlier before tucking him in with a promise that if his mother needed anything Little Cub would be the first one to know.

Devon was just dozing off again when Golden Eagle felt his hand being squeezed.

Instantly Devon was wide-awake as he scooted to the end of his chair so that he could lean against the bed. Golden Eagle ran the fingers of his free hand through Raven's short-cropped hair soothingly as his wife turned to him.

Raven licked her dry lips. "Little Cub?"

Devon smiled reassuringly as he chuckled shrewdly. Golden Eagle had known that would be Raven's first question. "Trevor is fine love!"

Devon reached over for a glass of water that he had waiting. He helped Raven sit up slightly so that she could drink it. Golden Eagle sat back after putting the glass down before placing his hand back in his wife's right hand again when she settled back. "Can you squeeze my hand again?"

Raven nodded as she squeezed her husband Devon's hand hard.

Devon winced playfully before teasing. "I did not mean quite that hard!"

Raven giggled for a moment before sobering as she remembered her ordeal. "Dream Dancer was here?"

Devon grinned in agreement before nodding. "Yes Dream Dancer was here, he has gotten quite powerful since he left Montana. Edward took over the doctor to help him set your right arm properly since the doctor could not do it on his own. The doctor was quite baffled by how he had managed to put it back into place; he does not know of course that he had your brother's help."

Raven frowned as she grimaced thoughtfully. "I know what you mean I could feel the power radiating out of Dream Dancer since he was with me the whole time; Edward helped me get Trevor to you before he fell with me. It was because of my brother's help that I found the buntline;

it stopped me from falling so far. I do not remember anything after blacking out."

The two decided to exchange stories first before Devon crawled into bed with Raven so that he could hold her close. Even when sleeping, Golden Eagle could barely stand to have her go any further than arms length away.

CHAPTER SIXTEEN

The day of the tournament was unseasonably warm for the middle of October. There was barely a cloud in the sky with only a light breeze. They were on the second of three rounds.

Edward was leading the pack with an unheard of forty-five over fourteen holes very hard to do on such a grueling course. Dream Dancer had a five-stroke lead on Willie Park Sr. who was playing exceptionally well; Willie was the earl's only real competition today.

There were twelve holes per round, for a total of thirty-six holes, with ten players in total. They were on the third hole of the second round.

Edward was to tee off next, suddenly the hairs on his arms stood straight up as a tingle of warning coursed down his spine. He looked up at the cloudless blue sky with a frown of irritability; a storm was coming, Dream Dancer could feel it; it was moving in fast too.

Suddenly without warning Edward's stomach clenched tight; he heaved as if he were about to be sick, but it only lasted a few seconds before disappearing. Dream Dancer had felt a little nauseated all day, but this was the first time that he had almost gotten sick from it.

Edward looked around perplexed not sure what that was about at all. Dream Dancer looked over at Dao, who was standing with Crystin holding her arm in support. The countess was holding her stomach as if she too was about to be sick.

Edward frowned grimly as he turned away; he walked up before putting his tee in the ground with Dream Dancer's new getta-percha ball on top, which was the new fad in England as well as Scotland.

Edward stood up as he backed away so that he was now behind the tee, as Dream Dancer lightly swung his golf club back and forth thoughtfully taking his time in no rush trying to relax so that he would forget about that little heaving sensation.

Edward still liked the wooden clubs James McEwan made for Dream Dancer, even though they were now going out of style since the getta-percha ball could take a harder club. Most were now using iron in their club designs.

Every club McEwan made had a Scottish thistle engraved on them they were highly prized. McEwan had always used ash or hazel wood common in England, until recently that is.

Edward had not liked the feel of the old clubs; he also did not like how easily they were chipped or broken. Last year Dream Dancer had hickory shipped down from his homeland so that McEwan could make him a set of clubs out of the harder hickory. Now McEwan would only use hickory.

Edward had also talked McEwan into a rounder club head with a slightly shorter shaft to help get Dream Dancer's hard rubber new designed golf balls up into the air better; without sacrificing distance.

Edward had nine clubs that his caddie carried around for him, which was the allowable amount; two drivers, one was for of the tee as well as a grass driver. He used two different types of spoons that helped him when he was on the fairway. Two Niblicks, which helped him in deep rough especially the one, Dream Dancer always referred to it as his get out of trouble club most of the time.

Three putters, the driving putter for severely windy days; it keeps the ball low for more control in the wind. An approach putter; with a lofted face for short shots to the green. Finally, the greens putter; used primarily on the green.

Edward cleared his thoughts of everything but the course now that he was relaxed. Dream Dancer frowned thoughtfully down the demanding third hole par five.

There was a deep gully with water below in front; it was hardly ever a trouble to the professionals. It could give a novice a lot of grief though.

In the distance, Edward could see the cardinal bunkers, three of them in total. A long huge bunker that nobody wanted to get near took up almost the whole fairway, with a slightly smaller one, several hundred yards behind that one. Finally, there was the one in front of the green it was the smallest of the three.

Edward knew that they were all very deep, when standing in them you could not see out the lip it was that high; they were almost impossible to get out of too.

There was two ways to get to the green from here the shortest way, which would be over the bunkers. Of course, that was also the most difficult one to negotiate because the first bunker was very big, so if Edward miss hit and ended up in that bunker it could cost him the championship. Of course, that all depended on how many strokes it took Dream Dancer to get out of there.

Although if Edward did get over them the green from there was sloping gently downwards; if his ball hit at the right angle it could run right into the cup for an eagle, which could gain Dream Dancer another stroke or two on Willie depending on how well his competition faired.

The other way was the safest way, but the longest with no guarantee that you would miss the other two bunkers since they were positioned in such a way as to give grief to the cautious golfer.

Once on the green from that angle though it was almost impossible to get your ball in the hole with one stroke or even two putts. The green from that position was a long upward climb, with a steep downward angle on the other side of the pin. If you missed the hole, you could be in big trouble because your ball would run right off down the other side into the rough, since the green was up on a slight plateau.

After careful thought Edward decided to go the shorter way, everybody hated a cowered Dream Dancer could not help thinking. That decision made, he started looking for a good place to put his ball.

Edward decided to hit his ball to the left so that it would roll as close to the front of the first bunker as possible. That would put him near the edge of the fairway, but he did not want it to get too close to the edge or it could roll into the rough causing him more troubles. Dream Dancer needed to avoid all three bunkers if possible, so that position would take the second bunker out of play for him hopefully.

Edward's strategy all planned out he walked up to the tee as he readied himself ignoring the prickly feeling he was still experiencing. With his full concentration on his form, Dream Dancer swung back and down.

Part way down in mid swing Edward's stomach clenched as he heaved again, which caused him to miss hit the ball. Unfortunately, right into the first bunker that Dream Dancer had hoped to avoid.

The heaving sensation only lasted a second, but it was enough as Edward watched his ball in irritation as it settled deep in the first cardinal bunker; Dream Dancer groaned in disgust.

The fact that Edward's ball got to the bunker in one shot was a feat in itself being a par five it should have taken Dream Dancer two shots to get there, but that did not matter. He turned after handing his caddie the club before marching over to Dao, as well as Crystin.

Crystin was slightly bent over obviously having a lot of trouble.

Dao looked up at the irritated Dream Dancer. "Crystin has been having morning sickness all day!"

Edward nodded as he tilted Crystin's face up already well aware of that, for some reason Dream Dancer was getting them right along with his wife. He remembered back to the night he had started looking for Crystin; he had figured after knocking himself out that the two of them were connected, now he knew for sure that he was right why else would he be feeling nauseated with the countess.

Edward turned back to Dao as Dream Dancer gestured towards the clubhouse in the distance. "Take her to the kitchen ask them for some dry bread for her to eat, it will absorb some of the acid in her stomach. I will give her something to help her when I finish round two."

Dao nodded as the Tianming Monk led a reluctant Crystin away.

Crystin really wanted to stay to continue watching Edward. His form, as well as his swing was beautiful to watch. The countess just hated to miss it; she left obediently though too sick to argue. She did not want to distract her husband either, which she seemed to be doing since the earl did not look pleased with her at all.

*****

Edward joined the procession that was going down to the fairway as the wind began to pick up slightly. Dream Dancer frowned as he looked up at the cloudless blue sky wondering if they were going to get through this round before the storm hit or if it would hold off until the end of the tournament.

Edward watched the others all hit before it was Willies turn. He frowned disgruntled as Dream Dancer watched Willies ball sail perfectly over the bunkers to settle a foot away from the green completely missing the other cardinal bunker in front of the green, it was in the perfect place for a chip in.

They finally got to Edward's ball; he stood there eyeing it trying to decide the best way to get it out of the bunker. Dream Dancer needed to dig deep into the sand to get under the ball fully in order to get it up into the air to clear the lip of the bunker.

Edward also needed enough of a club to get it over the other bunker so that it would be close to the green. Dream Dancer could only hope that it would miss the bunker in front of the green as well.

Edward's driver putter was out since it did not have any lift at all. His approach putter would have enough of a loft to get it over the lip, but he would not get any distance at all. Dream Dancer did not think either of his spoons would work either, so the niblick would have to do. Which one would give him the best advantage though?

Edward turned to his caddie as Dream Dancer held out his hand. "Give me the niblick, the one I call my get out of trouble club. Afterwards, I want you to go stand up on the lip of the bunker so that you can watch where my ball lands please!"

The caddie nodded in approval at Edward's choice of clubs before handing him the desired club; he trotted quickly around the bank of the bunker. The caddie was careful to make sure that he was out of the line of fire not wanting Earl Summerset to get a penalty stroke if he hit him with the ball.

Edward walked into the bunker. He made sure to dig his right foot deep into the hard packed sand, but kept his left foot elevated slightly.

This tilted Dream Dancer to the right so that once he buried his club in the sand; he would have no trouble getting under the ball. It would also give him the loft he needed to clear the lip, he could only hope anyway.

Of course, when setting up your club it was not allowed to touch the sand at all, this is why it was so difficult to get under the ball. Only after you swing could you touch the sand with your club.

Praying Edward swung hard, just as he hoped the ball sailed over the lip out of his sight. Unfortunately, Dream Dancer could tell by the angle it had risen into the air that it was going too far right; how far though was the burning question in his mind.

Edward stared up at his caddie hopefully, but knew just by his face that it was not good; obviously, Dream Dancer had gone too far right. He was not discouraged though; he knew by years of experience that once you got in trouble on a section of course it would follow you until you were finished the hole.

The hard part was putting it behind you so that you can carry on fresh to the next tee box. This is why most golfers failed to become professionals; they just could not put the last hole behind them.

Most armature players ended up frustrated after a bad hole so they were unable to play decently afterwards. Edward had never had that problem, Dream Dancer was always able to block out a bad hole so that he could continue on to the next.

Edward climbed up to join his caddie as he looked where the young man was pointing. He could not help but laugh in amusement, just as Dream Dancer had thought his ball had buried itself in the next bunker.

Edward turned to his caddie with a chuckle before Dream Dancer slapped him on the back in humour. "I guess I will keep this club my friend, I had to have at least one bad hole today!"

The caddie snickered in agreement relieved that Earl Summerset was not going to throw a fit of rage over his bad luck. Too many times, the caddie had to deal with angry nobles unable to handle a bad hole. Some of them were so bad that they would throw their clubs or smash them until they broke.

Edward managed to get his ball out of the other bunker in a similar manner. Fortunately, the ball settled just off the green between Willies ball as well as lucky for him the last bunker. It still took Dream Dancer two more shots to sink his ball.

Unfortunately, it let Willie gain two strokes on Edward. It still gave Dream Dancer a par, but Willie having a very good hole chipped in for an eagle.

Mercifully only one more incident with the gut clenching heaving sensation occurred at the Himalayan hole number nine, which again caused Edward to miss hit his ball. Dream Dancer still managed to birdie it, but Willie having a beautiful second round again eagled that hole.

Willie Park Sr. was now only two strokes behind Edward as the second round mercifully finished. Thankfully, Dream Dancer was still ahead of Willie as they all headed to the clubhouse for a needed break.

Edward frowned as he looked up at the clear blue sky just before entering the clubhouse for a bite to eat. Except for the wind picking up, no storm had materialized; it was still coming though Dream Dancer could feel it and he was never wrong.

Edward's timing had been off a few times, but never was Dream Dancer totally wrong. He just hoped it would wait until the tournament was over.

Once Edward entered the clubhouse he could see into the open dining room that was on the left; he saw Crystin, Queen Victoria, as well as Dao sitting at a table. His wife had her head in her hands; Dream Dancer could feel that queasy feeling returning.

Quickly Edward turned right going towards the back where the lockers were, his black doctor's bag was there. Dream Dancer had forgotten it this morning, which was unusual for him.

Edward changed out of his golfing shoes; the cleats were long they were made to be pushed into the ground to keep one from moving when swinging so they were too hard on the floors. He grabbed his doctor's bag before going to the dining room. Dream Dancer sat down smiling sympathetically across at his wife.

Edward looked up at the blue-eyed blonde hostess when she got to their table. "Can you bring me your special; I also need a cup of boiling water? I need to make my wife some tea for Crystin's discomfort."

The hostess nodded as she left.

Edward rummaged in his bag looking for the medicinal leaves he needed. When he had first come to England, it had taken Dream Dancer quite a lot of testing as well as talking to the locals to find their best medicinal plants here.

Luckily, Edward just happened to have what Crystin needed to help her with the morning sickness. Dream Dancer would have to make sure to start making his wife tea every morning to help combat the nausea.

That Crystin was getting morning sickness this late in her pregnancy did not bode well for her though. Unfortunately, there were some woman who suffered morning sickness throughout their entire pregnancy; Edward was hoping his wife would not be one of them.

Edward looked over at Queen Victoria as Dream Dancer grimaced slightly giving her a report since she had left them after the first round. "Well, my second round was a little more eventful. I ended up in two cardinal bunkers, but managed to miss the third one, which still gave me a par. Willie Park Sr. caught up by three strokes though, but I am still two shots ahead. I am just glad I kept the lead for the last round. There is a storm coming though, I hope it waits till the tournament is over, but I have a feeling it will not wait."

The prince consort came over, he plopped down disgruntled. Albert was third, only three strokes behind Willie; he was not too happy about that by the sour look on his face.

Queen Victoria ignored the look on her husband's face, as well as the fact that Albert ordered wine instead of food. Victoria gestured at Crystin instead curiously. "What is wrong with my goddaughter?"

Edward smiled his thanks up at the hostess before mixing in the medicinal leaves, with some rose buds as well as some hazel leaves to help take away the bitterness. Dream Dancer turned to the queen while he let them steep.

Edward had not told Queen Victoria that Crystin was pregnant. Victoria did not need to know that yet it would raise too many questions that Dream Dancer would not be able to answer. "Not sure, I think Crystin ate something that disagreed with her!"

Queen Victoria frowned in suspicion. They had all eaten the same thing, but no one else seemed sick. Victoria finally shrugged off her suspicion; Edward was the doctor after all.

Edward checked the tea; it was ready, so Dream Dancer put it in front of Crystin with another sympathetic look at the countess. "Here my dear drink this it will settle your stomach."

Crystin sat up straighter as she dutifully took a sip.

Quiet descended as everyone ate except the queasy countess.

The prince consort refused food as well, but Albert did order another wine.

*****

Raven walked towards the captain with her constant shadow following her. Trevor had stayed with her all week refusing to leave her side; if she needed anything, he would be the first one to fetch it. She had let Little Cub be knowing that it was just a reaction to the near mishap, it would not last long she was sure.

Raven was just thankful that the training she had given Trevor over the years had kept him from panicking. Since Little Cub was a toddler, she had been training him in the art of knife fighting, wrestling, warrior skills, as well as her unique fighting techniques. She was getting him ready to join the other Cheyenne braves.

Already Trevor was close to Raven's skills; she knew it would not be long before he surpassed her. At ten years old, Little Cub was already close to her height, she was sure he would be taller within the next two years.

Trevor was the splitting image of his father, Devon, but he had her green eyes with a hint of grey in them. He was three quarters English and a quarter Cheyenne, except for the high cheekbones one would never guess he had Indian blood in him though. Raven knew the woman would flock to him once Little Cub was older with that light blond almost white hair, as well as his greenish-grey piercing eyes, he was going to be gorgeous.

Since Raven had to forgo their usual exercise routine, it had not helped Trevor move past the incident. Both her hands had been wrapped until today since the sea spray kept irritating the rope burns on her palms. Her shoulders were too sore for it anyway; Dream Dancer had healed her enough so that she had full use of both arms, but she was still in a lot of discomfort. The doctor must have pushed her brother away too soon.

Thanks to Dream Dancer though, Raven was already as good as new, so they would be starting their routine tomorrow instead of being laid up for a month or two. Once their routine was back to normal Trevor would see for himself that she was all right, she was sure that afterwards Little Cub would once again go back to hounding the crew and Captain Roberts.

"Hurry up now! Get those hatches battened down as well as those sails lowered. We are running out of time!"

This is why Raven was on deck, the flurry of activity as well as all the yelling from the captain had brought her up here curious to find out what was going on. Captain Roberts had been screaming at his crew for almost an hour, much more than was his usual custom.

As Raven got closer to him, she could see that his face was red sweating profusely. "Captain, is there a problem?"

Captain Roberts looked at Raven with a worried frown as he pointed behind her. "That is the problem!"

Raven turned to stare in trepidation at the black, mauve, and purple clouds that they were heading straight for. She could see forks of lightning flaring out striking the water everywhere, the closer they got the bigger the waves were getting as the wind picked up; a huge gust hit them suddenly almost knocking her over.

Captain Roberts grabbed Raven to steady her. "Get your family into their cabins please, you better get ready for a bad one; I do not like the looks of that one little bit! It just figures so much for making it to England in under twelve days, but hopefully we will make it before the end of the twelfth day or early in the morning on the thirteenth day. If we do, we will still beat Lightning's time by three quarters of a day or so. Make sure you grab something to eat out of the galley. Once the storm hits fully there will be no food until it is safe!"

Raven nodded fearfully before grabbing Trevor's arm with no argument. She had not liked the last storm that they had, but the one coming looked way worse. She dropped her son Trevor off with the pastor, with the promise that she would return with food after giving Daniel Captain Roberts warning.

Next Raven rushed to her own cabin to get Devon to help her gather food, as well as some freshwater. They were getting low on water, but with the storm coming, it would fill their rain buckets.

They just got back to their room when it hit full blast!

CHAPTER SEVENTEEN

Edward grimaced as he looked to the west again in apprehension at the storm clouds coming. Dream Dancer did not like the looks of them at all, even though it was still a long way away yet!

They were on the ninth hole of the last round; lucky for Edward, he had managed to keep his two-point lead on Willie. How Dream Dancer had managed it, he was not entirely sure.

Edward was having a hard time concentrating on his game, which was affecting his usual love of golf. Dream Dancer just could not get the thought out of his mind that they should leave immediately.

Edward looked towards Crystin before going to the tee box; she had insisted that she was feeling better so had wanted to watch him win the tournament. Dream Dancer had given in against his better judgement knowing how much the countess had missed playing golf since his wife's parents were killed.

Even though Edward had given in, he still felt very uncomfortable having Crystin here, why he had no idea; it was unusual for Dream Dancer to pay any attention to spectators no matter who they were.

Edward shook off his unease, he smiled slightly in pleasure as he thought of the last six days; they had grown closer since they had gotten to Scotland. Dream Dancer was now getting more optimistic about their future. He hoped that someday his marriage to Crystin would become everything that he had ever wished for in his life.

Crystin was now five months and nine days into her pregnancy; Edward had laughed in delight the first time the countess had felt the babies move inside her. Now they both believed Dao although both still found it hard to understand why it had to be like this. Dream Dancer being shaman with powers was the first one to accept it. His wife had a little more trouble understand why, although being a witch's offspring had helped her to accept it finally.

No more did Crystin refuse to sleep with Edward, the last couple of nights Dream Dancer had even woken up to find his wife cuddled up to him. Of course, he had not said anything not wanting her to pull away again.

Edward had still made sure to keep a little distance between them though not wanting the evil in Crystin to try again to gain control of Dream Dancer again.

Edward shook off his thoughts again with a sigh of frustration, his mind kept wandering refusing to stay focused. He walked over to put his tee in the ground before putting the ball on top. Standing back, Dream Dancer lightly swung his club looking down the fairway trying to find the best place to put the ball.

Unfortunately, try as Edward might he could not settle his thoughts as Dream Dancer tried again to clear them of everything but the game.

Edward closed his eyes before taking a deep breath and releasing it slowly, as he did so he relaxed every muscle one at a time; finally, as Dream Dancer open his eyes the earl locked his gaze on the beautiful scenery that was around him, ignoring everything else.

It was a spectacular view from here with the Himalayan Mountains in the background.

Edward managed to clear his mind enough so that he now had a sense of where he wanted to place his ball. Dream Dancer stepped up to the tee positioning himself he got ready to swing.

Edward's club barely moved an inch before it fell to the ground instead as Dream Dancer turned racing towards Crystin with a cry of fear, but he was too late as his wife fell to the ground out cold. "CRYSTIN!"

Edward dropped down on all fours beside Crystin frantic.

Instantly as Edward's hands pressed against the Mother Earth Dream Dancer felt her pain, as well as a quiver racing through her.

Edward felt, as well as heard, an evil chuckle of satisfaction reverberate through the earth. Dream Dancer had heard that evil cackle only once before when he had went on his vision quest seeking answers to his lost dreams.

Quickly Edward checked Crystin over, but his wife was breathing normally with no trouble that he could discern. Dream Dancer sighed in relief as he sat back completely baffled, he needed his doctor's bag to investigate further.

Edward looked over at his teacher Dao in fear. "We need to get Crystin back to the clubhouse; there is something not right!"

Dao nodded already aware of that having heard the evil chuckle as well. The Tianming Monk looked at Dream Dancer in concern. "Are you going to forfeit?"

Edward nodded emphatically. "You better inform Willie for me, I will carry Crystin."

Dao frowned troubled as he jumped up immediately before doing as he was told. Once finished giving the bad news to the other players the Tianming Monk hurried to catch up to Dream Dancer as his student marched purposely along. It did not take them long to reach their destination since they were on the ninth hole, which happened to be the closest fairway to the clubhouse.

Edward stopped at the door as Dream Dancer looked towards the storm clouds, but they were still quite a ways away yet so the golfers should finish before it arrived thankfully.

The storm Edward had felt coming was not the one on the horizon anyway; he now realized that it was the one in his arms. Dream Dancer grimaced in fear as he shook of his apprehension before entering.

Queen Victoria having tea left it quickly as she rushed over in concern. "What happened?"

Edward shrugged unknowingly. "Not sure yet, sorry your Majesty, I had to forfeit on the ninth hole."

Queen Victoria waived dismissively. "It is only a game! Take my carriage I will be along as soon as I gather my husband; the Prince Consort won't like forfeiting but Albert has had too much wine anyway.

Just send the carriage back here when you are done with it we will see you shortly."

Edward nodded in relief as Dream Dancer looked over at Dao. "Can you bring my stuff, please; I will meet you at the carriage?"

Dao scurried away quickly.

*****

Within twenty minutes, they were back at Queen Victoria's townhouse.

Dao rushed ahead of Dream Dancer leading him to his room, the Tianming Monk brought Edward's doctors bag with them even though he was sure they would not need it.

Dao pointed at his carpet as soon as Dream Dancer entered; the Tianming Monk had laid it out as soon as he had finished unpacking. "Put Crystin on my carpet in the center please!"

Dao rushed around lighting all the candles, as well as his incense that he had positioned around his carpet. Once finished the Tianming Monk grabbed his training outfit, as well as Dream Dancer's; quickly they both changed. Edward's teacher went behind a screen though still not allowing Dream Dancer to see him unclothed.

Finished they knelt one on each side of Crystin before chanting they went deep into a trance. Dao and Edward opened their minds to each other so that they could find an answer that they both could see.

Dream Dancer with the Tianming Monk's help saw a ship with Crystin laid out in a bunk as they journeyed to England before going to Wales. Not once, did Crystin open her eyes; finally, they were in Edward's tepee waiting for something.

The vision dissipated, so both men sat back contemplatively.

Dao frowned as Dream Dancer disappeared before Edward's eyes once again turned green so that the earl was once more prominent. "We must hurry the evil is prevailing we do not have much time!"

Edward frowned thoughtfully confused. "But, why are we to go to England first?"

Dao shrugged perplexed as well. "I am not sure, but there must be a reason. The evil has taken over your wife again so until the healing

Crystin will remain unconscious. The twin's are fine so far; I did not feel any distress or loss of life. You must make sure to keep them all alive until we get to where we are going!"

Edward grimaced angrily hating what was happening to them, but knew there was not much he could do about it right now. It frustrated the hell out of Dream Dancer to feel so helpless!

Edward reached over as he tenderly stroked Crystin's white hair before pushing a few scraggly strands out of his wife's face. Dream Dancer tried to imagine her with black hair again, but failed.

Dao stood up as the Tianming Monk motioned to the door before explaining. "Put your wife in your bed for now Dream Dancer; we need to rouse the servants so that we are all pack up ready to go when the queen gets here. We will need Queen Victoria to commandeer a ship."

Edward nodded as he tenderly scooped his wife up into his arms. Crystin was such a tiny thing, barely weighing anything; Dream Dancer could not help but think.

Dao held the door open for Edward as Dream Dancer left obediently.

*****

Raven followed by Devon entered their cabin to put the food they had managed to scrounge away. They made sure that everything was secure, so that nothing spilt or rolled around as the sea got rougher.

The pastor, as well as their son Trevor, was settled in for the night with food and water; so there were no more worries there.

Raven disrobed with a sigh of relief getting ready for bed. Finished she took a step towards her bunk, but did not make it there as the ship heaved dropping into a deep trough making her stagger.

Devon just finished disrobing himself made a grab for his wife, Golden Eagle managed to snag Raven around the waist before pulling her tight against him trying to steady her so that she would not fall and possibly re-injure herself.

Raven giggled playfully as her husband instantly hardened against her buttocks in reaction, so she wiggled tantalizingly in invitation. "I feel drunk with all this staggering around!"

Devon groaned as his fully erect manhood settled perfectly between Raven's buttock cheeks as Golden Eagle chuckled enticingly. "I think I might like all this tossing around, as well as the swaying of the ship."

Raven groaned deep in her throat in agreement before bending slightly at the waist as she lifted up on the tips of her toes so that she was taller. She rubbed against Devon's manhood invitingly as she purred like a kitten deep in her throat. "It definitely has interesting prospects."

Suddenly Raven yelped in surprise as a huge wave made them both stagger towards the bunk. She dropped her arms quickly catching herself as she made a grab for the lower bunk. Now she was bent in half as she chuckled in amusement, as Devon fell with her.

Devon trying to keep them both from falling to the cabin floor ended up bent in half over Raven. Golden Eagle could not help laughing at how ridiculous they probably looked.

Getting an idea, Devon pushed himself up slightly as he bent his knees positioning his manhood at Raven's core. Keeping one hand on the small of his wife's back, Golden Eagle entered her from behind.

Raven cried out ecstatically as another wave pushed her husband Devon up even tighter against her. She shuddered in ecstasy as Golden Eagle entered her slick womanhood in one powerful thrust.

Devon hit his head on the upper bunk, so he moved his head out from underneath as he hooked his fingers between the wood as well as the mattress of the upper bunk to keep him from falling. Golden Eagle ground his hips against Raven as his wife pushed back against him in demand.

As another wave hit it drove Devon even deeper inside Raven. Golden Eagle groaned in disappointment as he erupted way too early. He had really wanted to prolong this, but they had not made love since boarding the ship.

Raven felt Devon lose control, which also triggered her own release! She pulsated around her husband's manhood so powerfully that she had to bury her head in the blankets as she screamed slightly in surprised satisfaction.

Devon feeling the powerful contractions Raven was experiencing grinned in pleasure; Golden Eagle would have to remember on their way back home how much his wife liked this.

Devon released his hold on the upper bunk as they both fell laughing onto the lower bunk still joined as one. Still slightly hard, Golden Eagle proceeded to make love to Raven once more.

Devon took his time now though, but kept their present position. It gave Golden Eagle better access to Raven's tender nub, as well as his wife's large full breasts even while still joined.

Raven hooked her leg over Devon's giving her husband more access to her bud of pleasure as she took Golden Eagle's free hand bringing it to her breasts.

They giggled as they played like first time lovers all through the night hardly even noticing the fierce storm raging around them anymore.

*****

Edward stood staring out to sea as a boom of thunder crashed in the distance. The ship they had managed to commandeer sped around the coast of Scotland. The black haired green-eyed six-foot ships captain had given them quite a hard time not wanting to sail with the storm getting ever closer.

With Queen Victoria vehemently insisting that the captain take them; as well as with Edward's assurances that if they stayed as close as possible to the coast going around the long way everything would be fine. Captain Smith had finally agreed reluctantly, but only because they still had blue skies over in that direction.

Captain Smith had warned them though that if he felt any threat from the weather between here and England that he would find the closest dock whether they liked it or not. The captain fervently refused to put his ship, as well as his crew in jeopardy for anyone not for a queen or any amount of money!

Edward frowned contemplatively they should be able to get to England by tomorrow afternoon at the latest he hoped. Afterwards they would catch a train to Northern Wales; luckily, there was a train station not too far from Dream Dancer's castle. Unfortunately, there was still no train service the further south you went in Wales.

Edward was still baffled by why they needed to go to England first though. They had stowed the horses in the hold this time, just in case not willing to take the chance of losing any of them to the sea if things got a little rough.

Edward could not feel Raven anymore, not since the ship's doctor had forcefully evicted Dream Dancer from his body. All that the earl could hear or feel now was the steady rhythm of three hearts beating; it drowned everything else out.

It had taken Edward quite a while to realize that he was listening to the sounds of Crystin's, as well as his babies' heartbeats. It was not until Dream Dancer was feeding his wife some broth that he had even figured it out at all.

Edward chuckled slightly although there was not much humour in it; again, he was feeding Crystin by using his mouth. Would they ever have a normal relationship he could not help thinking. Dream Dancer was seriously beginning to doubt it!

Edward shook off that unpleasant thought as he went back to thinking about how he had found out about the heartbeats he was hearing. Dream Dancer had noticed while feeding Crystin that every time the main artery in his wife's neck pulsed, which was a heart rhythm; he would also hear a thump in his mind before two more thuds followed it closely.

Getting curious, Edward had taken his stethoscope out. Once he put it on Crystin's belly Dream Dancer again heard a faint echo as the twin's hearts beat in time to the ones that kept echoing in his head.

To test out Edward's theory he had come up on deck unable to sleep anyway; so Dream Dancer stood here looking intently out at the black threatening clouds in the distance. The lightning show on the horizon was spectacular.

Even from here, Edward could hear the fizzle and crackle as the lightning flared hitting the water in multiple places before a huge boom of the thunder would echo eerily in the stillness of the night.

Edward smiled as he heard the thud of one before the next two thumped in quick succession, so Dream Dancer had been right even up here he could feel the pulsing of first one heart and another before finally the third.

It absolutely amazed Edward, but also comforted him knowing that if one of them were in distress Dream Dancer would know immediately.

Dao materialized beside Edward soundlessly. "Are you okay?"

Edward turned with a baffled smile of confusion to his teacher Dao. "Yes, I am not sure why, but I can feel Crystin's heartbeat as well as the twin's even way up here. I have been hearing it since we docked in Scotland, but I did not realize what it was until tonight."

Dao smiled knowingly as the Tianming Monk gestured reassuringly at his student Edward. "That is not unusual when one is connected Dream Dancer. Take you for example; I have felt your heartbeat since that long ago day in Boston at the stables when we first met. When you are in pain, I also feel it not as badly as you do off course; it is still very uncomfortable for me though. Since we are connected, I also can feel your need for me; if you are concentrating hard enough on that need, I can also see why you need me!"

Edward frowned in surprise before grinning in understanding. "Ah, so that is how you always know when I am coming!"

Dao chuckled as the Tianming Monk nodded. "Yes, now you know my secret."

They both stood in companionable silence at the railing of the ship watching the fury of nature as the black, mauve, as well as the purple clouds swirled around angrily. The two men could tell that the storm was not natural at all, as it stalked them unmercifully; trying to overtake the ship that they were on.

All they could do though was stand there praying that the ship would not falter as they seemed to gain ground one moment, but other times it seemed the storm was winning as the lightning came close to reaching them.

It almost seemed like a cat and mouse game, but with way higher stakes, since there were more lives involved. Unknown to Edward though was the fact that the stakes were even higher than Dream Dancer realized.

Dao knew it though; the Tianming Monk kept to himself the knowledge that every soul under heaven was in deep peril at this very moment! If that storm caught them there would be no light left in this world only darkness!

Dao also knew that it would not take long for Mara, the devil, to become released if the occupants on this ship were no more. The Tianming Monk was the only one who knew that the only thing standing in Mara's way right now was the six sentient stones; as well as one tiny Celtic Witch, with a belly full of the only thing that would keep the serpent contained until the appointed day of reckoning was at hand.

*****

In the end though, Edward was proven right as the ship stayed just one-step ahead of the storm that was trying to stop them. With no difficulties arising, they arrived at their destination before noon the following day. With both men still standing in the exact same spot, unable to sleep they prayed and kept watch until they docked safely.

CHAPTER EIGHTEEN

Crystin was laid out in the center of the tepee lying there as if dead, she had been in a coma for five days now. Thankfully, the countess' heartbeat as well as the twin's hearts was still beating strong.

Edward was getting frantic though wondering if they were going to be too late. Dream Dancer had made sure to keep Crystin well hydrated with water, tea, and lots of nourishing broth. The twin's were now five and a half months along; would they be strong enough to survive this healing?

Edward could not help but contemplate his worst fears though would Crystin come out of this at all now! If his wife did regain consciousness would she be the same person, Dream Dancer could not help his fearful thoughts as they kept echoing deep in his subconscious mind.

Edward shook off his unpleasant thoughts as he looked across the tepee; he smiled over at his sister before turning to the right to grin at his brother-in-law Devon who was sitting on Raven's left. They had arrived the day after Dream Dancer's group had gotten to England, which is why they had been told to go to England first in that vision they had gotten in Scotland.

Dao mysteriously disappeared the day after Edward's party had arrived; the Tianming Monk had returned later with Raven, Devon, Trevor, as well as the pastor.

Edward chuckled quietly to himself as he thought of the first meeting between Raven and Queen Victoria…

*****

Edward's mouth had dropped open in shocked surprise as Raven walked into the palace dressed in a flowing peach satin gown that was scooped low in front. A deep red emerald necklace with a teardrop pendant in the center nestled against her dusky skin; the pendant fit perfect between her breasts.

The dress swept the floor in a cloud of silk; it almost seemed that Raven was floating down the length of the reception room to Edward as his sister walked towards Dream Dancer with a lithe grace not seen in the pampered nobility.

Raven daintily took Edward's right arm as she let Dream Dancer lead her into the grand hall towards Queen Victoria.

With a swift flick of Raven's wrist, which she had diligently practiced in secret; Edward's sister opened the fan that was in her right hand so that nobody could see her talking as she whispered in aggravation to Dream Dancer. "If you breathe one word of this to anyone at home I will vehemently deny the fact that I wore silk!"

Devon walking behind them snickered in delight as his brother-in-law Edward choked trying not to laugh as they reached Queen Victoria. Just before they got to the throne, Golden Eagle walked up beside Raven.

Devon had stayed behind Raven at first wanting his wife to be the center of attention.

Immediately both men dropped to one knee with their hands on their swords while Raven dipped low into a perfect curtsy between them. It had taken her a week to get it right; of course, she would not fess up to that not even to her husband Devon.

Queen Victoria stared down at the three before getting up out of her throne; she regally walked down the dais so that Victoria could stand in front of them wanting a better look at Edward's sister Raven. "Rise!"

Queen Victoria frowned in irritation not having realized that she would have to look up even at Edward's sister and both men dwarfed Raven.

Queen Victoria waved her hand in aggravation as Victoria indicated the two men, but addressed Raven. "How can you stand to have such towering men around you all the time?"

Raven grinned as she stood up before looking at Queen Victoria in humour. She leaned forward dramatically pretending that it was a secret, but made sure that all the nobility standing around gawking could hear her. "Well, your Majesty, it is like this! If you find yourself getting a crick in the neck from looking up too long, all you have to do is give the offender a swift kick in the shin. When he bends down to massage his leg he will be at eye level with you, so all you need to do is reach out to grab a hold of his ear. Make sure that you give the ear just a slight twist as you are pulling him forward, that way he cannot get away, so will stay at eye level with you until you are completely done talking to him!"

Raven with a perfectly straight face put on an innocent mask pretending that she did not hear the gasps of outrage all around her. She snapped her fan open as she waved it in front of herself a few times nonchalantly as if she had not just shocked the whole royal court.

The two men standing one on each side of Raven choked coughing slightly as they tried not to laugh uproariously at her antics.

Queen Victoria laughed in delight before clapping her hands in approval. "Well, I will have to remember that! I think we are going to get along just fine Lady Raven, welcome to England my dear."

Raven winked at Queen Victoria outlandishly before snapping her fan shut dramatically as she swooped gracefully into a deep curtsy. With a husky chuckle, she agreed with the queen wholeheartedly. "I believe we will, your Majesty, I believe that we will!"

All night Raven had shocked the nobles as she kept Queen Victoria entertained. Edward knew that Raven would be the talk of the court for the next year or maybe even two Dream Dancer couldn't help thinking.

*****

Edward cleared his thoughts, which brought him immediately back to the present; Dream Dancer still could not help thinking about how they had ended up here three days later as his mind wandered once more.

The next day they had left Raven's son with Queen Victoria to look after before the five adults loaded Crystin onto a train. Now here they all were finally in Edward's tepee, in Wales. Preparing for what Dream Dancer still did not fully understand.

After Edward's sister Raven had gotten off the ship in England she had given to Dream Dancer the white buffalo hide that Melissa Brown had warn for over thirty years. Surprisingly Dao had requested that

Edward bring it in the tepee with them. The Tianming Monk had placed it under Crystin as soon they had put her inside so that now the countess was laying on it.

Edward shook off his thoughts again as he grimaced angrily at himself for his inability to stay focused. Finally shaking off all thoughts, he went deep into meditation. His eyes blackened as Dream Dancer was once again released!

Dream Dancer painted symbols of his Cheyenne people on his face, as well as his chest, before painting the Oriental symbols that Dao had taught to Edward.

Dream Dancer chanting felt the power in him surge all around him so intensely that he had a hard time controlling it. Control it Edward must though, his teacher Dao had warned him that it would be very hard to manage at this time.

Finished painting himself, Dream Dancer picked up the paint as he went over to his sister next so that he could paint Raven as well; Edward continued chanting rhythmically in Cheyenne through it all not relenting.

Dao had painted himself already with all sorts of Oriental symbols around a large cross that was surprisingly tattooed on the Tianming Monk's bare chest.

Dream Dancer had been slightly shocked to see the cross never having seen the Tianming Monk unclothed before now.

At this moment, the Tianming Monk was in the process of painting the pastor's chest with a cross as he chanted his own powerful song. When done, Dao added the doves of peace making sure that they surrounded the cross on Daniel's chest.

When the two most powerful men in history were finished painting everyone except Crystin they turned as one as they both knelt one on each side of the countess.

As Dream Dancer chanted, an image of an unusual black cougar cub with a white tip on its tail appeared to him. Edward obediently painted the cub on his wife Crystin's cheek knowing that now and forever the countess' Cheyenne name would be Black Cougar Cub.

Normally cougar cubs were gold to reddish brown with spots. Most people when they saw a black cougar referred to them as a panther, it was just a colour variation though. They were also much smaller; which is why people thought that they were a different breed of cat, but they were not.

The Tianming Monk painted a cross with Sakura blossoms on Crystin's other cheek, which was known in other parts of the world as the cherry blossoms; Dao put them all around the cross. The same flower was on the robe he had given the countess. They were also prevalent on his carpet.

The Japanese considered the Sakura blossom a symbol of beauty, many of their women had the flower in their name somewhere. The Chinese however considered the Sakura blossom to be a wild part of human nature, to them it symbolized lions, cats, or tigers.

The two men finished painting Crystin at the same time; they were just sitting back when Edward's wife Crystin shrieked as she sat up. The countess pointed at Raven as she screamed out a Celtic curse before falling back, unconscious once more.

Instantly Raven fell withering to the floor in agony.

Devon cried out in fear and despair as he gathered his wife into his arms. When they had first arrived, Dream Dancer had told them that Raven was needed for this healing. Golden Eagle had tried to talk her out of it though as a shiver of foreboding coursed down his spine.

Raven of course would not listen to Devon after finding out that there were a set of twin babies involved, especially when they were Edward's children.

Tears streaked Devon's face as he screamed out in horrified dread, as Golden Eagle looked up he begged pleadingly. "Not Raven, please God; do not take my wife!"

The Tianming Monk jumped up quickly as he rushed to his carpet. Dao had placed it off to the right when they had first entered the tepee; right beside the carpet waiting, was his sword.

Once kneeling, the Tianming Monk beckoned to Pastor Daniel Brown in command so that the pastor would be on the carpet as well. "Hurry now; come kneel in front of me Daniel as you do so pray to God for guidance!"

The pastor confused, disoriented, as well as afraid got up in a daze as he did as he was told. Daniel was not sure why or what to pray for, but suddenly he felt that he must. He dropped to his knees on the carpet facing the strange little Oriental man that Edward called Dao.

Dream Dancer rushed over to Raven, but he could do nothing to help his sister; Edward watched the evil possessing her helplessly. He could not use his healing powers without taking in the evil himself.

Dao had warned Dream Dancer not to do any healing until the Tianming Monk told Edward that it was safe to do so, or the evil would win; if that happened all of them would be lost.

In frustration, Dream Dancer stared impotently at his withering sister as Raven shrieked painfully. Edward finally turned away unable to watch any more; with both fists clenched at his sides helplessly the earl stared at the Tianming Monk angrily waiting for permission to help his sister.

The Tianming Monk waited until the pastor knelt in front of him on Dao's carpet before raising his arms in supplication. "Great Spirit let your servant Daniel see!"

The pastor gasped in awe and wonder as the Holy Spirit all of a sudden entered him. He knew that it was the Holy Spirit because he had felt it many times in his lifetime as Jesus spoke to him wanting Daniel to teach certain biblical passages to his congregation.

This time was different though; the pastor felt so full of the pure Holy Spirit he thought that he might burst from the joy. Unable to help himself, Daniel jumped to his feet on the carpet as he raised his arms to the heavens ecstatically before closing his eyes savouring the sensation. "Lord let your will be done!"

The pastor opened his eyes and saw Dao as if for the first time as the Tianming Monk stood up in front of Daniel. The Oriental had a glow above his head as well as a glowing sword clenched in his fist waiting patiently.

The pastor saw behind Dao a man, an angel. No, he gasped awestruck, as the man's name entered his mind; not able to hold it back another moment, Daniel thundered in wonder. "Elijah!"

In the bible, Elijah did not die; he was taken to heaven in a chariot of fire.

Behind Elijah was the pastor's wife, Pamela! Morning Star was beckoning enticingly for him to come to her. He stared in shock as another woman materialized beside his wife unexpectedly, she was also waving for Daniel to come to them; it was his mother, Melissa or White Buffalo to the Cheyenne.

Now the pastor knew why he had been ordered to take the buffalo hide to Edward, his mother had died soon after Daniel left for England.

Looking towards Elijah again, two passages in the bible flashed instantly in the pastor's mind:

'Two Samuel fourteen: fourteen—***All of us must die eventually. Our lives are like water spilled out on the ground, which cannot be gathered up again, but God does not just sweep life away; instead, he derives ways to bring us back when we have been separated from him.'***

The second passage made the pastor tremble already knowing what was expected from Daniel this night:

'Two Kings twenty: four-six—***God's sovereign hand is in everything. God is in control of the lives of all people, the Universe, and the course of earth's history directing it to his appointed ends. God's people should pray like God's son. "I want your will to be done, not mine."***

God's people are challenged to live in harmony with God's will and in the strength that he provides when we live for God's glory, whatever happens is also for our good.'

The pastor looked up towards heaven his face was full of peace, with such a glow of pure love it was almost blinding to see. His arms reached up higher in praise as Daniel began whispering in acceptance by the end though he was shouting in joy. "Your will be done, LORD! NOT MINE!"

Instantly, Elijah entered Daniel as he prophesied; turning he pointed at Crystin's belly as he thundered in warning it was so loud that the earth shook. "She will be called Cecille Luan Gweneal or White Buffalo to her people. She will bring beauty to the earth as she keeps the evil at bay for another forty years. In the new century evil will begin leaking out of its prison slowly, until the mists of Snowdonia are no more. When the last fragment of fog disappears, so too will the six sentient stones. By the end of the next century, it will have begun as wives kill husbands and children, husbands will kill wives as well as their own children; children will also kill without mercy! Sodom and Gomorrah will return as people turn away, refusing to listen. Wars will prevail as the earth changes for the worst; storms, fires, as well as diseases, will run ramped spreading across the land. Infestation of flies, grasshoppers, worms, and rodents will infest the land. The white buffalo will come back one last time as the rise of the Dragon begins! Twin's will be born to the White Buffalo line once more, but they will be separated at birth as the last white buffalo hide disappears. When the sword of truth and the carpet of the guardians disappears so too will the Tianming Monks. As they disappear every last one of the faithful will follow, once they are all gone it will be too late! There will be no turning back as judgement draws ever closer!"

Elijah left the pastor suddenly.

Daniel turned to Dao with a serene face as he nodded in acceptance, as well as farewell giving up his life willingly to save the others.

The Tianming Monk chanting drove his sword threw Daniel's heart, as soon as Dao withdrew the sword the Baptist Pastor fell to the carpet dead.

The blinding white light of the Holy Spirit exited Daniel's body filling the tepee as blood gushed out of the Baptist Pastor's chest before flowing all over the Tianming Monk's carpet saturating it as the first of three sacrifices was given willingly.

The blood soaked through the carpet into the ground as it pushed the evil mist back to its prison in Snowdonia. Everyone that was still alive in the tepee heard a wail of denial as a furious quake reverberated through the earth. The tepee trembled shaking angrily, but stayed standing.

The six sentient stones in Snowdonia turned grey once more; as the stones strengthened they were able to close the portal tight trapping Mara's minion again as they resumed their guard duty. Once the gate was slammed shut, the fog lightened again to a pearly grey.

The Tianming Monk turned to Dream Dancer and Devon as Dao pointed his bloody sword at them. "Hurry Devon, put Raven beside Crystin. Dream Dancer, I want you to kneel between the two women as you do so I want you to bring your healing power to bear. Put a hand on each of their foreheads to heal them, after they are healed, your powers will be gone. You must give them up voluntarily to save the two women! Your powers are the second sacrifice that must be given willingly so that the evil can be drawn completely out of the two women!"

Dream Dancer nodded without hesitation as Edward obediently knelt beside Crystin.

Devon carried Raven over putting her down on the other side of Dream Dancer. Golden Eagle quickly stepped back totally shocked, afraid, as well as confused by what was happening to them. He had watched horrified as Dao, Edward's teacher, killed Pastor Daniel right before their very eyes.

Devon was the only one unpainted, so he could not see what the others could since he was not trained to see with his inner eye. All that Golden Eagle could do was put his trust in his brother-in-law Edward in the hopes that Dream Dancer would make everything all right once more.

Dream Dancer obediently put his hands on the two women's foreheads before chanting desperately in Cheyenne Edward felt his eyes blacken even more, now there was no hint of green anywhere to be seen.

The pain was excruciating as Dream Dancer curled up slightly in self-preservation, but refused to relent or remove his hands as Edward felt the evil mist enter his palms for the second time in his life.

Finally, Dream Dancer sat up knowing that it was time he screamed in pain and determination as Edward brought both hands with the evil contained in them together in front of him in a prayer like motion.

Unsure why Dream Dancer did so, but feeling compelled Edward lifted them high above his head still with both hands pressed together as the most powerful shaman in history willingly sent all his power into his joined hands.

The Tianming Monk continuing to hold out the sword waited patiently until suddenly the sword of truth began to glow a deep bluish-grey once again.

The Tianming Monk watched a pure black mist exit the tips of Dream Dancer's fingers as Edward pushed against the evil evicting it from his body; because it also contained all of Dream Dancer's unique shaman powers it was now ebony black instead of a dark grey.

Fighting to get away the black mist was reluctantly drawn slowly from Dream Dancer into the sword before suddenly it entered the Tianming Monk's body.

The Tianming Monk threw back his head in pain as Dao screamed out determinedly. "I am Dao Ba Zevak Hajime a master of the Tianming Samari Monks who follow the 'Divine mandate of Shen's will!'. We are the truth, the way, the path or flow of the Universe! I am Dao, which means wielder of the sword of truth. I am Ba, which means, third. I am Zevak, which means sacrifice. And I am Hajime the beginning, which will lead to the end!"

The Tianming Samari Monk dropped to his knees in anguish unable to keep himself upright for a moment longer; Dao could not help but scream out eerily once again trying to hold onto life for a precious few more minutes. "I am the wielder of the sword of truth, I am the third sacrifice, and I AM the beginning that will lead to the end. I give up my life willingly to buy time for all humanity in the hopes that someday they will hear then repent!"

Suddenly without warning, the Tianming Monk reversed his sword before thrusting it into his own heart. As the sword entered Dao's chest he looked up for the first time so that he could see his lord.

For just a split second there was a look of complete shock written all over the Tianming Monk's face as Dao took the hand that was extended to him. "Your will is done!"

The Tianming Samari Master, Dao, gave up his spirit gladly.

The blinding white light of the Holy Spirit that was still filling the tepee disappeared suddenly as both the Tianming Monk and Dream Dancer dropped to the ground unmoving.

The Tianming Monk's carpet continued to glow though, as it thirstily drank up the blood of its master, as well as the leftover blood from the Baptist Pastor. When the last drop of blood fell, the light dissipated. As it disappeared no blood from either men was apparent on the carpet, but two more symbols joined the hundred others that marked the carpet as holy.

CHAPTER NINETEEN

Raven was the first to open her eyes.

With a glad cry of thanks, Devon rushed over before dropping down beside his wife Raven as Golden Eagle gathered her close thankfully.

Edward sat up next, turning instantly he watched Crystin hopefully. Dream Dancer gazed down at her in fascination as his wife's hair began to darken more and more, until it was pitch-black once more. Except for a small streak of white just over the countess' left brow.

It reminded Edward of the vision Dream Dancer had earlier of the black cougar cub with the white tip on her tail.

As Crystin opened her eyes, Edward could not help smile in satisfaction at the crystal grey eyes that his wife focused on Dream Dancer. Thankfully the evil was now gone completely.

Edward reached out before stroking Crystin's cheek in relief. Tenderly Dream Dancer scooped his wife up as he stood. He would check the babies carefully as well, once they were back in the castle.

Edward looked over at Devon. "Bring Raven inside, I will return after to bury my friends!"

Devon nodded in agreement, as Golden Eagle also picked up Raven before following his brother-in-law Edward to the castle obediently.

*****

An hour later Edward returned with Devon; they now carried shovels, both of them were not looking forward to the next several hours.

Edward had cleaned all the symbols off Crystin before listening to the twin's healthy heartbeats with Dream Dancer's stethoscope in relief.

Devon had cleaned up Raven lovingly as well.

As Edward worked, Dream Dancer had explained what had happened to the three very confused participants, since they had not been able to see everything that had taken place.

Edward had left his own paint on though knowing that this moment would come as Dream Dancer stopped to stare at the tepee sadly before reluctantly they went inside. He frowned undecided for a moment before turning to Devon with a pained expression. "I want to bury them in here; I will never be able to use it again anyway!"

Devon inclined his head grimly, understanding his brother-in-law's feelings, but did not say anything leaving it up to Dream Dancer since it was Edward's tepee.

Edward walked over beside the carpet before bending he moved it aside; Dream Dancer figured since the blood of his friends had soaked into the ground underneath the carpet that it must be holy ground, so this was as good a place as any as he began digging.

Devon joined Edward a moment later.

Dream Dancer chanted his Cheyenne burial song as he dug a grave for his friends. Edward felt the difference in himself almost immediately never again would his eyes change colour, now they would be a deep green forever.

Dream Dancer could not help feel a slight twinge of sorrow at losing a part of him, but he felt relief too. He had carried the burden all his life; now no more would Edward have to worry about misusing gifts that he had not wanted in the first place. He would never have to worry either about anyone using him because of his powers.

It took the two of them over an hour working together to get the grave deep enough, as well as wide enough for their two friends. Once finished they picked up the pastor first, tenderly they laid him inside. Dream Dancer continued chanting in Cheyenne, while Devon also said a prayer. Together they sent Daniel on his way to be with the Great Spirit.

Next was Dao's turn; Dream Dancer caught back a sob as they laid the Tianming Monk beside Daniel. Again, Devon prayed as Edward chanted while they filled in the grave solemnly.

The two men dismantled the fire pit so that they could pile all the large rocks all around the grave outlining it. When they were all done Dream Dancer wailed forlornly as Edward dropped down at the head of the grave.

Dream Dancer pulled his knife from the top of his boot as the Cheyenne grieving ritual for Edward began.

Devon silently melted away after picking up the white buffalo hide taking it with him. Golden Eagle left his brother-in-law to grieve for his Oriental guardian. Dao had not only been Dream Dancer's teacher since he was seventeen, but had also become Edward's friend and constant companion as well.

Devon would give Edward half an hour to grieve before sending Raven out to make sure that Dream Dancer did not over do it. They both knew from experience how easy it was to kill oneself by accident when someone was grieving that deeply.

*****

Raven, as well as a determined Crystin, marched towards the back garden in order to check on Edward. Raven of course, carried Dream Dancer's black doctor bag knowingly.

Crystin had quizzed Raven on the Cheyenne customs of mourning, so she understood more now on why she had found Edward all cut up that day. It seemed like a lifetime ago to the countess, but was really only two weeks ago!

Crystin needed to make sure that Edward was okay; Dao had talked to her in Scotland about making sure that if the Tianming Monk were to die she would take care of his pupil, so the countess had made a solemn promise. She had just not realized that it would be this soon though.

The two women entered the tepee looking around. Raven tisked knowingly as Crystin cried out horrified.

Dream Dancer was sitting Indian style at the front of the grave chanting, for some reason Edward had felt compelled to move Dao's carpet over so that he could sit on it. There was blood everywhere; it was all over the grave, carpet, as well as the ground, but mostly on him.

Raven marched over to Dream Dancer before grabbing the knife that was still clenched in Edward's hand; she tossed it into a corner. She turned to Crystin as she pointed towards where the fire pit was at earlier. "There is a canteen over there somewhere, please bring it here for me!"

Crystin nodded before doing as she was told.

Dream Dancer still in his own world never acknowledged them at all.

Raven nodded thanks as Crystin handed her the canteen.

Raven soaked the cloth she had brought before kneeling in front of Dream Dancer in order to wash away the blood. She needed to see how much damage Edward had done to himself.

Thankfully, most of Dream Dancer's cuts proved to be superficial though. Luckily, there were only two cuts deep enough for Raven to put a couple of stitches in. Afterwards, she made a paste that she lavishly applied to all of Edward's cuts so that no infection would set in.

Raven was just getting up off her knees when the hairs on the back of her neck stood up in warning. Suddenly in one swift motion, she spun towards the tepee door as she drew her knife from her boot at the same instant.

With an ever so slight whisper of sound catching Raven's ear, she crouched in readiness. Almost instantly, her arm was grabbed from behind.

Raven looked back at Dream Dancer as Edward kept his sister still before shaking his head at her in warning.

Raven nodded as she relaxed putting her knife back in her boot when Dream Dancer let her go. She turned back to the entrance of the tepee as she curiously eyed the white-robed figure standing in the doorway.

The person that entered was slight and short just over four feet, but covered from head to toe in a white cloth so it was impossible to know what gender it was. All that could be seen were two slanted deep brown sorrowful eyes. The figure in white reached up before removing the hood.

Raven frowned taken completely by surprise. He was only a boy around twelve she would guess; Oriental like Dream Dancer's teacher Dao had been.

The boy bowed deeply in greeting. "I see I am too late! My father Dao died bravely?"

Edward stood up instantly before bowing back at Dao's son. "He died four hours ago; Dao took his own life to save my wife and twin's!"

The boy stood back up before nodding in approval. "As it should be!"

The young boy turned to look at Crystin intently knowing instantly that she was the one before bowing respectfully. "Ah, the mother of the twin's. Just as beautiful as I knew she would be; having the Sakura as one of your symbols you could not be anything less than beautiful!"

Crystin smiled in confused delight at the compliment wondering what a Sakura was, unaware that she had one around her neck since Dao never got the chance to tell her about them.

The boy turned back to Edward once more as Dao's son bowed in formal greeting before introducing himself to Dream Dancer. "I am Shin it is Korean; because I have belief, faith, as well as trust. I am Chien, it is Vietnamese; it means fighter or warrior. I am Eiji; it is Japanese because I will be the protector of the two. Finally, I am Dao, which is Chinese; it means that I am now the wielder of the sword of truth! I AM Shin Chien Eiji Dao, a master of the Tianming Samari Monks who believe in the way as they follow Shen's will to the appointed end!"

Edward smiled at the boy. He looked a lot like his father Dao; except his eye-pouches were slightly bigger as well as darker showing a stronger Korean descent. Shin might end up short compared to his father, which spoke of his Vietnamese blood. His eye slant, the colour of his skin, as well as his nose, was exactly like his father's; it showed the Chinese and Japanese influences in him.

Edward bowed as he introduced himself, his wife, as well as his sister. "You can call me Edward, Earl Summerset, or Dream Dancer. My wife's name is Lady Crystin or countess if you prefer. My sister is Lady Raven; her husband, which you will meet when you come into the castle, is Lord Devon."

Shin eyed Edward for a moment before nodding decisively. "Dream Dancer, I think it suits you best!"

Edward laughed aloud in delight. "Your father Dao said the same thing when we first met in Boston."

Shin gestured at the carpet that Edward was now standing on before pointing at the sword, as he looked at Dream Dancer knowingly. "My father's?"

Edward nodded as Dream Dancer helped Crystin to stand before turning back to Shin. "We will leave you now to say goodbye to your father. Pastor Daniel is on the right; Dao is on the left. Come to the castle when you are done, we will talk there."

Shin nodded silently as the Tianming Monk watched them leave, thankful to have a private moment with his father Dao without having to ask.

Once the three were gone, the young monk walked over before picking up the carpet. Shin draped it in the center of the grave so that the carpet covered most of it. The Tianming Monk dropped to his knees onto the carpet making sure that the center of the carpet was assessable to him and was in between the two deceased men.

Shin could see Dream Dancer's blood all over the carpet, but he ignored it. The Tianming Monk sat back on his haunches as he picked up the sword of truth; it was still full of his father's and the pastor's blood, but that too he ignored.

Chanting the Tianming Samari Monks song, Shin brought the sword in front of him asking it to accept him. The young monk smiled in relief as he heard a slight hum of acceptance from the sword of truth.

Shin brought the sword in close before turning it so that the point was close to the center of the carpet. The Tianming Monk drove the sword as hard as he could down into the center of the carpet so that the point was now embedded in the grave between the two deceased men; all the while, the young monk continued chanting.

Shin with both hands on the pommel bowed his head so that his forehead was touching his hands; the Tianming Monk knelt there as he prayed. Finally, feeling the presence, the young monk looked up as he smiled at his father Dao.

Dao reached out placing his hand on Shin's forehead, but no words were spoken as the young Tianming Monk was shown his father's last day before Dao was gone now able to rest in peace.

Shin still chanting changed his song; his Tianming Samari Master at the monastery in his homeland materialized in his vision so he gave his report. Feeling his master's approval the young monk stood up pulling the sword out of the center of the carpet, it left a gapping hole dead center.

Shin touched the tip of the sword to the head of his father's grave causing the sword of truth to glow for a second. Once it was finished, the Tianming Monk looked down at the carpet now no hole was evident from where the sword had pierced it. Nor did the sword or the carpet have any trace of blood on them not his father Dao's, Dream Dancer's or the pastor's.

Shin stepped down off the grave before placing the sword on the carpet as he knelt. He rolled up the carpet so that the sword would remain inside until later. Once done the young Tianming Monk picked up the carpet as he turned to leave the tepee.

Shin could not help but pause at the entrance once more as the Tianming Samari Monk looked back at the grave one last time. "Goodbye father, until we meet again one day!"

Shin disappeared just as soundlessly as the Tianming Monk had appeared.

*****

Crystin frowned at Edward curiously, unable to keep quiet any longer now that the countess was done eating. "Who is that boy?"

Edward finished what was in his mouth; he was starving, so really did not feel like answering questions right now. Dream Dancer sighed slightly in resignation as he respectfully put down his fork before turning to his wife Crystin. "That is Shin, he is Dao's son; he will be our daughter's guardian, as well as her teacher once she is born. He will be your protector for now until that time arrives."

Crystin grimaced in irritation as the countess spit out in a huff. "I do not need a protector I can look after myself, thank you!"

Edward shrugged dismissively as he chuckled. He was reminded of why the black cougar cub had chosen Crystin; she was such a fierce little thing. Dream Dancer had no doubt that his wife could look out for herself most of the time. "That might well be, but Shin will be all the same."

Edward ignored his wife Crystin's grumbling as he went back to eating. The first thing Dream Dancer had done once he had entered his castle was go up to his room to wash off all the paint, as well as the rest of the blood.

Edward had reapplied the ointment Raven had used on Dream Dancer before going down to the dinning room for some much-needed food. Finally finished eating he pushed his plate away.

Edward looked up before smiling in welcome as Shin walked in.

Shin put both hands together as the Tianming Monk bowed deeply in greeting. "I hope you do not mind if I use my father's room Dream Dancer? I put the carpet in there already."

Edward shrugged not minding at all; Dream Dancer was not surprised either that Shin had found his father Dao's room already without help. "By all means use it, but we are only here for a couple more days. Raven and Devon have to go back to England; after they leave, we are heading to Llannor Castle on the Llyn Peninsula to reclaim Lady Crystin's castle. I have already sent a message to Queen Victoria; she will send me some of her army so that we can get Llannor back into shape and guard duty as the protector of the Southern coast of Wales."

Crystin grinned in delight at Edward as she reached over grabbing her husband's arm in excitement. "Really, you will help me reclaim my ancestral castle?"

Edward smiled at Crystin's pleasure before nodding as Dream Dancer patted the hand his wife had resting on his arm. "Of course, it is your home; once we have it all secured we will make a trip to England to get it all refurbished for the babies since we will be staying at Llannor for the birth of the twin's. I had a long discussion about your castle with your godmother before I left England, she wants Llannor put back as the guardian of the coast as soon as possible. Queen Victoria also wants it ready for her visit since I invited her for the birth of the twin's in three and a half months. Although she does not know that is why I invited her yet, so we have lots to do to prepare."

Crystin squealed in pleasure before jumping up the countess reached over hugging Edward ecstatically. "Oh, thank you!"

Edward chuckled pleased by Crystin's enthusiasm as he hugged her back. Once his wife sat back down, Dream Dancer gestured cautiously in warning. "That is why you must have a protector! I will not take any chances; I do not trust that cousin of yours one little bit, so I do not want any complaining from you. Shin will stay at a respectful distance! Once you get use to him you won't even realize he is there, okay?"

Crystin nodded vigorously in agreement not wanting Edward to change his mind about reclaiming her home. If the countess had to put up with a shadow so be it; she would do anything to be able to run around her home again, especially if her husband put it back into its original former glory; Ernest had run it down over the last two years.

Edward looked over at Shin before Dream Dancer gestured at an empty chair in invitation. "Sit, so that you can eat; when not entertaining we are not formal around here your father Dao always ate with us."

Shin nodded as he sat before accepting the food passed to him. The Tianming Monk wolfed it down half starved from his journey.

Edward watched Shin eat not one bit surprised that the boy was starving; the rest of the meal continued in silence.

*****

Edward crawled into bed beside Crystin totally exhausted from his ordeal. Ignoring his wife's vehement protests Dream Dancer gathered her close to him so that he could kiss the top of her head. "I just want to hold you, you gave me quite a scare the last week, so I need you close tonight!"

Crystin sighed as she gave in to her husband Edward's wishes; it was actually nice to be held. Especially by someone who needed you that much. Having been alone for so long it was hard to get use to someone always being around.

Crystin knew that she would have no choice but to get use to it though her new husband Edward was such an affectionate man. The countess had never met anyone like him in her life even her father had not been that affectionate towards her.

Crystin had grown up around the nobles that had attended her father's court until she was sixteen; the countess had always found the men to be rigid, with no affection toward the wives that sat beside them. Although the women were just as bad as the men were she had found.

Not Edward though Crystin's husband was always finding excuses to touch her it had made the countess slightly jumpy at first, but now she was beginning to like it. She had noticed that same need to touch in Devon and Raven as well. She wondered if it was an Indian custom, which is what her maid Edith had called the earl.

Crystin sighed quietly to herself that cannot be right either since Devon was an English Lord; he had grown up in England. Oh well, the countess could not help thinking it really did not matter why! It was just something she needed to get use to, that is all that mattered.

Hearing Edward's deep breathing that told Crystin her husband was asleep, the countess pushed back slightly so that she could watch him sleep for several moments admiring how handsome he was. Her maid Edith had called him a savage, but as far as she could tell, there was not one mean bone in his body.

Crystin grinned as she reached up before stroking Edward's cheek tenderly. Her husband had been so patient with her never demanding anything that she was not willing to give, but with the evil now gone would the earl become more demanding the countess wondered.

Crystin snuggled up against Edward with a contented sigh as she finally drifted off to sleep, but the countess' dreams were wrestles. A wicked chuckle as well as her Cousin Ernest's cruel face haunted her dreams.

At one point, Crystin clutched at her husband Edward in desperation as the countess moaned in fear still sound asleep.

Edward woke instantly as Dream Dancer pulled Crystin in closer before whispering soothingly to his countess. “Shhh love everything will be okay, I will protect you I promise!”

Edward felt Crystin relax against him in satisfaction as his countess drifted deeper into untroubled dreams; Dream Dancer finally went back to sleep content now as his wife snuggled even closer to him.

CHAPTER TWENTY

Edward smiled at Crystin's put upon expression before Dream Dancer tweaked his wife's nose playfully. "I promise that I will be back later tonight or early in the morning, love. I just want to scout the castle since we have to wait for Queen Victoria's men anyway. Once I get the lay of the land, I will go talk to the townspeople at Llannor village. I should know more about what is going on around there afterwards. Stay here please so that the captain of the queen's guard will also wait here for me."

They had arrived at Beddgelert last night, so had stayed in the local inn waiting for Queen Victoria's men when Edward all of a sudden decided to go scout the castle with just his own captain. Dream Dancer did not want to set off any alarms if her cousin was still holding her castle hostage, so figured just the two of them would be more inconspicuous.

Edward planned on going to the Llannor pub afterwards in order to find out some useful information. Crystin of course wanted to come, but until he knew more Dream Dancer wanted his wife to stay safe not wanting to have to worry about his countess; it would only distract him.

Sighing Crystin gave in reluctantly, but pointed at Edward in warning. "Queen Victoria's army should show up in the morning if you are still not here we will meet you part way. I am not sitting here waiting like a good little girl. That is my ancestral home I want it back now!"

Edward laughed in delight as his little cougar hissed at him in warning, but Crystin did finally agree to sheath her claws until either Queen Victoria's captain, or Dream Dancer showed up in the morning.

The more Edward was getting to know Crystin the more in love with her fire and spirit he was falling. Dream Dancer reluctantly nodded in agreement though. It might work out better that way for him anyway so he would not have to come all the way back here to get his wife; as long as they did not get to the castle too early.

Crystin frowned in discontent for a moment as she gave in grudgingly. Suddenly the countess grinned as she remembered her old nurse wondering if she still lived in the village. "Ed my nurse Marie lives on the southeast side of the village; if you tell her that you are my husband I am sure that she will help you out."

Edward nodded as he bent to kiss the tip of Crystin's cute little button nose before turning away so that his wife could not swat at him as Dream Dancer chuckled teasingly. "I will find her, thanks!"

Crystin smiled after Edward as she touched her nose in surprise. The countess had enjoyed his bantering, so she was quite disappointed when he did not try to steal a kiss. The more she was getting to know the gentle side of her husband, the more she was falling in love with him.

Crystin sighed forlornly now that Edward was gone; she turned to go upstairs to their room by herself. The countess' ever-present shadow followed discretely.

Shin took up a position across the hallway just down from Crystin's room, not too close, but near enough that if the countess needed him the Tianming Monk would be there instantly.

Of course, if Edward would have still been here; Shin would not have stayed here, but since Dream Dancer would be gone all night; it was up to the Tianming Monk to keep Crystin safe.

*****

Edward chuckled as he left the inn; Crystin had started calling him Ed on their journey here, Dream Dancer liked his wife's little endearment for him.

Edward's captain was already waiting for him at the stables, so they quickly saddled their horses before riding off.

Edward reached down to pat his stallion's neck in affection after Dream Dancer's horse was warmed up enough. "You up for a hard ride there Cheyenne, you are getting too soft in your old age!"

Cheyenne snorted as he bobbed his head pulling at the bit slightly.

Edward chuckled; he knew how much Cheyenne hated to walk, so he bent close to his stallion's neck as Dream Dancer loosened the reins. "Okay boy, run with the wind, lets see what you got in you!"

Cheyenne grabbed the bit in his teeth as he surged ahead, not needing any more encouragement from his master. The stud's powerful hooves ate up the ground as they flew through streams as well as over gullies; it seemed that they were barely touching the ground at all.

Edward let Cheyenne run as Dream Dancer whooped in exhilaration. It was the most stimulating experience being on a horse with such power and grace. For over an hour, they ran flat out.

Edward looked over his left shoulder to check on his companion, but Dream Dancer saw his captain's horse falling further behind them too exhausted to run anymore.

Reluctantly, knowing Cheyenne could run flat out for another hour; Edward pulled up slowing him to a canter before reining the stallion in once more into a trot to cool him off and finally to a walk.

Edward laughed at Cheyenne's snort of rebuke wanting to run further. "Sorry old boy, but not all horses have your stamina."

When his captain caught up, Edward looked at his sweat-encrusted horse with a frown. "I think we need to find you a new horse!"

Captain Davies laughed in agreement. "Old Tom here is meant more for carrying armour he was not bred for speed or stamina, but yes he is getting too old. I was getting kind of interested in that dapple grey you have been training."

Edward chuckled knowingly. "She is a fine one that is for sure. If you want her, I can take a little money each month off your pay for her."

Captain Davies grinned in pleasure. "Sure, I would love to have her."

They let the horse's have a rest for half an hour before they were off once more.

*****

Crystin heard the sounds of horses, as well as men, out in the courtyard. She jumped up racing out of her room in excitement before going down the stairs. The countess slowed in disappointment at the entryway as the brown haired grey-eyed six-foot-one captain of Queen Victoria's guard walked in instead of Edward.

Captain Jacobson seeing Crystin walked over before bowing respectfully. "Countess, I am so sorry it took us this long to get here. The train we were on derailed on the border of Wales, so we had to help unload passengers. Luckily nobody was hurt too badly, but we had to ride the rest of the way here instead of only a hundred miles."

Crystin smiled consolingly. "I am just glad none of you were hurt."

Captain Jacobson nodded in agreement before looking around, but did not see Edward so turned back to Crystin in question. "Where is Earl Summerset?"

Crystin waved in the general direction of her castle in aggravation. "Edward went to scout Llannor castle; afterwards he is going to go talk to the villagers to see what he could find out, but he is not back yet. If my husband is not back by morning we are to go meet him halfway."

Captain Jacobson chuckled at Crystin's angry tone knowing that the countess did not like being left behind, but he nodded in approval at Earl Summerset's good thinking. "Great, that will save us a good day if not two I am sure. My men are setting up for the night in the courtyard; Queen Victoria sent you a hundred men with the promise of more if it is necessary."

Captain Jacobson stopped talking as he frowned in suspicion catching movement in the shadows, so his hand dropped to his sword instantly.

Crystin turned to see what Captain Jacobson was staring at before the countess looked back at him in reassurance. "It is okay captain that is Shin, Dao's son; he is now my protector. You met Dao when we went to Scotland."

Captain Jacobson relaxed as he nodded. "Yes I did, is he with the earl?"

Crystin shook her head sadly. "No, Dao died four days ago!"

Captain Jacobson frowned in surprise before looking back at Dao's son. "You have my condolences Shin, your father was a good man."

Shin stepped forward as he bowed appreciating Captain Jacobson's words of praise that he had given his father Dao. "Thank you!"

Since they were away from the castle Shin now wore black with his sword strapped to his back as the Tianming Monk trailed Crystin, trying to be as inconspicuous as possible. He had made sure that Captain Jacobson had seen him though, not wanting any unexpected confrontation with him or his men.

Captain Jacobson turned to Crystin once more as he bowed. "Until morning countess, I will be with my men if you need me."

Captain Jacobson turned smartly before leaving.

Crystin still hoping Edward would return tonight went back upstairs to get ready for bed. She tossed around in her lonely bed restlessly having gotten too use to her husband sleeping beside her, the countess was quite surprised at how miserable she felt now without him there. Finally, she dozed off.

*****

Edward looked over at Captain Davies in surprise. "It looks abandoned!"

They had left the horses ground tied a quarter of a mile away in a cluster of trees; silently they had advanced looking for sentries up on the walls of Llannor Castle, but there was no one around. Edward was not sure if that was a good sign or not!

Captain Davies shrugged dismissively. "They could be hiding inside since the gates are closed."

They could be of course, but Edward had his doubts. "Let's go to the village, I want to talk to Crystin's nurse first. Afterwards, we can go to the local pub to see what we can find out."

Edward's captain nodded as they silently went back to get their horses. They mounted before skirting the castle still trying to be as inconspicuous as possible just in case Dream Dancer was wrong.

The village was about five miles from the castle; the two men arrived just as dusk was falling. Edward looked around in suspicion it was very quiet for this time of the day. There should have been children running around at least, but there were none.

The pub, as well as the stables, was on the right. Even there though it was too quiet; only one old nag was in the corral.

Edward frowned perplexed unless they were out in the fields, but Dream Dancer had not even seen any crops at all.

It did not take them long to find the cabin Edward's wife Crystin had told him her nurse lived in. Dream Dancer dismounted before dropping his reins to the ground. "Stand Cheyenne!"

Edward went to the door before knocking, nothing happened; he again knocked a little louder this time though, but still Dream Dancer got no response.

Edward was just turning away in disappointment when the door creaked open cautiously, so Dream Dancer turned back; all he could see was a bloodshot watery eyeball staring out at him fearfully.

The brown eyeball blinked once. "What do you want?"

Edward bowed slightly as Dream Dancer smiled hoping to put whoever was behind the door at ease. "I am looking for Marie. I am Earl Summerset; I am Mary Crystin Alexandrina's husband. She told me to come here to find her nurse."

The door opened quickly as a little grey haired woman beckoned Edward in hurriedly. "Come in, hurry now before HE sees!"

Captain Davies dismounted before dropping his reins knowing his horse would stay with the stallion. The two men entered the damp, dank, pitch-black cottage.

The little woman who Edward assumed was Marie went around lighting the three stubby little candles that she had left.

Marie picked up one of the candles before bringing it over; she held it up to Crystin's husband so that she could see him better. She cackled in delight at the tall handsome earl. "So my little dearie managed to escape did she? It looks like she found herself a fine figure of a man too! Where is she?"

Edward patiently let Marie check him out, but tried not to breathe in too deeply. Crystin's old nurse let off a foul odour it was almost making Dream Dancer gag. "My wife is waiting in Beddgelert at the inn. I needed to know how things stand at the castle as well as around the village before I bring Crystin here."

Marie sighed sadly before shrugging grimly in caution. "The castle has been abandoned, but Ernest is still lurking around. He comes every chance he gets to steal our food, horses, weapons, our young; as well as any crops we manage to harvest. Most of the townspeople have disappeared, left to find new homes. Only we old folks that have nowhere to go are left. We have been warned that should Crystin come here we are to let him know immediately or suffer the consequences, but I am too old to care about that!"

Edward frowned in grim anger really disliking this Ernest fellow even more now. To terrorize families or old folks did not show him as much of a man; it only painted him as a bully that needed to be stopped! Dream Dancer was just the man to put a stop to his reign of terror too.

Edward shook off his angry thoughts as Dream Dancer asked the old nurse about Crystin's cousin. "What about Pwllheli Castle do you know what is going on there?"

Marie nodded matter of factly. "My niece lives in the Pwllheli Village so keeps me informed. She visited me yesterday to bring me some food, so won't be back for a day or two. She said that there are about a hundred mercenary soldiers running around the village raping, as well as pillaging, the folks around there. I keep trying to get her to stay here, but her mother refuses to come with her so my niece will not leave without her. So far she has managed to hide herself whenever the soldiers are in town, but I am afraid for her!"

Edward grimaced, so Crystin's cousin was up to something; maybe they should go scout Pwllheli Castle as well. "How far is the castle from here?"

Marie pointed northeast. "Almost twenty miles from here; if you go back to Llannor Castle, it's only about another fifteen miles straight east from there it's right on the coast."

Edward turned to Captain Davies. "We will go scout it I think; if Llannor Castle is abandoned I will not worry about Crystin heading there in the morning. She said she would meet us part way if I did not return in the morning, so we have plenty of time to check it out before my wife gets here."

Edward turned back to Crystin's nurse before bowing in thanks. "Once my wife is back in the castle I am sure she will send for you, so pack up in order to be ready to go. Thanks for the information; I am sure we will see you in a few days."

Marie clapped her hands in glee once she put her candle down. "Oh how wonderful to see my dearie all grown up, as well as married. I have missed her dreadfully! There is a back entrance to the gardens that I left unbarred; you can get into the castle from there to open the front gate."

Edward opened the door, but Dream Dancer turned back hoping to lift the old woman's spirits. "In three months and two week you will be plenty busy, we have twin babies on the way."

Marie squealed in delight. "I will have my niece come to help me since twin's can be quite a handful; I am getting old you know. Oh my, I am such a mess I cannot let my dearie see me like this. I will get my niece to help me clean up a little. Crystin would die of shock if she saw me looking like this!"

Captain Davies followed closely by Edward quickly exited the foul smelling cottage; both took a deep breath of clean air in relief.

As they were mounting, Edward turned to Captain Davies with a chuckle. "I sure hope Marie cleans herself up, or the first place Crystin's old nurse is heading is in a tub whether she likes it or not."

Captain Davies snorted in full agreement as the two men went back the way they had come, again not a soul showed themselves. They did not stop at the pub since Marie had answered all their questions for them, plus according to her nobody would be there anyway.

Once out of the village Edward kicked his horse into a canter as they headed for Llannor Castle. Dream Dancer wanted to go through that back entry first; that way they could drop the drawbridge down so that Crystin as well as Queen Victoria's men could enter when they got there just in case the earl was held up at Pwllheli Castle.

It did not take them long to get back to the castle; they skirted the back wall looking for the garden, it was not hard to find. They tied their horses not knowing how long they would be, so did not want them wandering off.

Edward grabbed his pistol just in case, as Captain Davies strapped on his sword.

The two men cautiously slipped inside; they had to fight their way through the jungle of overgrown trees to get to the castle.

Twice Edward had to laugh as Captain Davies grumbled irritably about having to use his sword to get through the dense tangled vines. "Stupid trees are going to dull my sword I swear!"

Finally, they managed to get to the back entry of the castle.

Edward cocked his pistol just in case.

Edward's captain kept his sword out so that it was ready for use, as well.

Quickly the two men entered in a rush. Unexpectedly, the door slammed shut behind them causing all light to disappear instantly.

CHAPTER TWENTY-ONE

Edward cursed; he had not thought to bring a torch with him. Instantly he closed his eyes as he crouched opening his mind to his surroundings. When Dream Dancer opened his eyes again, he still could not see anything more, but he could feel his surroundings.

Silently Edward thanked Dao for the countless hours of training that Dream Dancer had done with a blindfold, which taught him how to use his other senses.

Dao had always taught Edward that everything had energy.

Edward stood up as he inhaled deeply; he could smell a faint old-burnt smell. Using his sense of smell, as well as his inner eye Dream Dancer traced the whereabouts of the torch, which was off to his left.

Trusting his instincts, Edward walked over as he searched the wall. Finding the torch at last, Dream Dancer pulled it out of its bracket before turning to Captain Davies. "Do you have flint?"

Edward's captain grunted in agreement irritably. "Yes I do Earl Summerset, but I can't see where you are at!"

Edward chuckled knowingly. "That's okay just hold out your hands as you strike the flint, I will do the rest."

The captain did as he was told, suddenly a torch flared to life right in front of him; Captain Davies stepped back instinctively in surprise.

Edward laughed at Captain Davies' startled face before turning away as Dream Dancer walked down the small hallway.

Occasionally Edward would pause to light another torch up on the wall. Finally, they got to a set of stairs leading up; they were damp, which caused them to smell mouldy, as well as rank.

Edward frowned irritably as a rat scurried past them; they had a lot of work to do in here he could not help thinking. The first thing on Dream Dancer's list was cats, big cats by the looks of the huge fat rats infesting this place.

When they got to the top of the stairs it took the two of them pushing, as well as shoving, with all their might to get the door opened wide enough for them to squeeze through.

Edward went first with his pistol at the ready, but again it was abandoned. Dream Dancer frowned grimly as he looked around it was in total shambles. Tables were busted; chandeliers, dishes, as well as candelabra, were broken before being thrown everywhere. Not needing the torch anymore now that there were windows, he could see quite well without it so he extinguished it before leaving it at the back entrance.

Edward looked around again thoughtfully; if he had to guess this was probably the guards dining area, or the servant hall, which would mean that the kitchen or another dining area would be next. Stepping over debris as well as more rats, they hurried into the next room.

Edward was right it was the kitchen, but again somebody had ransacked the place. He sighed angrily as he looked around; Dream Dancer had better prepare his wife before she got here Crystin was going to be furious the earl was sure.

There were two doors, one was to the right with one straight ahead; Edward figured the one to the right would be another dining hall probably for the servants. Dream Dancer was sure that the one he had just left would be for the guards, which would mean that the doorway straight ahead probably led to the main dining hall.

Kicking things out of his way when Edward could do so, he went as straight as possible, but Dream Dancer had to negotiate around the stuff that he could not move easily. He got to the archway finally before entering the main dining room.

Edward had to turn left since there was nothing but a blank wall to the right. Dream Dancer looked around in dismay as he shook his head in disgust, what a mess. He could not believe that anyone would do such a horrible thing in what looked like a hall that had once been beautiful.

After turning left, Edward could see an archway straight ahead; again, Dream Dancer had to negotiate around the debris.

Once out of there they came to a small landing with four stairs going down to a wider landing. Edward walked down the four steps before pausing to look around. If Dream Dancer continued straight ahead another set of four stairs went up, which led to another third floor landing. It probably held bedrooms, or maybe the library plus a den; it could also be servant's quarters.

Edward turned left, instead of going up to the third floor, to another set of stairs that were going down. Dream Dancer descended the twelve stairs, which brought them into the large foyer with the big front double doors straight ahead.

Edward could see doors on either side of the foyer; probably a ballroom or a sitting room for entertaining guests, but he was not interested in them right now. Dream Dancer skirted the broken chandelier as well as other debris, but continued walking purposely to the front doors.

The two men opened them before walking out to a small open entryway that had once had statues on either side, what the statues had looked like Edward had no idea since they were smashed to smithereens.

The little entryway was not very big it only took Edward four strides to get to the three steps that went down. They were now standing outside in the front entranceway, which would lead them to the courtyard.

Cautiously they stepped out into the open. Again, they were greeted with complete silence except for the squawking of indignant birds, as they flew away in anger.

Even here, Edward could hear the squealing of angry rats as they scurried away; the horrible sound echoed in the dead silence as Dream Dancer shuddered, it seemed to him that the reverberation travelled all the way down his spine.

Once reassured that there was nobody around they kept going as straight as possible, but still they had to skirt around more debris, busted buildings, as well as garbage that had been strewn all about.

To the right and left of the gate were guard towers, Edward could see huge bells at the peak of each tower for warning every one of intruders.

The torn apart stables were to the left with three other buildings that had been demolished positioned against the wall. If Edward had to guess Dream Dancer would say that one was a blacksmith shop, the other was possibly an armoury; one could also be an inn or a pub.

To the right against that wall, there were a couple dozen bungalows, shops or some kind of business' that had also been torn apart, Edward was not exactly sure what they were though.

The guard towers were all connected by a walkway that went all the way around before going into the castle; Edward was sure that there were more rooms up there. It was a huge castle it even made Dream Dancer's look small by comparison.

Now Edward knew why Crystin was so determined to get it back. It must have been beautiful at one time full of life with lots of character, now though Llannor Castle was only a shadow of its former glory.

They finally reached the main gate; Edward paused as he turned around to look at the castle from this perspective. Dream Dancer had not noticed a barn way to the right of the castle it would have been attached with a secret exit into the garden for a quick get away if the unthinkable should happen and the walls were breeched.

Now it was in ruins since Crystin's cousin had it knocked down in a fit of rage after she had disappeared. The castle horses would have been kept there, away from the publics horses.

Edward looked over at Captain Davies as Dream Dancer heard a sad sigh beside him.

Captain Davies looked at Edward grimly as he gestured around in dismay. "When I was a young lad my father brought me here. You could not imagine by looking at it now what it was like at that time. To the left were two barns one for the guards and one for visitors. A smithy, a huge inn, as well as an armoury was also along that wall; to the right were fresh product shops as well as exotic stuff brought in from the ships to be sold here! There were also bungalows for people who lived or worked in the castle year round, with a pub called the Hidden Pearle. People ran to and fro; archery contests with all sorts of warrior competitions were held here. Guards stood up at the bell towers watching for signal fires from all the small towers spread around this inlet ready to sound the alert of invaders by the sea!"

As Captain Davies talked, Edward closed his eyes; suddenly he could hear, smell, as well as picture the chaotic bustle of this place long ago. His vivid imagination heard the impatient stamping of the horses, vendors hawking their wares. Dream Dancer could also taste the exotic spices that were swirling around on the wind that for sale. He smelt the horse manure intermixed with the smell of food, sweat, and perfumes.

Edwards nostrils flared as his ears perked up at the whoosh of the furnaces as they flared up getting ready for the day as the smithy then blacksmith shops came to life. Dream Dancer could hear the tolling of the bells before a call of greeting came down from the guard tower as more visitors arrived.

As Captain Davies voice faded, Edward came back to himself reluctantly; Dream Dancer opened his eyes looking around in dismay at the garbage, as well as the broken down buildings, littering the courtyard.

Edward frowned angrily as Dream Dancer turned to his captain with a hard, resolute expression. "I vow that it will be back to its former glory by the time my children are born!"

Captain Davies grinned knowingly; he had no doubt that Edward would make it happen. He had been with the earl long enough to know that when he showed that determined expression things were done quickly.

Captain Davies nodded as he brought his right arm up before hitting his chest on the left where his heart was with a closed fist in the promise as he bowed. "I will gladly help you all I can, this I vow!"

The two men turned working together they dropped the drawbridge down over the small dry moat that was full of garbage, as well as more refuse. The moat went around both sides of the castle to the high towering back walls of the garden.

Once the drawbridge was down the two men quickly made their way back to the garden gate the same way they had entered, now familiar with the castle layout it did not take them as long to negotiate.

They left one torch at the back entrance burning though; just in case they decided to come this way later, it would burn itself out eventually. Both mounted as they headed for Pwllheli Castle next to scout it; they hoped to find out what Ernest was up to, if anything.

The sun was shining brightly as they ground tied their horses in a cluster of trees before stealthily making their way towards Pwllheli Castle. There was a small hill just ahead, so the two men climbed it slowly; they dropped to their bellies as they slithered on their stomachs the last few yards to the top as they looked down.

Edward frowned puzzled as Dream Dancer watched someone coming out of the castle pushing a cart full of dirt, as well as rocks, to a mound not far from the gates. There was actually several mounds all at varying stages of height; another cart came out as the other one went back in, again there was just rocks and dirt in it. Several more carts came out before going in.

Edward looked at Captain Davies, but his captain just shrugged not having any clue what that was all about either. There were guards everywhere some up on the walls, with a good fifty or so patrolling between the many rock piles; twenty more were scattered around the castle gates.

The two men stayed for about two hours, but nothing else interesting was happening so they climbed down the little hill before hurrying back to their horses.

Once on their way back Edward turned to Captain Davies thoughtfully. "Do you have any idea what they are doing?"

Captain Davies shook his head just as perplexed. "Nope I have no idea at all, unless they are building a trench in front of their gates getting ready for a siege. Why they would do it inside not outside the gates I have no clue, but nobody ever said that Ernest was smart only cruel; plus very unpredictable most of the time."

Edward grimaced as he looked up at the sun getting higher in the sky as he swore angrily. He was dead tired not having slept since Beddgelert, but he knew there would be no rest for him anytime soon as he thought of Crystin's reaction to her castle if Dream Dancer did not warn the countess in time. "We need to hurry, I need to waylay my wife before she gets to her castle and sees it!"

Captain Davies nodded in agreement; he had met Crystin when she was only two that long ago day he had visited her castle with his father. He could still remember the little tantrum the countess had pulled when she had gotten angry with her nurse over something. He could not remember now what it was about though.

Captain Davies waved Edward on his way. "You go ahead; I will meet you at the drawbridge in front of the castle. My horse cannot keep up with yours anyway."

Edward nodded his thanks before bending low over his horse's neck. "Come on Cheyenne, let's fly!"

Cheyenne snorted in agreement quite happy to oblige his master; he always hated these sedate walks or trots since he preferred to run. He pinned back his ears as he gladly grabbed the bit in his teeth; within seconds, they were flying as the stud opened his stride giving all he got.

Cheyenne raised for the first two years of his life in the mountains of Montana was born to run. The mustang, thoroughbred cross stallion would not stop until he dropped dead if his master would let him!

Edward raced towards Llannor Castle hoping to make it in time.

*****

Crystin frowned angrily as she rode along. She had been spitting mad this morning when Queen Victoria's guard refused to budge one inch from the inn unless the countess agreed to ride in the center of his army; so now over a hundred men surrounded her.

Shin had also given Crystin a hard time as her young guard absolutely refused to ride a horse, so trotted along not far from the left side of her horses flank. The countess had to admit though that he was doing surprisingly well, not once had Dao's son fallen behind.

The fifty soldiers Edward had brought along had not backed Crystin up one little bit either. They were all up ahead breathing fresh air while the countess ate the dust of a hundred horses.

Suddenly the procession came to a dead stop at a shout, as the dust settled Crystin could see the spires of her castle not too far on the distant horizon. The countess grinned in anticipation; she was almost home.

Crystin was just about to demand that they go on when a path opened up unexpectedly in front of her as a horse with its rider came toward her. The countess eyed her dirty bedraggled husband grimly, as well as his sweet-foamed black horse, in disapproval as Edward came towards her.

Once beside Mist, Cheyenne reached over to give Crystin's mare a teasing nip on her hindquarters.

At exactly the same moment, Edward reached out pulling a squealing Crystin off her horse. Dream Dancer deposited his wife in front of him before proceeding to give the countess a thorough kiss in greeting.

Crystin pounded her impotent fists against Edward's chest half-heartedly in protest, but only for a moment as her treacherous body melted against her husbands in surrender. She had missed the earl dreadfully last night, but the countess would never admit that to him.

Edward chuckled deep in his throat in satisfaction as he lifted his head before looking down at his dazed wife Crystin as Dream Dancer smirked. "I am happy to see you too, Black Cougar!"

The soldiers surrounding them whooped in pleasure as they banging their spears on their shields as they hollered their approval at Earl Summerset's antics.

Crystin slapped Edward on the chest in rebuke; the countess tried hard to hide a little grin of pleasure, as well as her flushed cheeks from everyone. "You can put me back on my horse now, you brute!"

Edward laughed in humour, not fooled one little bit by Crystin's show of defiance as Dream Dancer caught the wicked twinkle in the countess' eyes, as well as the grin of pleasure.

Instead of doing what Crystin asked though, Edward looked around at the soldiers surrounding them as Dream Dancer waved dismissively. "I need a moment with my wife please."

Instantly the soldiers around them turned their horses so that their backs were to the couple before they moved off respectfully out of hearing range.

Crystin scowled grimly as the countess looked up at Edward not liking the sound of his tone, or the deep worried frown that suddenly appeared on her husbands face. "What is the matter?"

Edward sighed unhappily, as Dream Dancer looked down at Crystin. "I have two good things to tell you as well one really bad thing."

Crystin grimaced resignedly before nodding decisively. "Good first, please!"

Edward inclined his head in agreement already planning to give the good first. "Your Marie is still in her cottage, she is looking forward to seeing you soon. She informed me that your castle was abandoned by your Cousin Ernest after you disappeared so there will be no fight to reclaim it."

Crystin squealed in pleasure before hugging Edward thankfully, but when he did not return her hug, the countess pushed back. She looked up in concern at the frown of foreboding on her husband's face.

Crystin tensed herself for the bad news instantly on guard. "The bad news is?"

Edward sighed resignedly readying himself for an explosion. "They ransacked the whole castle destroying almost everything in it, as well as everything outside of it. Most of the villagers are gone since your cousin has stolen all their food, horses, armour, as well as their weapons. Your fields are empty with no harvest coming in this year; all the young healthy men, women, and their children are gone. There are rats everywhere; the moat is empty plus full of garbage, as well as refuse!"

Crystin sat there stunned as she wilted against Edward in despair as she thought of her beautiful castle. Just for a moment though, as the countess digested her husband's words. Suddenly her back stiffened in outrage as she looked up at the earl before hissing in anger. "Well we will just have to see about that, I will not let that man win! Llannor is my home so I will put it back to the way it was; I swear!"

Edward grinned as his feisty black cougar cub hissed in outrage baring her claws to fight her bullying cousin; Dream Dancer nodded in approval as he reached up to tweak Crystin's nose playfully. "I was hoping you would say that, I just wanted to forewarn you of what I found. Of course, I have not been in all the rooms, but I am pretty sure that they are all the same."

Crystin looked at Edward quizzically. "Did Marie say whether her niece was around as well?"

Edward frowned puzzled, but nodded. "Yes she visits her every second day or so your nurse said, why?"

Crystin her mind already buzzing with plans smirked at Edward teasingly before reaching up the countess tweaked her husband's nose playfully in return. "You will see later!"

Suddenly Crystin pushed away from Edward; she dropped to the ground lithely chuckling as she got away from her husband before the countess quickly mounted her horse. "Lead on Earl Summerset, but for goodness sakes Ed get me out of the middle of all these soldiers; I am tired of eating their dust!"

Edward's eyebrow rose in surprise as Crystin expertly dropped from Dream Dancer's horse. Without missing a beat, the countess was up on her mare before the earl could protest that she could hurt herself. Especially being five months and nineteen days pregnant.

Clearly Crystin had jumped from her horses back before so knew how to land, his wife was just full of surprises. Edward could not help chuckling though, he could not wait to find out more Dream Dancer's countess was definitely not one of the pampered nobility at court.

Taking pity on Crystin's long-suffering face, Edward turned his horse to lead his countess to the front of the procession.

Saluting Queen Victoria's captain of the guard in hello, Edward rode to the front before raising his hand up; bringing it down suddenly Dream Dancer's men were once again on their way.

CHAPTER TWENTY-TWO

Crystin caught her breath in dismay; the courtyard had been troubling, but easily fixed. Except the outside stable attached to the right side of the castle that the countess was sure would take a lot of work to put to right.

Crystin walked to the bottom of the stairs leading up to the entrance of her castle, she stopped staring upwards in dismay. She could not help the tears from filling her eyes as she saw the beautiful pair of hand carved stone dragons gracing the front entrance that she had hidden behind many times to get away from her Cousin Ernest; they were completely destroyed. One had been female the other male, a person had to walk between them to get into the castle. Now they were unrecognizable; both had been smashed to bits.

Crystin sighed sadly, as she walked up the four steps before stepping over the debris as Edward's wife walked into her once beautiful castle. The countess looked around in rage this though was an absolute outrage!

Crystin grimly gazed around the entrance hall; the gorgeous chandelier that should have been hanging down just in front of the stairs leading up to the second floors was smashed. It was lying on the floor in front of the steps.

The beautiful tables, statues, vases mirrors, as well as all the other antiques that had graced this beautiful foyer were broken also thrown about half-haphazardly.

The second floor held the three dining rooms, as well as the kitchen on the right. With the libraries, dens, plus the servants quarters in the back for the ones that lived here year round on the left.

On the main floor to the right of where Crystin stood now was the ballroom; to the left was the sitting room. As well, as access to a set of stairs leading up to the third floor where the master bedroom and guest chambers were.

There was a fourth floor as well, but it was only accessible from the guard towers. The guard towers each had rooms for visiting guards, as well as a weapon and armour room.

The fourth floor of the castle held three small private bedrooms for the higher ranked officers of the army that should have stood on the walls. There were five large rooms with bunk beds everywhere; each room could hold up to twenty beds.

Further down it also had a meeting room for when Crystin's father had wanted to discuss in private defence, strategy regarding the little inlet, or when war was upon them. Finally, there was a gathering room for the soldiers when they were not on duty with an attached room that held the soldier's weapons and armour.

Crystin turned to her right first as the countess rushed into the ballroom; this room was huge it ran almost the entire length of the castle. It could hold up to fifteen hundred people; it had been used a lot when her parents were alive.

Now though it was in shambles with the grand piano, as well as all the musical instruments, broken; portraits of Crystin's family littered the floor, not a stitch of furniture had been left whole.

Crystin turned away in despair as the countess walked back out into the hall before going straight across past the entrance to the sitting room. This one was not as large since the stairs leading up to the third floor cut it off, but you could still put five hundred people in here easily.

Totally dejected Crystin looked around at what had once been one of her mother's masterpieces. The furniture had all been made in rose or maple wood all very old antiques that had been in the countess' family for generations. Again all the portraits that had graced the walls were now littered amongst the broken furniture.

A horrifying thought overwhelmed Crystin suddenly, with a cry of fear she turned sprinting to the doorway. The countess pushed her husband impatiently out of her way since Edward had followed her silently wanting to be close if she needed him.

Once back in the entrance hall Crystin turned left before running for the stairs leading up to the bedrooms as the countess took them two at a time.

Edward not liking the horrified look on Crystin's face followed his wife closely.

Shin, Crystin's constant shadow, followed closely behind Edward just as concerned by that look on the countess's face.

Crystin out of breath from the long climb barely paid any attention to the broken dragonhead's that had once graced the elegant banister top and bottom. The countess raced down the hallway ignoring all the open doors of the guest bedrooms, just with a quick glance you could see they too had been ransacked.

Crystin continued down the hallway jumping over or squeezing past obstacles; the hallway curved around the castle it was very long bringing you right around the entire castle until you were actually almost over the ballroom.

Once Crystin got to the end, another set of four stairs led up to another small hallway. Now you would be standing over the ballroom, here the countess slowed. Her bedroom was on the left, but she barely glanced at it her door was open it had also been ransacked.

Crystin's glanced quickly at her mother's peach and crimson private bedroom door; the huge thick door was still closed tight, so her hopes rose. There was no door handle on the outside of the door; it could only be used as an exit.

It was a safety measure Crystin's father had devised long ago so that nobody could enter his wife's private rooms without him knowing. This way if the walls were ever breached they could not get a hold of his wife or his daughter to use against him. They would have to go through him first, so both mother and daughter could be protected in there for a very long time.

Crystin prayed as she walked to another door at the end of the hallway. Shakily the countess reached her hand out to turn the knob, but it was still locked as she wilted in relief. This thick solid door was the only way to enter both these rooms.

Crystin could tell by the door that they had tried to get in, but only the countess had the key. Luckily, the huge thick old solid oak door had withstood their repeated attempts to break it open.

Crystin reached into her bodice pulling out her medallion, which she never took off unless sleeping. Every night the countess put it under her pillow; it was always the first thing that she put on in the morning.

Edward stared in awe, thoroughly fascinated by the medallion. Crystin must have kept it hidden because he had never noticed it before. It must have been under the chemise she was wearing when Dream Dancer had first found her since he did not remember seeing his wife wearing it even at that time.

It was a thick large circle of intricate open knots, you could see right through them. Except for the four connecting points where a cross was attached to the Celtic circle. It looked as if those four connecting points were all that was holding the cross in the center of the Celtic circle.

There were two large deep green gems; one was on the right hand side the other was on the left side of the Celtic circle; these were the first two connecting points. The arm of the cross, where Jesus' hands would have been nailed disappeared under both of those gems.

The gems were so deep a green they appeared almost black, when not in the light.

Edward had never seen gems like them before; suddenly he frowned in thought as he realized that they were the same colour as his eyes. The Summerset eyes as well were so dark a green that they appeared black when in different kinds of light. Dream Dancer shuddered in uncertainty, was it just a coincidence!

The cross was unlike any Edward had ever seen; entwining the thick center base of the cross was a dragon, which was the other two connecting points holding the Celtic circle to the cross.

The dragons head was partially embedded into the top of the Celtic circle; it was large enough that it hid part of the top of the cross also.

The long sinewy neck went under the cross before twining around the cross once so that its shoulders, as well as its upper muscular legs, now would be over the top of the cross hiding part of the upper center base.

The front legs of the serpent came down as they curled inside the opening on the right; there was enough of a gap to put an index finger inside the curled up legs.

The rounded belly of the dragon was prominent so was raised slightly. It almost looking like it was pregnant since it was in front hiding the center of the cross. It did not look as if it were attached to the cross at all though.

The wings actually covered most of the left center beam of the cross, as well as most of the upper left gap, where Jesus' right arm would have been. The wings were not embedded into the cross either they too just fanning over it.

In order to connect the left arm of the cross to the Celtic circle the tip disappeared under one gem holding it in place.

The long tail of the dragon entwined the lower part of the thick cross base twice before the pointed tip was embedded into the bottom of the Celtic circle. The dragon was mostly red with black entwining the scales, as well as its legs; there was even some black on the head.

The dragon's thick muscled lower legs came down ending in sharp claws; it almost looked as if the dragon was landing trying to perch on the right center beam, where Jesus' left arm would have been. It's talons actually looked as if it were holding onto the center beam, but if you looked closer you would notice that the claws only went part way around they did not actually touch the arm of the cross at all. The right side of the cross also disappeared under the right green gem.

You could see way more of the center beam on the right side of the medallion compared to the one on the left side since the wings covered most of it.

It was beautiful; the Celtic circle was pure silver by the looks of it. As was the chain holding the medallion that was also made up of Celtic knots but thicker. What the dragon was made out of was a mystery though.

There was even another little tiny deeper green gem for the eye of the dragon that caught the little bit of light entering through one of the tiny windows. It made all three gems flare so that the dragon actually looked as if it were aglow.

The gems were obviously real; Edward frowned in thought Dream Dancer had heard of a gem that was a deep green to black in colour called a malachite gemstone. They were very rare and could only be found in the mists of Snowdonia.

When Edward had first come to England, Queen Victoria had joked one time that his eyes reminded her of malachite, but Dream Dancer had not known what she was talking about at that time.

As the gemstones caught more of the sunlight, green brilliance reflected all around them, as well as up on the walls, casting eerie shadows everywhere.

Crystin turned the medallion backwards as well as sideways, holding tightly to the outside of the Celtic circle with her left hand. The countess put her right index finger into the curled up front legs of the dragon before putting her right thumb on the other side of the thick cross base were the tail entwined the cross, so that she was actually holding the dragon as she twisted.

Crystin made sure to hold the Celtic circle firmly as a soft click echoed in the deep silence as the base of the cross with the entwined dragon turned. As it turned, the knots twisted moving as they entwined once again to form images of doves.

Edward blinked thinking that Dream Dancer was seeing things; it also opened up two slots where the gems were situated. Unless the medallion was backwards though, you would not even see the slots.

Underneath hidden by the two malachite gems was the bottom and top of a key. That is what the wings of the dragon, as well as the gems, were actually hiding. This way nobody would notice that the small center cross beam where Jesus' hands would have been nailed, was actually separate from the thicker base.

Once the key was taken out, only the thick cross base with the dragon entwining it remained in the center of the medallion.

Crystin pull out the key; the countess put it into the lock before twisting it, they all heard a resounding clank as the old rusty lock reluctantly let go.

Crystin pulled the key out before snapping it back into place in her medallion. The countess twisted the thick intricately designed circle so that the slot that held the key in place was once again hidden; the doves mysteriously disappeared, as they become Celtic knots once more.

Now it just looked like an old Celtic medallion with a dragon entwining the cross in the center. The cross in the center proclaimed to other witches or warlocks that her family followed the one true God, not the Celtic Gods of old.

Edward had watched with interest; he was very pleased that Crystin trusted him enough to let him see it. Dream Dancer's curiosity was killing him to see what the countess had hidden in the room that was so important to his wife.

Crystin sighed in pleasure as she open the door to her parent's rooms before she dropped the medallion back under her chemise. The countess looked around in pleasure thankful that it was untouched by her Cousin Ernest's hands.

Inside Crystin had stashed old portraits, her mother's jewels, all the best dishes; as well as everything of special value that she treasured. Not only here though, but the countess had also hidden stuff in her mother's private bedchamber that had also been used as a nursery.

The adjoining door to her mother's room was further ahead in the corner of the master bedroom on the right. Both rooms were stuffed full there was barely even room to squeeze through over to the huge four-poster bed with dragons carved on the top of all four posts.

Of course, Crystin had help at first; Marie too had hidden whatever she thought her charge would want when she was full grown.

On the bed was a huge painting of Crystin's parents holding her when she was a baby, it was propped up so that the countess could come in here when it was safe to talk to her parents when she was lonely.

Crystin turned carefully, not wanting to dislodge anything, to her husband with a pleased grin. "I kept one portrait of each of my family member in here just in the case, now I am so glad that I did!"

Edward smiled in relief at Crystin's pleasure. "Good I will have the soldiers start cleaning out all the other rooms. I am sure we will find some things that are salvageable or fixable in all this rubble. We will leave these two rooms until we have the others all cleaned out. Afterwards, you can start putting the paintings back up where you want them. We will camp in the courtyard until we have a suitable room for us to stay in here. I will send someone to pick up your old nurse, as well as any cat that can be found for the mice and rats. Maybe Marie will know where I can find a couple of good hunting hounds too; we are going to need fresh meat since we have no harvest or animals to butcher. There is a nice forest not far from here that we hid the horses in this morning, so wild meat will have to do for now. I will also send a couple dozen men out to buy supplies as well. Once you are ready we will go to England to restock supplies, as well as for any furniture you wish to acquire; make sure you make a list of everything you want. At the same time, I need to hire more soldiers. We have the use of Queen Victoria's men for now, but eventually we will need our own. Hopefully, I can recruit some of the men from around the island. I will also send for my captain, as well as a hundred men from my castle in Summerset. It is peaceful there so I will just leave fifty to keep my estate running smoothly. I have several trusted servants there that I will send for as well to help here until we can find more."

As Edward talked, they made their way out of the room; when Crystin shut the door they all heard a loud click echo eerily as the lock reset itself.

They stopped at Crystin's room, but again everything was broken or destroyed.

Crystin looked over at Edward as the countess pointed towards her parent's rooms in explanation. "Once we have the master bedroom cleaned out, we can move into it; we can use my mother's bedchamber as a nursery. Luckily, I made sure to put all my baby things in there for safekeeping."

Edward frowned in surprise taken aback. "You would not mind us using your parent's rooms!"

Crystin grinned at Edward's startled look. "No, I would not, plus they would expect it. My parents would have approved of you I think. We are not true blue bloods you know, but are a strange mixture of distant Scottish, English, Welsh, Irish, as well as Cornish bloods. The only real claim to royalty we have is through my mother; she was rumoured to be related to Queen Mary of Scotland. Seems Mary's daughter was stripped of her rank, and was banished. Nobody talks about her now; it is as if she had never been because she married a Cornish commoner. They had one son; he married an English half-Scottish heiress, but she had no ties to true nobility she was a lady-in-waiting I believe. She saved the queen's life though, since someone shot at Mary while they were out on a hunt. The girl jumped in front of the queen having seen a rifle barrel pointing through the trees, so they were raised to a baron. They had one son who married a Scottish lady-in-waiting; they had two children. Their oldest son married another English heiress; they had three children. Their oldest son married my Cornish grandmother, which would usually have lost him his baron status. He only kept it because she saved my godmother's mother. My father's family was rumoured to come from the old Welsh king's mistress she gave him his first born son, so she was raised to a duchess; she was also rumoured to be a Celtic witch that had put a spell on the king. She was quickly married off to a high-ranking Welsh knight who was raised to a duke by the grateful king. She had three more children by him my great-great grandmother was her second daughter I believe. She married another Welsh commoner another knight that had been raised to a duke because he saved the king's life. Their son married a half-Welsh half-Irish heiress. The old English king, Queen Victoria's uncle, was not happy when my father wanted to marry a lowly barons daughter, but when my grandmother saved Queen Victoria's mother he allowed it. Through my mother's family, I have a very distant relation third or fourth cousin I believe to Queen Victoria, but it is all hushed up. With all the scandals surrounding my family's history nobody wants to admit we even exist; that is why we were given Llannor Castle here in Wales it keeps us hidden, as well as forgotten most of the time."

As they talked they made their way back to the stairs leading down, they peeked in doorways but never stopped for long.

Once back on the main floor Crystin turned left to the stairs leading to the second floor, they went up the twelve stairs before she paused. The countess did not really need to go to the dining rooms and kitchen since Edward had told her already what they were like.

Crystin turned left instead taking the four stairs leading up to the library, dens, as well as the servant's quarters. The huge library had been her father's joy; with an attached sitting room that had been her mother's place of refuge. The countess had spent many hours here with her mother as she read to her.

There were actually two dens one for Crystin's father, as well as one for her mother for semi formal meetings.

All the rooms were torn apart with only the top shelves of the library being spared since the books were too high up for them to reach. Crystin had destroyed the ladder many years ago after she made sure to put all their special books up as high as the countess could manage; now she was glad that she had done so.

Sadly, Crystin shook her head in sorrow before going to look in the next two rooms; the one on the right had been her father's office, the one on the left had been her mother's sewing room. Both of them had been ransacked completely, it did not look to either of them that there was anything salvageable in here at all.

The hallway was now curving with bedrooms on each side for the servants going all the way around the castle until again they stood above the ballroom. The master bedroom would be right above Crystin now.

Some of the servant's rooms were damaged, but not all of them.

They walked back the way they had come before going back down the four stairs to the landing as they turned right going down to the front entryway. They went around the chandelier, as well as all the debris to the front doors.

CHAPTER TWENTY-THREE

Once outside, the chaotic scene happening in the courtyard bombarded them.

Soldiers were erecting tents getting ready for a long uncomfortable night.

Already a big tent had been set up for the cook, as well as her helpers; delicious smells mingled with the smell of horse manure and human sweat. It filled the air making one unsure whether inhaling was a good idea or not depending on your sensitivity to each smell.

Edward led Crystin over to the two captains; they were trying to decide what to do after all the tents were erected.

Edward gestured at his own captain first, already having a list of things Dream Dancer wanted done first. "Take a few men Captain Davies, go see if Crystin's old nurse is ready yet; if she is not you can help her get ready, we will need her tonight. If her niece is there bring her along, the countess wishes to speak with her. Pick up any stray cats that you can find, it is probably best to look around the stables or forge in town there should be a few bring at least four; take one of the wagons. Send the rest of your men out to see if they can find us enough provisions for a week. I will send my page to Summerset so that they will bring us more."

Captain Davies saluted Edward before slipping away.

Edward turned to Queen Victoria's captain next. "You can send thirty of your men out as well Captain Jacobson, see if they can recruit soldiers for me and gather as much supplies as they can. Put twenty men up on the wall for now the rest you can put in groups of ten, two groups for Crystin, as well as two groups for me. The countess' group can start in the kitchen before going into the dining rooms. I will start in the back bedrooms then work my way to the stairs. Send ten men out as well to clean up the moat, afterwards send them out hunting when they are done. I want everything brought out that is unsalvageable to be burnt. What can be repaired can be set aside; my wife has the final say on what is burnt. Have someone who can write follow her around to make a list of everything she wants or needs."

Captain Jacobson saluted as he went to start organizing.

Edward found his page; Dream Dancer wrote out a hasty note to his captain in Summerset before sending the young man on his way.

Just as Edward finished the forty men Dream Dancer had requested arrived, as did a young freckled faced red headed fellow with pen, ink, as well as paper.

The redhead bowed to the countess, as well as to Edward. "I am James; I am the youngest son of Sir Walter of Cambridge."

Crystin smiled he was only about eighteen with a very serious face. She nodded in greeting as they all went inside before splitting up. The countess went straight to the stairs leading to the second floor with her twenty men as Edward turned left leading his twenty to the stairs going up to the third floor bedrooms.

Crystin split her crew up into two groups of ten. One group she sent to the kitchen, the other ten she started working in the main dining room. The countess went from one room to the other supervising, as well as helping, where needed.

Never having been afraid of hard work Crystin refused to stand on the sidelines watching others do it all. Before long, she had two piles of stuff stocked up, one for burning plus one that could be repaired if the countess could find a decent woodworker among the soldiers.

Crystin spun at a horrified gasp of shock; the countess turned hurriedly in excitement already guessing who it was. Her old nurse stood in the doorway with a hand over her mouth in stunned disbelief.

Marie dropped her hand as she sputtered in dismay. "My lady what for goodness sakes are you doing, your parents would be appalled to see you in such a state!"

Crystin with sweat running down her face, as well as a smudge of dirt across her left cheek, and a black spot on her nose grinned cheekily at her nurse. The countess giggled in delight before running over for a big hug from her old nurse.

Crystin pushed herself away so that the countess could see Marie's expression. "Marie I am so glad to see you here! Did you bring your niece? You know very well that my parents would be right here helping me, so no hysterics now there is way too much work that needs to be done. Your room was not touched or the one beside it, so you can move back in right away."

Crystin looked behind her nurse as she was talking; she saw Michelle standing there waiting impatiently for her turn to be greeted. She grinned in pleasure at the willowy tall brown haired girl with greyish blue eyes. She was a year older than the countess the two had grown up together. They had been fast friends until Crystin's cousin ran Michelle, as well as her mother off.

Squealing in pleasure, Crystin pushed past her nurse, not even letting Marie answer any of the countess' questions.

Crystin squeezed her friend ecstatically. "I have missed you so much Michelle!"

Michelle laughed boisterously. "I have missed you too lovey, you look radiant!"

Crystin stepped back as she rubbed her stomach even though she had been hiding the fact that she was now almost six months pregnant hoping that nobody would notice since her marriage had only been seventeen days ago today, she leaned forward as she whispering secretively. "I am going to be having two babies, twins."

Michelle's mouth dropped open in shock. "My aunt told me you were married, but she did not say anything about pregnant!"

Marie grinned unrepentantly not one bit sorry for not saying anything. "Of course not, I figured the countess should be the one to tell you that."

Michelle reached out to pull Crystin back into another embrace as she whispered emphatically in the countess' ear a blessing, as well as a promise. "Lovey, I hope your wee ones grow big and strong. I will stay here to protect you, the little ones also, this I swear to you!"

Crystin pushed away from Michelle with tears in her eyes as the countess smiled radiantly at her friend. "I know you will, I will have my old room made up for you, but for now you will have to move into the room beside your aunt. The whole castle is in shambles; my Cousin Ernest destroyed almost everything he could get his hands on. I will be right back!"

Michelle nodded as she let Crystin go; she frowned after the countess sadly wishing that she could confide in her friend. She was too afraid that her best friend would not believe her though; Michelle herself had found it almost impossible to believe when she had found out six months ago!

Michelle was scared that it would drive a wedge between the two friends, that she was not willing to chance at this time; especially now that she knew Crystin was pregnant! It had changed everything for her, Michelle must find a way to protect the countess no matter what; even against herself if need be!

*****

Crystin walked into the dining room, the countess clapped her hands to get everyones attention before making sure to speak loud enough for the ones in the kitchen to hear her too. "Okay everyone take a break go out to the tent to have something to eat. Make sure that you all grab something out of the pile we made for burning to take down to the courtyard. Everything has been sorted so now it is just the cleaning up. After you eat you can return here there are still two back dining rooms to do."

The twenty men all gathered around the pile, thankfully by the time they all left it was all gone.

Crystin went out to the hallway before grabbing Michelle's hand. "Come on I will introduce you to my husband Edward."

Marie interrupted the two girls, getting too old to keep up with the pair she chuckled as she waved the two girls on their way. "You two go ahead; I am heading out to eat also since I am half starved, I will meet you both in the food tent."

Crystin nodded as the countess shooed her young scribe off with her nurse.

Once everyone else was gone, the two girls giggling raced down the four steps. They turned left before racing down the twelve steps, once at the bottom they turned right.

Almost as one, the two young women stopped at the bottom of the stairs leading up to the bedrooms. The two girls looked at each other as they grinned in delight; fondly they both remembered the many years of trying to beat each other to the top.

Without a word needing to be spoken by Michelle, Crystin giggled knowingly as the countess began. "Get set, go!"

Lifting their skirts they sprinted up the stairs together, but it was not long before Michelle being malnourished petered out as she slowed.

Crystin surged ahead reaching the top first, the countess turned looking down at her friend in concern as Michelle breathing hard finally reached the top. In all the years that they had raced up the stairs, neither of them had ever actually won, always they had reached the landing together.

It was not until that moment that Crystin really looked at Michelle more closely; the countess noticed the bones, as well as the gaunt cheeks, for the first time in apprehension. "Are you okay?"

Michelle catching her breath nodded calmly in reassurance. "I am fine lovey; I have been giving most of my food to Aunt Marie. Just give me a few days to recuperate; I am sure that I will be back to my old self again before you know it."

Crystin nodded, but made a mental note to ask Edward to check Michelle and Marie out more thoroughly to make sure that nothing more serious was wrong with either woman.

Michelle leaned over as she whispered cautiously. "Someone's following, us!"

Crystin chuckled as she looked to where Michelle was indicating having forgotten about Shin. Turning her friend around Crystin beckoned the young Tianming Monk forward as the countess explained to her concerned friend. "You will get use to him that is Shin, he is my bodyguard. Shin this is my best friend Michelle."

Shin bowed gracefully with both hands pressed together respectfully. "It is a pleasure to meet you."

Michelle nodded in confusion as she turned to Crystin questioningly. "Bodyguard, but he is only a boy?"

Crystin nodded; the countess explained as they began walking down the hallway. "Yes, actually Shin will be my daughter's teacher when she is born. He is really protecting the twin's that I am carrying; it is a long story so I will tell you about it later. Even I have a hard time believing it, it's so very confusing."

Michelle frowned wondering how they knew that Crystin was going to have twins already; the countess was not even showing much yet or was she. It had been a year and a half since the two friends had seen each other; Michelle had just thought that Crystin had gotten a little fat. "So you are going to have twin girls? How do you know that?"

Crystin shook her head negatively. "No, according to Shin's father Dao who told me, I am going to have a girl and a boy."

Crystin was saved from any further explanations as they got to the back bedrooms.

Edward had started in Crystin's old room, now he was in the guest rooms having done three bedrooms already; Dream Dancer had just started working on the fourth.

Edward saw Crystin coming with a woman, so went over to see what his wife wanted.

Crystin smiled in pleasure up at Edward as the countess introduced Michelle.

Edward bowed in welcome at the introduction as Dream Dancer took his wife's friends hand before giving it a light kiss on Michelle's knuckles. "I am very glad to finally meet one of Crystin's friends. I hope you will be staying to help my wife out?"

Michelle giggled at the handsome earl before nodding decisively as Edward stood up. "Of course, you could not drag me away now!"

Edward grinned thankfully. "Good!"

Crystin gestured down the hallway back the way they had come. "We are going to go to the courtyard to eat, will you join us Ed?"

Edward nodded before pointing up the hallway in the opposite direction at the bottom of the four stairs to the master's suites. "Would you like to see what is in the burning pile first, the men can take it down when they go eat."

Crystin nodded as she walked over to the pile in order to inspect it, but of course, nothing was salvageable, so the countess inclined her head in agreement. "All of it can go!"

Edward nodded before calling his men together as Dream Dancer sent them on their way with a load. They followed the men down the hallway, but at a much slower pace. Still it did not take the four of them long to get to the tent for some much needed food, they all joined Marie as they ate hungrily.

Absolute quiet descended.

*****

Several hours later an exhausted Crystin walked towards the bed the soldiers had brought down from her mother's room since it was the only one usable. Thankfully, they had set it up in the countess' tent.

Crystin definitely would not have liked sleeping on the hard ground being as sore as she was; her lower back was killing her. They had worked for another three hours after supper, so the countess was almost dead on her feet.

Crystin was elated though now that Michelle was here to talk to, as they had worked the countess had told her friend everything that had happened to her so far.

A stunned Michelle had been flabbergasted by it all.

Crystin was not even sure if her friend actually believed her since Michelle had such a dubious look on her face after the countess had finished her story.

Edward heard Crystin's groan of pain, Dream Dancer frowned in concern before walking over. "You are doing too much my Black Cougar let the others do the work! Lie down on the bed; raise your nightshirt for me, I will rub your back with some cream it will ease the pain."

Edward went over to his black doctor's bag before pulling out the ointment that he had made; the Cheyenne swore by it. Dream Dancer would take the secret to his grave unless one of his children or grandchildren showed signs of being a doctor, which would make them a medicine man or a shaman in the Cheyenne culture.

Once Edward heard Crystin get into bed, he walked over to pull the blanket down to just below her hips. She had bunched her nightshirt around her shoulder blades, but ignoring his wife's protests Dream Dancer lifted it up as he pushed the nightshirt over the countess' head before throwing it in a corner. "I am a doctor my dear I have seen lots of women naked so just relax."

Crystin frowned perturbed at that thought. "Lots of women?"

Edward chuckled as he heard a hint of jealousy creep into Crystin's voice. Ignoring it, Dream Dancer began rubbing the ointment deep into his wife's muscles.

Crystin gasped in shock as the cold ointment hit the countess' hot skin before groaning in pleasure when it began tingling as it heated up.

Edward concentrated on Crystin's lower back first as he made his way up slowly massaging and rubbing his wife down lovingly. It was not long before Dream Dancer heard the countess' deep breathing that said his exhausted wife was asleep.

Taking advantage of the situation, Edward pulled the blankets off Crystin so that Dream Dancer could rub his ointment into his wife's firm buttocks before going down the countess' nicely shaped legs.

When Edward was done and sure that Crystin was in a deep sleep, Dream Dancer rolled the countess over onto her back.

Crystin murmured in protest, but did not wake up.

Instantly Edward hardened as he looked down at his naked wife. He chuckled at himself, but ignored his desire as he put some cream in his hands. Dream Dancer began at Crystin's shoulders before rubbing his ointment down the countess' arms then moved to her torso.

Edward unable to help himself lingered on Crystin's pert breasts that were just beginning to get bigger as they started filling out. The countess' nipples were a dusky pink now, but Dream Dancer knew that they would become darker as they enlarged filling with life giving milk to feed his children.

Crystin groaned in pleasure in her sleep, but still did not wake up.

Edward finally moved down to Crystin's stomach as he lovingly crooned to the twin's while massaging his wife's belly. Dream Dancer bent over the countess for a bit so that he could kiss her distended belly before laying his head on her stomach still singing a Cheyenne lullaby; once done he sat back up with a smile of pleasure not only had he heard their hearts beating, but they were moving around in there quit a bit.

Crystin had been trying to hid the fact that she was pregnant it was fairly easy to do right now since she just looked like she was putting on weight, but Edward knew that soon the countess would not be able to hide the fact that her belly was growing. A month more and she would have to stay at the castle to hide her self.

As Crystin's stomach grew bigger, Edward's babies would also start moving around a lot more; Dream Dancer could hardly wait to feel them actually kick not just move. His wife was already feeling it now, but they were not big enough for the earl to experience it yet.

Edward worked his way down to Crystin's hips; he paused for a moment not able to help the urge to touch his wife there as Dream Dancer gently massaged the countess' bud of pleasure.

Edward did not linger long though not wanting to wake Crystin; Dream Dancer moved down his wife's legs next as he messaged his ointment into them good before doing the countess' feet, as well.

Finally finished, Edward pulled the blankets over Crystin before crawling in beside her. He gathered the countess' naked body close to him lovingly. Ignoring his need for his wife, Dream Dancer cupped one of her breasts; he went to asleep content now as he held her closer.

CHAPTER TWENTY-FOUR

Crystin yawned as she crawled out of bed; she looked down at her naked body before grinning in pleasure. This getting up naked in the mornings was becoming a ritual she thoroughly enjoyed. For the last week as they worked to set the countess' castle back to rights, they had slept in this tent.

Every night Edward rubbed her down with his amazing cream that made her body tingle exquisitely. The countess' skin was velvety soft as well as a healthy pink from all the attention it was getting.

Crystin reached down as she stroked her rounded stomach in pleasure; the countess was showing more and more every week, as the twins grew bigger. It was also getting harder to hide it from others.

Crystin was now getting excited at the prospect of becoming a mother; the countess had begun wearing her mother's old clothes again, since they were too big for her it helped to disguise the fact that she was further along in her pregnancy than was actually possible.

Crystin had tried to pretend for a while that everything was all a lie, a dream that she had made up. Now though with her belly growing bigger, as well as her breasts hardening, the countess no longer doubted what Dao had told her; at first, she really had not believed that she was five months pregnant.

It was November third today so she had been married for just over three weeks, but was five months twenty-four days pregnant. A lot had happened in those three and a half weeks she could not help thinking.

Crystin looked around the tent once more in both pleasure, as well as sadness. Today it would be dismantled since they would be moving into the master bedroom. The countess was excited about that, but saddened also. They had grown closer here; she would carry the fond memories of their time in this tent for a very long time. This bed would now be moved back upstairs for Shin to use.

Shaking off her mood, Crystin pulled her medallion out from under her pillow; putting it around her neck, the countess turned as Michelle came into the tent in order to help her get ready for the day.

*****

Edward frowned grimly as he stared at the young black haired soldier that he had sent to Pwllheli Castle three days ago. Dream Dancer had hoped that the soldier would come back with some answers for him on what was happening over there or what had happened to the last soldier the earl had sent. "You can't get in the castle at all? Nobody in town seems to know anything or they are just too afraid to say; that would be my guess! What about Simmons, did you find out anything on what happened to him after he left here?"

The young soldier shook his head regretfully. "Nothing at all, he got in but was never seen again. There are no young men or women in the town anymore they are all gone. All the old people in town say the same thing. Once they go in, they never come back out. I checked in the next town it is the same there all the young people are gone. The only thing anyone knows is that soldiers show up; grab five or six young men or women, even some of the children if they are healthy before forcing them to go with them. Once they enter the castle they are not seen or heard from again!"

Edward sighed in frustration before looking at the three captains gathered around them listening. Queen Victoria's captain shrugged perplexed as Dream Dancer looked at him first.

Captain Jacobson shook his head at Edward completely baffled. "I have no idea!"

Edward looked at Captain Davies from his castle in Wales, but again Dream Dancer got a shrug of confusion. "I have no idea either!"

Edward turned to his captain from Summerset; he was the oldest one there. He had arrived five days ago with the much-needed provisions, another hundred soldiers, as well as twenty servants to help them get the castle back into shape. That was the only reason they had gotten the huge castle set to rights so quickly.

They now had over three hundred soldiers with more men showing up to join daily as word spread that more and more of the young were disappearing around the Island. Edward had made sure that all his soldiers spread the word around every town on this peninsula that Llannor Castle was a haven to anyone wishing to stay.

Tomorrow Queen Victoria's soldiers, as well as fifty from Edward's castle in Wales, would be leaving for England with them. The queen's men would not be returning with them though, but Dream Dancer planned to hire more soldiers once there; he hoped anyway.

Edward eyed his older captain hopefully. "Any ideas, Gregory?"

Captain Gregory frowned thoughtfully. He had gone to look with Edward just after arriving at all the dirt piling up around Pwllheli Castle. "Well all I can think of is that they are building a dungeon or maybe digging an escape route. With the amount of dirt as well as rocks though, I would guess both. If they are building a dungeon, it means that they are planning to have someone in it! You or Crystin I would imagine, but just in case anything goes wrong; they are building an escape route also. It should come out near the sea somewhere, so they would need a boat or a ship."

Edward grimaced grimly. "Maybe I should leave Crystin with Queen Victoria or my sister Raven in England; it will keep my wife out of harms way."

Captain Jacobson nodded in agreement before gesturing in encouragement. "I would seriously think about that if I were you. I can keep an eye on the countess there for you, if you wish!"

Captain Davies laughed knowingly at Edward. "If you can convince the countess to stay there that is!"

Edward frowned thoughtfully as Dream Dancer threw up his hands in frustration at the thought of his wife Crystin. "I might have to get Queen Victoria to lock her up, but I will try reason first!"

The others all laughed at Edward's aggrieved expression.

Edward just grinned before gesturing around. "Okay let's get all these tents put away now that the soldiers rooms are all done they can stay there tonight. I want these tents in the courtyard packed up for our trip to England tomorrow."

Everyone dispersed, so Edward left to go find Crystin; Dream Dancer was not looking forward to this discussion at all.

*****

Crystin frowned thoughtfully as the countess looked around at her mother's old room, it would now be the nursery; it was almost empty. She was just not sure where to put the last of the portraits of her family; finally, she shrugged in indecision.

Crystin turned back to her helpers in frustration. "You can take everything else down to the sitting room for now I think, I will figure out what to do with them later! I also need the bed in my tent brought up here for Shin; he can stay in the nursery until the twin's are born."

Shin stepped up before shaking his head in disagreement. "I would rather stay in the room that is just down these stairs on the left if you have no objections; that way I am close, but not in anyone's way."

Crystin nodded relieved; she had not really wanted Shin that close to them. Especially because there was no door handle on the outside door, so he would have to come in through the master bedroom all the time. Ed though had insisted that the countess put the Tianming Monk in here even though she had protested.

Crystin turned to her red haired scribe James. "Add another crib on the list please, that should be it for now. You can give the list to Edward so that he can go over it in order to add what he wants for himself too."

Edward walked in just as Crystin finished talking, having heard the countess' request Dream Dancer nodded. "I will look at it later, you can put it on my desk in my office please, James."

James nodded as he left.

Edward looked around before waving in dismissal. "Everyone can go down for lunch. The cook, as well as her helpers is setting it out right now. I need a moment with my wife please; Shin you can stay also."

The others grabbed the last few pictures obediently before carrying them out to be dropped off at the sitting room.

Crystin frowned as the countess looked at Edward's concerned expression. "Is something wrong?"

Edward gestured at the rocking chair that Crystin's mother had always used when feeding the countess as a baby. "Sit please, we need to talk!"

Crystin nodded perplexed as she sat before watching Edward pull up a chair to sit in front of her. The countess was getting a little nervous wondering what this was all about now.

Edward leaned forward before taking both of Crystin's hands in his as he told her everything that he had found out, as well as what conclusions they had drawn. After he was done, Dream Dancer told the countess that she should stay in England until she was close to term; when the twins were due, he would come get her.

Edward knew that Crystin had to be here at Llannor Castle for the birthing; Dream Dancer had seen it in a vision.

Crystin sat there staring at Edward in dumbfounded amazement before shaking her head in disbelief at how foolish the countess' husband was being. "You can't seriously believe that whatever my cousin is up to would have anything to do with us? Llannor Castle is not that important, there is no crown jewels here or treasure; even if there were he would have found it when he lived here! There is nothing important enough in the castle that would drive him to such lengths. He knows Queen Victoria suspects him of raping me, so he knows if I were to die that he could be suspected. Besides, now that I am married to you, your family would inherit this place when I am gone. I am just starting to show enough now that I am having a harder time hiding it, so some people will begin to suspect that I am pregnant. But, there is no way that Ernest could have known before now that I am expecting, because only three others knew about it! This castle is only used as a defence in order to keep pirates out of Wales or any foreign armies trying to invade

England by sneaking in through Wales. You already told me Ernest was doing all that stuff even before we came here, so it is more likely that he is digging himself a hole to hide in, since he is a coward at heart. Just in case I tell my godmother that he was the one that raped me, she told me that she had threatened to send him to Newgate if I ever remembered. I did not tell the queen because Dao told me that my cousin was used by the evil mist just as I was, to do what he did, so I have forgiven him. He was a rotten guardian, but I would not want to see him locked away for the rest of his life for something that was beyond his control."

Edward sat back reflectively thinking hard about what Crystin said, could the countess be right? Maybe they were jumping to conclusions. Dream Dancer had not known about the conversation Dao had with his wife either.

Finally, Edward shrugged uneasily; Dream Dancer really did not like that man or trust him one little bit. There was just something very wrong about Crystin's Cousin Ernest that had the earl on edge, he just could not help it.

Edward's eyes narrowed in warning before he nodded reluctantly giving in; Dream Dancer shook a finger at Crystin though. "Okay, maybe you are right about your cousin! We will be in England for at least a month, so I am leaving Captain Gregory to look after things here. He will keep me informed about what is going on at Pwllheli Castle. If, we feel a threat of any kind coming from your Cousin Ernest between now and our journey back here. You will stay in England for another month or until I say it is safe to return, understood!"

Crystin grinned in agreement, as the countess nodded not having any doubts that she was right. "As you wish!"

*****

Shin stood in his new room looking around in contentment. The Tianming Monk had chosen this room because there was a small balcony, so if he needed a quick escape he had one. Crystin's room also had a balcony, but this one was easier to negotiate to reach the courtyard below.

Everyone was in bed except for the guards; not all were sleeping yet though, so Shin had time. He went over to his trunk in order to pull out two carpets. One was used to cover up patterns the Tianming Monk did not want others to see. It had once graced Edward's bedroom in his castle in Northern Wales.

The other carpet vibrated with power as the earth spirit symbols of the chosen ones greeted Shin. For some reason the chosen spirits that were appointed by Shen, the Great Spirit could not find another to guide in this lifetime. They were held in this carpet until judgement day. His theory was that the Great Spirit had something very special planned for them. The young Tianming Monk knew that someday he would join them there as well.

The Tianming Samari Monks in Shin's homeland believed that all humankind had a soul or Hun. Hun refers to the soul that goes to heaven to be with the Great Spirit or Shen.

There was also a spirit guide from the Mother Earth; the Tianming Monks referred to the earth as Po. Most people did not know that they should have a spirit guide from the earth to guide them also.

The spirit guides were actually from a time long past. Only the Tianming Monks were aware of a time before even though some wondered. This earth was much older than anyone knew or could even imagine. The ones that found their soul, as well as their spirit guides also suspected since they were now whole so could see beyond.

When Jesus' was born it changed things as Mother Earth faded into the background, which caused humans to lose sight of their earth spirit guides. Now though was even worse as more people pulled away from Shen, which saddened the Tianming Monks greatly as the humans also lost their souls.

The Hun and Po were meant to make a person whole, without both there can never be harmony in mind or body. Once a person died the soul separated from the spirit, the Hun returned to the Great Spirit to be judged; the Po returned to Mother Earth until one was born again that was worthy to be guided by it.

The natives around the world had found so encouraged of their spirit guides, but in the process; they had lost sight of their soul. The whites around the world had concentrated on their soul completely forgetting about their spirit guides losing half of themselves. They wandered around aimlessly most felt the void, but did not know what the cause was.

Shin's people too had found their spirit guides, but had lost sight of their soul. Until the white man came that is, they re-taught his people to find their soul. Unfortunately, most abandoned their earth spirit guides in the process, which was also happening to the Indians.

Only through believing in the Great Spirit, as well as letting your earth spirit guide you, could one find actual peace. To find them both and balance the two within oneself was difficult.

Some people seemed to have no trouble at all, not even realize that they had found both. Others took years to find peace within them. For example, there were the ones who found both unknowingly, but thought it was their subconscious or sadly even believed it was destiny guiding them.

While others never finding their inner peace died angry, fearful, with bitterness locked in their souls. They never knew that it could have been different for them.

Take Crystin for instance; she has a beauty that spoke loudly that as a young child she had found both her Po as well as her Hun, but had not even realized it. Since the stronger half of the countess' family was Celtic, they had always believed in the earth spirit guides.

Crystin's great-great grandmother who was a witch had converted over to the Great Spirit having also found her soul, so had passed down those beliefs to her offspring's. Because the countess had grown up knowing both of them, it gave her an unusual inner beauty; that is why the evil had tried to get a hold of her.

It was also why Crystin's Cousin Ernest was influenced to rape her first; there was no way with that kind of strength it could have penetrated the countess' shield. Only through her defiled body would it be able to use her.

Shin frowned thoughtfully as the Tianming Monk again contemplated the disappearing Mother Earth spirit guides. Especially now, since most were unable to find their soul, as they pulled away from Shen the Great Spirit.

It seemed to Shin as if there were something not quite right about all of this, or a piece of the puzzle was missing. The Tianming Monk wondered if the Great Spirit actually wants the earth spirits to disappear for some reason!

On the other hand, Jesus' birth could have caused an unintentional consequence that nobody had foreseen; not even Shen. When Shin had said goodbye to his father while taking control of the carpet, as well as his sword, there had been something Dao had tried to tell him. Could it be the missing link to the disappearing Mother Earth's spirit guides or to Shen's inability to keep people from straying?

Finally, Shin shrugged if the Great Spirit wanted him to know Shen would show him the truth! If not, so be it; the young Tianming Monk's job was not to solve puzzles, but to help raise the one not yet born. He was optimistic though that she could help others find their spirit guides.

Everything living had an aura you just needed to know how to see it in order to read that aura to know something about that person, animal, or thing. Even a tree had an aura; once cut down to be made into a table or a chair it still gave off a very faint aura that said it was once alive. If people learn to see with their inner earth spirit, they would be able to see that aura everywhere. Unfortunately, most had lost that ability.

Shin shook off all thoughts as he put his spirit carpet just off to the left of the balcony spreading it out so that he could use it. He took out the other carpet before putting it by the door. The Tianming Monk went back into his trunk looking for his ink containers as well as his brush, so that he could paint his symbols of protection in the nursery.

Shin found them, so he put them by the door with the carpet that he planned to leave in the nursery. The young Tianming Monk went back to his spirit carpet; he knelt once again in the center praying as he waited patiently.

*****

Crystin sat on the edge of the bed; she watched Edward go over to dig in his bag for his cream. The countess cleared her throat to get her husbands attention. "You do not have to put that on if you don't want to, I am not that sore tonight."

Edward turned with a jar in hand before smiling placatingly. "I want to it is good for the skin too plus you enjoy it, so I do not mind."

Crystin nodded pleased, she had hoped that Edward would do it again; the countess loved how it made her feel in the mornings. With no hesitation she stripped off her nightdress before crawling into her parent's huge bed waiting, she was hoping to stay awake this time.

Edward sat down beside Crystin before lowering the blanket as he began massaging her. Dream Dancer had lovingly done this for his wife every night for the last week. He patiently massaged just her back waiting until he heard the countess' even breaths to lower the blanket further as he did her legs next.

When Edward was sure Crystin was asleep, he turned her over massaging both arms, as well as her torso. As Dream Dancer moved further down, he felt his wife give a little intake of breath so he knew that the countess was not asleep.

Since Crystin was not objecting Edward continued down to her breasts, but this time only messaged around his wife's breasts; Dream Dancer bent his head as he lightly flicked his tongue across the countess' erect nipple teasingly. He played with one for a few minutes before changing sides to play with that one also.

Edward felt Crystins breathing deepen, but still she did not protest; he continued massaging down to her stomach. Crooning to the twins Dream Dancer sang them a lullaby in Cheyenne before kissing the countess' distended belly as he moved down further.

Edward massaged from Crystin's feet up to her knees on both legs working his way up further. Dream Dancer made sure to go around the inside of his wife's thigh so that his hands only lightly brush up against the countess' inner heat; first one thigh then the other one.

Crystin's eyes open slightly as she groaned in pleasure half-asleep; the countess opened her legs further so that Edward would have better access to her inner heat.

Edward looked up; he saw Crystin watching him, so he brought his hand further in as he played with her curls teasingly before moving up slightly. Dream Dancer bent once more in order to draw a nipple into his mouth. He suckled gently on it as his finger found the countess' bud of pleasure, so he massaged it lightly with his fingertip.

Crystin groaned in desire as the countess lifted her hips in demand.

Edward moved his head slightly so that he could reach her other breast as he moved his fingers down to find Crystins opening. Dream Dancer inserted two fingers to wet them before bringing them back up to massage the countess' bud harder until he heard her cry of ecstasy.

Edward put his fingers deep inside Crystin so that he could feel her climaxing around his fingers; Dream Dancer groaned in pleasure against the countess' nipple.

Crystin ran her fingers through Edward's short hair it was just barely long enough now to get some hair between her fingers before bunching her hand into a fist the countess pulled her husbands head up for a deep demanding kiss.

Edward chuckled letting Crystin have her way as he kissed her deeply, enjoying his wife for the first time. Dream Dancer finally disentangled himself as he crawled in on her other side; he pulled the countess in close as he kissed her on the forehead lovingly. "Go to sleep now."

Crystin too tired to protest fell asleep almost immediately.

Edward sighed contentedly from this day forward no more would Dream Dancer allow his wife Crystin to pull away, now that they were settled in what would now be their home it was time to become a married couple in every sense. He could hardly wait, since tomorrow was the beginning of the rest of their lives

Edward joined Crystin in sleep a few minutes later, as Dream Dancer once again ignored his need for his wife.

*****

Shin feeling the castle as well as all its inhabitants sleep got up as he gathered the carpet by the door, his ink, as well as his brush; quietly he made his way up to the nursery. The Tianming Monk had made sure to prop the door open so that he could get in without having to go through the master bedroom. He let himself in before closing the door; afterwards he put the carpet down in order to move the crib out of the way.

Shin sat on the floor, exactly in the center of where the crib would be; humming softly he began painting symbols. A white buffalo was first since the Tianming Monk had seen it in a vision in his room.

Next Shin painted Dream Dancer and Crystin's earth spirit guides, as well as his own. These symbols would help protect the baby girl's sleep. The Great Spirit's angels followed before the Tianming Monk put Oriental protection symbols entwining everything. He kept turning as he painted until he had gone in a complete circle.

The final symbol was the Celtic cross Shin had seen Crystin wearing. Now he was back to where he had started. The Tianming Monk sat back still humming his song as he waited for the paint to dry, as well as for the symbols to begin glowing slightly as they came to life.

Satisfied Shin got up to go over to the carpet. He picked it up before draping it over the symbols hiding the glow that would dissipate by morning; until the day Cecille would be placed in her crib, at that time it would come back to life. The Tianming Monk set the crib on top of the carpet.

Shin painted symbols on the crib next before walking around the room painting flowers with the occasional animal around the walls. The Tianming Monk was not worried about which child was going in this crib; he already knew since this one was full of girl's toys. Crystin had once slept in it as well so the countess' daughter would now be the one to sleep in it.

Shin finally left the nursery room shutting the door; he walked around the little hallway painting protective symbols over all the doorways before going down the four steps. The Tianming Monk turned as he painted more symbols on each side of that doorway.

Shin's song changed unexpectedly as he turned walking down the long hallway. He stopped periodically to put more symbols every once in a while on a wall before turning to the opposite wall the Tianming Monk would add another one there as well.

No torches were burning having been extinguished earlier, but every time Shin added a symbol, he could see more. The Tianming Monk's inner eye had no trouble picking up the slight metallic in the paint as it glowed for him.

Others would not see it except for Dream Dancer who had been trained by Shin's father Dao on how to see with his inner eye. It took the Tianming Monk half the night to get every room, as well as every hallway in the castle. Finally, finished he changed his song again as he floated back up to the third floor.

The castle now came to life as Shin went inside his room. If intruders should enter, he would be the first to know. The Tianming Monk knelt once more on his spirit carpet giving his report to his master in his homeland before crawling into bed. He slept now with no worries.

*****

Edward woke sweating profusely as he gathered Crystin against him in relief. He had dreamt that he was in a forest. The trees were so big that Dream Dancer could not put an arm around them it would take several people together to get their arms around the base. The trees towered so high in the sky that they completely blocked out the sun, leaving deep murky shadows everywhere.

Edward searched diligently, but he could not find his wife or his daughter. Dream Dancer could hear them giggling though, but all he could see was the bottom of a fringed doeskin dress flirting among the giant trees every so often.

Edward called out desperately, but it was not in any language he recognized; it was foreign to him. Try as he might, Dream Dancer could not speak in English or in his native Cheyenne. He tried again, but it was no use; the earl could not use another language.

Edward suddenly caught sight of the dress again; this time he saw several strands of black hair flying in the wind as Dream Dancer heard another giggle, but again they were gone as they flirted through the trees teasing him.

Edward woke just as he caught sight of two pixie faces staring at him around the tree; one he knew instinctively was his daughter. The other one made Dream Dancer cry out in denial at the dusky skinned black-eyed woman staring back at him with a grin of mischievous laughter. The love shining brightly in her eyes was hard to miss as it lit up her whole face.

Edward bent his head as he kissed the top of Crystin's head sadly; this was not the first time Dream Dancer had seen himself with another woman.

Was it a warning of the future, Edward could only hope not. The fact that his daughter was there, but not his son scared him as well! Would Dream Dancer lose his son too or is there a different meaning?

It could be that the young girl, as well as the older girl was both the same person. It might be the Great Spirit's way of telling Dream Dancer to train his daughter in the native traditions not in the English way.

Maybe it was Celtic Edward was speaking; he shuddered at that thought, the only place that might have trees that big here could be Snowdonia inside the mist. Dream Dancer did not remember seeing any trees, but that did not mean anything they could be deeper in the mist. He would hate to have to live in that mist for the rest of his life, the earl could not help another shiver of dread at that thought!

It could also be that the two girls were Edward's daughter, as well as a granddaughter. Since his son was not there, it could mean that Dream Dancer's daughter would be leaving England, but his son would stay here.

Edward frowned in frustration; there was always way too many different ways to interpret a dream. He would have to meditate to see if he could find the answers in the next few days; sadly, Dream Dancer no longer had his tepee to hide inside now.

Oh well, Edward was sure that he would find a quiet corner somewhere. Nor could Dream Dancer go into the future to see since he no longer had his powers, so finding an answer would be difficult he could not help thinking.

Edward finally drifted off to sleep, with no more dreams to trouble him.

CHAPTER TWENTY-FIVE

Edward, Crystin, as well as Queen Victoria's soldiers had started the ride at dawn back to Beddgelert before heading to England. They had arrived in London after two long days on horseback and five hours on a train, they pulled into the train station around ten o'clock in the morning.

Edward's group had split up as they waved goodbye to Queen Victoria's captain, it took another hour for them to get to Raven and Devon's townhouse. They would be staying with them while gathering supplies for the castle.

Crystin hugged Raven in excitement. "It is so good to see you!"

Of course, the first discussion the two women ever had alone was a little strenuous at first because Raven had seen what Crystin had become when the evil mist forced the countess to trap Dream Dancer.

Lucky for Crystin, her new sister-in-law was not the type that held grudges; as soon as Edward assured Raven that all the evil was gone from the countess it did not take the two women long to become fast friends.

Especially once Edward told his sister Raven, that his new wife Crystin was pregnant with Dream Dancer's babies. Everything had been instantly forgiven; twins were not unheard of in the Cheyenne tribes, although sadly successful deliveries were seldom reported.

The two women had talked for a long time exchanging stories, while Edward had been busy burying Dao and Daniel that long ago day. Now, Crystin had a better understanding of who her husband was; it had helped the countess get past the reluctant bride issue they had faced at first.

Crystin had learned all about the extraordinary gift that Edward had carried around all those years, but had given up to save her. The countess had not told her husband about that conversation though wanting their relationship to progress naturally with no outside influences added.

Edward had decided on their way here that it would be a good idea to visit with Raven and her husband Devon since Dream Dancer had not had much chance to be with his family while they were in Wales. With all the commotion that had to be dealt with, as well as the passing of Daniel and Dao, it had put a damper on their visit.

Raven turned to Edward next; she gave her brother a huge bear hug in excitement. "How long are you staying Dream Dancer?"

Edward groaned in mock pain as his overzealous sister Raven squeezed him so hard that he felt his back crack slightly. Dream Dancer chuckled in delight before stepping back. "Not sure yet Crystin's cousin totally destroyed almost all her castle furniture, paintings, chandeliers, and whatever else he could get his hands on; so I am sending you two out shopping. I would say it should take the two of you a week or two to get everything we need. I would like to be back at the castle within a month if possible. I need to hire soldiers to come to Wales also."

Raven clapped in glee as Edward's sister smirked in pleasure. "I love shopping, how much can we spend?"

Edward laughed knowingly already very much aware of that; Dream Dancer also knew that Raven had impeccable taste, so he had no worries about the quality his sister would demand from the shops. "Whatever it takes!"

Raven chuckled mischievously as she put a hand up to her mouth covering part of it as if it were a secret so that only her sister-in-law Crystin could see her lips moving. She made sure that she spoke loud enough for Dream Dancer to hear her though. "Edward is going to be sorry he said that!"

Crystin laughed in delight as Edward groaned in horror. She really liked her sister-in-law Raven so she had been delighted that Ed wanted to stay here instead of in the Summerset townhouse.

Raven dropped her hand trying to look innocent as she grinned crookedly at Dream Dancer before putting her hands on her hips in demand. "What seems to be the problem Edward; are you in pain somewhere? That is twice now you have groaned, they did not sound very healthy either. Maybe I should check to see if you have another boil on your buttock cheek! With all the riding you did the last couple of days it would not surprise me at all, you use to get them quite frequently in Montana!"

Edward sputtered indignantly as Dream Dancer turned red slightly.

Crystin quickly covered her mouth trying to hide her giggles of delight as Edward's cheeks turned red in embarrassed because his sister Raven was teasing him unmercifully; the countess had never seen her husband blush before now.

Devon chuckling in sympathy came to his brother-in-law Edward's rescue as Golden Eagle stepped forward. "Come on Raven lets get our guests into the dining room for breakfast they would probably appreciate something to eat before freshening up. Afterwards, you ladies can go shopping."

Raven laughed teasingly at Dream Dancer's grateful look that she saw her brother Edward give to Devon, so giving in she turned beckoning them to follow her. Once she seated her brother, as well as his wife Crystin; Raven having been aware of the two shadows following turned to them before gesturing in invitation. She knew who Shin was, but was unsure who the tall brown haired girl was. "Both of you sit with us, we are not formal here."

Crystin made introductions quickly remembering that Raven did not know her friend. "Raven this is Michelle she is my childhood friend, as well as my maid."

Raven nodded in welcome before turning to Devon thoughtfully. "We will put Edward and his wife Crystin in our adjoining room; Shin as well as Michelle can take the two guest rooms across the hall from them."

Raven waited for Devon to nod in agreement before she turned to Dream Dancer with a scowl of incredibility. "Edward, did you know that the nobility here in England do not share their rooms with their spouses; isn't that a shame! I hope you two do not follow that tradition a wife belongs with her husband."

Edward laughed at his forthright sister Raven. "No, we do not, Crystin sleeps with me."

Crystin went red in the face as a fiery blush darkened her cheekbones as she remembered her wedding night.

Raven nodded relieved; she did not agree with that custom at all. She was glad Dream Dancer had more sense than to follow it. "Good, as it should be!"

Two servants walked in with trays, which held bowls of porridge a dish of strawberries, as well as milk.

Edward grinned over teasingly at Raven as Dream Dancer indicated the porridge set in front of him. "Your doing I take it?"

Raven smirked as she nodded vigorously. "Of course it is! Believe me Devon's cook was not at all pleased when I invaded her kitchen to show her how I wanted her to make it. They eat what they call pease porridge here in England. Yuk, I am so glad that I brought ours, theirs is made out of peas; can you believe that! I brought enough with me to do us until we get home."

Edward showed Crystin what to do with the strawberries before putting on the cream. "Be careful though the porridge is hot!"

Edward turned to his brother-in-law, Devon. "How long are you two staying?"

Devon shrugged grimly not really wanting to stay, but they did not have much choice in the matter right now. "Not sure yet; Queen Victoria has confirmed our son Trevor as the next Earl of Rochester, so that is done. I have several interviews in the next three weeks for a steward to take care of our son's estates until he is old enough. Once a reliable one is found, we will be heading back; Little Cub will return on his sixteenth birthday in order to attend school, as well as take over his estates. I am hoping to be gone within the next three weeks, a month at the very most. We want to get back as soon as we possibly can."

Edward gestured in caution. "The sea will be pretty unpredictable at that time; you might want to wait till spring to leave. The end of November would be the latest that I would recommend; even so you will still be taking a chance at a pretty rough voyage since the weather can be so volatile at this time of the year."

Devon shrugged dismissively. "Well hopefully we will be gone before the end of this month, but we have to get back by the end of this year regardless. The ranch has been left too long as it is; there has been a lot of whispering of war coming recently we do not want to get caught in that."

Edward sighed sadly; Dream Dancer had heard those rumours as well. All they could do was hope that rumour is all it was.

Raven showed everyone to their rooms; she gestured in warning over at Crystin before she left. "I suggest you wear a split skirt we will be doing a lot of walking. When I first arrived in pants, it did not go over very well, so I switched to the split skirt in order to blend in a little."

Edward chuckled in delight; Dream Dancer could well imagine the stares Raven had received upon arriving.

Crystin nodded perplexed wondering why any woman would want to wear men's clothes, but shrugged not wanting to offend her sister-in-law Raven.

They went into their room in order to freshen up.

*****

Two hours later Edward laughed in delight as Raven walked towards him. She was wearing a split skirt all right, but had her black Stetson firmly on her head; she was also wearing moccasins. Her long hunting knife that she had made herself was in its beaded pouch on her hip.

Edward knew Raven well enough to know that his sister probably had a derringer hidden somewhere on her. Dream Dancer was just surprised that she did not have her six-shooter on her hip as well.

Edward had put his Stetson away not wanting it to become wrecked since there was only two in existence that he was aware of anyway. A man by the name of John B. Stetson had made one for them after Raven had helped him recuperate from a fall. He had broken his leg, so had stayed with them for over a month.

John Stetson had been on his way back home to Philadelphia; he had told them that he had came west for health issues, but now that his health was better he wanted to go home. In thanks, John had made them each a hat out of cow fur-felt; it had a wide brim to keep the rain or sun off; a high crown to keep an insulated pocket of air on the head so a person did not sweat while wearing it. The crown was even big enough that you could carry water in it.

John had told Edward that the fur-felt made it lighter, it also kept its shape better, plus using felt there was no tanning of hides needed so a lot less work. It was a new design that he was working on, so when he got home he was planning to do more experimenting to get different shapes and styles. As far as Dream Dancer knew, there still were no others in existence yet.

Raven ignored Dream Dancer's amusement as she walked over to Crystin before handing the countess a pair of newly made moccasins, she had just finished them two days ago. "Here try these on; they are better for walking long distances compared to shoes."

Crystin eyed the intricately designed moccasins in admiration; the beadwork was spectacular. A black cougar cub dominated the front. When the countess took them, she could not help stroking the velvety soft hide in amazement.

Raven grinned in delight at her sister-in-law Crystin's obvious pleasure. "They were suppose to be a going away gift, but I figured now would be a good time to give them to you."

Crystin reached out to give Raven a grateful hug. "They are beautiful, thank you; I will treasure them always."

Edward looked over at Raven in gratitude as he helped Crystin to put them on. Dream Dancer stood up before bowing with a grand sweep of his arm, he shoed them to the door. "Okay you two off you go your carriage awaits, but try to be back by dark. I am heading down to my office down at the docks I have neglected my patients recently. I will take Devon with me. Make sure that you have the clerks write down everything including the price. Let them know I will send wagons, as well as my lawyer, to collect the items later."

Raven nodded as she grabbed Crystin's hand in glee pulling her out to the waiting carriage. She absolutely adored shopping, so she did not want to give Dream Dancer a chance to change his mind.

Michelle was already in the carriage waiting; Shin climbed up with the driver.

*****

Two hours later the three women stood in a chandelier shop.

Shin stood at the doorway watching his charge closely, but not participating.

Raven frowned disgruntled. "It is too gaudy looking, not suitable at all!"

Raven turned away in disappointment they might have to find another shop for the last chandelier. None was good enough for the beautiful entryway in the castle that Crystin had described to her. She left the clerk turning towards the door.

Suddenly Raven gasped as she grabbed Crystin's arm before pointing in excitement. "Look in that corner!"

Crystin looked obediently before inhaling in surprise. "Oh, it is beautiful!"

The three women rushed over as they oohed and ahhed in delight as the chandeliers crystals sparkled, it would be perfect in the entryway. They had not noticed it until the sun now an orange fiery ball had begun to go down enough to reflect through the window off it, drawing their attention.

They now had all five that Crystin needed, so the countess turned to the clerk. "Make sure you pack them really good since they will have a two day overland journey by wagon that they have to make."

The clerk nodded as he took all the information down he needed; he had a delighted grin on his face that would stay for a long time. The commission off those five chandeliers would feed his family for the next year or so.

Now the clerk was glad that he had not gone with his first instinct, which was to kick them all out. Especially the one with her funny looking hat, she had a lethal looking knife at her hip, which had made him extremely nervous at first.

The only thing that had stopped the clerk was the youngster standing at the door watching him suspiciously. He was dressed all in black; he had a peculiar looking outfit on with a deadly sword strapped to his back. Not once had he taken his eyes off the three women.

Once outside the three women turned right before continuing down the sidewalk. They were so use to their ever-present shadow now that none of the women even realized that at every store they had been in the clerk at first was very reluctant to deal with them.

Shin though was very aware of this, but did not say anything not wanting to wreck their shopping trip, as the Tianming Monk silently followed keeping a discreet distance.

Crystin looked over at Raven on her right as the countess pointed. "There is a baby shop just down here. I want to go there next; we can cross the street to the woodworkers shop afterwards."

Raven nodded in agreement; it was a little crowded on the streets today, so Michelle stayed close behind them with Shin following behind her.

A red headed young man stumbled between the two women unexpectedly.

Instantly Raven dropped into a crouch, putting her leg out she tripped him. Spinning around she stood back up to her full height before stomping a heavy foot on the groaning man's chest as he lay on the ground in a daze.

The thief looking up in consternation unsure what had just happened.

Raven pulled her knife out threateningly as she held it in her left hand before holding out her right hand palm up. Her voice was deadly as she looked down at the unfortunate carrot-red headed, golden-eyed thief in his early twenties. "Give me back my purse. NOW!"

Reluctantly the thief held the purse up as he stared in surprise up at the green-eyed woman. He remembered a similar pair of eyes, but darker. He also could not help remembering the funny hat from ten years ago; at that time he was held by the scruff of his neck though being only a boy.

The thief had been extremely grateful to Earl Summerset for not calling down the police on him that day; he had never forgotten that incident. Edward had thrown a coin on his chest, so he had kept that silver dollar above his bed as a reminder to stay clear of the Summersets

Raven took her foot of the thief as she sheathed her knife before pulling out a silver dollar; she dropped it on his chest. "Here, get yourself something to eat!"

The thief could not help his grin of delight as the woman tossed a coin on his chest just like the earl had done that long ago day.

The young thief sat up before laughing good-naturedly as he saw the Oriental standing behind the woman with his hand on his sword threateningly. He had not noticed him at first because he had been behind the tall brown haired maid or he would not have gone anywhere near her. "You must be related to Earl Summerset!"

Raven frowned down at the thief in surprise as she nodded. "Yes, Edward is my brother. I am shopping with his wife, Crystin."

The thief stood up as he looked over at Crystin intently for a long moment studying her. Immediately he noticed the slight hint of a thickening waist that she was obviously trying hard to hide. He had heard the rumours of course, but this was the first chance Tomas had to get a good look at Earl Summerset's wife.

The thief dug in his pocket as he handed Crystin a purse before bowing in apology. "I am deeply sorry countess it will never happen again; please give my regards to your husband, as well as my apologies."

The young thief put two fingers to his mouth as he whistled shrilly. Several young men detaching themselves from the crowd before they all turned disappearing without another word.

Raven looked at Crystin in surprise that the thief had returned the countess' purse without prompting. She could not help but chuckle in humour though because he had kept the silver dollar.

Crystin had not even realized that he had taken her purse as well, so he could have gotten away with at least one. Why a thief would willingly return a purse had both women baffled.

Crystin shrugged at the confused Raven as the countess tucked her purse back in her pocket. "I don't know who he is!"

Raven grimaced; she would have to speak to Dream Dancer about the thief later as they continued on ignoring the gawking stares of passers by.

CHAPTER TWENTY-SIX

Edward and Devon walked into Dream Dancer's warehouse by the docks that he had converted into offices, as well as a small makeshift hospital, for the poor or needy. Dr. Summerset grinned at his blonde haired, blue eyed, burly clerk.

Edward had tried a woman at first Dream Dancer thought that people would be more comfortable, but it had not worked out at all. She fainted twice at the sight of blood; when anyone needed physical help she would not even touch them.

Edward had found a young man by the docks one night drunk, so had sobered him up; it was the best thing Dream Dancer had ever done he could not help thinking. "Afternoon Samuel, how are our two new doctors working out?"

Samuel grinned in delight at seeing his boss. It was his lucky day when Edward found him a drunken mess by the docks. Not only did Dr. Summerset help him to quit drinking, but he also gave him a job that he loved. He would do anything for Earl Summerset without one second of hesitation. "Fine Doctor Summerset, you have three new students from Oxford as well."

Edward nodded pleased; Dream Dancer had arranged with all the universities in England that trained doctors, nurses, and other health professions to do their hands on training here free of charge. It had worked well for Dr. Summerset; it also gave the new doctors a taste of what being a real doctor was all about now. If they could not make it here, they would never make it on their own.

Edward had been quite surprised, as well as pleased, when two of his students returned last year after finishing school because they wanted to stay to continue practising with him. That is why Dream Dancer was able to leave when needed; Dr. Summerset did not have to worry about his patience getting the help they needed when he was gone.

Edward was seriously considering building a real hospital around here. There were two old warehouses over two blocks before going up another four blocks that were falling apart. Dream Dancer was in the process of negotiating with the owner of the land to buy both pieces. Dr. Summerset wanted to tear them down to build his hospital; so far, he was not having any luck since the owner did not want to sell.

Edward introduced the two men before gesturing hopefully at his clerk. "Anything for me, Samuel?"

Samuel nodded with a grin as he reached into his desk; he pulled out a packet before handing it to Edward. "Yes there is Dr. Summerset, from Lord Greystone it arrived two days ago, but nobody knew where you had disappeared to!"

Edward took the letter in excitement before opening it immediately. Dream Dancer read the letter, he whooped in pleasure as Dr. Summerset waved the letter unable to contain his glee. "Finally he sold me both properties, here are the deeds. Get ready Samuel we are building that hospital after all!"

Samuel grinned in pleasure, already aware that Greystone had sold out to Dr. Summerset. His brother had made damn sure that he would do so, like it or not. "You want me to talk to my brother?"

Edward nodded eagerly in agreement. "Yes have him meet me at the sight tomorrow, nine o'clock in the morning. Oh get a hold of Lord Chester for me as well, I met him at Oxford he is a whiz at designing buildings. Have him meet me there tomorrow anytime after nine. I will stop on my way home at all the universities to find us the best builders, woodworkers, bricklayers, etcetera. We will need equipment as well, see where you can find me the best!"

Samuel was writing down everything as fast as he could go as the excited Dr. Summerset rattled off a list of to do's for him.

Devon waited patiently for Edward to run out of steam before interrupting. "Do you want an investor? I can have my lawyer look into my finances in order to help you out since my money has just been sitting dormant all these years anyway. The Montana ranch meets all our financial needs, so the money here is just piling up."

Edward grinned at Devon before nodding in pleasure. "I would be happy to go into business with you, blood brother!"

Devon smiled in excitement as the two men clasped arms in the traditional Cheyenne way sealing their pact. Edward beckoned to Golden Eagle once Dream Dancer let go of his brother-in-law's arm. "Come on Devon, I will show you around. Afterwards, I will take you over to show you where I want to build my hospital."

Devon nodded as he followed dutifully; coming to England had just given Golden Eagle the boost that he had needed. With a possible war on the horizon, a business investment here would hopefully carry them through the rough times that were sure to follow if war did break out.

*****

Two hours later, both men stood at the warehouses discussing plans as they walked around before going in-between the two buildings. As they entered the alleyway between, five men materialized in front of them unexpectedly.

Devon instantly crouched in a fighting stance, but relaxed as his brother-in-law Edward caught his arm in caution before shaking his head in reassurance as Golden Eagle looked at Dream Dancer inquisitively.

A carrot-red headed man in his twenties, with golden-brown eyes detached himself from his group. He walked forward before bowing deeply as he grimaced in frustration. "Doctor Summerset, I just had the pleasure or should I say misfortune of meeting your sister today; as well as your lovely wife."

Edward laughed knowingly at the thief that he had at one time caught red handed, but Dream Dancer had let him go instead of throwing him in jail. It was just after the young earl had disembarked from the ship he had taken to get here.

Edward could well imagine the scene had been very similar to what had happened that day. Dream Dancer could not help chuckling at the thief's put upon expression. "Did you return Raven's purse Tomas?"

Tomas laughed good-naturedly as he gestured in humour. "Your wife's as well, with my heartfelt apologies of course! I also couldn't help noticing that the countess is expecting, is she not?"

Edward nodded pleased to hear that the thief had returned Crystin's purse, Tomas had found him when Dr. Summerset had first opened up his practise at the docks. The young thief had been severely wounded in a fight in order to take over the thief's guild that he ran with and Dream Dancer using his powers of healing on the half-dead thief had given him back his life. Now whenever Tomas had a chance to repay the earl, he took it. He was not one bit surprised either that the observant thief had noticed his wife's condition.

Tomas' expression turned deadly serious in caution all of a sudden. "You know there is a hefty reward out on the capture of your wife. I have let it be known in my guild that if any of my people touches a hair on her head that they will have to answer to me personally. I sent out notices to all the other guilds as well, but I cannot guarantee someone from there won't try to snatch her!"

Edward stiffened instantly in fear as Dream Dancer spat knowingly. "Lord Pwllheli's doing, I suppose?"

Tomas shrugged grimly. "Not sure; it was a mercenary who did the contract on her no lord's name was mentioned, but with the merc's there usually is a lord or lady hidden in the background somewhere."

Edward nodded in agreement before changing the subject. "I was going to come see you tomorrow, will you put the word out on the street that I am looking for soldiers; I need them to come to Wales with me. No questions about their past will be asked if they wish for honest work, my wife's castle is in short supply right now. You can tell them I can be found at Lord Rochester's townhouse for the time being. I also wanted to let you know that I have now acquired both these warehouses, so I will be tearing them down to build a hospital here. If any of your people or their families want to work for me let me know, I will be back and forth here constantly for the next few weeks. Hopefully a month will be the most, I have pressing things to finish in Wales yet."

Tomas laughed in delight. "You said that he would give in eventually."

Edward grinned in pleasure as Dream Dancer rubbed his two hands together in satisfaction. "Well I knew he was in financial trouble so he would sell sooner or later, it was just finding his price."

Tomas saluted in farewell. "Until we meet again!"

All five men turned disappearing soundlessly.

Edward turned to his brother-in-law, Devon. "We better go find our wives; with Raven and Shin with Crystin I am not as worried, but it is better to be safe than sorry!"

Devon nodded in agreement, so the two men trotted back to their carriage quickly.

*****

Raven grinned at Crystin before nodding in approval at the cute stuffed toy her sister-in-law showed her. They had spent several hours in this store browsing, as well as buying baby stuff.

Raven knew that there was no going to the woodworkers shop today, once done here they would be heading back for supper.

They had gotten almost everything for the twins here, but they had not found a suitable crib yet. Oh well, it would have to wait until tomorrow.

Crystin tucked the toy under her arm. "I can't find anything else here that I want; I am sure though that we will find another baby shop somewhere along the way, but right now I am starved!"

Raven laughed in agreement. "Okay let's finish up; afterwards we will go back to the carriage it is time to go anyway."

They went up to the counter, again Crystin gave a grinning clerk all the information before leaving the store quite pleased with their shopping trip today.

As they walked back up the street, Crystin pointed across the road. "We can start at the woodworkers shop tomorrow, Raven; afterwards we can go to the furniture shop to see if they have a crib."

Raven nodded before stiffening in alarm as a dozen young men surrounded them not even ten feet from their carriage. Instantly Raven put herself in front of Crystin pulling her knife out. She had a derringer, but she would leave that for a last resort; there were way too many people on the streets right now to chance hitting an innocent bystander by mistake. She could see the driver of her carriage being held at gunpoint by somebody so he would be no help to them.

Shin drew his sword covering Crystin's back. They kept the countess sandwiched between them waiting for the men to make the first move.

Michelle was on Crystin's right, but had nothing to help protect Crystin with at all. She held her ground though growling fiercely at the man waiting for an opportunity to get past the towering brown haired maid.

Shin's sword whistled in warning as the Tianming Monk twirled it threateningly as one of the men tried rushing in to grab Crystin.

Quickly the man jumped back as the sword cut clean through his shirt. Lucky for him the point only left a red furrow behind that bled, but his quick reflexes saved him from being cut completely in two.

A man tried to get past Raven, but jumped back with a squeal of pain. The woman's knife had found its mark burying deeply; it severed the muscle in his extended left forearm when he had tried reaching for the countess.

Raven heard the sounds of a carriage barrelling down the street; she sighed in relief as she heard her husband Devon screaming out threats at the kidnappers.

The dozen men scattered suddenly as a furious Devon followed closely by Edward rushed out of their carriage before it could even stop fully. The two rescuers arrival filled in the two holes so that now Crystin was surrounded with Michelle now protected as well.

Edward growled in fury at the men as they regrouped for another rush. Dream Dancer gestured with his head towards his carriage as the earl hissed grimly at his sister in demand, but soft enough so that the men starting to come at them again would not hear. "Raven hurry now before more men show up, get into my carriage I want you to get Crystin out of here!"

Raven grabbed Crystin's hand needing no further prompting as she pulled the countess along quickly. The three men stayed close to the women protecting them as they got to the carriage.

Raven went in first pulling Crystin in after her before Michelle got in sandwiching the unfortunate countess between the two women protecting her still.

The three men braced for another rush, but suddenly two dozen men showed up attacking the others. Edward saw a carrot-red head in the attacking group, so sighed in relief.

Shin sheathed his sword quickly, but pulled out a dagger before swinging onto the back of the carriage keeping the rear guarded; while Devon followed closely by Edward crawled up with the driver.

Quickly the driver snapped his whip with a loud bellow of urgency. "Get up there now!"

Soon the carriages was barrelling down the street full tilt; a few minutes later Raven's carriage caught up since the thief holding it hostage had been disarmed by Tomas' men. It did not take them long to get back to Devon's townhouse. Quickly the men jumped down before rushing the three women inside; nobody relaxed until everyone was safely inside.

Raven beckoned to them, so they all followed her silently into the sitting room before finding seats as they all sat. She looked over at Edward grimly. "What was that all about?"

Edward told them about the warning he had received from Tomas.

Crystin shook her head incredulously as the countess interrupted Edward heatedly. "That does not make any sense at all, what would he want me for?"

Raven looked at her sister-in-law in sympathy. "Some men are just down right evil Crystin; they will never give up when they want something! I remember many years ago in Montana a wealthy rancher who decided he wanted a certain woman who was married already. He went to great lengths to get her; including kidnapping her, as well as killing her husband!"

Crystin sighed in exasperation as the countess shook her head in disagreement. "My cousin would not want me that way, he does not love anyone!"

Edward frowned thoughtfully as Dream Dancer pointed at Crystin's belly. "Maybe not, but it could be that the evil still has a hold of him some how. Which would mean it is trying to get to you, or maybe now it is after the twin's."

They all stiffened anxiously at a pounding on their door.

Instantly the three men rushed into the entryway.

Shin pulled his sword out as the Tianming Monk stepped behind the door in readiness.

Edward opened it cautiously; when he saw a man standing there on the doorstep holding a letter out Dream Dancer opened it fully as he relaxed. "What can I do for you sir?"

The man handed him the letter as he bowed before pointing over his shoulder at eight others standing below the stairs. "I have an introductory letter from Tomas, he sent us to you."

Edward opened the letter reading it quickly. 'Doctor Summerset I was upset to hear what was happening this evening, so I have intervened on your behalf. I also found you nine men who I know are very reliable, they all want to become soldiers. Please use them to help protect your wife; they would also like to go to Wales with you. Sincerely Tomas.'

Edward smiled in welcome as Dream Dancer looked up. "Your name is?"

The man saluted smartly. "Names Griffin, my lord."

Edward nodded in approval; he could tell by the salute that this was not the first time he had been a soldier. Dream Dancer looked past Griffin at the others standing in a row waiting for his approval

Not seeing anyone among them more suited, plus knowing Tomas the way that Edward did Dream Dancer knew that the thief would not entrust a letter to just anyone, but only to the most reliable one of the bunch.

Edward decided that Griffin would make a good captain. Suddenly getting an idea Dream Dancer grinned in humour. "Okay Captain Griffin you will take charge of my wife's personal guard, we will call your men the Black Cougar Guards. I will have special uniforms made up proclaiming your new roles in life."

Edward looked behind the door at Shin. "Come on out; you will train these men, so they will be your responsibility!"

Shin sheathed his sword before stepping around the door; the Tianming Monk walked down the stairs with Dream Dancer to inspect his new students, as well as to become acquainted.

*****

Several hours later Crystin crawled into bed waiting in anticipation as Edward brought his cream over. She tried again to stay awake, but with all the excitement that had happened today, soon the countess was fast asleep.

Edward crooned his lullaby to the twin's before crawling in beside Crystin. Holding his wife close to him in relief at having her safe, Dream Dancer fell asleep instantly.

CHAPTER TWENTY-SEVEN

Crystin got out of the carriage followed by Raven before Michelle disembarked last. Instantly the countess' Black Cougar Guards in their new gold and black uniforms surrounded them on three sides.

The black cougar was prominent on the front, as well as the back, of their golden shirts. Their pants were black with a golden strip down the outside pant leg.

The captain of Crystin's guard had a slightly different uniform from the rest; his was mostly black with a golden cougar on the front; with one on the back of his shirt as well. His pants were the same as the others though.

Crystin's captain always stayed in front, while Shin guarded the rear.

Shin had surprised them all when he had painted a black cougar on the front, with a golden cougar on the back of his white flowing robes, which proclaimed the Tianming Monk the master of Crystin's guards.

Crystin's mouth had dropped open in astonishment when she had first seen her bodyguards in their fancy uniforms. The countess was not sure, if she should laugh in delight or if she should slap Edward silly for making her the center of attention wherever she went from now on.

After the initial shock had worn off though, Crystin had laughed in pleasure giving in to Edward's wish that the countess keep her guard with her at all times.

This was their last day shopping having spent two weeks going up and down these streets hitting every place once, sometimes twice.

Edward had said less than two weeks, but Raven having a great time had drawn it out a few more days. The women had actually been done several days ago, but had continued so that they could spend more time together; which was fine by Crystin she had thoroughly enjoy every moment of it.

Most of the items that Crystin had purchased were already on their way to Wales with the new soldiers Edward had recruited throughout the month of November. The earl had sent the new soldiers ahead so that Captain Gregory could begin there training right away. Dream Dancer knew that his captain from Summerset would eventually want to go home. There was close to a hundred of them already; another ten had shown up last night.

Devon had managed to find a reliable steward last week, so as soon as Edward and Crystin left for Wales; Raven, Devon, as well as their son Trevor would be heading back to Boston before going to their home in Montana.

Edward had tried to talk them out of it of course since they would be on the ship the last two weeks of November, as well as the first part of December; very dangerous time to travel Dream Dancer knew. Raven had promised to send a telegram as soon as they arrived safely in Boston.

Their last shopping trip today would be spent mostly at the dressmakers; a complete new wardrobe had been ordered for Crystin on their second day so today she would do a final fitting. Even though the countess' belly was distended, they had made allowances for it. Everyone could now see that she was expecting there was no hiding it anymore, but she still wore baggy clothes trying to hide how far along she actually was. She was now six months and twelve days into her pregnancy.

Crystin being so tiny, but tall still did not look as if she were having twins even though the countess was over six months. It had amazed them all especially Raven as she laughed good-naturedly teasing the countess as she remembered that she had been twice that size with just one baby inside her.

Crystin had a lot of pressure in her lower back though, so Edward figured that was why. The countess was carrying the twin's very low;

Dr. Summerset knew his wife would have a great deal of back labour because of that.

Crystin turned to Raven as they walked along. "I am going to miss this, as well as you, when you go back home."

Raven nodded in agreement. "I will too!"

They turned into the dressmakers shop. Instantly the guards surrounded the shop door; nobody would be allowed in except women.

Only Shin, as well as the captain of Crystin's guard, entered with the countess' party.

*****

Edward looked around in approval at his two bare lots; not a thing was left from the demolition of the two warehouses. Not even a nail could be found on the ground anywhere.

Edward turned to his clerk's brother before Dream Dancer nodded pleased. "Your men did an excellent job, Mathew."

Mathew bowed in pleasure; he was totally opposite of his brother being short, as well as fat, with a head of curly blonde hair with deep brown eyes. "Thank you, my lord. After you helped my brother it's the least I can do for ya!"

Edward dug in his pocket in order to pull out the bank note he had waiting before handing it to Mathew. "Here is the money I owe you; as well as a bonus, for getting the job done so quickly."

Mathew took the note before looking at it. His eyes got big at the hefty bonus; he looked up at Edward in appreciation. "Anytime ya need me Doc., don't hesitate to let my brother know it!"

With that statement, Mathew turned before trotting back to his cart that held the last of the rubbish to be dumped; as well as the men in his crew.

Devon chuckled at his brother-in-law, Edward. "I did not know that a man's eyes could get that big around."

Edward laughed in agreement before turning to his architect without commenting on Devon's humour.

Edward took the rolled parchment that Lord Chester had waiting. "Let's see what the finished plans look like, Andrew."

The three men gathered close together, Edward unrolled it so that they could study the plans closely as Andrew explained it to them. They only had an hour before the foreman as well as his workers began to arrive, so anything that needed changing would need to be made now.

*****

The guard standing in front of the dressmaker's door stiffened as he watched seven young people approaching. There were three women being escorted by four young men; all the men were done up in their Sunday best, so were obviously suitors.

The seven young people stopped uncertainly as the guard in front of the door stepped forward. "Women only please no men are allowed in today!"

The youngest of the three women eyed the handsome guard in his unusual uniform; she could not help the urge to flirt, even with her beau standing beside her. "Aren't you a handsome one? We want to buy a dress for Queen Victoria's ball next week if that is okay with you. You would not happen to be going, as well, would you? I would be very happy to save you a dance or maybe even two!"

The guard blushed, but stood his ground as he ignored the young pretty girl's suggestive tone. "Go right in ladies, but the gentlemen must stay out here!"

One of the blond blue-eyed dandies trying to impress his woman dropped his hand to his sword before sputtering indignantly. "I will have you know sir that I am the son of Baron Lancaster if I wish to shop here for my lady, I have every right!"

The seven other guards sensing trouble walked over to surround the seven youngsters that were trying to enter the shop.

Instantly the woman who had flirted with the guard stepped up as she put a consoling hand on her escorts arm. "It's okay Lord Lancaster we will go in ourselves! There is no need for you to get all excited since we will not be long. I am sure madam Claire's got my dress ready for me by now, so just wait out here!"

The young nobleman wilted; Lord Lancaster looked around at all the tense waiting soldiers as he nodded before wisely backing away.

The three women tittering all entered the shop giggling about the handsome soldier's forceful attitude.

Shin, as well as the captain of Crystin's guard, looked at the three women entering suspiciously for a moment. It did not take the two men long to dismiss the giggling trio as they went back to watching their charge closely.

*****

Edward handed Lord Chester an envelope in pleasure before rolling up his plans satisfied that they only had to make one adjustment, so Dream Dancer was extremely pleased by that. "Thank you, Andrew; you did an excellent job as usual."

Lord Chester opened his envelope, giving the banknote a quick scan; Andrew looked up nodding his thanks at the generous earl as he saw the nice bonus attached. "If you have anymore questions or another job for me please do not hesitate to call on me at any time, Doctor Summerset!"

Edward turned to his brother-in-law Devon as soon as Andrew was gone. "How are we doing on time?"

Devon pulled out the pocket watch that Raven had gotten him years ago just after they were married; it had an eagle on the front, and played a beautiful tune. "About fifteen minutes or so, I would imagine."

Devon barely got that out when two wagons with about two dozen men pulled up. Golden Eagle pointed chuckling in humour as he snapped the lid back down on his watch before putting it back in his pocket. "Well maybe now by the looks of it, it is always nice when the help shows up early."

It did not take long for the wagons to empty as the men encircled Edward and Devon. Within moments, they were completely surrounded. Dream Dancer frowned puzzled as he looked for his foreman, but did not recognize any of the men around him.

A few minutes later, several more wagons pulled up.

A man in the crowd shouted out in warning suddenly. "Those are not our wagons!"

Instantly the men surrounding Edward pulled out knives as they unexpectedly attacked, as all hell broke loose.

The men in the arriving wagons yelled out in anger as they charged into the gathering men around Earl Summerset, now it was a free for all.

Edward tried to reach his brother-in-law Devon, as Dream Dancer knocked out the man attacking him, but could not get away as another man attacked him instantly.

Devon desperately tried to get to his brother-in-law Edward, knowing that the attacking men were really after Dream Dancer. It took Golden Eagle some manipulating, but finally he managed to get to the earl. He got behind Raven's brother so that he could protect his blood brother's back.

The two men now standing back to back fought off all comers as they heard more wagons coming. Neither of them knew who was friend or foe as they fought for their lives.

Edward swore grimly, how many more wagons were going to show up here. Dream Dancer hollered back at Devon in anger. "Damn! Are they ever going to stop?"

Devon's low chuckle held no amusement at all as Golden Eagle yelled back. "Doesn't look like it!"

The two friends, brother-in-laws, as well as blood brothers fought on!

*****

The black-haired blue-eyed soldier who had waylaid the seven youngsters still stood in front of the dressmakers shop door guarding it as he watched the four men grimly. He had a sneaky suspicion that if he were to move away from the entrance at all the youngsters would make a dash for the door to try getting in. He stayed in front of the entrance refusing to move as the four men wandered around waiting for their women to come back out.

The soldier frowned in aggravation as he watched another group of men with their women approaching suspiciously. It just figured that they would have to be here just before a ball.

Obviously, this was a favourite dressmaker's shop by the amount of women trying to get in here today. It also seemed to be a day for suitors since all the women so far had men with them.

The soldier glanced over at the buffoon that had tried showing off, he just happened to see a quick gesture towards the others that were getting closer. Instantly he yelled a warning, but was too late as a sword pierced his chest.

The guard did manage to scream out one word though. "TRAP!"

The seven lounging soldiers quickly drew their sword, but were too late to help their comrade. More men began pouring out of the alleyways attacking the unfortunate Black Cougar Guards.

*****

Shin, as well as the captain of Crystin's guard, instantly raced outside to help their men as screams rang out.

Shin instantly drew his sword, as well as one of the Tianming Monk's dragon daggers; they both whirled singing their deadly song as they cut through bone or tendons with ease. Neither of the blades stopped moving as blue and green streaks of light flared all around them as the deadly weapons caught the sunlight.

Shin went from one fighting group to another hardly slowing or noticed. The Tianming Monk twirled before spinning in time to his fatal dance of death, which nobody was immune to at all!

As Shin danced, he could not help but remember his teachers or his last day at the monastery before they sent him to find his father Dao so that the Tianming Monk youngster could help him, as well as to protect the one yet to be born.

On that day, Shin had received a gift; two dragon daggers both made secretly by Masamune just like the sword his father Dao carried. They had just a slight curve in the blade; the thickest part was at the pummel until the curve in the blade began afterwards it got thinner until you reached the tip.

It was razor sharp if you looked close you could see serrated grooves on the opposite edge, so that if you did not pull it out the same way it entered it was almost impossible to remove especially if it hit bone.

There was a dragon, as well as Japanese symbols, on the thicker part of the blade that matched the sword. It also matched Crystin's necklace Shin had noticed, but never mentioned.

The hilt had a dragon entwining it with the head of the dragon on the very end of the pommel protruding outward; the eyes had two very deep green gems embedded, they were the same colour as Edward's eyes…

*****

As Shin sat in front of his master head bowed in prayer, his master had put the two daggers in front of him. "If these blades accept you they are yours! Your journey will be long with many dangers, but we have faith in you. You are young so have many new things to learn, always seek the Great Spirit's counsel when troubled it will never steer you wrong. Go my son your father Dao needs you, I just pray that you will arrive in time his passing is near!"

Shin had picked up the daggers in awe before twirling them experimentally. A blue-green fire swirled around the young Tianming Monk's hands from the gems, as well as the blue from the blade as they accepted him. They would be his now for the rest of his life until another guardian took his place.

*****

Shin's mind returned to the present as the Tianming Monk completed his deadly dance. It was not long before bodies littered the cobblestone pavement, as all the assassins lay dead or dying.

Shin spun at a horrified cry from inside the shop as Raven holding her bleeding head raced out the door. "They took Crystin, as well as Michelle! I tried to stop them, but could not hold them off by myself. The girl's that came in earlier opened the back door before I could get to them. Five men were waiting on the other side there was just too many for me!"

Shin followed closely by the captain of Crystin's guard raced inside before going out the back with Raven close behind. The three ran down the alleyway, but they were too late as a carriage raced by knocking the three would-be rescuers into the building as it careened passed them.

*****

Edward looked around sadly at the dead and dying men littering his lot as Dream Dancer shook his head grimly totally confused by why!

The first two wagons had been assassins, but lucky for them Edward's foremen had also shown up with two wagons full of workers. The last wagons had thankfully been sent over by the thief Tomas to help them build the new hospital.

Edward heard a groan of pain off to his left, so he walked over before kneeling as Dream Dancer turned the unfortunate assassin around.

Edward looked up as Dream Dancer heard his brother-in-law Devon come up behind him. "My black bag is in the carriage can you please get it for me."

Devon turned trotting away obediently.

Edward opened the man's shirt, but knew just by looking that the assassin was not going make it. Dream Dancer bent down to ask angrily the burning question in his mind. "WHY!"

The assassin took a ragged breath; knowing that he was dying, he spat out in grim pleasure. "We were to capture you if at all possible. Failing that a diversion to keep you here, but we did not expect your men so quickly!"

With that, the assassin's eyes closed in agony as he drew in one more breath of life before his chest stilled forever.

Edward got up frowning thoughtfully, why would they want to keep him here! Suddenly Dream Dancer was racing over to the men that Tomas had sent.

Edward grabbed the brown-haired brown-eyed leader of Tomas' group of helpers by his arm in desperation, Dream Dancer pointed towards the wagons. "Hurry, gather all your men, follow me!"

The thief nodded without question as he whistled shrilly to his men so that they would follow him; he did not like the look of fear on Edward's face. Obediently his men trailed him as they all jumped back into the wagon.

Edward beckoned to his brother-in-law Devon as Dream Dancer ran for the carriage before shouting one word. "Crystin!"

That was all that needed to be said as they both jumped in the carriage before racing at break neck speed to the dressmaker's shop where they knew Crystin was getting her wardrobe made.

Devon jumped out of the carriage before it even stopped followed closely by Edward; they both knew that they were too late though. They looked around at all the dead bodies sadly.

Raven followed closely by Captain Griffin rushed up to them. She grabbed her brother, Edward's arm in apology. "I am so sorry I tried to stop them, but they knocked me out taking the two girls!"

Edward looked around grimly in fear. "Where is Shin?"

Raven frowned as she pointed south. "Shin went after them said to tell you that he would bring her back to the townhouse or die trying!"

Edward sighed in relief having no doubts that the Tianming Monk would do everything that he could to bring Crystin home safe.

Edward turned his sister Raven around before moving her hair aside to see how dire she was hurt, but it was not serious since it had quit bleeding already on its own. "It's not too bad; I will look after it later when we get back to your townhouse, by the looks of it we have several more serious injuries to attend to."

Two guards needed stitching up, the rest were all superficial wounds and would heal in time; luckily, only one guard had died thanks to Shin.

Edward sent Tomas' men back to his foreman with the plans, as well as instructions on what Dream Dancer wanted done first; his foreman would have to look after things for now, the earl would be useless to him until Crystin was returned to him safely.

Edward gathered the Black Cougar Guards along with Dream Dancer's family before going back to Devon's townhouse to wait for Shin to bring Crystin back to him.

It would be the longest night ever in Edward's recollection as he paced like a lion trapped in a cage with nowhere to go, as well as no outlet for his fear; with no powers any longer Dream Dancer would not be able to spirit walk in order to find Crystin. Like it or not he had no choice but to wait!

CHAPTER TWENTY-EIGHT

The Tianming Monk made a quick stop at Devon's townhouse to change into his black Ninja assassin robe, the white Samari robe he was wearing was too easily seen in the dark. Shin was not worried about Crystin's whereabouts he would be able to find her anywhere, as long as she was pregnant that is!

The Tianming Monk was directly connected to the baby the countess was carrying. The closer Shin was to Cecille the deeper her heartbeat sounded to him, so all he had to do was find which direction the heartbeat was the loudest to know where her mother Crystin was.

The Tianming Monk shook off his thoughts as he left the townhouse. Silently finding the direction he needed Shin broke into a ground-eating trot; he pulled his hood down before vanishing, as he become just a passing shadow in the night.

*****

Crystin looked around grimly; the two women were tied to chairs in what looked like a dungeon. The countess shifted uncomfortably as the twin's in her belly kicked at her. Both were extremely wrestles right now, she knew that they were feeling her fear. She whispered soothingly hoping to calm them, as well as herself. "Shhh my precious little ones, Shin or your father are on their way be calm now it is only a matter of time until we are free!"

Crystin took deep breaths as the countess comforted herself with the knowledge that the two men would find her soon. It seemed to work as the twins settled once more.

Crystin looked around again at the dingy damp walls, but there was really nothing to see. She had been blindfolded when first brought here, so the countess had no idea where they were.

All Crystin knew is that it had taken them quite a long time to get here, several hours the countess had guessed, so figured that they were not in London anymore.

Michelle groaned as she woke.

Crystin was not sure when her friend Michelle had been knocked out or even why! They had both been awake when they were put in the carriage. She must have tried to fight or run when they were taken from the carriage; why else would they have knocked her out.

Crystin wondered why they had taken Michelle as well unless the kidnappers did not know who the countess was, so took both women just to be on the safe side. She shook her head very confused. That made no sense though since they would have had to take Raven too if they had not known.

Raven had black hair the same as Crystin, but Michelle's was brown; the kidnappers must have known they were looking for a black haired woman at least, so the countess' sister-in-law Raven would have been a more logical choice.

Michelle looked over at Crystin, but her vision was blurry as she grimaced in fear at her friend. "I am so sorry…!"

That is all Michelle had a chance to say as Ernest walked in regally; he ignored his cousin Crystin's bellow of rage.

"WHY!"

Ernest turned to Michelle before slapping her savagely. "Bitch, I told you what I would do if you disobeyed me, so now your mother is dead because of you! Good thing I never trusted you, so had others watching or I would have missed a golden opportunity to capture my cousin."

Michelle's head snapped painfully to the left; she spat out blood as her teeth cut the inside of her lip. She looked up defiantly at her tormentor. "I told you that I would not help you as soon as I found out that she was pregnant! Do with me as you will, if my mother is dead so be it at least she is away from the likes of you. I am glad she is no longer in any pain!"

Ernest lifted his hand to hit Michelle again, but turned away in rage instead; He would deal with her later Lord Pwllheli had more interesting plans for her.

Ernest turned to face his cousin Crystin next before walking over to stand in front of her; Lord Pwllheli smiled down at the countess evilly. "Well my dear we meet again; plus carrying my baby no doubt!"

Crystin turned her face away quickly before her cousin Ernest could see her shocked look. So, that is why he wanted her; he figured the countess was pregnant with his baby. Clearly, Michelle had lied to him or just had not told him everything.

Crystin sighed mentally in relief as she put on an expressionless face before looking back up at him. If Ernest found out the truth, she knew that he would kill them both, so the countess played along in order to buy more time for her husband or Shin to get here. As long as her Cousin Ernest figured it was his baby, it would keep the two women alive.

Crystin grimaced in rage as the countess put on a good show trying to convince Ernest that she meant every word. "Yes, but if I could have done so, I would have ripped it out of me!"

Ernest rubbed his hands together in glee. "So, now I have a legitimate claim to Llannor Castle how nice. Once the baby is born I will not have anymore need of you though, so you better hope for a long pregnancy."

Crystin could not help the shot of fear that coursed through her at her Cousin Ernest's cruel smirk. The twins instantly started kicking the countess savagely once more. She took a deep breath calming her self as she pictured her husband. "My husband will have something to say about that!"

Ernest chuckled negatively in pleasure. "Your husband will be dead soon, it has all been arranged. We will be leaving for my castle in Wales by dawn; once we get there, nobody will be able to save you. As soon as we arrive and I get confirmation that Earl Summerset is dead, we will be married. I made you a nice comfortable set of rooms in the dungeon deep in my castle; you will stay there until the baby is born. If you are a good little girl, I will even leave you there to live out your life. If you are a bad girl and cause me too many problems, dead will do just fine!"

Crystin grimaced in pain as the twins again kicked at her unmercifully as apprehension for her husband took over. The countess took a big calming breath as her Cousin Ernest finally turned away from her.

Ernest went to the door before calling in two guards. "Take Michelle up to my room and tie her up on the bed; when I am finished with her your men can have her since she is no longer any use to me!"

Michelle screamed in terrified defiance as she fought her captors, but it was no use as she was carried forcefully out of the dungeon!

Crystin with tears streaming down her face fought her bonds for a moment, but could not get away to help her friend. The countess froze instantly as her Cousin Ernest walked back over to her.

Ernest stroked his Cousin Crystin's smooth cheek with an evil grin. "Just think we will have lots of time to get reacquainted once we are at my castle. I look forward to it my dear!"

With that Crystin's cousin disappeared as the countess sobbed in helpless panic!

Crystin groan in pain as the twins started kicking her savagely in the back again. If she did not find a way to remain calm soon the twin's might rip the countess wide open now; causing a premature birth that she knew her babies would not survive as tiny as she knew they were!

*****

An obscure figure flirted from one victim to the next leaving a trail of blood, it was the only indication of a presence! Not a sound could be heard; even if looking directly at the shadow of death you would never see it, not until it was too late!

The twenty-five guards stationed on the high wall never had a chance as the Tianming Samari Monk danced with the wispy cloud cover that ever so often hid the full moon. Shin never stayed in one position long so that the other guards did not notice anything amiss.

One by one, the mercenaries silently died where they stood unaware that death was stalking them! After the last one was dispatched the

Tianming Monk crouched where he was as Shin looked down letting his senses broaden, but not one living person could be seen or heard now.

The Tianming Monk stood up readying himself; he curled himself into a ball as Shin spun in midair trying to be as small a target as possible. Staying in the shadows of the trees, the young monk landed lightly cat like in a half crouch with one leg stretched far back behind him ready to spring into action if necessary.

The Tianming Monk stayed there for a long moment as he kept his left hand pressed firmly on the ground feeling for any vibrations that would tell him others were near. Using all five of his senses Shin waited patiently in silence.

The Tianming Monk about to rise to continue on paused suddenly; he could sense something coming, but was unsure what it was at first. He frowned uneasily dogs, six of them in total three on his right with another three on his left. Shin just hoped that he could get rid of them before they raised an alarm.

The Tianming Monk waited patiently, at the last second he drew his two daggers. Streaks of blue-green were all that could be seen as Shin turned right first, since those three dogs were the closest and again he danced with the shadows; all three dogs died within seconds, thankfully without a sound.

Crouching in the darkness once more the Tianming Monk waited as the other three dogs came into view. The dogs sniffed at the ground as they went over to their three dead companions sniffing and nudging them in confusion they tried to get them to rise. Before the dogs even realized what was happening Shin jumped between them as the young monk quickly buried his two daggers deep into two of them.

The Tianming Monk unable to extract his knives fast enough though reached up just in time as he caught the third one by the throat as it lunged for his juggler. Holding on tight Shin reached around to grasp the dogs muzzle as he gave a quick jerk snapping its neck before dropping it.

Quickly the Tianming Monk extracted both his daggers before Shin wiped them clean on the dog's coats. Silently the young monk continued on thankfully still not seen or heard.

The Tianming Monk dropped to one knee suddenly as he heard rustling off to his left. Shin flipped his right dagger backwards so that he was holding it by the blade as he waited patiently.

Both daggers were perfectly balanced for use in hand-to-hand combat or even for throwing. All of a sudden the Tianming Monk threw one at a guard coming out of the bushes, the dagger easily found its target.

The unfortunate guard was still doing up his pants after going to the washroom, as he instinctively grabbed at the dagger protruding from his throat; he tried but was unable to make any sound except for a gurgle.

In satisfaction, the Tianming Monk watched the dagger buried itself deep into the man's throat so that he could not call out for help. Shin ready jumped up before rushing to catch the guard so that he would not make any noise when he fell to the ground.

The Tianming Monk slowly lowered the guard to the ground before Shin extracted his knife from the man. He continued on silently as death found every man on watch, one at a time!

The Tianming Monk had no remorse as a dozen more guards died without a sound. Finally, Shin was at the back door; he looked up at a balcony two floors up that had its doors open, instantly he scaled the wall.

It did not even seem as if the Tianming Monk touched the building at all, it was almost as if he was walking on invisible stairs; the young monk made it look that easy before grabbing the balcony Shin vaulted over it, he silently disappeared inside as the phantom of death entered!

*****

Raven fidgeted in apprehension watching her brother Edward pace. She felt helpless, for the first time in her life, her training had failed her. It was now the wee hours of the morning; none of them had slept a wink or even tried.

Raven would never forgive herself if something happened to Crystin or the babies; she could not help but feel responsible. None of them had a clue where the countess had been taken so helplessly they all waited, powerless to do anything else!

Raven got up needing something to do; she turned to Edward as she gestured towards the kitchen. "I will make break…!"

Suddenly Raven stopped what she was going to say as the three instantly froze for a moment. Quickly without a word needing to be spoken by any of them, they made a rush to the center of the room to stand back to back.

The three instinctively drew their knife as they moved before waiting tensely knowing something was not quite right, but not one of them was aware of why at first.

Edward tensed grimly as he heard glass breaking, as well as the door being kicked in, as a dozen sword-wielding men rushed into the room. Dream Dancer knew that there were more on the way; he could hear them in the hallways.

The three fought fiercely keeping their backs protected as they fought for their lives. It seemed as if the assassin's would never stop coming as more and more bodies piled up around them.

*****

Michelle was laying tied spread eagle on the bed sobbing hysterically, when suddenly she stopped as a shadow entered through the balcony. She held her breath waiting unsure if she had imagined it as the minutes ticked by with nothing happening.

Michelle could not help the little squeak of surprise as the shadow materialized beside the bed. Immediately she quieted as a figure dressed all in black held up a finger to his mask where his lips would have been to silence her.

The Tianming Monk sliced at the ropes to free Michelle before reaching down to help her up. Putting his hand up once more to indicate silence Shin silently beckoned her to follow him.

The Tianming Monk went to the door before cracking it open slowly hoping it would not squeal; luck was with him as it opened soundlessly. Not seeing anyone Shin slipped out the door to make sure nobody was around.

When The Tianming Monk was satisfied, he went back to the room to get Michelle. Pulling out an extra knife that he had tucked in the back of his sash, Shin handed it too Crystin's maid so that she had something to protect herself with.

Silently beckoning to Michelle once more the Tianming Monk led her out as they stealthily made their way down the hallway. They came to a set of stairs leading down so Shin held up his hand to halt Crystin's maid and he went down alone to make sure it was all clear.

When the Tianming Monk was satisfied he motioned for Michelle to come down to him, once she was behind him again Shin turned left leading her down another hallway slowly.

All of a sudden, the Tianming Monk stopped dead in his tracks waiting. He cocked his head listening intently; at the last moment, he pulled his right dagger out. At the same time, he put his left arm back to push Michelle out of his way. Shin spun left so that he was now standing beside Crystin's maid facing the opposite way. He held her tight against the wall as he threw his dagger in one swift motion at something that was behind her.

The guard gurgled as he reached up trying to pull the dagger out of his throat, his lips moved trying to call for help, but nothing came out.

The Tianming Monk let go of Michelle and raced to the falling soldier to catch him before he could make too much noise. Shin eased him to the floor; he knelt as he extracted his dagger from the dead soldier.

Michelle gave a little squeak of shocked surprise as someone grabbed her from behind holding her by the throat.

The soldier chuckled suggestively in Michelle's ear. "Bloody hell, now how did you get out of those ropes woman? Now that you are here though we can have a little fun before the other men get a hold of you!"

The soldier had come out of a room directly behind Michelle so did not see the Tianming Monk at all until too late. He looked away from the woman about to pull her back into the room that he had just vacated. It was not until then he saw his comrade lying face down. He frowned in surprise, but that is all the time his brain had to register anything; suddenly he grunted as a knife protruded from his right eye socket and he saw no more.

Michelle let out a slight squeal of astonishment before the soldiers arm tightened around her throat in death; he pulled her backwards with him causing them to both fall with a loud bang. Lying on top of the now dead soldier Crystin's maid dug her nails into the man's arm pulling at it trying to pry it from her throat as she choked seeing spots in front of her as all air was cut off immediately.

The Tianming Monk raced forward to help Michelle, but just as he got beside her; more soldiers hearing the commotion ran into the hallway. There were six on his left, with four more on his right. He only had a split second to make a decision, so Shin crossing his arms reached with both of his hands into his robe. He pulled out six stars three in each hand.

The Tianming Monk knew that the eight pointed shuriken stars would not kill a grown man. He hoped though that they would give him the distraction he needed for the few precious minutes Shin would need to help Michelle.

The Tianming Monk flung both his arms out releasing the shuriken throwing stars. Just as he had planned, the soldiers in front squealing in pain stopped dead detaining their comrades as they tried to pull the eight pointed stars out of their chests.

The Tianming Monk took the opportunity to reach behind him with his right hand withdrawing his sword. In one swift motion, he brought the sword down severing the arm that was keeping Michelle hostage, before he brought it back up. Quickly he threw the sword to his left hand since there were more guards on his left; Shin pointed the sword dripping the dead guard's blood towards the six guards. His right hand had already withdrawn his other dragon dagger so it was pointed to the right threateningly towards the other four soldiers trying to get to them.

Thankfully hearing Michelle take a life giving breath of air, the Tianming Monk spun away no longer paying Crystin's maid any attention as Shin danced dispatching the guards quickly.

Michelle could not help squealing in revulsion as the severed arm released its hold on her. She pushed it away in disgust as she took several cautious deep breaths of air out of her bruised throat, but remained where she was so that she would not get in Shin's way.

The Tianming Monk finally walked over and helped Michelle up before pulling his dagger out of the guard's right eye. Shin looked at her with a frown of worry. "Are you okay to continue on?"

Michelle nodded decisively before reaching down to pick up the knife that she had dropped. She watched as Shin went around collecting his stars, but never said anything. Crystin's maid was unsure how she felt about all this, in one way she was thankful to the youngster for saving her life, but the monk frighten her as well.

The Tianming Monk beckoned to Michelle. "Come on, but stay close to me they know we are here now!"

Michelle rushed up behind Shin as she followed closely, it did not take long to reach the dungeon where the final dozen guards were positioned to keep them from getting to Crystin.

The Tianming Monk dispatched them quickly before the two of them entered the room to find Crystin still tied to a chair with her Cousin Ernest behind her holding a knife to her throat.

Ernest growled grimly in warning. "Drop your sword, as well as your dagger whoever you are; or I will slit Crystin's throat!"

Instantly the Tianming Monk did as he was told. Afterwards, Shin held up his hands in reassurance to show that he held no more weapons. "It is over let the countess go; if you do I will spare your life!"

Ernest laughed in disbelief before pointing at Michelle cowering behind the man dressed all in black. "Pick up those weapons woman and bring them to me so that he will not be tempted to try anything stupid!"

Michelle hiding what she was doing from Ernest, hid the knife that she still had in the pocket of her split skirt before walking around Shin; she picked up the monk's sword then the dagger as she brought it over to Crystin's cousin.

Ernest not trusting Michelle either pointed to his left. "Drop them over there; afterwards, come kneel here beside me!"

Once Michelle was kneeling beside him, so was out of his way Ernest reached down to pull out an old duelling pistol that he had before pointing it at the stranger. Lord Pwllheli could care less who the stranger was; all he wanted to do was to get rid of the little man. So far, the strange man dressed in funny black garments had managed to wreck all his well-laid plans.

Ernest grinned in pleased satisfaction as he waved the pistol around for a moment before aiming it at the man dressed all in black once more. "When you get to hell give my regards to Earl Summerset for me, let him know that I am taking good care of his wife…"

All of a sudden, Ernest screamed before dropping the gun; he grabbed the knife protruding out of his left side that Michelle had managed to drive home while he was occupied with the stranger.

The Tianming Monk without hesitation grabbed his other dragon dagger out of his sash before throwing it. Shin watched in satisfaction as it embedded deeply into Ernest's thick skull.

Lord Pwllheli fell backwards dead before he hit the ground.

*****

Edward fighting for his life, as well as the lives of his family, heard shouts suddenly followed by screaming throughout the hallways. Dream Dancer sighed in relief as reinforcements arrived.

Suddenly it was all over as Crystin's Black Cougar Guards, as well as Tomas, came charging in the room dispatching the last three men. Edward looked around at all the dead men sadly before turning to give his sister Raven and his brother-in-law Devon a quick look to make sure that neither was hurt.

When Edward was satisfied that both were okay he turned grinning in relief as Dream Dancer looked over at Tomas. "Well it is about time that you showed up!"

Tomas laughed in delight. "Better late than never I always say. I heard that they had taken your wife Crystin so I was busy trying to find her, but when my men got there she was gone! Every single man there was dead except one; all he could tell my men before he died was that the spirit of death was stalking him!"

Edward hearing a cry of relief turned knowingly as he looked towards the door before bracing himself as a crying bundle flew into his arms.

Dream Dancer looked over at Shin in thanks as he stroked Crystin's hair in comfort as she clung to him.

Edward lifted Crystin's chin as Dream Dancer looked down at his wife assessingly. "Are you okay, love?"

Edward put his right hand down to stroke Crystin's belly; Dream Dancer felt a healthy kick of one of the twin's in satisfaction.

Crystin nodded as the countess looked up at Edward. "I am now!"

Edward looked over at Tomas and Shin before disentangling himself from Crystin. He stepped over bodies to get over to the two men so that Dream Dancer could shake Tomas' hand in appreciation, but he bowed deeply to Shin. "Thank you both, I am forever in your debt!"

Tomas shook Edward's hand before shaking his head negatively. "We are now even, Doctor Summerset."

The thief Tomas turned to his men. "Get rid of all these bodies boys so we can go!"

Within an hour, all traces of the assassins disappeared; it took another hour to clean up the mess before everyone crawled thankfully into bed.

Edward held Crystin close for a long moment before Dream Dancer kissed the countess deeply. "Goodnight love."

Crystin now content snuggled close to Edward before closing her eyes; instantly the countess fell into an exhausted dreamless sleep.

Edward held Crystin close for a while longer as he took the opportunity to pray silently, thanking the Great Spirit for keeping his wife safe. A few minutes later Dream Dancer also slept; he was beyond exhausted.

*****

Shin dropped onto his carpet before giving his report to his masters. No more would Crystin's Cousin Ernest threaten them as he lay in a pool of his own blood staring up sightlessly.

Shin informed his masters that they were leaving to go back to Wales tomorrow; the Tianming Monk could feel his masters approval, they all knew that Crystin's time was getting closer she must be in Wales for the birth it was predetermined.

Finished with his report Shin got up as he closed his eyes in concentration; thankfully, he felt no more disturbances as everyone slept. The Tianming Monk crawled into bed as he fell into a very light sleep.

Even at rest, Shin was always aware of every little sound not even a mouse could sneak by without the Tianming Monk being instantly aware of it.

CHAPTER TWENTY-NINE

December 24 1860

Edward stood on the balcony in Wales contemplating the fact that deep down he knew that Crystin was going to die. Without Dream Dancer's powers there was nothing he could do to change it.

Edward knew though that if it were Crystin's time he would not have stopped it even if he still had his powers. As much as it hurt him to let her go, Dream Dancer would never go against the Great Spirit's will; it would alter the future with disastrous results he was sure.

Edward had given Crystin a sedative, a mild one just to give her a bit of a break. Hopefully, it would help his wife to sleep for an hour if possible. The countess had been in labour for almost two days now; today was the twenty-fourth of December.

Edward sighed dispiritedly as he thought back over the last month…

*****

Edward remembered sadly standing at the dock with his wife Crystin as they both said a final goodbye to Raven, her husband, as well as Dream Dancer's nephew Trevor a day after the attack as the trio boarded a ship heading home to Boston, from there they would catch a train to Montana.

Edward had gone to see Queen Victoria afterwards to inform her of Lord Ernest's death, as well as to give her a report on everything that had happened. The queen had tisked angrily regretting the fact that she had not arrested Pwllheli the day he had shown up at Dream Dancer's castle in Wales.

In compensation, Queen Victoria had given Edward Pwllheli Castle with all the lands that surrounded it. He had laughed teasingly at the queen accusing Victoria of giving him more headaches.

While Edward was there, he also informed Queen Victoria that Crystin was pregnant; he had fibbed a little though telling her that his wife was not due until the end of March. Dream Dancer planned to invite Victoria to come to Llannor to check out the renovated castle as an excuse to get the queen here when it was getting close to the countess' time. He knew that the queen needed to be at the birthing he had seen it that long ago day when he had gotten that vision of the twin's birth

Edward had argued for over a week with Crystin on whether Michelle could be trusted again, but of course, Dream Dancer's wife had won. Now both mother and daughter were living with them at Llannor Castle.

Shin had stood up for Michelle as well, which had surprised Edward. To convince Dream Dancer the Tianming Monk told him how Ernest had died, as well as Michelle's part in it.

Edward had gone to Michelle to thank her personally for helping to save his wife and unborn children.

Edward knocked on Michelle's door wanting to talk to her in private to get her side of the story. Dream Dancer had been furious at first when told that Crystin's friend had betrayed her, but after talking to Shin he needed to hear her side before deciding if she would be staying.

Michelle opened the door; she frowned hesitantly unsure why Edward was here. "Yes my lord is there a problem?"

Edward gestured inside not wanting others to hear what was being said. "May I come in, we need to talk?"

Michelle nodded as she stepped back holding the door wider before closing it behind Crystin's husband Edward. "What can I do for you Earl Summerset?"

Edward turned to her as Dream Dancer frowned grimly. "I want to thank you for saving Crystin, but you need to know that I am also very angry with you. I am finding it very hard to allow you to stay now that I know you also betrayed my wife. I need to know why you did so in order to make a final decision!"

Michelle looked at Edward sadly, as she sighed dispiritedly before sitting on her bed as she fidgeted nervously wondering if she could trust him with the truth. She understood the earl's feelings, but she was scared that he would still send her away if he knew the whole truth.

Michelle grimaced, she did not have much choice; Edward would send her away for sure if she did not tell him. "I am sorry my lord you will not think very highly of me after I tell you, but I want you to know first off that I love Crystin very much. At the same time, I must admit that I was also very jealous of her most of my life. We were the best of friends, but always there was a distance between us; she was high born, a lady with all the privileges in life that I was denied. I did not know that it was Ernest who sent us away, we were told that Crystin wanted us to leave now that she was older she did not need us anymore. I should have known better of course, but jealousy has a way of eating at you as time moves on. When Ernest found us, we were totally destitute with absolutely nothing, not even much for food. He took us in and fed us, at first he was like our saviour. I was sworn to secrecy though so could not tell my aunt our good fortune, but I brought her some of the food that I pretended to eat whenever I could. Lord Pwllheli came to me one day to tell me that Crystin was back in Llannor. He asked me to find out what was going on here as a way of paying him back for his help, of course I said that I would. When my mother found out, she was furious with me, to try to stop me from helping Ernest she told me a secret that she had harboured since I was born. Crystin is actually my younger half sister, my mother was her father's mistress before he fell in love with Crystin's mother then married her. So, I informed Lord Pwllheli that I could not help him; in retaliation, he took my mother hostage locking her in the dungeon that he was building to keep Crystin in until she had the baby. I had no choice but to come here in order to spy on my half sister to save my mother. When I found out Crystin was pregnant I refused to help him again, but he took me down to the dungeon to show me that they had beat my mother really bad; so again I reluctantly came back to do his bidding, but I lied to him as much as I possibly could in order to keep Crystin safe! Please do not tell Crystin that she is my half sister I want to do it someday, but I am just not ready yet."

Edward had agreed to keep Michelle's secret for now with a warning that she must tell Crystin after the babies were born by the latest. Once she did, Dream Dancer would also make a decision on whether she was staying or going.

Queen Victoria showing up for a surprise visit had also intervened on Crystin's behalf when the countess told her godmother what was going on.

Queen Victoria listened to Edward's fears; of course, Dream Dancer did not tell Victoria Michelle's secret. Afterwards, the queen talked to Shin. Later she had taken Michelle aside to hear her confession in private.

Michelle was made to swear an oath on her life to Queen Victoria that from this day forward she would be Crystin's protector.

Edward was finally satisfied, so Michelle had been forgiven with the slate wiped clean never to be brought up again.

Queen Victoria arriving the last week of November to celebrate Crystin's pregnancy had surprised them all, especially when she stayed for a whole five days, it had caused quite a delay in getting Llannor Castle back into shape.

As soon as the ballroom was finished, of course, Queen Victoria had to have a ball. Even though Victoria knew that Edward hated them, or maybe that is why she did have one. Sometimes Dream Dancer swore the queen did it to spite him, why he did not understand.

If that were not bad enough, Queen Victoria insisted on having a jousting competition to relieve her knight's boredom. Later just before the queen left, they had an archery competition that Edward won easily.

Edward, as well as Shin, had shown off their skills as they danced the Tianming warriors dance. Queen Victoria as well as his wife Crystin was absolutely delighted by their performance since neither had seen it before.

Edward had taken Queen Victoria to Pwllheli Castle the second day of her visit to have a look around, as well as to help him get in without a fight. Once they got there, Dream Dancer realized that it would not have been a problem anyway since they found it abandoned.

Of course, as soon as word had reached Pwllheli that Ernest was dead the mercenaries had all disappeared with whatever they could carry in lieu of pay now that their master was dead.

They had found Michelle's mother at Pwllheli Castle; thankfully somebody had let her out of the dungeon so she was only a little malnourished with a few bruises, but still very much alive.

All the survivors of Ernest's cruelty had disappeared back to their homes. Slowly Edward was finding them to try bringing them back so that Dream Dancer would have some staff at Pwllheli, not wanting to deplete Llannor Castle again.

Queen Victoria had come up with the bright idea of making the Pwllheli lands a golf course, being that close to the sea it was ideal. Once they were finished hashing out the plans the queen left to go back to her castle in London, thankfully taking her court with her.

The Prince Consort Albert had not come with Queen Victoria this time around since he had been complaining lately of stomach pains. Victoria did not want to leave him alone too long; she was quite worried about him.

Edward gave Queen Victoria a potion in the hopes that it would help her husband. Victoria had promised to be back at the end of February to help Crystin before the birthing. After the queen left, they finally finished putting Llannor to rights.

Crystin was ecstatic at having her home set back to its former glory as an operational castle. Guards now stood in the towers once more watching for signal fires from around the little inlet of intruders or pirates.

Edward finally left for Pwllheli Castle in order to begin the construction of the golf course. Dream Dancer had decided to make it nine holes since it was too small for any bigger. He spent four days there planning before leaving unexpectedly for England on December fifth.

Edward went for two reasons; one was to check on his hospital, the other was to gather supplies for the golf course. He had left Crystin in Llannor this time since she was too uncomfortable to travel far plus they were still trying to hide the fact that her pregnancy was way too advanced.

Edward spent a week in London as the construction on his hospital continued. Not wanting to leave his wife too long though Dream Dancer left the two doctors in charge of finishing up, as well as adding staff so that it would be fully operational when it was ready.

Edward hurried back to Pwllheli Castle with his equipment for the golf course that Dream Dancer had bought, having been gone way too long.

Edward at first could not decide whether he wanted to use Pwllheli Castle as a clubhouse, but finally decided against it since it was just too big. So, Dream Dancer found a foreman to begin construction on a clubhouse.

Edward made sure to hire as many locals as he could to help dig sand traps where he wanted each green to be. Unfortunately with Ernest killing off so many of the young he did finally have to go further a field to find more help. Dream Dancer was optimistic though that some of these workers would stay to settle on the peninsula since the population had plummeted over the last two months.

Edward took several locals into the forest to show some of them what young trees would be best to plant in-between the fairways in order to keep them separated. Dream Dancer was not sure how the new trees would fare so close to the sea, but if need be he would try others until he found the right combination that would grow there.

Once Edward was satisfied that the men knew what Dream Dancer wanted he returned home for a bit to be with Crystin.

Edward after thinking about it for a while decided to make Pwllheli Castle into a hotel instead, so he went back to Pwllheli to find workers. He walked the castle writing plans, as well as drawing pictures of what he wanted to change.

Everything was coming together nicely as Edward jumped from one project to the next supervising, as well as helping where Dream Dancer was needed.

Once the twin's were born, and Edward's wife was up to travelling again; Dream Dancer planned to take Crystin shopping since his countess would have the final say in decorating the clubhouse, as well as the new hotel.

Periodically Edward would run home to give his wife a report on how things were progressing, spend a few hours or one night with her before racing off back to his projects once more.

For over a week Edward ran himself ragged trying to get as much done as Dream Dancer possibly could despite the weather, of course there was no way it would all be finished this year.

Already construction on the golf course had been suspended now that there was too much snow; the construction on the clubhouse had also stopped until nicer weather prevailed.

It was more likely that Edward would be lucky to have it completed before the next golfing season, without any problems arising that is.

Two days before Edward was at Pwllheli looking over some of the work already completed when a ferocious storm blew in halting any chance of them accomplishing anything outside. Only the inside renovations on the hotel could continue.

Edward stayed though wanting to do more once the storm moved off, but a rider with a note from Shin to hurry back had changed his plans.

*****

Now here Edward stood on the balcony in the storm needing an outlet for his fear.

Edward had sent a note to Queen Victoria right away that Crystin was in labour already, but way too early. Victoria had arrived this morning without all the fanfare; with only her personal guards, as well as her husband who seemed to be doing better with the medication Dream Dancer had sent him.

Queen Victoria had gone to the dining room a half hour ago to eat with her husband, but had promised to be back shortly.

Edward braced himself as the wind picked up once more as it howled angrily, immediately Dream Dancer went inside as an icy cold sleet started falling again.

The storm had intensified the day Crystin went into labour; it had steadily gotten worse almost as if it were feeding off Edwards wife's pain. Occasionally though it did give them brief respites, but not for long.

Edward closed the balcony doors before walking over to stare down sadly at Crystin.

Shin had spread his special carpet under Crystin wanting to capture the birthing blood so that it would soak into it. The white buffalo hide sat by the bed waiting patiently for the birth of the next White Buffalo.

Crystin woke as she felt an intense stare; she smiled up sadly at Edward. She was also very much aware of the fact that she was going to die. The twin's were ripping the countess apart inside she could feel it.

Crystin was about six weeks earlier than the countess had anticipated and it was taking way too long now.

Crystin knew that Edward would be okay though having just had a dream of Dao as he showed the countess the twin's in the future, as well as her husband's life away from England.

Edward wrung out a cloth before kneeling as he gently wiped the sweat off Crystin's forehead as he kissed her tenderly. Dream Dancer sat back to look over at Queen Victoria as she walked back in, but turned back to his wife quickly in concern.

Crystin moaned in agony as another contraction ripped through her belly; she sat up slightly as the pain intensified. The countess tried to ride out the pain without screaming knowing that Edward was worried enough.

Once it was over Crystin fell backwards panting in exhaustion, the countess was getting weaker with a lot more difficulty as each contraction hit.

Suddenly one hit Crystin unexpectedly before she had time to prepare, this time the countess could not help the scream that ripped out of her as the agony overshadowed her worry for Edward.

It seemed to Crystin that this one would never stop as her back arched fighting the pain as she felt something rip deep inside her. The countess screeched again as the agony became unbearable for a long moment, but finally the pain subsided as she panted trying to regain her breath.

Crystin thankfully had a bit of a respite, as her body now weakened even more tried to gain enough strength back to get through the next contraction. The countess did not know how much more of this she could take as she panted heavily catching her breath.

Crystin knew though that she had to continue to be strong; there was no way she was going to let the twin's die inside her. The countess inhaled resolutely before drawing a determined breath as the countess braced herself for another contraction.

For another two hours, Edward watched helplessly as Crystin struggled through the worst birthing pains Dream Dancer had ever seen even as a doctor.

It was eleven-thirty at night, the twenty-fourth of December, when Edward's son crowned. Within fifteen minutes, a healthy baby boy dropped into Dream Dancer's hands. He was a little small at around four pounds, but he gave out a lusty healthy cry once the umbilical cord was cut.

Edward passed his son to Queen Victoria after cutting the cord that connected the baby to its mother before turning back to Crystin knowingly as the countess wailed pitifully in severe agony.

Crystin determined to see that her daughter was safely delivered sat up slightly as she propped herself on her elbows to give herself more leverage; the countess pushed frantically.

Crystin's daughter ripped savagely through her belly tearing her mother apart inside as the countess felt another rupturing sensation deep inside her. She heard the gong of the grandfather clock as the midnight hour came.

Urgently Crystin bore down persistently; straining the countess was panic-stricken knowing deep down that her daughter must be born at midnight! She gave one final heave as her tiny daughter thankfully dropped into Edward's hands just before the clock finished its last chime.

Crystin gave a huge sigh of satisfaction as her daughter was born at midnight on the twenty-fifth day of December in the year of eighteen sixty.

Suddenly Crystin screamed in agony as a gush of blood followed her daughter out. She fell back on the bed unable to hold herself up as the lifeblood drained out of the countess, saturating the carpet.

Edward cut the umbilical cord, in satisfaction he heard his daughter draw in a life giving breath as she cried out. Not needing any other assurances that his daughter would live Dream Dancer quickly handed his daughter to the waiting Shin before rushing over to the head of Crystin's bed in order to be with her as the countess slowly bled to death.

Edward had time to give her one last kiss in farewell as Dream Dancer whispered brokenly. "I love you my Black Cougar Cub! The Great Spirit will take good care of you now my love!"

Crystin smiled up sweetly at him in satisfaction as the countess mouth one final time. "I love you too, Ed!"

Edward wailed in denial as Crystin's eyes glossed over for a moment before finally rolling back in her head.

Crystin saw both her parents standing at the end of her bed beckoning to her as she died; gladly she took their offered hands as she went willingly to be with them.

Gathering Crystin close to them her parents lead the countess into the light as all three disappeared.

The carpet soaking up Crystin's lifeblood added one more spirit symbol as it joined the many others gracing the beautiful rug. When it was over, not a drop of blood could be seen anywhere on the carpet or bed.

CHAPTER THIRTY

Edward reached up sadly, as he closed his wife's unseeing eyes; he got up before walking over to the twins. As much as Dream Dancer needed to grieve right this minute he had to see to the twin's first; his grief would have to wait until after.

Edward went to his son first who was now sleeping peacefully in Queen Victoria's arms. Dream Dancer smiled at the light blonde fuzz knowing that he would look just like all the other Summerset earls. "Edward William Charles Summerset, welcome. You will be called Charles after your great grandfather. You will be the next Earl of Summerset after me. Your godmother and godfather will be Queen Victoria as well as her husband Prince Albert; if they have no objection that is?"

Edward had made that decision quite a while ago knowing that someday Dream Dancer would be leaving England; so he needed to make sure that his son would succeed him as the next earl.

This would also protect his son from Prince Albert since Queen Victoria's husband did not like Edward. Dream Dancer could only pray that now because Albert was Charles' godfather, it would stop the prince consort from transferring that hatred to Charles. Especially once Edward was no longer around to protect his son.

Edward knew though that Prince Albert was also very sick. Of course, Dream Dancer could no longer predict how long the prince consort had; nor could he help Albert now that his powers were gone.

Edward had given Queen Victoria's husband more of that potion since it had worked for him, but this time after examining Prince Albert thoroughly Dream Dancer had also added a slight painkiller to the mix.

Edward knew that the prince consort was in a lot of pain, but was trying to hide it from Queen Victoria. Dream Dancer would be very surprised if Albert managed to survive for another six months; if Prince Albert did make it past that, a year would be the longest Dr. Summerset would give him!

Edward had not told Queen Victoria or the prince consort his suspicion because he knew that Victoria would expect Dream Dancer to heal Prince Albert as he had her, but now he could not!

Edward could be wrong about that of course, without his powers he could not be one hundred percent sure. Therefore, just in case some miracle happened and Prince Albert was still around for another twenty years Dream Dancer needed to take this precaution. Especially if the prince consort managed to still be alive after the earl was gone from England.

Queen Victoria nodded in agreement; she would have her priest baptise Charles before she left. Victoria would proclaim him the next earl once she arrived back at Buckingham Palace.

Edward turned to his daughter next, he stared down at her reflectively; she was small compared to her brother, probably about three and a half pounds at the most he figured. She had a full head of black hair with no white apparent from his vision. Dream Dancer sighed thankfully, maybe that meant the vision was wrong so she would not be blind either.

Edward looked closer as he noticed a silvery white tip on the ends of her hair, well so much for that hopeful thought; Dream Dancer frowned grimly he could only pray that as she got older it would disappear.

The baby girl opened her deep green eyes; it was rare for a baby to be born with such unusual eyes; babies typically started with brown or bluish-grey eyes. Edward could see instantly that there was a light milky film over them. Dream Dancer sighed sadly, as his other hope plummeted as well. He knew beyond a doubt that she was blind, as he had seen in his vision.

So what did the colour variation mean for Edward's daughter, was it a good sign or a bad one? Dream Dancer could only pray that it did not mean Dao had not removed enough of the evil!

Time would tell Edward supposed there was nothing he could do about it now anyway; not until she was a little older then Dream Dancer would know for sure. "White Buffalo, welcome! You will be called Cecille Luan Gweneal as foretold by Daniel; we will call you Cecille that means blind in Welsh."

Shin nodded thoughtfully. Cecille meant blind, but Luan meant Warrior in Gaelic; Gweneal meant white angle or blessed angel in Welsh. The meaning of her name suited her since she was blind, but with his help she would become a warrior; white angel or blessed angel also suited her because of the white tips on her hair; it would give her a unique look when she was older.

Shin could also feel an innocent purity about Cecille. Like her mother, she would find her spirit guide, as well as her soul with ease. She would not need any help to balance her inner self, which was a good sign.

Shin could also feel a great power lying dormant, as Cecille grew it would get more powerful until her powers peaked at puberty. Only time will tell what White Buffalo will become in the future. The Tianming Monk could thankfully feel no evil in her aura at this time, which gave him hope that the evil mist was completely gone from Dream Dancer's daughter.

They cleaned up the twin's before bundling them up good and tight since both were so tiny, as well as premature, they needed to be kept as warm as possible; afterwards, they were taken to their room.

A wet nurse would have to be found right away.

Michelle given that responsibility rushed out knowing that the twin's would need milk as soon as possible, a couple of hours would be too late. Leaving the castle quickly she hurried to the guard tower; having a woman in mind she went to get Carissa's brother to take her to the village to recruit his sister.

The poor woman had lost a baby girl three days ago, Michelle had heard Carissa's brother telling one of the other guards yesterday that is how she had found out about it. Since Michelle knew her family personally, she was confident that the woman would be perfect for the twins.

*****

Edward frowned in aggravation as Queen Victoria cornered him unexpectedly. "How is this remotely possible, you and Crystin have only been married for a little over two months?"

Edward bowed sadly to Queen Victoria needing to take Crystin away in order to grieve. "I will let Shin explain it to you your Highness; he will tell you the whole sad story I promise just let me get the countess out of here first please!"

Queen Victoria nodded impatiently as she stood back to wait.

Edward turned to Crystin sadly before he cleaned her up; chanting in Cheyenne, he got the countess ready for her journey to the Great Spirit. Dream Dancer wrapped her up in a blanket tenderly.

Edward lifted Crystin before stopping to talk to Shin quietly on his way out. "You must deal with Queen Victoria!"

Shin already aware of that nodded in reassurance at Edward. "Go I will deal with the queen and her husband."

Edward sighed in relief as he took Crystin out of the bedroom. He went down to the chapel in the back of the castle, since he still did not have a tepee set up here where he could go to be private this would have to do.

Dream Dancer laid Crystin on the altar before sobbing he took out his knife as Edward began his grieving ritual.

*****

Shin turned to Queen Victoria as the Tianming Monk bowed respectfully. "Your Highness, the earl has taken Crystin to his chapel to mourn so we will not see him for the rest of the night!"

Queen Victoria waved her hand in exasperation. "You will tell me since Earl Summerset refuses to answer my question how it is possible for Crystin to have two babies survive when she has only been pregnant since the second week of October at the earliest, but yet this is only December twenty-fifth! That is only two and a half months; it is not possible, is it? I also want to know why that carpet on the bed has no blood on it at all even though my goddaughter Crystin bled all over it!"

Shin smiled calmly as he bowed again respectfully to Queen Victoria and her husband Prince Albert as he waved in invitation for them to sit on the bed. "Your Highness, Prince Albert sit I will tell you a sad little story."

Queen Victoria looked at her husband Albert in expectation.

Prince Albert shrugged at his wife Victoria's look. "Don't look at me you are the one who insists on knowing!"

Queen Victoria scowled in aggravation at her husband before going over to the bed as she sat in a huff. Prince Albert dutifully sat beside his wife as they both looked up at the son of Dao, who they had found out only yesterday had died in Wales soon after leaving them in London.

Shin smiled pleased as the two sat on the carpet without realizing where they were. The Tianming Monk would need the power of the carpet to do what needed to be done next. "Your Majesty, Prince Albert I need you to close your eyes so that you can visualize as I tell this story it will explain everything to you."

Shin's voice drowned on soothingly for another few minutes talking nonsense as the Tianming Monk slowly hypnotized the pair. Once he felt that both of them were deep enough in a trance, he began humming bringing the guardian's spirit carpet alive. "It was so good of you both to come all this way to see Doctor Summerset for Prince Albert's ailment. Now that Prince Albert is recovering, you both had a nice visit with Earl Summerset as well as your goddaughter Crystin. Tomorrow you will return to Buckingham Palace after Charles is baptised not remembering the birth of the twin's or the death of Countess Summerset once you leave this castle. On May fifteenth, you will both remember going to Wales on May first to witness with sadness the death of Countess Crystin Summerset after she delivered a premature boy of four pounds twelve ounces. You will write the birth of Edward William Charles Summerset as of May first, he will be the next Earl of Summerset. Queen Victoria as well as Prince Albert will then remember the christening as you are named as godmother and godfather. There will be no other children born to Earl Summerset only one boy. You will follow me now to your room, when I leave you at the door and say goodnight neither of you will remember any of this. You will both get ready for bed as you talk in excitement about how happy Earl Summerset and his Countess seem to be as well as how pleasant your visit had turned out, forgetting everything bad that happened here tonight. In the morning it will just be a part of a nightmare."

Shin turned as he continued chanted, he led the dazed Queen Victoria and her husband Prince Albert to their bedchamber before bowing in farewell. "Goodnight your Highness and Prince Albert."

Queen Victoria nodded regally in goodbye as she took Prince Albert's arm as they entered their room. "Well that was definitely a nice visit…"

Shin grinned in satisfaction as the closing of the door cut off Queen Victoria's sentence. The Tianming Monk turned away with no more worries that the queen or her husband would remember until the appointed day.

Shin hurried back to Edward's bedchamber before taking his carpet off the bed as he walked into the twin's room with it. He moved Cecille's crib over in order pull the decorative carpet away so that the now glowing symbols were revealed. The Tianming Monk had painted them before going to London.

Shin took his own carpet that was full of spirit guides and spread it out on top of the glowing ink. The Tianming Monk made sure that his carpet completely covered the symbols as humming he prepared himself. He went to Dream Dancer's son Charles first since he was the first-born.

The Tianming Monk took Charles over to the carpet before laying him in the center, kneeling Shin prayed to his master in his homeland, as well as to the Great Spirit. He introduced the first twin.

Feeling an urge the Tianming Monk nodded in obedience; Shin knew instantly that it did not come from his homeland because his master would have spoken directly to him. It must have come from Shen, the Great Spirit that was the only explanation the monk had.

The Tianming Monk unwrapped the blanket from around Edward's son before taking his special intricately designed dragon dagger out to prick Charles finger with; Shin let a drop of blood fall onto the carpet in the center.

Charles cried out in pain not liking that one little bit.

The Tianming Monk picked him up crooning soothingly; Shin held tight to the finger giving it just enough pressure to stop the bleeding, but not enough to stop the circulation.

Once Charles quieted, the Tianming Monk checked, but there was no longer any blood; Shin quickly wrapped him back up before taking him back to his crib.

The Tianming Monk went to Dream Dancer's daughter next; he picked her up with the white buffalo hide still wrapped around her. Shin brought her to his carpet before laying Cecille in the center.

Chanting the Tianming Monk pulled down the buffalo robe before using the same dagger pricked Cecille's finger letting two drops of blood fall beside where her brothers had fallen. Instantly the blood ran together; the little red bloodstain curled as it moved until an image formed.

From this day forward, every time a birthing happened in White Buffalo's line of descendants another drop of blood would be added; until a full image would appear to take over the center of the carpet, of what the Tianming Monk did not know. Right now, it just looked like a blurry image possibly of an animal, but until it was full size it would stay unrecognizable.

Cecille whimpered, but did not cry out when her finger was pricked. Within minutes, the injury disappeared with only a tiny red dot left to mark that Dream Dancer's daughter had been cut.

The Tianming Monk eyed Cecille's finger in fascination; would she be able to heal herself anytime or was it just this once? To find out Shin would have to cut Edward's daughter again, but at this time, he was unwilling to do so.

The Tianming Monk would watch her closely though, for the time being Shin would keep that thought to himself; time would tell. It was an exciting prospect though, if Cecille could heal herself could she also heal others as her father Dream Dancer at one time could.

If Cecille could do so, that would make her a medicine woman or a shaman in Dream Dancer's Cheyenne culture.

The Tianming Monk pulled out the necklace with the little Sakura blossom that he had taken off Edward's wife Crystin, while Dream Dancer was outside; he put it around Cecille's neck. Shin would teach her never to remove it so that her dreams would be safe. As she got older nightmares could influence her, so this would protect against that happening.

Next, the Tianming Monk pulled out the Celtic medallion that he had also taken from Crystin before putting it around Cecille's neck. When he finished he lifted her up high as Shin chanted introduced her to his master and again to the Great Spirit, he felt approval from both.

The deep green gems of the medallion caught fire glowing as it encircled Cecille accepting its new mistress.

Lowering Cecille the Tianming Monk moved the buffalo hide aside further; he crooned to Dream Dancer's daughter before kissing her on the left shoulder above her heart. A little red dot appeared for a moment, but disappeared just as quickly now they were connected. From this day forward, Shin would be able to find the White Buffalo anywhere.

Wrapping Cecille back up, the Tianming Monk took her back to her crib. Shin took the medallion off her to drape it so that it was above her head against the headboard of her crib there it would stay until she was old enough to wear it.

Cecille opened her unseeing eyes before closing them as she fell asleep, content.

Shin removed his carpet; he put the decorative one back over the glowing symbols before moving Cecille's crib back over top of the symbols. The Tianming Monk gathered up his spirit carpet as he left the twin's room. He would give Dream Dancer one more hour by himself before going down to bring Edward up to bed.

Shin was just about to enter his room, but stopped when Michelle with the new wet nurse in tow walked passed him to the stairs leading up to the nursery.

Michelle paused at the stairs as she turned to Shin first though to introduce the two, knowing that the young monk was Cecille's guardian so he would have to approve of her choice. "Shin, this is Carissa; she lost her baby three days before so will now feed the twin's with your permission!"

Shin eyed the brown haired, blue eyed, chubby five-foot woman with huge breasts assessing her quickly. He could feel a sad, hopeful, emotion radiating from her. There was no sinister or angry aura around Carissa, which would affect Cecille. Nor could the Tianming Monk feel any illnesses from the wet nurse that would transfer from the milk to the twins.

Shin finally nodded in approval as the Tianming Monk bowed gracefully. "Thank you for coming to help us on such short notice; I am deeply saddened by your loss. I hope the twins can help to heal your pain at the loss of your little one."

Shin turned to Michelle next as he gestured towards the master bedroom. "You will have to go through Edward's room; he is elsewhere mourning for his wife so just go right in. I will go find a servant to bring the nurse a bed, so leave the nursery door ajar please."

Michelle nodded as she led the way up the stairs.

Carissa turned to follow Michelle up the stairs, glad to get away from the intense examination of the funny looking youngster. She could not help wondering why she needed his permission; when it was the earl's babies, she was to feed.

Michelle led Carissa into Edward's room before taking the wet nurse to the nursery door. All thoughts flew from the nursemaid's head though as she heard one of the babies start to cry in hunger. Immediately she rushed to him before picking Charles up so that she could put him to her right swollen overflowing breast.

Carissa sat in the rocker before smiling in thanks as Michelle brought the baby girl to her, eagerly the wet nurse shifted letting Michelle help her to position the little one so that Cecille could feed off her left breast at the same time.

Carissa sighed in relief as the pressure in her breasts eased as the babies slowly drained them. Unknown to the nanny was that even one more day without a baby to suckle would have been too long for her; she would have died of milk fever.

*****

Edward laid part way over his wife as he sobbed; blood soaked her blanket, as well as the table, from his many cuts. Dream Dancer looked up in misery as he felt Shin's presence all of a sudden.

Shin tisked in disapproval before helping the reluctant Dream Dancer up as he took him out of the chapel up to his room where the Tianming Monk had a bath waiting.

Edward crawled in the tub with a thankful sigh. He smiled sadly, as he remembered Shin's father, Dao doing this many times for him in the past. There was even healing oil lacing his bath water, it would soak into his sores so that it would work overnight to help in the healing of Dream Dancer's many cuts.

Once Edward was done soaking to his satisfaction, Shin came over with a bucket of water to rinse him off excess oil before helping the earl out of the tub. He walked over with a healing salve spreading it generously on Dream Dancer's cuts before holding out his white training rob. When ready the two went to the Tianming Monk's carpet as they sat quietly.

Dream Dancer went deep into meditation; he smiled as he felt Crystin's joy at being reunited with her parents before sighing sadly, as Edward said a final farewell to his wife.

Shin nodded in satisfaction as he felt Dream Dancer's mood shift to acceptance as his wife left this earth to be with the Great Spirit; the young guardian was satisfied. He helped Edward up tucking him into bed before the Tianming Monk disappeared silently with his carpet.

Edward sighed dejectedly, as a healing sleep overtook Dream Dancer.

*****

Not once had Shin spoken respecting Dream Dancer's need to grieve, the Tianming Monk would tell Edward about the wet nurse in the morning. He had made sure to get her a bed before going to get the earl. He had cautioned Carissa not to enter the earl's bedchamber tonight.

Shin would also mention the need for a door handle so that the nursemaid Carissa could enter without having to go through Dream Dancer's room all the time. The Tianming Monk would also tell the earl about Queen Victoria and Prince Albert's memory lapse tomorrow as well. Edward would also have to keep Cecille away from the queen as well as the prince consort.

Shin shook off his thoughts as he entered his room; he knelt on his carpet giving his report before crawling into bed he fell into a deep sleep exhausted.

*****

Shin sat up instantly sweating profusely; he had dreamt of a forest with huge trees all around him. He was lost as he searched for the White Buffalo flirting around the trees teasing him. The Tianming Monk tried again but could not find his way to Cecille.

Suddenly Cecille was gone; Shin could not sense her anymore. He screamed out White Buffalo's name to no avail as he tried to find his way out of the forest, but the Tianming Monk received no answer.

Shin knew that if he did not find Cecille he would die; afterwards, his soul would wander the earth lost as the Tianming Monk's purpose went unfulfilled.

If Shin failed, not only would the evil ultimately win with no guardian around to help keep it at bay, but also there would be a hole in the carpet. Once the chain was broken, no spirit soul would ever be able to enter it again.

What was the dream trying to tell him? Shin needed to figure out that question as quickly as the Tianming Monk possibly could! There had to be an answer in the dream somewhere.

Shin finally got up; he dropped onto his carpet in order to meditate looking for answers, but surprisingly there were none as the Tianming Monk's master refused to or could not help him.

Shin prayed to the Great Spirit next hoping for an answer, but again he was frustrated as no answer came to him. Finally, the Tianming Monk got up as he went back to bed with no more dreams to haunt him.

*****

Edward again dreamt that he was in the forest searching for his daughter, as well as the woman that he was meant to seek out. His dream played out like before, but suddenly the dream changed as Dream Dancer finally caught the woman.

The woman looked up at him with love shining out for all to see.

They were standing in a small clearing with the sun shining brightly as Dream Dancer bent to give her a loving kiss, but paused suddenly as a shadow fell over them both. Edward frowned as he backed away from the woman calling out to his daughter desperately as he searched for Cecille.

The woman grabbed Dream Dancer's arm pulling at him trying to get him to come back to her, but Edward pushed her away still looking for his daughter Cecille.

The woman stared at Dream Dancer sadly for a few minutes, finally with tears streaming down her face she turned away from him before disappearing; Edward knew that she was gone forever.

Edward wailed in denial as he woke himself; sweat drenched his sheets. He sat there shaking as he tried to interpret the dream. Was it a warning that Dream Dancer would lose his daughter Cecille; or was it that he would let White Buffalo come between him, as well as the woman that he was destined to love losing her forever?

Edward sighed grimly; obviously, he would have to tread very carefully in the future. He had to make sure that his love for his daughter Cecille or his fear of what she could become if Dream Dancer did not keep White Buffalo close to him did not ruin a love that was being offered by the woman in his dreams.

Edward laid back down, well at least now he knew that it was a native woman in his dreams so thankfully he would not have to go back into the mist of Snowdonia. It was half an hour before Dream Dancer could finally go back to sleep.

EPILOGUE

April 25, 1871

Edward stood staring out at the vast sea contemplatively; time seemed to have run away with him. His wife Crystin had been gone now for ten years and four months today, now here Dream Dancer stood at the bow of a ship heading to parts unknown.

Edward had managed to hide in Wales for the first five years totally ignoring the outside world by finishing his golf course at Pwllheli. Dream Dancer had also completed the castle given to him by Queen Victoria; it was now called Pwllheli Hotel.

Queen Victoria's husband Prince Albert had died the year after Crystin did so she had pretty much left Edward alone for a time. Of course, after five years Victoria started hounding Dream Dancer to go back to London.

A year later Edward finally did, but Dream Dancer hid at his hospital for another year staying completely away from court, much to the anger of Queen Victoria.

Running out of excuses though, Edward had given in as he returned to court reluctantly. For the next year Queen Victoria paraded one woman after another in front of Dream Dancer trying to marry him off to one of Victoria's ladies; of course, he would take none of them.

They had finally argued, so Edward had stormed off to his hospital in a fit of rage.

A year later Queen Victoria sent armed guards to escort Edward back to the palace like it or not, when he got there he was given an ultimatum.

Either Dream Dancer married the woman Victoria had picked out for him, or he could go to Manitoba in Canada to take over the small fort that was beginning to have Indian trouble again.

Of course, Edward would only be there as a diplomat as well as a representative of Queen Victoria's court. Since doctors were in such short supply there, Dream Dancer could fill in as a much-needed doctor as well.

Edward's earldom would be passed to his son Charles immediately; Queen Victoria would act as Dream Dancers son's guardian until such a time came that he could take over the lands himself.

Edward of course, had taken the banishment; knowing that it was the will of the Great Spirit pushing him towards the woman that he had seen in a vision. Not once but twice, before and after his wife Crystin had died. So, Dream Dancer went home to Wales without his son Charles to get all his affairs in order.

Edward had also made a quick trip to his castle in Northern Wales to dismantle then burn his old tepee. After it was all cleaned up Dream Dancer made sure to put a cross where he had buried Pastor Daniel and Dao to mark the location before heading back to Southern Wales.

With Edward's daughter Cecille, Michelle, and Shin in tow; they had found a ship heading to Quebec Canada where Dream Dancer would catch a train to Montreal Quebec. Once there a trapper would meet him to guide them to Manitoba.

Edward had left his horse Cheyenne behind being too old now for such a long journey, as well as his late wife Crystin's mare. In their place, he had taken a three-year-old stallion sired by Cheyenne, also black like his father. Dream Dancer bought Michelle a palomino quarter horse mare, which he would breed to his three year old later. He had also found a black and white pinto mare for his daughter Cecille that he planned to breed as well.

The mare was very unusual being mostly black with two white markings one on each side of her front legs. The only other white she had was just above her tail, the white continued down her tail about halfway before turning black for a bit then it again turned white once more. Her mane surprisingly was black until about three quarters of the way down; it was very long, afterwards it turned white. She was a beautiful long legged three-year-old filly; Edward could not wait to see what kind of foals she would produce when bred to his stud.

Already Edward's daughter Cecille had her horse wrapped around her little finger. White Buffalo had named her mare Saya, which means swift arrow in Japanese.

Edward had also bought two more mares that Dream Dancer was using as packhorses right now, but would breed later to his stallion.

Edward heard a tinkle of laughter; Dream Dancer turned to watch his daughter Cecille as she scurried up the ratlines. Shin of course was right behind her; the Tianming Monk had a rope tied to his waist with the other end tied to White Buffalo. There really was no need though she was as surefooted as the sailors were.

Watching Cecille, a stranger would never believe that White Buffalo was totally blind.

Shin was using the mast as a teaching tool so that Edward's daughter Cecille would learn balance, flexibility, as well as how to use her inner eye when there was nothing around White Buffalo except space, some rope, or a few poles.

Edward watched as Cecille stood on the arm of the tallest mast with her arms outstretched; she walked forward as if she were on a tightrope. Dream Dancer chuckled in humour; White Buffalo would make a great circus performer he could not help thinking.

It really amazed Edward how quickly his daughter Cecille adapted to her surroundings. It had taken White Buffalo two days to put her walking cane away, which is how long it took her to memorize every part of the ship. Now Dream Dancer's daughter did not need it anymore.

The sailors had watched Cecille in awe for two days as the young girl walked the whole ship memorizing it. They now made absolute sure that nothing was out of place so that the blind girl could move around freely without help.

It had not taken Cecille long to wrap every one of the sailors around her little finger, they would do almost anything for White Buffalo. The captain had laughed in delight never having seen his ship so well maintained or clean before; he had asked jokingly if he could keep her.

Cecille's uncanny knack for languages amazed them all, even her father. She could speak several different kinds already; Edward was flabbergasted sometimes by her ability. Welsh and Celtic, which was a form of Cornish, languages White Buffalo had learnt from Michelle as well as her nanny. Various oriental languages she had learnt from Shin her tutor. Cheyenne from him of course, one of the sailor's was now teaching her French with one teaching her German.

Shin had also taught Cecille how to see with her inner eye, so that most of the time Dream Dancer's daughter did not have to use the walking stick. It was not just a cane though; inside was a lethal rapier that White Buffalo was becoming an expert in handling.

Cecille had also taken to the Tianming Warriors training; White Buffalo could do things with her body Edward had never seen before, it just amazed him to watch her. Dream Dancer's daughter even surpassed Raven when it came to flexibility.

Cecille could pop every bone out of joint before wrapping her limbs completely around herself until she was in a ball and could actually roll around. Back flips, cartwheels, somersaults, standing on her hands walking around, or bending completely backwards until White Buffalo's feet touched the deck were no problem for Edward's daughter even on a swaying ship.

Every time Cecille began her exercises, the crew that were off duty would come to gather around her watching in fascination. Before long, they were clapping or singing to encourage White Buffalo trying to help her out.

Edward heaved a sigh sadly, as he shook of thoughts of his daughter Cecille. Dream Dancer missed his wife Crystin dreadfully sometimes, so a future with another woman right now did not appeal to him at all.

Of course, Edward did not know for sure if this woman was meant to be loved by him. He did know that she would love him though since he had seen it in her eyes in both dreams. He was not sure though if Dream Dancer was meant to love her in return, he just knew that he would meet her someday. She would also influence his life somehow; good or bad was yet to be determined of course. What would be would be he supposed even if he did not like it.

Edward had learnt that the hard way on that fateful day that he had not only given up his powers to save his sister Raven and wife Crystin; Dream Dancer had lost his friend, teacher, as well as his long time companion Dao.

Edward still missed Dao fiercely although his son Shin seemed to be taking over; it was still not the same. Dream Dancer had a feeling that he would mourn for his friend forever always feeling a hole in his life, even more so than for his wife Crystin.

Edward stiffened in apprehension suddenly as a shiver shook him; Dream Dancer looked up in dread. His daughter Cecille was standing on the lookout platform at the very top of the mast balanced precariously on the very edge of it with arms outstretched; White Buffalo's face glowed in joy as the clouds above her start to churn.

More clouds raced towards the others as they massed into one huge purple, mauve, as well as black thundercloud. The sky all around the clouds turned a deep orange suddenly making it almost impossible to see what was happening; it was as if it was trying to hide what was taking place from the decks below.

Shading his eyes with his hands Edward moved into the shade of the mast as he stared upward in horrified fascination; even in the shade Dream Dancer had to keep his hands in place in order to follow what was happening above him.

*****

Shin frantically tried to coax Cecille down, but he could not reach his charge White Buffalo; if the Tianming Monk tried pulling on the rope both of them would fall to the decks below. All he could do was watch helplessly as the heavens opened up around them.

Several lightning bolts came straight down before flaring all around Edward's daughter keeping Cecille directly in the center, but seemingly not touching her at all; it was as if it was teasing White Buffalo or maybe it was fighting her.

Shin gasped in horror as Cecille began to glow brighter and brighter; it seemed to the Tianming Monk that White Buffalo was drawing in the lightening, actually forcing it to enter her small frame.

As the lightning reluctantly entered Cecille, it seemed that the clouds above were getting smaller before finally dissipating as they disappeared. Within seconds, the sky turned a deep blue once more allowing others to see the top of the mast.

Shin leaped up ignoring his own danger as he carefully made his way forward. The platform was not very big, so with the two of them on it, it was even smaller. The Tianming Monk reached his charge, but he did not dare touch White Buffalo; Cecille still had a slight glow all around her.

Cecille looked up at Shin as White Buffalo smiled serenely. "I am ready to get down now, my father needs me!"

Shin looked down; he could see Dream Dancer running towards the mast heading to the ratlines so that he could climb up if they did not come down immediately. The Tianming Monk nodded knowing Edward would be furious, the two of them carefully went down.

Edward saw Shin leading his daughter Cecille back to the ratlines so backed away from the ladder waiting impatiently for the two to come all the way down.

Shin reached the deck first; he jumped down the last few feet before facing an over anxious father as the Tianming Monk lifting his hands in caution to stop Edward from advancing. "Do not touch White Buffalo yet Dream Dancer, she is okay!"

Edward frowned forebodingly. "No more climbing that mast!"

Cecille jumped down the last few feet, lithely White Buffalo landed in front of her father. "I am sorry ni-hoi for scaring you! I could feel your fear for me, but I was in no danger. A storm was coming, so I needed to divert it since we are almost there, but the storm would have pushed us way off course."

Edward stared at Cecille in shock that was something very new. Dream Dancer watched in fascination as his daughter's eyes now black glowed for another minute. Slowly they began to lighten before going back to their customary deep green with a film over them, which was the only indication that White Buffalo was blind.

It seemed that every time Cecille's eyes turned black that White Buffalo could actually see everything as long as they stayed black, once they went back to their original deep green they filmed over once more.

Cecille's hair was ebony black unless you looked closer; you could see a silvery white frosting on the tips of each hair about an eighth of an inch on each one. Edward had cut her hair many times trying to get rid of the white frosting, but within a day or two, the silvery white again covered the tips; Dream Dancer had finally given up. The only other indication that the lightning had touched White Buffalo was that the silvery frosting on the tips of her hair were glowing as well before finally that too dissipated.

Cecille was not a beautiful girl, her face was a little too long; White Buffalo was also a little too skinny, but Edward could see potential for beauty when his daughter was older. Her face was a little too white, so her midnight black hair actually made her look almost ghost like.

Several gifts were now beginning to show themselves as Cecille got older. She had a great affinity towards animals that was uncanny, even wild animals would flock to her if she called to them. White Buffalo could also coax a flower to bloom or get a seedling to sprout it was amazing to watch.

Edward had often wondered if Cecille could get a flower to grow if she could also make it die, but not wanting to encourage the dark half of his daughter to blossom; Dream Dancer had never asked White Buffalo to try it.

Edward looked around to see if anyone were watching them with a fearful look; it would tell him whether they had seen anything. Thankfully, though most of the crew were below in the galley having lunch. It did not look like the ones that were on deck had been able to see what Dream Dancer's daughter Cecille was doing, lucky for them.

Edward knelt as Dream Dancer took his daughter Cecille's two hands in his before squeezing them gently, but kept his voice firm trying to convey to White Buffalo how serious this was without scaring her.

Edward remembered a conversation similar to this that he had with Devon in Montana, but this was much more serious since it looked as if his daughter Cecille was going to surpass Dream Dancer in power.

If Edward could not make his daughter understand that some things were just wrong, they would all be in big trouble. "Cecille this is very important so listen closely to me please! You cannot go around changing things, everything happens for a reason. Storms bring much needed rain for fresh water to drink. If you stopped the rain people and animals would die of thirst; trees, as well as flowers, would die too. Shen the Great Spirit makes things happen for a reason, so for us to tamper with nature could cause a catastrophe. We are all born, so we must all die, but only the Great Spirit can decide when or how. For you to stop someone or something from dying when it is their time is very wrong, even if it hurts us to see it. It is all part of the life cycle, but none of us can predict when or why. You must always think of the consequences before you do something, think of who or what will be affected. You are a special girl White Buffalo, but you must hide that from strangers or people will try to use you. I know that you would not want or like that love!"

Cecille nodded matter of factly as White Buffalo also squeezed her father Edward's hands, but in reassurance. "I know that already ni-hoi; usually, I would never stop a storm that is natural, but we must make land tonight. This storm was not meant to be father; I am not sure where it even came from. Po, the Mother Earth informed me that she did not bring it to life it was unnatural. Po asked me to put a stop to it, Mother Earth even told me how to do it. She said the storm would have made the ship crash against the shore, so all the sailors would be killed even though it was not their time yet!"

Edward frowned in surprise. "Mother Earth talks to you?"

Cecille nodded decisively. "Yes all the time; Po tells me when things are not right, as well as when I am not to interfere. Mother Earth also tells me when she needs my help with something that she cannot do herself."

Edward looked at Shin grimly. "Did you know about this?"

Shin shrugged unperturbed as the Tianming Monk nodded. "That Po talks to White Buffalo, yes I did. I was not aware that she was asking Cecille to do things for her though. I will talk to my master tonight about that."

Edward scowled angrily. "You do that; you also need to find out who or what is sending storms to stop us from getting to where we are going. I am not happy either that Mother Earth is asking my daughter to do things already, White Buffalo is only ten years old after all!"

Cecille let go of her father Edward's hands; reaching out White Buffalo put her arms around Dream Dancer in comfort. "Ni-hoi, Po would never ask me to do something I could not do, she is teaching me many things. Please do not worry so, I was born to help keep this earth beautiful and the evil at bay, it is my destiny father!"

Edward sat back on his heels after his daughter Cecille let him go; he stared at White Buffalo's earnest pixie face. He remembered telling his sister Raven that at one time it was when Dream Dancer was leaving for Boston in order to go to England.

Raven had been worried that Dream Dancer was going alone, but Edward had been sixteen years old at that time. Cecille was only ten for goodness sakes; White Buffalo was way too young!

Edward sighed unhappily at how quickly his daughter was being forced to grow up, Cecille's responsibilities were making White Buffalo way older than her age made her; it saddened Dream Dancer greatly.

Edward reached out stroking Cecille's cheek tenderly. "I know love; we will talk more about this later. Why don't you run down to the galley to get some lunch, you have not eaten yet."

Cecille nodded eagerly as she undid the rope that was still tied around her waist. She closed her eyes for a moment remembering the ships layout from where she was at; White Buffalo finally turned scurrying off with no assistance to the door before going down to the galley.

Edward followed his daughter Cecille slowly with Shin walking beside him. Dream Dancer turned to the Tianming Monk grimly. "Any idea's about that storm or who would have enough power to get passed the Mother Earth?"

Shin shrugged unknowingly. "I will see what I can find out while you go have dinner with White Buffalo, I will join you shortly."

Edward nodded as Shin turned away going to his cabin.

Edward continued on, hearing his daughter Cecille's infectious giggles Dream Dancer could not help but smile as he went into the galley in order to eat.

*****

Shin entered his cabin; usually he did all his reports at night, but if there were a force trying to stop them the Tianming Monk had to find out why now, as well as who was doing it.

Shin went to his bunk; he reached under pulling out his carpet. He laid it out before dropping down in the center, chanting the Tianming Monk went deep into meditation to talk to his master at their hidden monastery in his homeland.

Shin's master materialized in front of his young pupil immediately, as if he had been waiting for him. The Tianming Samari Master had a deep frown of foreboding. "Shin you must keep a special watch on your student and charge as a force that is unknown begins to show itself. Po, the spirit of the earth will be unable to stop what is coming. The Tianming Monks are dying mysteriously one at a time. Confusion is abundant in the heaven's because Shen the Great Spirit, our sovereign master, has disappeared leaving us to fend for ourselves! Nobody seems to know why this is happening. People are crying out to Shen, but there will be no response. With prayers no longer being answered, cults will now begin to form everywhere. There is another born to your father's line, he will one day produce a guardian; so far, we have not been able to get to him. The war in Japan caused a lot of damage here as well as change. We are not sure what is coming for us now since we no longer have any power among our people. Po, the spirit of the earth is also waning so your charge will be all that stands in the way of the unknown force brewing. What will become of all of us is uncertain if your charge is not strong enough to hold the forces back until the appointed time!"

Shin frowned troubled. "Is the waning of Po's power the reason my charge is being asked for help from the earth spirit already?"

Shin's master nodded decisively. "Yes! Keep in mind that the powers will die with your charge, no other will be born until the one is needed. You will stay with the White Buffalo descendants until your appointed end. We can only hope to find the next guardian in Japan when he is born. We are not sure, but we think the unknown power is after Po, the spirit of the earth. If that is so, who knows what will happen to the earth if it succeeds, sparks of change are everywhere; where it will lead us only Shen the Great Spirit knows!"

Shin sighed grimly as his master in his homeland disappeared. He stayed where he was for a long time as the Tianming Monk continued to meditate searching for what, he was not sure. Finally, unable to find any answers to who or what this unknown power was, the young monk put his rug away before going to find Dream Dancer to give him the sad news.

*****

Several hours later Shin with Edward standing beside him were both on the deck watching Cecille do her daily exercise routine; they were also discussing quietly what the Tianming Monk had found out from the Tianming Samari Master.

Edward frowned in frustration at Shin as Dream Dancer gestured towards his daughter Cecille. "White Buffalo is too young for all of this; she needs to be a child first!"

Shin sighed grimly Dream Dancer was fighting a loosing battle if he kept up his instance that White Buffalo was only a child. Edward needed to accept his daughter the way she was before he drove her away. The Tianming Monk had to find a way to make him see the truth. "Dream Dancer I know that you hate what your daughter is becoming, but she is not just any child. Do you even realize that your daughter's IQ is way above normal? The Chinese people have a game called Xiangqi it is similar to chess, but more complicated. It is a game of war played at the Tianming Monastery. It takes years to master the intricate battle strategies and techniques needed to play this game. Even at the monastery, this game is not introduced until a child has been in training for at least ten years. Of course, there are exceptions to the rule; I have been playing this game since I was eight years old. Cecille on the other hand has been playing this game with me since she was five years old. Not once since the first day we began to play have I been able to beat her. That puts her in the category of a genius. Her ability to learn languages, as well as her need to understand everything now, plus her knowledge of the outside world is phenomenal. It also puts her in the genius category. You must help her to become everything that she is meant to be, not hold her back. If you continue on this course, in time it will only make her resent or hate you for trying to stop her being who she is!"

Edward stared at Shin in shock; Dream Dancer had not realized any of that. He had been trying so hard to keep Cecille as his little girl; White Buffalo was now the only link Dream Dancer had to his wife Crystin.

Edward scowled angrily at himself is that what the dreams he had been having lately been trying to tell him. Could it be that not only would Dream Dancer drive his new love away, but also his daughter Cecille. All because he refused to see White Buffalo as anything but, his little girl!

Edward turned away from Shin as Dream Dancer turned to watch his daughter reflectively. As usual, there was a big crowd watching Cecille dance as they clapped along encouraging White Buffalo.

Edward had noticed that in the last two years, his daughter Cecille was showing many signs of being a shaman or a medicine woman. He had pushed his suspicions away though not wanting it to be true. Instead of teaching White Buffalo all that she needed to know about being a doctor or shaman as Dream Dancer should have been doing, he had tried to suppress it instead.

Edward turned back to Shin with a grateful smile as he bowed to the Tianming Monk in gratitude. After rising Dream Dancer gestured in reassurance now willing to go beyond his first inclination, which was to protect Cecille. "Thank you my friend, you have given me much to think on; I did not realize until now what I was doing. I had noticed the last year or so that White Buffalo is showing a lot of potential in regards to being a shaman or a medicine woman. I will need to find her someone in Canada that can teach her, until I find a suitable shaman or medicine man I will begin her training as a doctor. She can decide for herself later which one is right for her."

Shin sighed in relief glad he had decided to interfere on Cecille's behalf as the Tianming Monk nodded in agreement. "You are making a wise decision Dream Dancer; your daughter needs guidance not hindrance. I believe a shaman is what the Mother Earth has planned for White Buffalo so that she can teach others about the earth's spirit guides. Like you though I can also see Cecille's potential as a medicine woman, maybe she will combine the two within herself."

Suddenly one of the sailors up in the crows nest shouted out. "Land ho!"

All the men surrounding Cecille dispersed as they headed to their posts eagerly to begin preparations to dock.

Edward left Shin to continue watching Cecille as Dream Dancer walked over before going up to the quarterdeck. "How long captain until we dock?"

The mousy brown haired five foot six ships captain shrugged as he looked over at Edward. "About two hours if all goes well, we still have to negotiate a very narrow channel yet."

Edward nodded in relief before going back to gather Shin, as well as his daughter Cecille; they went down to their bunks to pack. Afterwards, Dream Dancer took their packs below to get the horses ready to disembark as he put saddles, bridles, and packs back on them.

When Edward was done, Dream Dancer left the hold to go get his daughter Cecille so that they could watch as the ship negotiated the channel that would bring them into Quebec Canada.

Cecille giggled in delight as she pointed towards a school of dolphins escorting them to the narrow channel. They jumped as they frolicked in front of the ship; one even jumped up as White Buffalo reached out, surprisingly it almost touched her hand.

The ship was a little too high for the dolphin though as it squawked falling back into the sea. As they got closer to the narrows, the dolphins stood up on their tail; paddling backwards, they waved their fin in goodbye as they flipped themselves backwards in a spectacular aerial show before disappearing.

Cecille clapped in wonder as she waved back before sighing forlornly when they disappeared. She watched in fascination as the captain expertly negotiated the narrow channel. White Buffalo could tell by the way that the canal was formed that humans had made the last part of the channel.

Cecille did not feel any pain from Po, the spirit of the earth, so she knew that whoever had made the canal had known their spirit guide. If one was familiar with their spirit guide, as well as their soul, an affinity to the earth and its animals happened. When it did, the person would work with the earth instead of scaring her.

Edward touched his daughter Cecille's shoulder to get her attention. Dream Dancer had enjoyed watching White Buffalo's face light up as she watched the dolphins performing for her. "Come love, we need to get Michelle so that we can leave the ship."

Cecille nodded as White Buffalo turned to follow her father.

*****

An hour later Edward helped Michelle up onto the deck in sympathy, the poor girl had been sick the whole way here. Dream Dancer had given her something to help with the nausea, but she had refused to come up on deck even once. Even though she was raised on the coast of Wales, she was still totally terrified of water.

Cecille followed her father staying close behind Edward. White Buffalo had a hold of Dream Dancer's coat tails; she also used her cane to negotiate the narrow plank going down.

Edward continued helping Michelle all the way down the plank before leaving her with his daughter Cecille as Dream Dancer went back to help Shin unload the horses. With three sailors helping, they got all five horses unloaded in no time.

A man in his late forties, thin with sandy blonde hair, and just shy of reaching Edward's height stepped forward inquisitively. "Are you Earl Edward Summerset?"

Edward nodded with a grin as Dream Dancer reached out to take his new lawyers hand in greeting. "Yes sir, you must be Monsieur Chiasson? My lawyer in England said that you would meet us here."

Michel smiled in approval liking the earl instantly as Edward vigorously shook his hand. He had met many English nobles over the years, but this was the first time he had been greeted with such a friendly smile or even a handshake. "Yes I am my lord; I will take you to your hotel it is not far from here. In the morning I will take you to the train station, my brother Pierre Chiasson will meet you in Montreal to guide you to where you need to go."

Edward waved away the lord nonsense irritably. "Just call me Edward, I am not a lord or earl anymore my son now has that distinction. Here, can you take one of my pack horses please and lead on; it is nice to be on solid ground so we will walk if you do not object."

Edward inhaled deeply in pleasure as he sighed; it reminded him of Boston, so it was almost like being at home. Dream Dancer heard a yell from the coach driver for his horses to giddy up as it raced out of town heading for parts unknown. The smell of horse manure, human sweat, the bellow of the forges, as well as the hawking of wares even this late at night filled his senses.

Unfortunately, they would not have time to explore Quebec tomorrow, but Edward did plan on stopping at a store for clothes so that they could get out of these English fop clothes at least. Dream Dancer would unpack his Stetson first thing in the morning he could hardly wait. He also had two sets of buckskins, but he would wait for a bit for that not sure what Canada was like when it came to Indians or half-breeds.

After dropping their horses off at the barn, they entered the hotel. Within twenty minutes, the lawyer had them all booked in. He left with the promise of returning in the morning in order to take them shopping before going to the train station.

Edward dropped onto his bed thankful that it stayed still and did not sway. Michelle, as well as Cecille, was in the adjoining room. Shin was here in this room with Dream Dancer since the lawyer had arranged to have an extra bed put in here for the Tianming Monk.

Exhausted Edward slept for several hours before suddenly a dream snagged him.

*****

Edward heard a strange sound; it reminded him of a sinister hiss of laughter of something. It was completely different than the evil mist they had fought against in England though, relieved by that Dream Dancer searched trying to find the source of the new threat.

Edward was just about to give up when Dream Dancer saw three men standing beside a tripod made of wood, it was cone shaped like a tepee.

They all had a rope tied to one foot; one at a time they lifted before dropping their foot back to the ground turning something connected to the tripod that dug deep into the earth's surface.

Suddenly, the men backed away as steam billowed all around them as a different kind of contraption replaced the men; it was able to dig even deeper. A few more of the tripods popped up they seemed to be getting bigger as time moved on, but still there were not many.

All of a sudden, they changed again as they become huge; they towered so high into the sky that Edward could not see the top of it. Now the contraption was made of steal or metal of some kind as they continued to dig into the earth, now able to go even deeper yet!

As it dug deep, black stuff sprayed everywhere as the Mother Earth wailed in pain. As the black liquid settled, Edward could see animals covered in it. He could also see lakes and streams flowing with an oily substance on top. The animals tried to get away from it, but instead died a horrible death. He saw children drinking the tainted water; Dream Dancer cried out, but it did no good as they continued drinking.

Edward watched the humans on the gigantic monster as they shouted in joy as more of the black substance spewed out. Unexpectedly the great beasts began dotting the earth until the ugly contraptions covered every inch. As they dug further down unknown to the people was that they were stealing the earth's very lifeblood, scaring the Mother Earth forever!

Even the oceans were not immune as Edward saw the earth covered in the metal contraptions from one end to the other. Dream Dancer cried out in fear and denial as he felt the Mother Earth dying all around him.

Suddenly a bright light exploded in Edward's head before his dream vanished; all he felt now was an empty void. Instantly Dream Dancer woke as tears streamed down his face. It was the evil of greed that he had heard chuckling at the beginning of the dream. The humans would ultimately destroy the earth themselves unaware that in doing so they would also destroy them selves.

Edward looked over to see if he had disturbed Shin, Dream Dancer saw the Tianming Monk watching him sadly. The two men had the exact same dream, but neither commented as they turned away from each other. It took both men until dawn to fall asleep once more, thankfully with no more dreams to haunt them!

*****

Here ends the book Dream Dancer & the Celtic Witch
Coming soon, my fourth book in the White Buffalo (New Beginnings) Series

Twin Destinies

In the North West wilds of Quebec Canada, only three days from the border of Ontario. Spirit Bear, the medicine man of a mysterious hidden Cree Tribe, watches helplessly as his people begin mysteriously dying one at a time.

It forces Spirit Bear to turn to Matchitehew who was once a brother he loved. After his brother had changed his name to Powaw when he had become the priest of their tribe, a twist of fate alienated the brothers.

Now the twin brothers must put their hate for each other aside, in order to go on a vision quest together to find answers. The two men are stunned by a vision that neither were prepared for at all!

Cecille or White Buffalo to the people now full-grown and at the peek of her power as the most powerful shaman to walk this earth in over a thousand years, disappears with only her guardian at her side. Her spiritual purpose in this life is to help heal the earth, its animals, as well as any person wishing to find their spirit guide.

White Buffalo is drawn unwillingly into a struggle between two brothers. Will she be able to heal the unknown illness that is spreading like wildfire throughout the skin-walker Cree lands? Or will Spirit Bear's people be driven to the edge of extinction before Cecille can figure out why!

NOTE TO MY READERS

I hope everyone approves of the new direction my novels are taking. I will try to keep the western theme to my books for now, but as you can see they are taking on more of a fantasy flavour as I bring my books closer to the new world that I wish to create.

—I did take the liberty of changing the name of the county in England. In England, it is called Somerset, but I did not want to be directly linked to this place. So, I did change the name to Summerset for my main character. Please note that as far as I am aware there was no earl in Somerset, but there was a duke.

Somerset (i/'sʌmərsɛt/or/'sʌmərsɨt/) is a ceremonial and non-metropolitan county in South West England. It borders Bristol and Gloucestershire to the north, Wiltshire to the east, Dorset to the southeast, and Devon to the south-west. It is partly bounded to the north and west by the Bristol Channel and the estuary of the River Severn. Its traditional northern border is the River Avon, but the administrative boundary has crept southwards with the creation and expansion of the City of Bristol, and latterly the county of Avon and its successor unitary authorities to the north. Somerset's county town, Taunton, is in the south.

For more information go to: **http://en.wikipedia.org/wiki/Somerset**

—Queen Victoria (Alexandrina Victoria; 24 May 1819-22 January 1901) was the monarch of the United Kingdom of Great Britain and Ireland from 20 June 1837 until her death. From 1 May 1876, she used the additional title of Empress of India.

Victoria married her first cousin, Prince Albert of Saxe-Coburg and Gotha, in 1840. Their nine children married into royal and noble families across the continent, tying them together and earning her the nickname "the grandmother of Europe". After Albert's death in 1861, Victoria plunged into deep mourning and avoided public appearances.

For more information go to: **http://en.wikipedia.org/wiki/Queen_Victoria**

—The Enfield Pattern 1853 rifle-musket (also known as the Pattern 1853 Enfield, P53 Enfield, and Enfield rifle-musket) was a .577 calibre

Minié-type muzzle-loading rifle-musket, used by the British Empire from 1853 to 1867, after which many Enfield 1853 rifle-muskets were converted to (and replaced in service by) the cartridge-loaded Snider-Enfield rifle. The term "rifle-musket"; meant that the rifle was the same length as the musket it replaced, because a long rifle was thought necessary to enable the muzzles of the second rank of soldiers to project beyond the faces of the men in front, ensuring that the weapon would be sufficiently long enough when fitted with bayonet to be able to be effective against cavalry, should such an eventuality arise.

The British .577 Snider-Enfield was a breech-loading rifle. The firearm action was invented by the American Jacob Snider, and the Snider-Enfield was one of the most widely used of the Snider varieties. It was adopted by British Army as a conversion system for its ubiquitous Pattern 1853 Enfield muzzle-loading rifles. It was introduced in 1866, and was used by the British Army until it was superseded by the Martini-Henry rifle in 1871.

For more information go to; **http://en.wikipedia.org/wiki/Pattern_1853_Enfield**

—Kusari gusoku (chain armour) is the Japanese term for mail armour. Kusari is a type of armour used by the samurai class and their retainers in feudal Japan. When the word kusari is used in conjunction with an armoured item it usually means that the kusari makes up the majority of the armour defence. For more information go to:

http://en.wikipedia.org/wiki/Kusari_(Japanese_mail_armour)

—Masamune, also known as Gorō Nyūdō Masamune, Priest Gorō Masamune, c.1264-1343 AD), is widely recognized as Japan's greatest swordsmith. He created swords and daggers, known in Japanese as tachi and tantō respectively, in the Soshu tradition. No exact dates are known for Masamune's life and he has reached an almost legendary status. It is generally agreed that he made most of his swords in the late 13th and early 14th centuries, 1288-1328.

For more information go to: **http://en.wikipedia.org/wiki/Masamune**

—The Open Championship was first played on 17 October 1860 at Prestwick Golf Club in Scotland. The inaugural tournament was restricted to professionals and attracted a field of eight golfers who played three rounds of Prestwick's twelve-hole course in a single day. Willie Park, Sr. won with a score of 174, beating the favourite Old Tom Morris, by two strokes. The following year the tournament was opened to amateurs; eight of them joined ten professionals in the field.

For more information go to: **http://en.wikipedia.org/wiki/The_Open_Championship**

—A Ball for the Masses: The introduction in 1848 of the gutta percha ball (or often called the "gutty") did an enormous amount to restore golf as a genuinely popular game. Gutta percha is a gum, which is tapped from a tree indigenous to Malaya. The substance is malleable when boiled in water and it becomes hard on cooling. Soon over time, the "gutty" became the ball of choice, not so much to the greater distance which can be attained with the "gutty" but rather because of its cheaper price. The process involved in the manufacturing of the "gutty" was a great deal simplier and its price was about a quarter that of the price of the feathery. The "gutty" cost about 1 shilling a ball in the 1850s. It was in this age when golf in Britain became more of a game for everyone. The increased leisure time created by the prosperity of the Industrial Revolution was another vital ingredient that enabled the sport to catch the imagination of the nation.

—Club making came of age with the invention of the "feathery" ball in the early 18th century. Clubs no longer had to withstand the impact of striking a solid wooden ball and exquisite wooden clubs could be fashioned from ash, thorn, apple and pear wood. Clubs then were made of wood because iron would cause too much damage to the delicate "feathery". When the gutta percha ball appeared in 1848, iron head clubs began to surface. The irons were more suited to the gutta percha ball however and wooden club makers had begun searching for harder materials to make clubs out of.

For more information go to:

http://library.thinkquest.org/10556/english/high/history/hist05.htm

—John B. Stetson was born in 1830 in Orange, New Jersey where his father Stephen Stetson was a hatter. He worked in his father's shop until he went West for his health. Prospector's hat: Stetson created a rugged hat for himself made from thick beaver felt while panning for gold in Colorado. According to legend, Stetson invented the hat while on a hunting trip while showing his companions how he could make cloth out of fur without tanning. Fur-felt hats are lighter, they maintain their shape, and withstand weather and renovation better. Stetson's western adventures came to an end in 1865. Stetson, now 35 years old, and in better health, returned east and established his own hat firm in Philadelphia, Pennsylvania, which produced high quality hats for outdoor use.

For more information go to **http://en.wikipedia.org/wiki/Stetson**

—Prince Albert of Saxe-Coburg and Gotha (Francis Albert Augustus Charles Emmanuel; later The Prince Consort; 26 August 1819-14 December 1861) was the husband of Queen Victoria of the United Kingdom of Great Britain and Ireland.

On 9 December, one of Albert's doctors, William Jenner, diagnosed typhoid fever. Albert died at 10:50 p.m. on 14 December 1861 in the Blue Room at Windsor Castle, in the presence of the Queen and five of their nine children. The contemporary diagnosis was typhoid fever, but modern writers have pointed out that Albert was ill for at least two years before his death, which may indicate that a chronic disease, such as Crohn's disease, renal failure, or cancer, was the cause of death.

For more information go to: **http://en.wikipedia.org/wiki/Albert,_Prince_Consort**